THE FLOURISH

MURDER IN THE FAMILY

HEATHER SPEARS

EKSTASIS NOIR

Ekstasis Editions

National Library of Canada Cataloguing in Publication Data

Spears, Heather, 1934-
    The flourish : murder in the family

ISBN 1-894800-36-2

    I. Title.
PS8587.P255F46 2004   C813'.54   C2004-911270-5

Cover design: Carol Ann Sokoloff
© 2003, 2004, Heather Spears

Printed in Canada

Published by:
Ekstasis Editions Canada Ltd.   Ekstasis Editions
Box 8474, Main Postal Outlet   Box 571
Victoria, B.C. V8W 3S1   Banff, Alberta ToL oCo

THE CANADA COUNCIL | LE CONSEIL DES ARTS
FOR THE ARTS | DU CANADA
SINCE 1957 | DEPUIS 1957

BRITISH
COLUMBIA
ARTS COUNCIL
Supported by the Province of British Columbia

The Flourish has been published with the assistance of grants from the Canada Council for the Arts and the British Columbia Arts Board, through the Cultural Services Branch of British Columbia.

THE FLOURISH

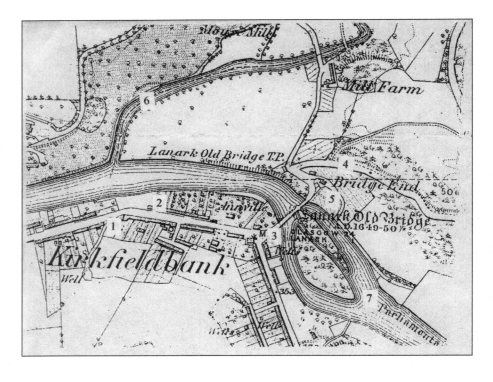

The village of Kirkfieldbank, ordnance survey map, about 1850, showing the Old Bridge and Annville.

1. Location of Kirkfieldbank Church and school
2. IOGT Hall
3. smiddy
4. Brae road to Lanark
5. Clydesholme Braes footpath
6. River Mouse
7. River Clyde

for my niece, Holly Spears

INTRODUCTION

Charlotte Muriel Spears—Auntie Moo—was 94 years old and the last of my father's generation. She had suffered a stroke. Visiting her in Vancouver I would bring her old family photos, and though very confused about the present, she could recognize them as if it were yesterday. I knew all the names but one—a young woman, definitely a Spears, who appeared in a picture with Moo's Aunt Annie.

"I know that's Annie, but who is it beside her?"

"Oh," said Auntie Moo darkly, "that's Aunt Charlotte. We don't talk about her—she was murdered."

When Moo died in 1990 the story might have died with her. What remained was the picture, now named, and a photo of Matthew Spears' family gravestone in Glasgow; her name appears there as well:

CHARLOTTE, HIS DAUGHTER,
DIED 23RD NOVEMBER 1883,
AGED 36 YEARS.

I was in Glasgow for a conference in 1996, and curiosity took me to the Mitchell Library, to look up newspapers from the day after her death. Perhaps the murder would be mentioned, if it had occurred at all. Sure enough, there was the story—several columns of it—set in a village called Kirkfieldbank which I had never heard of, up the River Clyde.

Since then I have been in Scotland many times. As well as looking at collected records, I have visited graveyards, church closets, and private homes. Microfiches of *The Hamilton Advertiser* provided a detailed chronicle of Lanarkshire society during the three years of the story, and (with the census for 1881 and some Glasgow references) the names, and sometimes valuable details, of all the characters. The collected letters of Gavin Scott supplied an intimate record, almost contemporaneous, of agricultural life in the valley.

Added to these written sources were the words of those, now elderly, who as children had heard something of the story told.

I would like to thank the many people who assisted me with information and encouragement, among others Iain MacIver, Reference Librarian at the Hope Institute, Lanark; Moira McKay, Archivist of the University of Glasgow; Mrs. Margaret MacGuinness and Mrs. Alison Rankin of Kirkfieldbank; the staff of the Lanark Museum; Ruth McKnight and George Hamilton of Stonehouse and Harry Carty of the Stonehouse Heritage Group (even to the turning over of fallen gravestones); Mrs. May Morris (nee Sneddon) of Glasgow and Mrs. Cairnes of Lanark; Margaret Dyment, Peter Weinrich and Jay Macpherson for invaluable editing and, in Vancouver, my brother Tom (as well as my cousin the late Isabel Spears) for a trove of family letters and photographs—including, among Isabel's father Gilbert's papers, several more unnamed pictures of Charlotte.

Finally I would like to acknowledge with gratitude the assistance of the Hawthornden International Retreat for Writers, Midlothian, for a residence in 1997, enabling me to begin to write the story I had found.

The events in this story are true. The characters all lived. My task as storyteller has been to provide motives, particulars, and narrative continuity, always and necessarily convinced that the parts I have imagined are true as well. For readers interested in the factual as it is intermingled with the fictional, quoted texts are italicized, and endnotes and an afterword provide sources and further information.

ILLUSTRATIONS

20. King-street, Stonehouse, from the Cross, 1880's. The Browns' draper's shop facing on right.
21. the Elders' house and smithy ca. 1920 with steps over the "airie" to the door.
22. the same house today.
23. The Vagus Nerve. Illustration from *Bristowe's Anatomy*, p. 40.
24. Willie's schedule for Session 1880-81. Glasgow University Archives.
25. Laying of the Cornerstone, the Poorhouse, June 7 1878, detail. Presumed to be Andrew Hamilton (standing, foreground) and his daughters Catherine (10 years) and Isabella (6 months). Lanark Museum.
26. discovery of a girl in distress: illustration from *The Girls' Own Annual*, 1884; and (insert) Katie's last message, assembled by the author from contemporary Lanarkshire handwriting.
27. my grandfather and his family, about 1902. From left: Gilbert, Robert (my father), Tom. Centre: Muriel (Auntie Moo), Thomas Spears Sr., Agnes. Front: George. Tom and George died in the Great War.

THE FLOURISH

MURDER IN THE FAMILY

PROLOGUE

*November 24, 1883: in which a dreadful vision
is glimpsed through a door.*

Young Mr. Cassells, veterinary surgeon, was riding back to Lanark after a late professional call. It was a black night with Clyde in flood and the rain, driven by an east wind, gusted in his face. He was getting through Kirkfieldbank and making a weary job of it, not thinking of much except home and a dry bed. Then rounding the Kirk bend he saw a number of lights along by the bridge, and knew something was the matter. He urged on his mare. Near the end of the street, passing a high palisade on the left she shied badly, almost unseating him.

A crowd was assembled in front of the blacksmith's house, which abutted the bridge and faced directly into the road where it turned to cross Clyde. He jumped down and gave his reins to a lad with a coat flung over his night shirt. Folk were all hastily clad and looking desperate and he heard more than once the word "murder." He pressed through, recognizing the village constable Roderick Munro in his helmet, standing in the porch; both were members of the Anglers' Club.

A short flight of steps crossed the "airie" to the living quarters. The constable's bull's-eye lantern revealed long black or brown smears on the steps and the lower part of the front door.

"For God's sake, Roddy, what has happened?"

Just then Inspector Falconer from Lanark emerged, looking grim and pulling the door shut behind him, but not before Cassells had one glimpse of the room beyond: something of the form of a female lying under a blanket against a great red fire, with backlit figures between her and the door, men in boots and two females supporting each other, whom he took to be the inmates of the house. The Lanark doctors, Kelso and

Gray—Kelso with his black apron on—were standing a little apart and looking very serious. The prostrate female's hair was all dishevelled and undone so she seemed no more than a lass, and her feet stuck out at the end of the blanket, one in a stocking and one bare and both darkened with earth or worse. There were two great lads on the bench under the window, heads down, huddled together, and a third near the lass's head, kneeling.

The latch fell. Only a moment had passed.

"Was that the body?"

Munro had been exchanging a low word with the Inspector, who now plunged into the street. He said hurriedly, "Oh, aye, but she's no dead. Sinking. The doctors have done what they could. Her throat was slit from ear to ear."

He stopped to cough, then went on in a stronger voice to say it was even worse—two more discovered dead and all from the same house, Annville, and the force would be questioning the three lads. He told Cassells her name.

"Where's her father then? Has he been fetched?"

Munro looked blank at that, so Cassells very properly volunteered to go after him at once. He knew the family and where they lived—out beyond Lanark on the Loch-road. Thus *to him was entrusted the duty of informing the parents of what had befallen their unfortunate daughter.*[1]

On the way his courage failed him. His mare stepped smartly over the brig and eastward up the long Brae and, thinking she was to bring him home, turned into Hope-street. Cassells therefore *very wisely got his father to accompany him on the sorrowful mission,*[2] but time was lost in making the old man understand what was wanted and getting him dressed. At last they were away in the trap, rattling up Lanark High-street, past the "Oot" Kirk and out the Loch-road, reaching Crosslaw Cottage something before two o'clock.

It was a sore thing to have to impart such news at the door, speaking as mildly as possible, with the trap lantern cruelly illuminating the parents' distracted faces. They got away again with the poor father between them sitting well forward, a dirty greatcoat over his shoulders and his stockingless feet stuck into his boots. While a wee shirted lassie about five years old, clinging to her mother, stood roaring in the cottage door.

So they hastened with him down to Kirkfieldbank, *arriving there about fifteen minutes after his poor daughter had breathed her last.*[3]

CHAPTER 1

In which Miss Spears is received at Annville.

Charlotte braced herself with both hands as the carriage plunged abruptly downhill. In the early twilight she could just make out the village below: a steeple and a crowd of houses beyond the pale curve of the river. Uncle John leaned across to point out Annville—a square white house near the bridge, rather isolated in a dark garden of wintry trees.

"Hang on, now, there's a sharp turn at the tollhouse, at the bottom of the Brae!"

Then they were right again and rattling over Clyde.

"If you'll watch over this side you'll see Nellie at the winnock. The upper one. Aye, there she is!" A round white face and a curtain falling.

Then her Aunt Helen was in the door, arms lifted, pinning on a large bonnet. A trellis darkened the porch, and a pair of urns stood one each side of the step. Uncle John, who had got out to open the carriage gate, handed Charlotte down himself.

She would have liked the harmonium brought in at once. The rain had already soaked the felt, and there had been a great lurch at the turning. But the postilion unstrapped her box first, and her aunt hastened forward into the drive and embraced her there, and asked at once after poor Mother and Annie and Tom, in Glasgow. A lad came down the path and held the horse, without a word, while other folk peered in at the wicket gate.

"Here, Jock Stark, will you come down and give me and Kay a hand with the instrument? I believe it's what you call an American Organ."

All along the front, a dwarf-dyke surmounted by a green-painted palisade hid the road. Charlotte saw shrubs dismal in the rain, and over on the left a strange, black tree. The lad, not giving her a glance, brought the horse around at the end, by a stone shed.

She and her aunt walked in after the harmonium, through a glazed inner door, and stood still for a moment in a large, square lobby: Charlotte could make out brown wainscotting in the gloom, a wardrobe, a stag's horn with a summer straw perched on it, an ottoman, an umbrella spill. At the far end a stairway led to the upper flat.

"There my dear, your box is in and that's you. You'll be wanting a wash up, and we'll have our tea. Now, give John your wet cloak—and your travelling felt as well—he'll kindly hang them in the kitchen." Aunt Helen's breathy voice paused as she surveyed her niece's costume. Charlotte was of course in full mourning.

"My dear! I've thought to bring over a nice half length of the new arophane! From the shop. It doesnae crumple even after a journey, but keeps as sleek as a blackie's wing. We'll spread it all out the morrow and see what can be done. And I've new weepers in the crape-line as well. Now, here's your rooms."

She preceded Charlotte through the door on the right, and they stopped so Charlotte could admire the furbishing and the wooden venetians "which are fitted to all our windows, both here and upstairs. This is your sitting-room." A smaller room, at the back, was quite filled by a washstand and plumped-up bed.

"You and I will make the tea, and you can see the arrangements, and then we'll sit down in the parlour and be comfortable—and you must tell us all about Tom and his new place, and poor Mrs. Spears and Annie."

Aunt Helen unpinned her bonnet as she spoke, a steel gray invention which was mostly hat wire and feathers. She laid it on the ottoman. Her back was turned, thick, leaning a little forward and the wool gown, a deep braided purple with elaborate flounces, stretched across her bottom. "Marrying money," Charlotte's father had said of her more than once, not unadmiringly.

The kitchen was in the lower flat. "The ground's steep down to Clyde, so we've an extra storey along the rear of the house. Mind the turn."

Charlotte followed down narrow stone steps under the staircase, and Helen hurried to turn up a lamp on the scoured table.

"We take our breakfast downstairs, and sup here as well—John's aye here if he's late coming through, and it saves a fire. It's cool as a dairy in the summer, and you may walk straight out into the orchard. The coal is under the stair."

A range filled the hearth on the west wall and the room was well warmed, though close and steamy.

"Here's the drinking water, it's from the kirk well. Folk say it's the sweetest." The kettle, brought forward from the back of the range, began immediately to hum.

"You're familiar with a range?"

Charlotte said there was a range at Corunna-street.

"Oh, aye, of course, and a fine one, I mind John said so, for you gave them all a dressed meal after the funeral."

A short silence followed, during which Helen fetched down a tray and set out cups. Charlotte's eyes took in the sink under the window, the steels ranged on their board, spoons, bowls and hollowware. A high-backed chair and a smaller one faced the range, and a wee stool, a "creepie," was tucked under the table. The Bible and Concordance, both well-worn, lay prominent on the dresser. Behind the door was a curtained, set-in bed.

Charlotte moving nearer the window could make out the walled garden: leafless branches and black, delved beds. Farther down, what must have been a bleaching green, pale with the last light from the sky, and a shed or greenhouse gleaming whitish at the bottom. The twin arches of the "auld brig" showed over the east wall, and then the rise of the Brae, and directly across the river was the dark, steep wood Uncle John had called Nemphlar when they came down. Between Aunt Helen's bursts of chatter she could hear the river.

Fortunately she had seen her uncle on the platform at once, despite her fears, and must cry out, "Uncle John!" rather loudly, and was stared at by two ladies who had got on at Carluke. He had actually waved his cap as he hurried forward. Then the entire way down in the carriage pointing out the sights—"You'll have all the society you could wish for in Lanark!" Directing her to look first at St Leonard's near the station (while staring studiously away from the imposing pile opposite, which Charlotte guessed was the Roman Church) and after that the Parish

Episcopal at the bottom of the High-street, and the famous statue of William Wallace. Then they were hurled away down Bloomgate and past the grand new United Presbyterian and finally, increasing pace— "Watch now or you'll miss it—" the "E U" or Evangelical Union, Westport, a little away from the road on the left hand.

"Our own kirk now." Charlotte had just time to glimpse a plain building with three narrow windows, a "gathered" church set side-on to the road, before they were dashed downhill.

She turned back into the steady glow of the kitchen lamp. Gone was the whirling sensation of the cars, and she had an idea of the ground under Annville, packed tight under the kitchen and against its deeper wall of white-limed stone.

Aunt Helen emerged from the pantry with a tin of Christmas cake and a chip of sugar. Again looking Charlotte up and down.

"You've no call to wear your gloves to tea, dear. You're to be quite at home, you're with family after all, and we're very glad to have you."

Quite ashamed to be seen standing still like a visitor, Charlotte drew off her gloves. Annie, after the funeral! she had an image of her sister's plump hands in the black-dyed kids, the bits of wet slack at the tip of each finger. "Take those dreadful gloves off, Annie, do," Mother had said as soon as she could. Her own hands, long and slender, extended for the octaves: "Miss Spears, with her taper fingers," as Mr. John Fulcher had said more than once, at the Ladies' Day Classes at Ingram Street Assembly.

"That's better, then! Will you lift down the caddy, the kettle's jumping. And over in the scullery you'll find jellies in the press. You'll discover a good grosset or strawberry nae doubt. I'll be away on up with the tray, and give the tea a chance to mash."

Aunt Helen lifted the kettle to swill the pot, and the exposed flames chafed the brasses, and brightened the blackened underside of the chimney and her round, flushed face.

Charlotte took the lamp and stepped across the flags at the foot of the stair. The scullery was close and chill, and smelled very disagreeably of old apples. Coppers and tubs stood about, barrels of meat and pots of lard. Something loomed at eye level, and holding up the lamp she beheld a great ham hanging in front of her nose. As she stepped aside her heel sunk into a spilled apple, into the flesh.

Aunt Helen peering for her at the stair turn: "Go canny. It's narrow till your feet are used. But you'll soon be running up and down with no trouble at all." Charlotte rubbed her boot heel against the stone as she came up.

In the lobby her aunt told her kindly she need not have taken preserves from this year's store, till they were through with the old.

"Maddie's fixed on very nice labels, look: *RASPBERRY ANNVILLE 1880*. She's a fine running hand, and she's a better gummer than she's a skimmer on a hot day! Ah well, it's the same with the apples, we're aye endeavouring to use up the back lot, and you could argue we never eat a sound fruit from one year's end till the next. Anyway, I try to take those as are quite firm, but with a wee bit bruise or a mark, for they'd no keep. The gone ones we give to Gruntie."

She preceded Charlotte into the parlour, moving rather sideaways, one stout hand for her skirts and one for the jar.

Helen had been married, shortly but profitably, once before, and widowed, and had set herself up as a milliner in the town of Stonehouse, in a small way but well-doing. Before she took John Brown for a husband, with his brood and his poverty. Charlotte remembered what Mother[4] had said: "John Brown will pass as a draper well enough, spruced up as he is now, but for his great hands"—for it would be a wonder, she went on, if they could ever fold silk without snagging.

In her lace cap Aunt Helen looked her age: there were little tucks and folds in her face and a blur on her upper lip. And Uncle John wee and restless pulling on his cutty pipe. Helen was some years older, but nobody knew how many; Father had said once he believed she was a "Year's Bairn," as they called the ones born in the droughty year of '26.[5] If so, she would be fifty-five.

Now Aunt Helen said she had no doubt that Charlotte would take to Annville.

"There's a woman, Margaret Tennant over at the Hotel, comes in to do the rough; she'll fetch the water if you've no a mind to it, though it's just along the street. She carries a raik up from Clyde every evening, for the cistern. Of course you'll no be wanting a fire, other than in your sitting-room, during the week."

Charlotte could see that the parlour, where they now sat, was little used. The two horsehair chairs and the lounge were draped in brown Holland and a folded felt on the stool had doubtless covered the cottage piano. Though the room was nicely furbished there were no books lying carelessly open, as if by chance. She came from a reading and writing family. There, one need never have displayed an open book for effect; Father's and dear Robert's papers had lain about always, everywhere.

A dining table stood in the gloomy back half of the room, with the chairs pulled in and the sideboard so close it would be difficult to seat oneself in any comfort. The table was covered with thick crash and obviously seldom used; over it hung an old-fashioned chandelier with burnt-down candles.

"She's aye willing to sleep in the house during the week, if she's wanted. And we'll be down again at the week-ends. I doubt Maddie will visit so often however, for she assists in the shop, and very efficient, and of course dear Willie's at his medical studies." Charlotte's cousins Magdalene and Willie were now quite grown-up, nineteen and twenty-two years old.

"But you'll no come to any harm," went on Aunt Helen, "for there's a stout sneck and keys for both doors."

"Annville's a tight house," said her uncle complacently.

When Charlotte had satisfied them about Tom's new place with Mr. Francis Sprite Apothecary and General Merchant, and described the new flat in the Great Western Road, and given a good report of Mother and Annie, she looked across at the cottage piano, which she had heard about but of course not yet tried. It stood turned a little into the room, rosewood, nicely polished, with an open latticed front lined in pink brocade, and candles each side of the rack.

"Will you give us a hymn, Chattie?"

"Do you no play yourself, Aunt Helen?"

Her aunt rose. "Why, I'll lead the way if I must. I'm no firm on more than 'Rock of Ages.' 'Caller Herrin'' I can render. Would it be suitable, however?" eyeing Charlotte's crape.

"Oh, 'Rock of Ages,' please," said Charlotte.

Uncle John came forward to light the candles with a Runaway match from the mantel. The stool, as Aunt Helen leaned, creaked in

sympathy. Her uncle's voice came and went: "—*cleft for me—hide!
myself in Thee*"—roaring our suddenly on the high, determined
"hide."

Then Charlotte took her aunt's place and threw off "Almost
Persuaded," always a favourite, Uncle John word perfect, Helen coming in with a shaky soprano. The cottage, she had heard immediately,
was out of tune, rather worse in the upper octaves, and the F and G
under middle C were silent.

"There's one stiff key," said her aunt. "It's never been right since the
flitting."

Charlotte played on.

"You've a beautiful touch, has she not, John? You'll be much in
demand, when you begin to go out again, for we've no musical
ladies—except for the Misses Allan in the Wellgate, who teach at the
Lanark Ladies' Seminary, and they'd no hold a candle."

Charlotte touched a series of chords and runs in F Sharp Minor
to avoid the stuck notes, and Aunt Helen said:

"That was lovely. Is it what you'd render at a soirée?" So Charlotte
gave them Number Three of the *Consolations* though she heard the
missing notes, or their absence, and the sharpness of the upper keys.

Mr. W M Miller had said, "It's a gift, to have absolute pitch, Miss
Spears." When she, for the umpteenth time, had set them right at the
Tonic Sol-Fa, half-way through and the intonation inevitably slipping.

"It may be a gift to you, but it's no gift to us," Miss Syle-Paton had
remarked in the lobby. Miss Alison Syle-Paton smiling.

"Put it under the bushel, Miss Spears." They were very familiar at
the Sol-Fa. Unlike The Choral Union, where Mr. Henry Lambeth kept
them in strict order, and even at rehearsals the organ roared forth
under the capable fingers of Mr. Berry, or he'd pull out the *Voix Celeste*
to hold them steady.

"Aye, it's grand to have the house full of music. Willie's the musical
one. Maddie will sit down and pick out a tune, Willie of course never
has the time, with his studies."

There was a pause.

"You may not care for John's pipe? He's an idea it cleans the air.

If there were any of the animalcular life floating about, as some maintain, the reek would kill them I'm sure."

Charlotte said that Robert had been prescribed tobacco at one time.

"It's the strong ailment demands a strong remedy," said Uncle John. Aunt Helen only sighed. For Robert, there had been no remedy.

"*My flesh and my heart faileth*," went on Uncle John in a firm tone, "*but God is the strength of my heart, and my portion forever. Psalms.viiv.26.*"

"Aye, and you were your brother's best nurse, my dear," said Helen, "I'm sure, if ever I were ailing, and I'm not, so you'll no have me to practise on, I couldnae wish for a kinder. And then your dear father taken so soon, you'd scarce be out of half-mourning? He's gone to a Better Land, come, dry your eyes, here's Margaret Tennant on the stair with water for the morrow. John will fetch the Bible up the night for a treat and we'll say our prayers by the fire."

Charlotte, recovering herself, had risen quickly. "May we first move the harmonium? Then it will be done, and out of the way."

A little rain water had darkened the lobby floor. Aunt Helen folded back the Turkey carpet and fetched the drugget out from under Charlotte's bed, to save the waxed cloth. "For it's no got casters to run about on? The cottage has."

Watched carefully by the servant, who had set down her pitchers and was standing at the stair foot with arms folded across her bosom, Charlotte and Uncle John grasped the handles and lifted with a "one, two, and awa'," while Aunt Helen rucked the drugget underneath.

"We could have kept George Kay," said John, straightening, "You're a strong wee body, Chattie, to be humphing this great contraption about. Could you no have taken up the flute?"

"Now, John. Where's it to go, then? Goodnight, Margaret! I'll just run after her, and mind her to fetch up hot water for you in the forenoon."

Charlotte hastened to say there was no need. "I always take a cold sponging."

"Ah, that's very wise. Goodnight, Margaret! then, and you may bathe hot whenever you please in the kitchen, there's a zinc tub under the stair. Margaret, goodnight!" Having shouted, Aunt Helen turned up the lamp and looked about. "Where's it to be, then?"

Her uncle said, "I'll push it back here the now, behind the door, but you'll no be able to get into the davenport."

Charlotte said, "Everything is a wee bit disarranged till I have unpacked. I am sure it will fit very well."

Her aunt lingered, as though she would wish to see Charlotte into bed, but perhaps would content herself in witnessing the opening of the box.

"Aye, it's but a week since I put away my black barathea," she said suddenly. "I hope you find the dark lavender suitable?"[6]

Charlotte, lifting out her polonaise and a neatly folded night-gown, murmuring her approval of course.

"Have you no rolled up your collars in your night-gown? That keeps them ever so smooth. You lay them out cross-wise, and the rolling-up holds the shape."

"They are in my other night-gown."

"Oh, aye, I was sure they would be. I've plenty of the crape-line, if you should wish to slot your under-linen. But perhaps it's of no consequence. You'll find every drawer has been fresh lined, and the bed's turned out this very day, so you'll no feel any damp."

She closed the door behind her at last.

Charlotte straightened her back and stood quite still. She must be thankful that she had not succumbed to tears! But she must not, at least till she had practised and made her other arrangements. The arophane!

She fingered her crumpled crape, stitched and stitched over her gown of dull black bombazine, comforted by its familiar, tawdry fall. Her aunt would not understand. She ought to have spoken at once: "Dear Aunt, I want to wear out these weeds for my father."

And for her brother, though that time of mourning was long by. She could scarcely explain it, yet she had not mourned Robert truly, till Father's death. Her chemise and drawers should be generously slotted with the crape-line, she resolved. This labour she would happily submit to, as a kind of penance—to wear slotted undergarments in room of flashy arophane.

Having settled their niece in, Helen and John were free to return to Stonehouse. Helen would get a hire up to the 3:8 Lesmahagow train:

"for that will be us all the forenoon, John dear, with showing Chattie about, and the patterns for the arophane." But John would be off much earlier—"driving his own pair," as he said by way of a joke. Charlotte would not hear him, he added, for he would be away well before five. He'd walk through the village and away up the Hazelbank Braes in the silence and the dark and meet the colliers coming in from the pit at Auchenheath, and some of them he knew, for he had wrought there. He'd be through Blackwood by six and from there it was not five miles to Stonehouse.

John was never lonely on his long trampings, for the world was bonnie in all weathers, and he was still amazed at these new spaces in his life which the purchase of Annville had supplied, when he had feared it would be but trouble and difficulty. He had a wonderful memory; a choice of Psalms, from which he had learned to read as a lad, brought him over Nethan Water, and stirring hymns like "Dare to do Right!" or "Brightly Beams our Banner" helped him up the steep climb out of Auchenheath dale. Then Revelation.xii for the last mile, coming in along Spittal-street with the two rows of low houses set tight against the road, and the light behind him strengthening. Stonehouse awake now, reek of the midden, past the Cross into King-street with the smiddy banging and the rumble of early barrows and vans. And there would be their own white sign, and Maddie taking down the shutter or standing up from her scrubbing-out and pulling her kilted apron round and perhaps smiling to see him, and away in to pour him his Camp Coffee.

Now, climbing into bed after his wife, he listened intermittently to her comfortable murmurings about Chattie, and how fortunate it was they could invite her to come to them, so Annville would not stand empty all the week, and the garden would be properly seen to, and they'd bring down those broody banties Mrs. Henderson had promised, from Mouse Mill. Annville had been purchased over two years ago, and it was difficult if you weren't aye there to see to things yourself. For it was dreadful what was neglected at Glessart—Helen owned property outside Stonehouse too, which was rented.

As for Chattie's coming, that was truly a stroke of luck, though it could be said, over-soon after poor Matthew went, to be flitting so far off. She was aye a quiet lassie at home. However, she'd be a very determined one as well, to judge by her correspondence.

Aunt Helen's letter of sympathy, on the nice black-bordered paper, had just suggested the possibility of Charlotte's coming up to Annville one day, though before directing it she had written a Post Script:

"I have talked it over with John, and he agrees that Annville could do with a capable House Keeper. Dear Chattie would be very welcome, whenever she likes, if she would not find it lonely." Fancy Charlotte's replying at once:

"There is nothing to keep me in Glasgow."

Charlotte had also written,

> Tom has advised our leaving Corunna-street for one of the large new flats in the Great Western Road, so that he will be near the shop. And since it is likely to be, my coming away to Annville at the same juncture would lessen the necessary difficulties we must face, in the task of ordering Father's papers and books, and a great many of Robert's as well, and all the ordinary packing and flitting. My second reason for closing with your invitation, is that I am eager to commence my Career as teacher of music. I have been advised that, there being no person of this Profession in Kirkfieldbank, while a School and a Church, the field could be said to be ripe for the reaping.

Then that sentence: "There is nothing to keep me in Glasgow." Almost as though. Helen doubted there'd be something not talked about. It was just as well Chattie was come to a quiet village, out of harm's way.

She looked a fair sharp lass, Helen went on aloud, but perhaps it was only her hair, which had a reputation for temper. She believed this to be far fetched; there were those with awful red locks who were as douce as lambs.

"It's her eye," said John.

"Aye, there's a bit of a skelly cast in it, that gives her a fairy look. That's no her fault. She'll do her best, I'm sure. But her hair's no settled down at all and she's past thirty. It'll be the sort that turns from red to white at one go—a pity, for she'll have to put up with it some years yet. She's otherwise a fine bonnie lass, she's her dear mother all over the back. Nothing of the Spears in her but for the hair; look at Annie's great mug, then, and Tom's got the Spears shallow eye, all fleshy round about.

"And the now Mrs. Spears, Annie's mother, you couldnae say Matthew picked her for her looks! Even then she had a face like a saucepan. I can't look at her but I think, I wouldnae find a bonnet to suit you, if I went through my stock a hundred times. I've thought on it now and then, whether he chose her for the bairns' sakes, for dear sister Lottie was the bonniest lass, that died poor soul and left him with them all."

John, who was similarly wearing his second wife, did not challenge this. But he defended Charlotte's brothers: "Tom's no bad looking, Helen. A big braw chield, and Robert was bonnie."

"Ah, he was that! Over-handsome, some would say, and over-clever. It was a brain fever in the end."

"No, now, Nell, it was a straight-forward consumption. And if you're fretting over Willie with his cramming, you'd do best to leave him in the Lord's hands. *God shall supply all your need*, Matthew.vii.34. Besides, when Robert took ill his studies were lang forbye, and though University Librarian and all that, his schooling would be nothing, in comparison with the Medical Preliminaries." John spoke reverently.

Helen, chastened, returned to Charlotte. "Well, she's a sight to see after both Tom and Annie, bless them. I've a great sympathy for the red hair. I always advise shades of violet, not over-bright, the hair worn extremely smooth or with a covering cap. The weeds are no her colour, poor lass. She'd be scarcely out of them after Robert, and then her father taken! She'll be pleased, however, when we have made up the arophane."

Charlotte lifted out her music and laid it on the bed in two great bundles, that sank into the bedspread. Kneeling, she untied the one and extracted Elliott's *Voluntaries*. A day of travel had meant a day without practise. Overhead, she heard her aunt murmuring, the clink of the chanty.

They had called Stonehouse "hame"—there was "hame" and there was Annville—the draper's shop in Stonehouse and the house in Kirkfieldbank. Uncle John said "King-street" rather than Stonehouse: he was "away hame to King-street the morrow."

Would Annville ever be "hame" to her? No more Corunna-street now, with the others flitted to the Great Western Road! No dear Father, no dear Robert evermore, to listen and smile away her cares! She drew a chair up to the harmonium. For some, there could perhaps be no "hame" on this earth; their lot was to be sojourners, that they might set their eyes more steadfastly on the Home Everlasting.

With the backs of her knuckles, Charlotte pushed in all the draw-stops, then played the second *Voluntary* right through with her feet poised soundlessly over the pedals. The digitals could not answer, though they knocked away rapidly, little deadened hammerings.

The effort stayed her tears, and she said her prayers calmly and climbed up into the strange bed. It was the first time she would sleep alone since she was six, when baby Annie had got too big for the cradle. Except of course the four weeks Annie was in the Royal with Scarlatina. Stretching out her feet, Charlotte was minded that she had not removed the heaps of music, which pressed heavily against her through the quilt, like two great stones.

CHAPTER 2

In which Charlotte inaugurates her career.

MISS SPEARS, Annville House, will commence a Singing Class in the Village Grand Templars' Hall, on Tuesday First. Twelve Lessons, 3s.6d. Harmonium and Piano taught (at pupil's residence if required). Terms Moderate.

The Hamilton Advertiser, April 16th, 1881.

Charlotte in moonlight, returning from the Co-operative Social Meeting in Lanark, walking down the Clydesholme Braes between the parks and the brairded drills, with the river dimpling and gleaming. After the lecture she had been asked to accompany the singing; the piano was tolerable and she'd been given a hearty vote of thanks.

"We'll be taking advantage of you, Miss Spears, take care," said Mr. William Munn with the red mulberry stain across one cheek and twinkly blue eye.

Now treading along the river path she saw no colours, only brilliance: white, silver, glowing shade. Yet she could make out every divot, every stone in the shallows, every reed where the water wimpled. Through Brig End farmyard between the sheds, the cattle moving and lowing in the byre—they were restless to lie out now on the new grass. She passed between sleeping farmhouse and bothy and walked on to the brig. For a moment she paused to stand in one of its pointed recesses, built so that foot-passengers could step out of the way of passing vehicles or, she supposed, mounted brigades in the old days, thundering across to find Covenanters and kill them. She had herself been startled once by rapid hooves, and had stood into a recess as several young Voluntaries dashed by, home from practise up on Lanark Moor.

She leaned with her arms on the cool stone, gazing over into Annville's garden swelling towards the flourish. The plum would soon be nearing its height, the pear overtaking, the apple preparing to bud.

The advance was timid—each branch putting forth single buds, opening one by one against the patterning of dark twigs, not a leaf anywhere and the ground still bare under the blond raspberry hoops and the sticks of the grosset bushes. Charlotte, going down the garden, desired only to look into each infant bloom and admire its perfection. The flourish! Soon, in no time it seemed, all to be mingled and swollen and rushed forward into glory. Like the crack choir, she decided, that is indeed made up of individual voices, but in which no single voice is heard beyond another; all are blended in "the burst of general joy." Dear Robert would have understood.

An owl called out in Nemphlar, and went on calling monotonously as she came off the brig. The forge door stood wide at the foot of the smiddy ramp, and a carriage lamp cast a sharp yellow beam outward, turning the blue-white night to ordinary darkness. She heard men's laughter, a female squeal of happy indignation. Probably Agnes Elder.

> Advertisement. Visits, including School (2). Chairmanship. Invitations. Pamphlets and Handbills. Rental of Hall. Reminders. Refreshment. Diagrams and hand-signs. Modulator and Suspended Tables of Tune, Other Tables. Sol-Fa Tune Books. Cards of Membership, Subscription and Attendance Book.

Charlotte, carrying her modulator, walked briskly up the village towards the IOGT Hall, counting over these completed tasks. Her Lecture,[7] which this very night was to introduce the Method and inaugurate a new Adult Singing Class, she was well towards knowing by heart. And that "Sea of Expectant Faces," which Mr. W M Miller had so often brought before the inner eye of his pupil-teachers, had taken on a gradual, almost disconcerting clarity. Sub-Inspector Munro's moon-like visage. Wee Janet Sneddon who hung about and ran in with the milk in hopes of a farthing, the very picture of a waif till you saw her canny eyes. Postmistress Simpson as she spelt out Charlotte's

Advertisement in a slow, high voice, in the dark little shop across the way. Miss Paul and Miss Lillias Paul, who had called and left a yellowish card—though perhaps they were far too old to sing. Stout Mr. Cameron the Minister with his narrow black eyes, and his ever-watchful Managers. Busy Mrs. West, an annuitant sister on one arm and a blind one on the other, and wee Sarah Hopkins their "grand-niece" from London!—to which of them did she really belong? These, and many more, might attend her lecture. She recalled again the advice copied so arduously, nay, ardently from Mr. Miller's Class.

"Have an understanding with a few young people in different parts of the room, beforehand, that their prompt answers will lead the rest—for in some neighbourhoods the people are very shy of letting their neighbours hear their voices."

Charlotte had questioned her conscience on the propriety of this, which Tom would have denounced as a cheap music-hall trick, had not Robert more mildly said, "One's friends would be there, and seeing a pause or silence would answer of course." Alas, she could dearly wish for a friend or two, even an understanding made, as it were, "beforehand." Could she trust the schoolmaster, with his smattering of the new Method? But she dared not ask him.

"In conclusion," she murmured aloud, then paused to nod pleasantly to Mr. Carmichael in the greengrocery door. *"In conclusion. You have now had a taste of our Method, and of the results which can be attained. No system is so well adapted for popular use, no method so well graded, no machinery so economical in cost as the Tonic Sol-Fa Method and Notation. Our Method is easy, cheap and true. Wherever God has given a vocal organ and a human heart, there we go."*

The Grand Templars' Hall, Kirkfieldbank, was modest.[8] It contained of half the ground floor in a two-storey at the westward or "Dublin" end of Kirkfieldbank, on the north side of the High-street. Mostly, the local Templars attended Tuesday meetings of the Order in Lanark: Greenside-lane was where the large soirées and entertainments took place. The Kirkfieldbank Hall was used for Band of Hope meetings, and rented out. Mrs. Reid, from the other apartment, brought her into the common lobby, which was narrow and dark, with a row of sad coats and mantles hanging above some disreputable boots. Curling and other gear was stacked farther back under a circular stone stair.

"You may keep the key, for we generally use the back way and won't be troubling you. There's our weavers in the garret go out the back as well."

"I hope you'll honour me by coming to the Lecture, Mrs. Reid, and that the weavers will come too."

Mrs. Reid pulled her apron round. "Well, that's them, they may come as they like. It's my two wash days and I've been at the boiler and am no done yet. I'll be seeing to your tea, however, so I'll be in before you break-up. I'll put the kettle on my own fire. I must tell you, our lassies are that eager. They're clamouring for singing lessons, and a pianoforte." Charlotte assured her the children were most welcome, and that she would be delighted to teach them.

"Our eldest is only ten. She'll set the Templars' kettle on the swee for if it's needed. There's cups and a caddy and an old loaf of sugar in the press. I've lit the fire early—for it's a boisterous cold day, but the room warms quite nicely. There's coals in the scuttle and counted."

Charlotte folded her cape over a pile of chairs by the Hall door, and paced across the boards to the fire. A tall schoolroom pulpit stood askew and as she was straightening it Mrs. Reid turned the gas up. Over the fireplace the IOGT banner loomed into prominence, with its gaudy trimmings and tasselled cords, and here and there she could make out the subordinate insignia of other associations—the Ornithological and Horticultural Societies, the Anglers' Club, which also boasted a plaque with some sort of mummified fish glued upon it. Between the street windows was a framed oleograph: an angel bending over two children dangerously near an abyss, and opposite hung a grayed verse worked in stitch: "FLEE ALSO YOUTHFUL LUSTS." Besides the chairs, there were rout seats front and back the length of the room, under windows hung with yellowed summer poplin.

Charlotte said, "I have asked Mrs. Cooper to send the refreshments over from the Hotel about nine."

She leaned the modulator carefully against the pulpit, and gathered together a pile of Congregational hymnbooks, Old Edition, from the table. "Might these be put away into the press?"

The two women then walked about slowly, Charlotte spreading her hands down her crape and Mrs. Reid imitating the gesture on her own stained apron. Overhead, the looms rattled and rattled.

"What's that then, is it Diagrams you'll be showing?"

"Aye, and the modulator, which scrolls down and is very large. Where is it to be hung up?"

"You'll find a cleik over the pulpit, and there's one here at the back they use for the Dissolving Views, this being the wall with no fire. You may want to turn the room around, so to speak, and make your address from this end, if you're to show Diagrams and such. The pulpit can be brought down, and there's a slate out in the lobby you could have in."

Charlotte saw that she must arrive early to see to these last arrangements, and said that the lamps might be extinguished till she returned. "*Besides the rent,*" she remembered, "*there must be calculated a small gratuity to the Hall-keeper.*" Counting, she walked back to Annville against the wind.

The rain had turned to untimely snow, with the road already wetly whitened, and the flesher's yard, its usual spill of straw and blood hidden, appeared for once clean past the arched gate. The road was unblemished but for the two wavering black streaks left by a trap, which looked as if faintly traced to contain the skittering hoofmarks between. Charlotte stepped up into the road, and walked within the lines as they filled and disappeared.

How changed was the Hall in the bright gas light, with extra candles all along the valances, and filled with happy voices! Some folk had come in as early as Charlotte, well rowed-up in top coats and mufflers, stamping their feet, then happy to assist with the pulpit and the seating, and the hanging up of the modulator—this last task executed by the village constable, Sub-Inspector Munro, from an unsteady chair.

"Now what can it be, it's doubtless very Scientific," were the remarks as it was scrolling down from its mahogany rod, nearly to the floor, revealing on its white-sized surface the emblem of the Unicorn, the Sol-Fa scale, and finally, at the bottom, the name and patent of the Inventor, Mr. Curwen. Ancient Mr. Curwen had once spoken a few words to Charlotte, after a lecture at the Andersonian.

She straightened the modulator, then moved to the door to welcome Reverend Mr. Cameron, who as Chairman would sit at the table beside her, and rise to make the Opening Remarks. She was glad to see the schoolmaster Mr. Dunlop, and the Managers here and there, though their presence—especially that of a red-faced farmer in a shiny suit, and craggy Mr. Carmichael—seemed to quench the spirits of those who found themselves nearby. There were children as well, and she managed to whisper to two stout girls, sisters, with brown ribbons in their hair, that she would like them to help with the cups when the time came for tea.

As folk began to find their seats she saw faces she did not recognize—scrubbed colliers and power loom weavers who worked from before dawn till after dark. Yet they had come away from their fires to hear her! And there was Mrs. West leading the one sister in, the blind one, and seating her busily. The wee grand-niece, too, standing half-hidden behind Mrs. West's ample waist. Charlotte resolved to ask the child's help as well. She offered up a silent prayer, even as she smilingly took the hand of the great-aunt: "May whatever I say be so simple, and so directed, as to be received by this innocent child!"

"This is rather like The Writing on the Wall," Mr. Cameron was remarking.

"Then we must hope that it is as prescient, rather than as incomprehensible," said Mr. George Thomson cleverly, smiling down at his wife in her tippet fox. He was a law clerk.

Mr. Cameron had caused the hymnbooks to be produced and a tired rendering of "Whither, Pilgrims, Are You Going?" was got through. Then he gave his Remarks, inviting Miss Spears to make clear what was, as yet, but Seen through a Glass Darkly—here he gestured towards the modulator—which no doubt she would most capably do.

Charlotte, impatient through the mournful rendering of the hymn yet thrilled to catch more than one strong, sweet voice in the general clamour, now rose to her feet. Surely the field was hers for the harvesting! She grasped the pulpit with both hands and began.

When it came to the Demonstration, she taught them Tallis' Canon by pattern—first in unison, then with herself supplying the second. Mr. Dunlop had happily assisted with the Mental Effect—had even paused to allow one of his scholars, Marne Reid, to give the answer.

From then on they were with Charlotte; she felt it, and when she chose two "monitors" for the canon—Manager Carmichael, whose tenor she had made sure of, and then, for effect, wee Marne Reid herself, a gazette of the performance would surely have read:

"(Sensation)."

Charlotte took the third. The canon was a success, threatened to continue, was suppressed and repeated more steadily to finish in a long, loud chord: *Doh, Ray*, with Charlotte's *Me*, followed by a burst of pleased laughter.

Eight ladies and eleven gentlemen subscribed at once, and several others hovered undecided; these might look in Tuesday night with no obligation. Manager Adam of Greenhill, who had waited patiently, took her aside to question her about Congregational Singing. Charlotte sipped her tea and said she regarded the praise of God, by *all* the people, to be the chief feature of devotion. Mr. Adam was a prosperous farmer with a large, long head and a yellowish complexion. He nodded slowly and walked off.

Wee Sarah Hopkins was allowed by the other girls to peer about after cups that needed refilling, which she could not very well do, being too small to see into them and too shy to ask. But Charlotte took time to sit down and ask her, taking her hand, whether if there were a Juvenile Class, she would like to join it. Sarah had the kind of fair hair that would never be subdued by a ribbon, a narrow chest and a plain, adult little face.

"Yes, I would. I sing at Sabbath School, Miss, and the Band of Hope."

"What form are you in?"

"I will be in the Fifth."

Charlotte was surprised.

"Then you could help me with the Attendance Record, for you would be one of the eldest. Do you have a good hand?"

Sarah did not know, but Aunt said she was to remain at school, whereas Izzie and Aggie (nodding towards the bigger lassies) were being set to the loom after Fair Day.

"Then you must be clever, and I will be very glad of your help."

Outside, the weather had turned and the unseasonable snow was melted away. A new sweetness filled the air, and the smell of wet earth steeped Charlotte's nostrils as she walked along the High-street— among the villagers, yet a little apart. By the time she reached Annville only one cluster of folk remained ahead of her, going past the brig end to the Ramath cottages. Behind her were Mr. Elder the blacksmith and his wife, and their big daughter Agnes who had subscribed as one of the first. Their house at the brig lay so deep that they got in across a bridge of steps. They bade her quietly goodnight as she turned into Annville gate.

CHAPTER 3

*In which spring advances, the Singing Class is established,
and Charlotte seeks advice.*

The flourish was forbye, the ground outside Charlotte's sitting-room window soaked with pink-brown apple petals. She could not call the prospect pleasing, with the palisade so near, and the ugly monkey-puzzle tree. But very early now, when she first drew back the curtains, the sun would come around at an odd angle and for a brief time pick out in relief the beautiful varied grays of the stones in the dyke, and dance among the branchy shadows on the wood. Towards noon only the highest of the liliac candles were alight—one shrub greenish-white, one mauve. They stood just within the wicket gate with its two stone posts with ANNVILLE cut into them, that faced the High-street. Down in the shade the yellow lilies, which seemed to grow anywhere, were past their prime. She had been around the garden twitching off heads, with the banties at her skirts.

Now, seated at her escritoire, Charlotte heard a gentle drumming thrill from the middle of the monkey-puzzle tree.[9] She leaned a little forward; the venetians were partly lowered to hide the sight of it from her chair. Up went its trunk black as the foliage—if foliage it could be called. It was rough and sticky-looking, and seemed to absorb the light.

Uncle John was proud of the tree however; it had been planted by Mrs. Eliza Fairlie of Hamilton, and there was not another on Clyde, excepting the two at Corehouse, and this was largest. When she heard children cry out in the road, Charlotte guessed the Smith bairns were giving each other a bash; and sometimes late at night there would be sudden rough laughter, even profanity, or a bump against the palisade—men in their drink getting home from the Inn, pleased with the excuse to strike a blow for passing a monkey-puzzle tree.

The woodpecker, which her uncle said returned every spring, was the only living creature to go near it, and the comfortable dunting tamed the tree somewhat. She could not make out the bird among the branches.

She would have liked to put her head in her hand, now, but she would not allow herself. She was expecting her poorliness. It was Tuesday, and she had been working on her Class Books, which now lay before her. Alas, her *Account Book*—so smart it had looked and felt when she purchased it at More's! bound in limp black leather, the cream-laid paper with its faint blue lines. Already spoilt by her many crossings-out—Charlotte wished that Mr. Miller had advised using the lead pencil. But Mr. Miller had envisioned a handsome Secretary smiling over the accounts, entering shillings and pence with a confident sweep of the hand.

Robert, writing away—he always had an Address to make for some Society or other. Sometimes he would chuckle over a phrase and stand up, waving the page, and submit them to a short rehearsal. "It is but for the Greyfriars'; I hope I do not cast pearls before swine," with Father beaming. Why, Robert's papers were covered with addings-in and crossings-out! Heartened, she dipped her pen.

No report of the Lecture had appeared in the *Hamilton Advertiser*.

Perhaps she should be content. The Method was in some places still looked upon as a freak of fancy—"*a method of 'killing' time rather than of 'keeping it'*" had been the supercilious leader in the *Herald*, though they later came round. Last year Mr. John Leishman, having embarked on his classes in Stonehouse, had got the following report: "*Mr. Leishman gave a lesson on music using the new method of manual signs of teaching, reading music from his hand opening and shutting to a certain form.*" Charlotte of course would prefer silence to that!

It was the Secretarial Duties, rather than her musical tasks, before which she trembled. Already she had spent an hour tracing a penny ha'penny, and found she had failed to record the purchase of the *Elementary Secular Tunes*. And Miss Janet Paul had complained that a sheet of her music was lacking. Had it never been sent? Had Mrs. West, ever sorting and shaking down the new scores, inadvertently dropped it into the fire?

If there were but a Secretary!

Mr. Miller took it for granted that each of his pupils, when they went forth, would secure one of course. But Charlotte had none and perhaps no hope of one. It was all very well in "toun"—one might require the assistance of a friend, or choose among the Members. An image of her Singing Class rose before her eyes, their various faces, some eager, some sly, some watchful, some foolish. Mrs. West who so dearly wished to help, and for ever getting in the way! Charlotte could never align herself with this woman who, like herself, was an incomer, settled with those of her family to whom she could be useful. There the likeness surely ceased—in age, in profession, in general prospects! Even were Mrs. West suitable, two women at such an enterprise would never do!

Happily, the "Particulars of the Certificates," also assignable to the Secretary, did not yet pertain. But the day would come, and the Certificates, devised by the Reverend Mr. Curwen himself, were rather like Darwin's Evolutionary Tree, with Elementaries and Intermediates waving in all directions, and Tunes, Sight-tests, Ear-tests, Rhythms and Voluntaries suspended aloft like fruits ever higher and more splendiferous.

And the ideal Secretary of course to be a man! "*Let him be a musical man.*" None she had encountered had lived up to Mr. Miller's ideal, though his own Mr. Macbeth perhaps came closest. Smilingly opening the door at The Cedars, having taken on the delicate organization of The Select Choir for the more advanced pupils. That evening, the grand in the darkened parlour, and Charlotte come early to play through the entire *Jagdsonata* for Mr. Miller at his particular request. Mr. Macbeth's pale face at the portiere, just as Mr. Miller was demonstrating the positioning of the wrist of the left hand for the new Phrased Fingering—his discreet withdrawal. A Secretary saw many things, doubtless, which would not bear recording in his neatly lined Books!

But how could Charlotte, spinster, request the assistance of a man? Sub-Inspector Munro would never do, though he was always early, moving the chairs into position without being asked—it had all begun with his hanging up the modulator at the Lecture. Waiting, too, to see that the lamps were extinguished, the door secured! Although this was of course his policeman's prerogative. And was to begin singing lessons! His large, slow signature on the "Agreement to Observe the Rules!"

As for Mr. Weir the barrister who did not practise, there was something shady about him, said Aunt Helen, the way he strutted about, frequenting the Hotel, and his new wife twelve years the elder, she had heard—that was where the money was, and taking her on while he still wore the arm-band, and her to go into half-mourning for a woman she'd never known and there were two girlies as well. But he was clever, Chairman of the School Board. If he should, as it were, offer himself—but the Members would not take to him, nor the Managers!

Two of the Managers were her best tenors and a third a less capable bass. Separately, she saw them—or more correctly heard them—as voices emerging from their familiar positions in the Hall. But as Managers they were like a dense shadow within her mind, absorbing light, impenetrable as the monkey-puzzle tree.

No, she must deal with everything herself, and if she must she could. The *Subscription and Attendance Book*, at least, was in good order, gummed with brown paper in two thicknesses for strength and carefully lined. "Number, Name, Subscription, Inducement, Attendance." The voice noted as well: a wee *T, B, S,* or *M* after each name. Already she could recall each one, its range and quality.

She ought soon to draw up the Attendance Diagram, and a Certificate List with the Requirements to be ticked off. For, as Mr. Miller said, "*Emulation sets in, and is the very thing you wish to provoke.*"

Was emulation Christian? Ought one not, rather, provoke in the Members, if provoke was the word, a love of music and of excellence? "It comes to the same thing," Robert would have answered. Charlotte knew, from experience, how competitive Members could be. At times, it seemed to her she had been trained as a Lion Tamer in the circus, and was now for the first time entering the tent, or rather the cage itself. The thought was unkind. A Christian thrown to the lions—but not without warning.

All but John Nugent (*B*) had paid the subscription, and he had promised it for tonight. There were two "absent" marks after Duncan McBeau (*T*), who called himself a tailor but was, said her aunt, but a hawker and travelled the roads with his wares. The possible loss of a Member brought on a gripping sensation in her chest, just behind the top of her stays—an old familiar ache that came and went, remembered even from childhood. Charlotte imagined, without thinking about it, that its location was that of her soul.

She rose impatiently, and mounting the staircase entered her uncle and aunt's bedroom above, satisfying herself with a glance that it was in order. The drawn winter curtains let in almost no light. This week would see them replaced with summer muslin from the shop. She opened the medicine chest and got out a stopped bottle—Aunt Helen's sal volatile—then paced about, awaiting some effect. "Mrs. White" the china chanty was peeping from beneath the bed and she moved it in with her foot.

Like Charlotte's the room had a front window, but here above stairs one could see quite over the palisade. The house opposite, called The Cottage, did not open straight into the road like the Hotel and tenements on the Ramath side, or the High-street houses on the other, but stood well back on its slope, with a raked grushie-red path leading up to the door between strawberry drills. The occupants were Mr. and Mrs. Allen, themselves well on in years. Behind it was a bothy in which their boarders were kept—four old ladies, all more or less daft.

Now Mrs. Raines, the most peculiar of these, appeared leading Miss Temple, nearly blind, around The Cottage. Miss Temple clinging to her but at the same time doing her best to steer her askint. Their skirts brushed the earth beds. They reached the road and Charlotte could see Mrs. Raines' spreading face beneath an ancient black bonnet with flying weepers; she was looking in a bewildered way up and down the road, her mouth working; then she seemed to gaze directly up at Charlotte, who hurriedly drew back. An attempt was made towards the brig but Miss Temple, scowling and determined, wheeled them about. They got into the public path under the palisades and Charlotte could see only the bonnet and a house-cap bobbing along beyond.

These two often walked off together, haphazardly; if they got as far as the school they'd go around it peering in at all the windows, and

Mr. Dunlop would have to despatch a merry scholar or two to lead them home.

Charlotte went slowly downstairs and into the parlour. Margaret Tennant had, as requested, opened the windows, and a draught sucked at the fringes of the front drapes just over the sill. Charlotte pushed the frame right up and set the stick straight, then, pulling her skirts aside, got around the table and did the same at the back. The venetians clacked, and she unwound the cord and refastened them higher. The tassels bobbed and the fresh air, tinged with a sour smell from the river middens, poured past her.

She breathed gently, and gazed. Separate white and dark gray clouds stood over Nemphlar Wood, and the romantic gables and chimneys of Sunnyside Estate peeped through the trees. The river rushed and gushed, and the fulsome, separate greens of oak, birk and hazel swelled in the sunlight. Flowering hawthorn had overtaken the flourish—a duller white shading into green, wild among the plantings and thick in the hedgerows. She could see sheep with well-grown lambs, white specks in the far upland parks. Nearer, just across the river, a mist of cerulean hung among the hazels—the bluebells of Nemphlar Wood. It was time for the yearly turn-out; tomorrow she and Margaret Tennant would get at the rooms.

Her music fluttered on the piano behind her and she went over, shivering a little, and sat down to practise. For two hours she played, first from the *Czerny Exercises* and then the last movement of the *Jagdsonata*, concentrating on the phrasing, the fingering Mr. Miller had penned in: 1,2,3,4 and a star for the thumb. She was minded of that lesson despite her resolves. The cottage was nicely fixed and tuned by Mr. Haddow of Hamilton who had been happy to come, having, he said proudly, several other instruments—including the Organ at the Episcopal—to see to in Lanark. The cottage responded well, though of course it was nothing to the beautiful old instrument in the Albertsonian library, which she had once been allowed to try, or Mr. Miller's splendid grand. The slightly tinny notes of the "hunt" carried down the garden and Margaret Tennant picked up the rhythm as she beat the worst from the blankets against their washing, the stour sparkling up in the sunshine. Already women were trooping down the "johnnie" that ran along the wall, getting to Clyde with their bines, jostling and laughing. Right below Annville there was a sandbar with space for the fires and the tramping. "That's Miss Spears at her instrument," the women said, standing still to listen. The music stopped.

Charlotte, within doors, stood up abruptly and held out her skirts, and went across to her rag drawer for a clout.

She was below stairs to an early tea when she heard a knock on the back door, and opened it to Sub-Inspector Munro. He followed into the kitchen and stood by the press, helmet in hand—as at the Lecture and the Singing Class or, she guessed, any public function, he was dressed in his constabulatory uniform with its faded braid, the belt passing rather under than across his stomach. His grand silver belt-brooch was highly polished however as were the two rows of buttons down his breast. Over the stiff collar his neck and head emerged in one unit, as if squeezed out. A police officer is always on duty, she supposed, and perhaps this was the only respectable outfit he owned.

"Concerning the singing lessons," he said after a short silence. "I've brought the subscription."

Charlotte, pleased, asked him to sit down and he took the smaller chair, setting his helmet on the flags between his feet and squaring it carefully. She saw that his mouse-coloured hair was sparse at the crown, his scalp very pink. He sat back and looked at her with rather a helpless, expectant expression. He is very shy, she thought, wondering whether he would be able, on his own, to produce a note.

"I'm sure with training your voice will be good. You are a true baritone, as are several of our bass singers, and Mr. Carmichael who sings tenor." It was always a puzzle with these between-register voices, but Charlotte was firm; no one, once placed, was permitted to change to another Voice.

"You will continue to sing bass in the Class. But for private lessons you may cultivate your own Voice, and sing from a baritone repertoire."

"A baritone repertoire," repeated Sub-Inspector Munro respectfully. "If you think it would do."

"Aye, it will do exactly. And you will learn some pieces suitable for solo, for example, at a soirée." Charlotte believed that one's pupils should always have the star of a performance to work towards, however distant it might gleam.

Sub-Inspector Munro nodded seriously, taking this in his stride.

"Public singing also improves—" she was going to say, the social graces. "It makes all the public appearances easier. Should you be called upon to speak in a meeting for example."

"I make my Weekly Reports to Superintendent MacGillivray, and have appeared in court from time to time. I have been called upon to give the Intimations at the Lodge."

"There you are then, you see. You are accustomed to an audience already, and singing can only provide more confidence and a clearer articulation."

He was suitably impressed and they agreed he should come to Annville Mondays at eight o'clock. He counted out a quarter's sub-scription, eight shillings and sixpence, for which Charlotte would make him a receipt at the Hall. It being time to set forth, he followed her upstairs and waited in the lobby, admiring the cathedral glass on the glazed door, while she fetched her music and put on her hat and gloves. He himself bore the modulator down the High-street—furled of course, but emerging from his arm in a stiff, military manner, so that three of the Smith bairns, playing outside, marched along for some distance close behind him.

Sub-Inspector Munro lived in what was commonly called "the Gaol," a one-storey row house of good proportions, raised from the High-street on the south side next the haberdashery. The gaol proper was his parlour on the left, mostly unused except for tying flies of an evening, or a game of draughts. Charlotte had formed some idea that he lived with his mother, but he was the sole occupant. Music had, as it were, burst into his solitary life, and at age forty-one he was suffer-ing a sea change, was certainly to be numbered among those of whom the Reverend Mr. Curwen had said, "*It will be like having a song bird in every house in England!*" In Scotland of course, as well.

The Class began with the Breathing Exercises, her Members familiar enough by now to follow without giggling or embarrassment. They must first loosen any constriction of clothing about the throat. Hands were then placed over the chest with the forefingers just below the col-lar-bone. Taking a deep breath and holding it, the Members struck their chests rapid percussive blows with the flat of their fingers to the count of four. Then four to breathe out and take the next breath. Then percussion again, lightly.

"One, two, three, four. Out, two, in, four-and-again. One, two, three, four."

Charlotte percussed before them, her white fingers moving so smoothly and rapidly against the crape of her bodice that they seemed but a blur. The noise was something like the woodpecker's. She herself struck quite hard, but warned her Members that they must work up to it over several weeks.

"You may also percuss your chests at home."

Some of the men hammered away roughly, not to be outdone, and both Mr. McConville, a collier, and Miss Euphemia Grindley ended up coughing.

She allowed them to be seated, and gave them the canon *Wakefield*. Mr. Nugent and Sub-Inspector Munro struggling to get down—the basses, as a group, were by far the weakest. Mr. Carmichael, quavering but true, bore the tenors onward, and the contraltos and sopranos were steady; indeed she must be grateful there was no single, piercing soprano among them, the bane of so many choirs.

The Paul sisters were allowed to "look over" just this once, till Miss Janet Paul's missing notes arrived. These two, almost as frail, were the nieces of the ancient sisters who had called at Annville, and looked strikingly like them, the same rather sheep-like length to their faces, with the eyes high up and the nose straight from the forehead. There was a wee daughter, or "niece" in the household as well, with white-gold curls: a little lamb.

The usual problems, to be firmly repressed at the start, Charlotte now dealt with. Miss Elder and Miss Grindley making eyes at young Thomson the joiner, who boarded with the Smiths. She spoke generally to the Members about there being no talking during the lesson. Mr. Lambeth had been known to suspend a Member summarily for whispering. "*You must be master of the room, or nothing,*" he said. "*Whispering between the pieces should be absolutely forbidden. It breeds disrespect, and is more fatiguing to the nervous system than ten times the amount of singing.*"

Charlotte had from the first detected a certain insubordination in the look of Mr. Weir the barrister. Though she had yet to catch him making a remark, or nudging his neighbour, there was that in his eye which told her he would require firm handling. "Mr. Weir, I am afraid I must ask you to leave the Class." Said in her head clearly, as if rehearsing it. But it would never come to that, if she could settle him now. He had a swagger about him, head back and a slight tendency towards the pigeon chest, long side-whiskers and a continual half-smile under the corners of his trimmed moustaches, a brown-eyed man with middling brown hair, well fitted out, shooting his cuffs, taking his time with his top collar-button when they prepared for the Free Passage of Air. And she did not like his look when she advised them to sing with mouths open "*sufficient to admit the thickness of two finger tips*," and all were trying this, the ladies as delicately as possible, and he had looked directly at her almost as though.

"A disappointed man." The phrase came to mind suddenly, she was unsure why, for he was surely prosperous.

He looked indeed rather rakish and citified; there had been several such gentlemen at the Choral Union, who gathered in the lobby afterwards, smoking. Some of them came to rehearsals wobbling along on Ordinaries, which were all the rage, and stood about outdoors looking at them. Mr. Lambeth of course had no trouble keeping such gentlemen in order.

But here there was only Mr. Weir in that class and perhaps Mr. Thomson the dapper little law clerk. Charlotte had expected these two to gravitate towards each other, a kind of imitation of the Choral Union dandies, but they did not. At tea afterwards, Mrs. Thomson hung prettily on her husband's arm. At one point Charlotte saw the two men standing exactly back to back, almost as if about to fight a duel. She wondered whether they had quarrelled. Perhaps there was some hierarchy however, and a barrister, even one who did not practise, despised a law clerk.

No one besides, except the schoolmaster, could have been called an educated man. Those who were also Members of the Kirk Choir gathered, others formed lesser groups. There were the three Managers. There were wives, who moved towards their husbands. The two big lasses stood close, eyes darting, and Charlotte took the opportunity of speaking to them about silence between the pieces. They apologized but Agnes Elder looked sulky. She had a loud soprano voice, rather full and watery as if coming through a sluice. Her figure, vigorously lashed by stays, seemed almost like two balls tied together, and her gown, in wide vertical stripes of green and russet sateen, was unbecoming. Her face was large and round, pleasing but for the expression, the skin unblemished and of that unearthly white which characterized the blacksmith's trade and which, in the Elder family, seemed to have affected even the wife and child. Euphemia Grindley had the lank red hair and pinkish eyes not uncommon in the lowlands, the only one in her family so afflicted. She was also severely laced, and her costume declared a haphazard sort of half-mourning, the skirts rather scanty, her big boots sticking out and the oily fibres of the weaving floor stuck to her hems and around her boot-buttons. Like many a village lass, she would have been in and out of these clothes through most of her growing up, Charlotte thought pityingly; her mother would produce a wean every two years or thereabouts, and few that lived. Euphemia was the eldest, and would surely be hard wrought all her life.

Charlotte now moved resolutely towards Mr. Weir and he turned to her pleasantly, speaking before she could get a word out. He was eating a large bun.

"You must compliment Mrs. Cooper on the baps, Miss Spears. She's been blethering to me about whether Archie should bring them along later, as we're no allowed our refreshment till we break-up."

Charlotte said, "It is best to put away the music before taking tea. I hope"—gathering courage—"that you are satisfied with the Class in other respects?"

"Oh, aye, you wouldnae want butter on the music. You'll need to keep a firm hand on us, you ken, Miss Spears, for it's well known what gets up to at the Evening Singing Classes, it begins with butter and who knows where it will end?"

Charlotte, inclining her head over her cup, walked slowly but firmly towards the fire so that he must follow her. The empty grate rather dulled the effect but she turned to him and spoke as severely as she could.

"Mr. Weir, discipline in the Class is essential. I am glad to hear that you agree, but I am quite serious. Singing is pleasant of course but only if we work seriously can we progress, and find true pleasure in what we achieve. Perhaps it could be said that the Teacher, newly come into the area, should rather wait and see how the Class comes on, but no Class comes on at all unless discipline is maintained."

"You've an iron hand, to be sure, Miss Spears." He was smiling.

"Aye, in this respect."

"Well, I'm sure you'd no find a Member among us would quarrel with you for that, though it didnae look muckle like iron the night, fluttering like a wee dove against your breast. I'm speaking of the percussion exercise, of course."

"No Member," said Charlotte, trembling, "who cannot submit to ordinary discipline, will be permitted to remain in the Class."

"Ah, well, we are at your command."

He may have looked a little discomfited as he turned away. Charlotte's heart was pounding. She swallowed a scalding mouthful of tea. "Mr. Weir, I must ask you to leave the Class—" almost, she could have said it! She determined not to speak to him alone again, for he would not have dared to be insolent had she spoken generally.

Mr. McBeau the hawker had returned, bawling away among the tenors with a will. Mr. Nugent had not yet produced his subscription. He promised to come to Annville the next day, casting his eye towards Sub-Inspector Munro and directing his words as much to him as to Charlotte, as if taking an oath before a magistrate. "It's the agent, he had no work for us till Monday last, but I'll have my end in the morrow."

Mrs. West voluble as always, bearing down now on Charlotte, wagging a finger. "Oh, Miss Spears, you do go out, aye you do—I know that a teacher must teach, whether or no—however it's no that, which I refer to. And we would be so delighted by a call. My sister is unable—she is, I must tell you, quite unable to take personal care, without assistance, she is very distressed about it, but as the spark flies upward, I like to say. She is however over-eager to make your acquaintance. We have been quite the song birds at home since the Class started, and Maria knows all the tunes. And as you were so good as to play at the Cooperative Soirée in Lanark, which not being the same as a kirk soirée—so we have presumed? Perhaps when Mrs. John Brown is at home, and the weather being fine, we will call, that is, Maria and myself, not Miss Taylor, and leave you our card, for we all use the same one, I will confess to you, and Miss Taylor's name stands, I told her, you'll no be expected my dear, till you improve, but your name stands. Your name stands, you see, Miss Spears, it is a kind of encouragement though between us I do not see there is any great hope. Though we have a great reliance on Whelpton's Purifying, but oh aye, her earthy bigging is crumbling down—and that is the verdict of Dr. Gray. I ought not to say verdict, it sounds like a death sentence and she is far from that, her stomach is in fact still very sound I am satisfied to report—" this last to Miss Sym the schoolmaster's assistant, who had stopped beside Charlotte for a moment; and Charlotte, turning away to place her cup on the green baize and beginning to assemble the books, was thankful she was not yet going out, despite the Co-operative Soirée.

Over the boiler Aunt Helen saying: "So you've Roddie Munro on your list of singing scholars, I hear. Aye, John told me, Roddie sometimes comes by for a crack when John's at Annville, he's no afraid of the kitchen at any rate. And he's a very faithful angler, we've had a bonnie brownie from him often enough. Of course he's no one for the Inn, well, he wouldnae be, would he? Unless he were fetched." She paused significantly. "He's no been a constable all his life, he was pensioned off from the Chelseas in '73.

"He sees the darker side of life," she added, as she lifted the blues on the stick and scrutinized them. "We'll leave these a wee, for they've no quite revived."

Roderick Munro not as comfortable coming to the front door then, for his lesson. Charlotte had the lamp lit in the parlour, and the two candles on the cottage as well though it was not yet dark. He was her only singing pupil so far, the others being scholars who came to study the harmonium or the piano. She had been surprised by his composure: when he sang, it was quite without his normal embarrassment. He stood well, one plump hand resting lightly on the top of the cottage, assuming the regimental "at ease" posture, lifting his head high. She complimented him.

"Are you a member of the Yeomanry?"

"No, Miss Spears, I do nae ride. I sustained an injury."

There was an odd dent on his left temple, half hidden by a lock of hair, and Charlotte wondered if this was the injury he had, as he put it, sustained. Had he been struck with a broadsword by an enraged native, or fallen from his charger into a spike or fence? The dent would not however prevent him from riding, unless it had perhaps affected his balance.

Aunt Helen did not know. She was not sure he had even seen action. "John could find it out, I'm sure, if he would take the trouble. I do believe it's a thing regarding his head at any rate, so he neednae be bashful about it. He'd want to be over-careful down Stonebyrnes Linn, with the angling, there's a terrible run over the Loup." Charlotte had a vision, not quite serious, of Sub-Inspector Munro pitching forward into the water.

After the exercises they had chosen some music. "Choosing the Music" was a popular subject for engraved illustrations in *The Ladies' Journal* and Charlotte was careful to stand well away from Sub-Inspector Munro, with the draped corner of the cottage separating them. She wished him to work on a tune he was unacquainted with, using the Sol-Fa notation. He chose "Now by Day's Retiring Lamp" and they went through it slowly.

"You'll soon find you'll no need a visual score, and be able to rely on what is called the Mind's Eye Modulator," she said.

"Oh, aye, Miss Spears, I'll have the tune in my head before that."

The Cedars, Glasgow, May 3rd, 1881.

My Dear,

You must not call this fellow a gentleman, for he is patently not one, however well educated he may choose to be. And I beg you never to apologize, in seeking my advice or counsel, if I can assist you in any small way. Indeed, you have done well to consult me, for as a female teacher in a new area, you must be singularly unprotected from the insinuations of such a Person who, having paid his Shilling Subscription, considers you a fair mark. It would seem he has no further objective than to make an Annoyance of himself, and therefore I do not judge you to be, God forbid, in any danger (knowing your character and your spirit!)

You say you have also confronted him, which was very brave of you, knowing as I do your extreme distaste for anything of the sort—for we all, of a sensitive nature, would naturally prefer to avoid rather than speak to or advise, those who would purposefully cause us discomfiture.

In one sense, you must consider yourself happy if he does become so objectionable, as to merit his ejection. But I would by no means urge you to allow this. If he shall continue, you can be sure it is for his own Amusement and a very mean game.

You say that he seems to be acting like a child, to try how far it can go. I say, treat him then as the naughty child he emulates. Rebuke him, and give no more thought to it. As Teacher, you have power to do so. Chastise him before the Class, make him a laughing stock.

Alas, on rereading these stern words, I cannot see how they might be carried out, by you, who are already so cast down. Were it I standing there, I could do so! But I am not there, and must temper my indignation to suit your circumstances.

I would beg of you then, my dear, to speak quietly to him once again, if you can bring yourself to do so. You have called him a gentleman, and such he may consider himself given the limited Society he moves in. Appeal, then, to his gentlemanly spirit, for he would be a poor specimen if he did not have a spark of it left, or aspire at least to be seen as such! If not, he is a rascal, and a short Note of Suspension, delivered by your Secretary, will do the trick. Believe me, he will not quarrel with it, for he will know in his heart he has been in the wrong.

Your clear voice is much missed amang the warblers of the Select Choir. I trust you continue to practise the pianoforte diligently and not deny yourself, or your present Society, the pleasure of your very superior performance, and that your music in all aspects flourishes as it should.

In closing, I beg you to give me the assurance, having weathered *this shadow on the path*, of writing to me again with better News when convenient to do so. I hope that my poor words have been of some help, though I admit to being written in some haste and agitation. We are all well, and Isabel begs to be remembered. As you no doubt have read, the *Oratorio*, went off well, being gazetted as "no less than what we have been led to expect." The Choir is now busy with rehearsals for the up-coming performance of *Norma*, of which I sadly cannot hope, with your new Duties, you will be enabled to attend. Courage! Yours ever sincerely,

W. M. Miller, Esq.

CHAPTER 4

Charlotte, attending the Evangelical Union Kirk in Lanark with her uncle and aunt, was not privy to the discussions concerning her in the vestry at Kirkfieldbank, where the Managers sat after service with the *Roll of Seatholders* open before them, waiting for the rents. Many Members of the Kirk Choir belonged to her Singing Class, and some had evinced dissatisfaction with the Kirk singing, now that they had the swelling tones of the Class to compare it with. "Torwood," the new Voluntary Charlotte was teaching them, sounded quite as though it ought be sung in the Kirk. Mr. Carmichael before service, putting out the hymnals and fancying himself alone, had tried out the first lines softly, then louder, in the nave, surprising the beadle who paused in sweeping the walk and leaned suspiciously on his besom.

> *No longer hosts encountering hosts*
> *Shall crowds of slain deplore.*
> *They hang the trumpet in the hall*
> *And study war no more.*

As performed by the Singing Class it was indeed fit for the Kirk. Ancient Mr. Whiteford at the harmonium could not wring such sounds out of his Choir, and during the hymns, the congregation was aye a good half-beat behind.

"Mr. Whiteford, though a long service in the Kirk, had of course not the benefit of a toun education."

One difficulty was whether, with a strong Choir, the congregation would be quite left out. The Managers knew Mr. Cameron's views and were largely in agreement: he firmly upheld congregational praise, though permitting an anthem from time to time. A concert or soirée was, he felt, the place for *listening* to sacred music; besides, these events were good money-getters.

Mr. Alexander Adam, instigator, said that he had already "sounded out" Miss Spears on the matter. "I didnae mention more. Only what she considered was the place of congregational singing."

He could not recall Miss Spears' exact words, but she was strongly in favour. It would be wise not to get up her hopes. Mr. Whiteford, despite his unfortunate collapse across the harmonium last week, was perhaps good for a year or so yet. It would be possible perhaps to examine her further. They could invite an interview without committing themselves. They could then form an opinion.

The vestry was off the nave at the front, forming on the outside a short abuttal towards the schoolyard. Within, it was high and dark, with a tiny lobby to the yard making it even darker, and but one window against the bank. It was lined nicely with Lebanon cedar, lot-ends the joiner had lying after the finishing work on the Lanark U P. Mr. Cameron, who as yet had no manse to live in, kept his surplice and a change of bands here in a narrow cupboard, and till he had got himself properly into them they smelled rather damp. He had worn them at his ordination in Edinburgh. Here was the press lined with musty kirk books, the stout chest containing the communion vessels, and a barely sufficient assortment of chairs, even with the precentor's chair brought in from the choir. A photograph hung over the chest: Mr. James Burness the previous minister, who had died so very young, looking rather miserable as well he might, thought Mr. Cameron hanging up his surplice. He sat down in his ordinary cassock.

A few members of the congregation, in arrears, had been in and paid their seat lettings for the half-year. Across from him Mr. Carmichael, having spilled out the two pouches on the table, was counting the collection with irritating slowness. He had been a grocer. A long arthritic finger separated out a worn farthing. The widow's mite, Mr. Cameron could not help thinking. The congregation had risen to the enormous effort of building their Kirk, and called him to them on the overtopping of this long and prosperous wave; now it was as though their energies as well as their coffers were emptied, and the idea of the manse had faded *"as a dream, Fades at the opening day."*

Indeed, a kind of exhaustion had fallen over the Managers after not only the exertions of building but, following on this, a long suit filed by the builder's family. Builder Simpson had been called to his Heavenly Home soon after being awarded the contract, with no warning to the Managers, who had spent an entire winter evening awaiting him in the vestry, for an explanation of his getting behind schedule. At the end of which time they had passed a resolution *"that his conduct was highly reprehensible."* Little knowing that, even as these harsh words were entering in the *Minutes and General Business Book,*[10] Simpson was keeping another Appointment. Death had revealed him a bankrupt and certain payments had been swallowed prematurely by another creditor; more were demanded. Mr. Stein Esq of Kirkfield House had taken up the pen for the Kirk, and long and bitter was the battle, the sum in question being nearly one hundred pounds. It was no wonder that plans for a manse must wait. And did they need, at this time of steadying, a new precentor, above all a young woman?

The decision was, however, to interview Miss Spears. Mr. Russell would convey this message to her in the form of a letter, after Tuesday's Singing Class.

Mr. Barr of the Dublin end of the village had voted against. Sitting back, thumbs in his waistcoat. "She's trouble. I'm saying it the now, that you may recall my words in the fullness of time. For *there is nothing covered, that shall not be revealed; and hid that shall not be known. Matthew.xx.25.*"

Mr. Barr, not a Member of the Singing Class, was a sour, muscular man a dull, boiled eye and a shaven chin raw red above his Sabbath dickie—a prosperous farmer with twenty acres and four men employed to work them. Mr. Carmichael rose to Charlotte's defense.

"Miss Spears is very strict and no-nonsense with the singers. And if you think she would lean too far over to the Evangelical, being a Congregationalist, why, she'd no take the post anyhow."

"As Christians," said Mr. Cameron, "we cannae but hear Miss Spears' side of it. It could be," stroking his clipped beard, "that she's just the ticket, for a musical soirée can bring in a pound or two to fall in a dry place." He eyed the collection, now piled in neat wee pillars and nary a shilling among them.

"There's the earthing to the turnpike road all falling down," added Mr. George Steele. The Inn stood out to the road, and a good dyke below the Kirk would do his west gable a deal of good, with the water aye leaking by.

So it came to pass that Charlotte received a letter in the IOGT Hall after her next Class.

Sub-Inspector Munro patient at the door, seeing her on the single chair under the cracked gasolier, very straight and solitary, holding the page out as if she were reading one word at a time, so long she sat, with her carroty hair sleeked down into a bun at her neck and her dull black gown, and the bare boards all around her.

The Managers were pretty evenly divided, though others had misgivings less irrational and violent than Mr. Barr's. There had already been a disruption last fall and they had been forced to dispense with the then beadle, Mr. John Stark, a young man, who had been shown to be of unsteady habits. An older beadle, like an older—indeed, a very old—precentor, could better be controlled. David Reid, if he had to be admonished for bringing in the fires the very Sabbath he was hired, while still September, had otherwise turned out well, and was satisfied with the same salary as his predecessor, being five pounds, five shillings per annum.

Admittedly they had, in Mr. Cameron, a young minister; this being his first Calling, he was as yet eager to please. But a young woman, a single woman certainly not to be termed middle aged! They could not voice their worries on this score, but Mr. Cameron being as yet not only without a manse, but without a wife—it was perhaps a blessing that Miss Spears was a Congregationalist.

Mr. Cameron, unbeknownst to his Managers, was however safe from any designs on the part of Miss Spears, for his heart was given to Williamine Stuart of Govan, a girl of yielding temperament and Presbyterian principles.

He had made love to her through a series of letters on which he spent, it must be admitted, as much care as on his sermons. The engagement would not be blazed about, however, till she came of age and the question of a home were settled. His prospects were till then not "such as he would presume to ask a young lady to depend upon," despite her pretty protests. He boarded with the widow Capie in the High-street, and though it must be said his material wants were supplied, it was a rare day he dined on other than collop. And of course he saw nothing of the famed venison enjoyed by his predecessor, owing to the Managers' unfortunate falling out (before his time) over a subscription, with the Cranstouns of Corehouse.[11]

Mr. Cameron had come to Kirkfieldbank on his expectations, for he was not yet ordained when he stepped into the shoes of Mr. Burness as interim preacher. There had been a flare-up from the Mission Fund, Glasgow, whose grant to the new church stipulated an ordained minister; the word "underhand" had been used in the correspondence. Mr. Stein of Kirkfield House had smoothed the troubled waters.[12]

Mr. Cameron was ordained in due course, and had in fact by this means avoided the discomforts of "sheltification." But he still felt, quite reasonably, that every shilling he received was begrudged him, though he did get it, he made sure of that.

"My dear Thomson," he wrote after the meeting, seated at his desk in the corner of his sitting-room:

> I was delighted to read in the pages of the *Advertiser* of the great success of your Soirée at Haywood, (300 counted!) which of course I heartily second, having had the pleasure to assist with my Reading which however was overlooked in the report, though the "original" poem, which I cannot agree was as "effective" as all that, except as an Inducement to Slumber, and the harmonium rendering of the Marche Flambeaux

(here he consulted Mrs. Capie's newspaper for the spelling)

> were duly praised. Your Labours to gather about you, and keep about you, such lights, while even a small village, are an example to your compatriots labouring in the field, Matthew.v.16.
>
> In this respect my excellent Managers have persuaded me, not entirely against my will, to interview a Lady newly

arrived at the village, not being entirely young, in respect to the position of Precentor, for our dear old Mr. Whiteford is sorely failing. I was Chairman to this lady's Lecture at our IOGT Hall and was suitably impressed by her command of her music, and her sentiments regarding the promulgation of music among the Common People, which as you know is the "signal-flag" of our "Sol-Fa" enthusiasts.

Her moral character is undoubtedly beyond reproach. She is now teaching a Singing Class which most of our Choir attend and speak highly of, including three of the Managers, and it is these who urge the step. One other of the Managers is dire in his foreboding, however he cannot have Reason behind him, his only concern being (I should guess) whether a Lady with such red hair can be quite the thing. She is however one of our E U sisters from the Westport, and lives very properly as housekeeper for the Browns of Annville House, who have, I believe, a son studying at Glasgow University. Her name is Miss Speirs.

I write you under the threat of supper, which is sure to be bread tea! I trust you are happier with yours! and leave you to enjoy it.

By the way, all this fashing over the settlement of the earth bank between the Kirk, and the Road, must postpone my natural anxiety on the question of the Manse. As you are in a similar (but culinarily speaking, happier) situation as lodger with your good Park's, you will sympathize with me. But I am in the humble position of one who has gone, as it were, to *sit down in the lowest room* Luke.xiv.8, etc. in faithful hope that I shall be called to go *up higher*, meaning, in my case, *Manse*, of which I have further Reason to wish for, more of which hereafter, I remain,

Yours faithfully
Walter Cameron.

CHAPTER 5

In which Charlotte receives a further advancement not unanimously approved, and establishes her Juvenile Class.

Charlotte dressed carefully, pressing her small black bonnet down over her hair and arranging the fall smoothly across her shoulders. Her dyed collar and cuffs were nicely revived, and the crape, neatly ironed out, restitched to her black merino gown. She would carry nothing but a black silk parasol of her aunt's, rolled tight. If the Managers wanted a selection of suitable pieces for the harmonium, she had any number in her head.

The evening was warm as she walked up the village, the air smelling strongly of hay, the sky down the dale bleached of its blue—pink-white and cloudless. The street was quiet. After a long day at the berry beds, a squad of bothy Donnegals sat on the Inn step or lounged against the wall, pulling at their cutties, and a few village kimmers stared from their doors. She could hear Clyde tumbling beyond the houses, for it was always biggest at loosing—or "lousing"—time when, Uncle John had explained, they let the water off up at the New Lanark Mills. Two women were getting down the well path with their raiks as she stepped around the earth bank, and they wished her a good night. She knocked on the vestry door.

It was very dark within. The parsimonious Managers had spared a lamp, though they would presently light a candle or two, when the evening deepened. Like her they were dressed in black; indeed, the open book and those unhid portions of their faces, and their severe collars, were the only other areas of pallor in the place. Like an oleograph, thought Charlotte, in darkest tones, or a painting so heavily varnished there was no colour left.

She was invited to sit, and took the chair across from Mr. Cameron, he and the Managers all sitting down again, except for the one whose chair she had usurped. The room disagreeably crowded, even the table nearly hid under the pages of the *Precentorial Duties*[13] and their large folded hands.

At first she could not help feeling she was here to defend herself, and bit her lip. "Rob," she spoke in her heart, "these gentlemen are really no more fearsome than the deacons at Elgin Place—or Mr. Senior, or dear Mr. Batchelor! They have all received "the right hand of fellowship"; why, any one of them might be Tom himself, for he is a deacon now!" She was then able to look bravely across at Mr. Cameron's broad countenance with its thin curved beard describing a line of jaw he did not possess.

When they questioned her, she answered quietly and sensibly. This was after all her profession; it was but her competence they required.

Her evening prayers were grateful, for it had been much of an ordeal, despite fancying Robert's gentle encouragement. Surely, from that sunny Realm, he was still interested in her struggles here below? It would have been a relief, even, to have talked it over before and after with Tom and Annie, made light of her trepidation.

"We neednae appoint Miss Spears till September, for she'd no have special duties to observe through the summer. She'd best be left to her Singing Class, and if we dismiss Mr. Whiteford the now, we'll save the four months' salary."

"Aye, and have no one to play at the services."

Mr. Adam put in: "Let it be resolved, that she be appointed for September First, and Whiteford to go then, and we neednae be putting the sheet round for him again, for his salary is paid lang syne. We must trust to the Lord's grace he'll be here to earn it. The Singing Class in the meantime, could very well begin to study for a soirée in the fall, when the other kirks would but be beginning to practise for Christmas. Miss Spears has already been speaking of a concert, and some of the selections are very blithe and suitable."

"The Choir willnae be over-pleased about that," said Mr. Barr. "And I hear you have Mr. Duncan McBeau in your Class, it would be the first time such a one has darkened our door. There's also a Baptist among you, I understand. And if I remember right, John Harvey is under a suspension for intoxication, he wouldnae look very nice singing in a soirée."

He went on to warn them gleefully that, for all they knew, any mendicant passing along the turnpike road might join the Singing Class over at the IOGT Hall, and thus be discovered in the choir box in the fall. "The *Duties of the Precentor* reads '*and friends,*' and who are we to ken the friends of Miss Spears?"

Mr. Cameron pointed out that according to said Duties the Precentor was (he read out) "'*subject to the control, and bound to obey the orders of, the Managers.*' I trust that the Managers are sufficient unto the task." He looked around severely.

Charlotte's salary was to be the same as her predecessor's: five pounds per annum. Her not being a Member of the Kirk was no stumbling block, the Congregational Psalmody being almost identical. Charlotte's interview, meant only to sound her out, had been satisfactory, and the vote—after she was gone—was in her favour though not unanimous. Mr. Russell delivered the letter the following evening, standing for a moment within the laden, scented porch with his hand raised to knock, to allow the strains of the piano to come to an end, a melody he recognized but could not name. Miss Spears appeared, squinting, framed by thick clusters of yellow roses.

"Miss Spears, I have been designated by the Session to deliver this letter to you. And may I be allowed to congratulate!"

Charlotte thanked him, taking it. As he turned to go, he added, "If I might enquire, what's the piece you were playing? for I'm sure my mother sang it, when I was a wean."

Smiling: "'Werena my heart licht I wad dee,' by Grizzel of Jerviswood."

"Aye, that's the very one! Now I will tell you something you did-nae ken. It is our own Jerviswood on the Mouse. There's no but a ruin up there the now."

He went off with a sprightly step, humming the tune, and

Charlotte, thinking of its aptness for him and other elderly Members, turned eagerly to her letter.

Little children liked Charlotte, who gave them her attention. Her pupils now included, for the harmonium, Mary and Mabel Adam, Robert and Jane Gilchrist, and Susan Jane Capie; and for the pianoforte Sarah Hopkins, Catherine and John Ross, and Marne and Grace Reid from next the IOGT Hall. They came to Annville eagerly, with their music more or less rolled, and worked with a will. None, unfortunately, had a particular talent. The Reids had just hired a pianette from Cramer and Co. on the Three Years' System, and except for the Gilchrists the others had a harmonium in their parlours; Rab and Jane were allowed to practise in the Kirk, with their father to let them in. He would tend to the front bank in the meantime, for he had planted it and except for the slippage it was doing nicely.

These pupils were all present at the first meeting of the Juvenile Singing Class, to be held Tuesdays at six, before the Adult Class.

She kept Sarah Hopkins at her side writing carefully into the centre page of the *Attendance and Subscription Book* with the lead pencil, keeping within the lines Charlotte had made for her.

"Miss Spears, what must I write under *Indu, cement*?"

Charlotte smiling told her to leave it the now.

"I could write, 'His Mother is in the Adult Class' but it would be crampit."

"Perhaps we can find a way to shorten it, Sadie. Is there space for 'Mother, comma, Adult'?" Sarah wrote.

Several Members of the Adult Class had come with their children. The Stein laddie, John, spruce in a Sabbath suit and trousers, walked smartly up to the table all on his own. "I'm to see if I take to it," he said to Charlotte. "And there's my brother, but he's probably too wee."

"How old is he?"

"He's no but six."

"Of course he can join. Where is he?"

"Out in the carriage, bubbling. Lindsay brought us, and he's to wait for us, but he'll be away to the Inn if you'll agree to Archibald."

Half way out he turned and ran back to say, "May he take off his boots, Miss? For it's as much them he's bubbling about."

"Of course he may. We don't sing through our boots!"

John Stein gave her a wide smile. "I've chucked mine already at the fit," he said, and ran out.

He spelled his brother's name slowly for Sarah, watching every letter jealously while Archibald, at the door, struggled to get out of his boots and stockings, and pushed the lot under the roup seat. Then he ran up, and stood close beside John and stared at Charlotte—a smaller edition of his brother, similarly starched and suited, his stubborn, teary face now calmed. While John the little esquire dug their subscription money from deep in the pocket of his narrow breeks, and handed it over quite as if possessing, and parting with, two whole shillings were a matter of indifference.

They all stood before her now, lassies in big white bows and summer pinnies, laddies cap-in-hand, in their breeks and jerkins, a stiff collar showing here and there. A few close-cropped from having lain with fevers, and all barefoot except Sarah, who wore winter stockings and black boots as if her office required it. The array of limbs, though knobbly and scratched, were surprisingly straight. Even the poorest of village children had the better of the bairns of the tenements in toun, with their crooked legs and bulging white foreheads. The faces before her were sun-darkened from pulling ground fruit in the hot weather. Except those of the two Adams girls, who wrought indoors, and they all looked fit but sickly Janet Dickson from the Close and a rocking, down-looking laddie called Bernard McBride, wedged between his two bigger sisters who had him fast by the hands.

"He's tongue-tucked," Sarah had whispered when they'd come in.

Charlotte asked if everyone could sing, and all except Bernard cried out: "Aye," and if they sang in School or Sabbath School or Kirk or the Band of Hope and she heard more "Ayes" among them. This time, she had some adult Members on hand who had brought their children, and if they were a little surprised to be called on to demonstrate, they did very well. Charlotte kept them busy as monitors of groups, and in among the children clapping and singing. The others, a few sisters or servants, sat on the roup seats and watched. On one final note she caught an especially beautiful, sweetly piercing voice among the throng, but it did not come again and for once she could not tell which child had produced it.

She finished the lesson with a hymn the children knew, and they

sang lustily, taking big breaths as she had taught them, to Fill The
Lungs, while she pointed the position of each note of the simple tune
on the modulator, to get them used.

> *When he cometh, when He cometh*
> *To make up His jewels,*
> *All His jewels, precious jewels,*
> *His loved and His own.*
> *Like the stars of the morning,*
> *His bright crown a-dorning;*
> *They-ey shine in their beauty,*
> *Bright jewels for His crown.*
>
> *Little children, little children,*
> *Who love their Redeemer,*
> *Are the jewels, precious jewels,*
> *His loved and His own.*
> *Like the stars of the morning,*
> *His bright crown a-dorning;*
> *The-ey shine in their beauty,*
> *Bright jewels for His crown!*

CHAPTER 6

In which the former acquaintance of the two cousins is related.

Charlotte had first seen Willie and Maddie when Aunt Helen visited at Corunna-street, to show off John Brown. That was about the time of the first reading of the banns and John, though newly fitted out, was an awkward fellow who did not know where to look. He said he was a clerk and gas collector in Stonehouse but Father, who'd been a bookseller for Uncle George in Edinburgh before employing as a timekeeper and clerk in Glasgow, was unable to engage him in conversation. John's children had been motherless for some years. Mary Alston Brown had wasted away of phthisis: of her six children only these two survived her.

Willie at that time was a plump little lad just out of frocks. Even in breeks and with cropped hair he looked the more girlish of the two; Maddie was a plain Alston Brown with a steep face and small mouth. Robert said, they must have got their faces traded and Charlotte, innocent, thought, they aren't twins so they couldn't have, but it was true Willie was the bonnie one even then.

The visit was "teedisome." If Willie or Maddie, with Annie sitting bodkin between them on the settee, shuffled or swung their legs, John Brown would pipe up and tell them to sit still "or you're due for a leathering"; Annie looking across at Charlotte with round eyes. The only time Father had ever thrashed *them*, was when they made Annie be *Rashin' Coatie*[14] in the ashpit, in the back close at Aldington-street.

Mother suggested a walk up Kelvingrove to the Park, and Charlotte and Annie were glad to escape with the wee ones, and after the Park they went up Sauchie to see Tom in the shop—he had just entered his indentures with D.A. Cuthbertson, Provan and Strong. When they walked in Tom was not to be seen; he was probably in the back rolling pills or suppositories out of powders, which was what he mostly did, he said. Looking for him, they had walked the length of the shop. Willie had got in close to Charlotte's side, and she felt his hand pressed into hers. He was staring at the row of great glass jars on the high shelf, with their transparent mixtures and the Latin labels gummed to the insets. A trick of light from the windows across Sauchiehall-street caught the sun and lit them through—royal blue, russet and deep turquoise green. Willie was pulling at her hand and when she leaned down he asked, "Is that the Happy Land, where all them bo'tles is?" [15]

She had seen him again at fourteen; he'd come in for the Athenaeum Lecture by Mr. Thomas Hughes who was to speak on "Perspective of Life." Mr. Paterson had recommended it. Mr. Paterson, the UP minister in Stonehouse, seemed to be rather a hero among the Stonehouse lads.

Willie was still small for his age. He wore an adult suit too big for him and an inflexible stand-up collar and brand new cap, surely secured for the occasion out of the draper's shop. He had a habit of kicking at things experimentally with his tackity-boots, and of glancing round-eyed at you, sideways. His voice had not yet broken. He was one of Mr. Paterson's "lads o' pairts" by then, studying for the Higher Certificate. He had walked all the way to Blantyre where he'd got a hurl in with a milk van, which he had not asked for, he said, for he could easily have walked the rest. He ate a large tea. Both Tom and Robert went to the lecture as well, and afterwards Robert said that young Willie "deserved every encouragement." Willie walking up and down the room, biting his lip and darting his eye towards Robert now and then, obviously fired by the lecture, and pleased by his older cousins' attention. He slept in their bed and was away early in the morning.

Mr. Thomas Hughes was the author of *Tom Brown's Schooldays*. His lecture had concluded:

> "*Understand yourself—know what you are best suited to do; this is the first rule of success in life. We grow up unawares, rising from the playthings of children and the games of schoolboys to the most serious of human pursuits. In short, the secret of arranging things in our minds according to*

their real situations and values ... (is) finding that true stand-
point outside ourselves, from whence we may look patiently
and firmly through the tangle, drift and whirl of life, certain
that, to the steadying gaze, the mist will disperse and the
mirage vanish away."

Willie had entered these words, in lead pencil, in his *Blackwood's*
Shilling Scribbling Diary. His profession was already determined and
was surely the most serious of human pursuits. He was to study
Theology and become a Minister of the Kirk. Robert, who was
University Librarian, would introduce him to the Dialectics and other
Young Mens' Associations. Robert wanted him to come and lodge
with them at Corunna-street, when he entered the University.

This last had however come to nothing. The next winter Robert
was in Bavaria, already more ill than they knew. Later Willie, in lodgings
in Endelsie-street, had often run up the stair, a flash of scarlet, his dark
hair rumpled and cuffs stained with ink, and stayed for long, earnest,
theological discussions with Robert. His eager voice rising to a shout.

"Do not allow him to tire you, Rob."

"He does not tire me, Chattie; he's a breath of fresh air."

Willie was still small, brisk, restless. He wore the scarlet cloak of
the *togati* in the usual raffish fashion, high across his throat, and was
encouraging a moustache. Charlotte thought him very young. Robert
had many other visitors, and it was Charlotte's business to receive
them, and to allow or refuse them upstairs. Mr. William P Dickson
from the Library, official and apologetic, with rolls of papers from the
New Catalogue, who was not to be turned away, Robert said. Then
there were David Hartley and his other friends among the Sol-Fa
Choir; and from the Elgin Place Kirk Tom's crony "W P" who prayed
with him, even Mr. Senior from the Music Committee, and Miss
Rough, and of course their dear Reverend Henry Batchelor with his
great, white mane. These visitors were, unlike Willie, formal and gentle.
They sat often downstairs, uncomfortable, speaking in low, cheerful
voices. They were careful not to overstay themselves.

Willie, borrowing Robert's dumbbells, attended gymnastics
instruction three days a week under Mr. Benson who carried out the
McLaren system in its entirety; Willie was also a member of the Junior
Bowling Team and the Dialectics. He read *The Nature of Atonement*

and Sir Charles Lyell on the stratification of the earth. He was buffeted by the strong winds of higher criticism questioning the authorship of the Pentateuch, by opinions socialistical and nullifidial. At Robert's bedside, through arguments that were playful even while in earnest, he felt himself tested in the clarity of truth and guided, when science failed to console, into the simplicity of faith. Sometimes they were silent and if Charlotte looked in, Robert's head would be turned aside on the pillows, and Willie sat nearby, hunched over—he'd give her that sideways look then, angry and helpless. Sometimes when Robert was feeling better, they romped: the others would hear high, silly laughter, the crash of a chair. Willie was studying Tyrone Greek, Logic and Moral Philosophy the year Robert died.

After the funeral, when the men came back to Corunna-street, Willie's face was raw red with greeting. He told Tom that he had put off speaking to Robert about the decision he had reached—to abandon the study of Theology and to enter Medicine. After that, he did not return to the house.

They had gathered at the harmonium. They had sung "There is a Happy Land, Far, Far Away," Charlotte remembering Willie in the Sauchiehall shop. She and the boys—and then Annie too—had been told when they were very young that those great jars contained unborn babies, which mothers purchased from the chemist's. Then, she had almost thought she could glimpse the tiny weans paddling about deep in the bright fluid. Was this why Willie had called it the Happy Land, confusing the idea of bairns glorified, with bairns yet to be born? His own brother Andrew and sister Catherine Spence, whom he would just remember, and before him another William and a John, neither of whom had lived at all, were safe in the Happy Land.

There was a medical doctor called Gairdner at the University, whose lectures were enthusiastically attended, also by *togati* who were not planning to enter medical studies. Willie heard him whenever he could. Gairdner was widely esteemed for a transparent truthfulness, a grand simplicity of mind. "*The patient is not a mere specimen of disease,*" he said, "*but an afflicted man, worthy of the patience and kindness with which suffering must be helped.*"

When Willie, almost stammering, praised Dr. Gairdner, Robert had chuckled and said that though a great man he was notoriously absent-minded, and that he had more than once been denied access to the Library because he could not find the books he had borrowed. After that Willie could not quite speak of how strongly the doctor's lectures affected him.

To Willie, his ten-years-older cousin Charlotte was only Robert's sister and a spinster. She was always there when he ran in to visit Robert; if Annie or Mrs. Spears let him in it was because she was upstairs, or coming down with a tray or going up with a poultice in a basin. She had a smell of soap and fomentations about her. Pausing on the stair in a clean apron, saying quietly, "I've just to bathe him," or, "He has a visitor." Willie almost felt she liked it if she could delay him; then, he would throw down his cap and loosen his cape and sit in the straight chair nearest the stair till she was through, or the visitor came down. She was aye busy about Robert, and whatever she did he would thank her, though Willie thought he would sometimes sooner be left alone. Once Robert said, when she had gone down and Willie had drawn up the chair, "Chattie tires herself out, she is too good. I wish I were not so helpless." And smiled. When he returned from Egypt, he was so much weaker that he could not be got over to the chair by the window, unless he were carried. Charlotte, when Willie came after her into the room, would step aside, because Robert wanted to be up every day when Willie was there, and Willie carried him. Then she would help settle him in the chair, and leave them. That last week, it exhausted Robert so much to be carried out of bed, that they did not converse.

"Shall I read to you?" But Robert could not exert himself to answer.

"Willie, ought you to move him?"

"He wishes it. What difference does it make?" Charlotte with her back to him then, turning out the bed. Robert's lightness in his arms, the awful sharpness of the backs of his knees through the rug. The fierce radiance of his look.

He had received a letter from a friend in Egypt, a nurse at Alexandria, Mr. Khalil Salih.

Will you be kindly enough to send me the following books as I know if you buy them your self they will charge you less

than what they charge me if I write to have them myself. You
can draw against me for value and I shall pay it as soon as I
receive any remarks viz.
  The Lovers' letter book
  How to make money
   " to dress on £15 a year as a lady
   " we manage without servants
   " to make soup
   " to dress Salad
   " to make cakes
   " to make Pickles
   " make Hash and curry cold meat
  Breakfast Luncheon and Tea
  Infant nursing
  two thousand familiar quotations
  Common things of every day life
  The Law of Bills
  How to cook eggs
   " " " Rabbits
  the invalid Cooks
 I hope you are better and you have now a better health
than what you have had here before, I am Dear Sir etc.

They giggled about the letter, Robert's beard pointed up in the air, his breath catching in a little sigh.

"Shall I buy these books and send them for you?"

Robert's eyes saying, "Aye, thank you."

The room at the top of the house had a remarkable stucco ceiling. The light changed on it, setting it in relief. Robert, laid back into bed, his dark wasted hands on the quilt and his beard pointing, watching it with that terrible concentration.

Downstairs, Charlotte gave Willie money for the books and the post. He did not think she approved and he thought, surprised, "It is because she does not know the man in Egypt, or anything about Egypt, or how Robert was nursed when she was not there." As she was counting out the money, he noticed the extreme whiteness of her hands.

After Robert died he did not see her again till he saw her at Annville.

CHAPTER 7

*In which Willie Brown pursues his university career,
and is taken with a fever.*

Charlotte's aunt and uncle were full of Willie of course, for he was just now cramming for the session examinations. It was, as far as John could understand, Junior Anatomy which was giving the difficulty. Though anyone who had managed the Preliminary Examinations so well was surely past the worst. They had included such subjects as Euclid and Algebra, and Statistics, Kinetics and Hydrostatics. What could Anatomy, *Junior* at that, have to be feared?

The break-up of the University sessions was in early April, and Willie sat the examinations the following week. The students would then be on holiday till the sessions recommenced in June.

The Browns were however disappointed in seeing Willie, whom they were daily expecting at Stonehouse or at Annville. Instead a scrawled card arrived, that he had accepted a job at the Western Infirmary for the interim, and would remain in toun; "which convey to Mr. Paterson"—for Willie, since he had abandoned Theology for Medicine, was sometimes stricken in conscience to be still receiving the bursary. Though Mr. Paterson when applied to had named the great Christians in Medicine and forestalled Willie's own arguments before he dared to voice them. And had refused Willie's then fairly safe offer to renounce the bursary, and said with a twinkle:

"You'll recall that our Saviour was a medical man."

"Willie's no to be overwrought," said Aunt Helen, turning the card around. "He'd be better taking his holiday after all the studying."

"Aye, but it'll no be his brain that's overwrought—he is to go about the wards, which is what he will do when he's become a doctor, you ken, and will prepare him the while. Mark.v.9."

Charlotte, sitting down at the harmonium to ready herself for a pupil, was surprised at her relief. Her hours of teaching and practise were already very neatly slotted into the house keeping, and Willie would have required sit down meals more elaborate than her own hastily dressed dishes; she had even begun to consider what she would feed him. She and Aunt Helen had spent a day on the empty upstairs room though it had suffered spring cleaning already, dusting the ceiling with a turkey's head brush, wiping down walls and furniture, turning the mattress and making the bed. John had even carried up the gate-legged table, previously in Charlotte's sitting-room, to stand ready for his books. She would bring it down again the Monday.

Willie passed his examinations: Pathology, Materia Medica, and the Junior Anatomy he had failed last sessions.[16] Except for one visit to Stonehouse, to pick up a straw and new linen, and for Saturdays "up the Watter" with his friends and some ladies, he remained in toun.

The work at the Western was physically arduous but a refreshing change from his books, just as his father had foreseen. Though it did not do to be fastidious. Unless one inhaled a good lungful of dripping camphor going in, which rather knocked out one's nose for a time, the wards weren't much worse than the emanations from Annacher's midden or the killing shed in Stonehouse, the stench of blood and offal he'd grown up with, that hung so heavy over the back road of a summer afternoon. He was never qualmish.

He worked as clinical clerk to Professor Leishman, following him about the new Ward for Diseases of Women on his morning visitings at half-past nine. The sister in attendance, the nurses and lady nurses at attention, the day-spreads pulled tight across the silent rows, not a crease showing. Later, if he was lucky, he did the dressing for Dr. Grainger, but the nurses were nimbler at it, and many a time he was glad of their help, when the great man was expected and they were in a fash to get the work done.

The lady nurses had no time for him, but he saw that they were kind to the patients, not above emptying a vessel either. They got no salary so it was truly a Christian calling. There was a bonnie one with white-blond hair, who began about when Willie did, but she did not last and the others said she was gone back to her dancing and her landau and good riddance. Willie wished he had spoken to her however, for she would have needed perhaps but a little persuasion to understand the good she could do, and the spiritual reward.

Glasgow in the summer time with the daylight early and late to show it off, the scrape of the scavenger's broom and the bangs in the back close with the midgie-men at the ashbins and emptying the tips; then came the early water-waggon and by the time Willie emerged from the close, vans and carriages were rattling past, and on Buchie omnibuses rearing over the other traffic, with bonnie nursemaids already perched under their parasols with their charges, heading for the 'Tanics, their ankles nicely hid by the modesty board along the upper deck.

Willie's digs were at the bottom of Elderslie-street, near Buchie where it runs into Argyle below the Park. He walked to the Western by his usual route, for the Infirmary stood high up over the south end of the Park, its spires mingling with those of the new University beyond.

He had tickets to the Western and knew his way about, but clinical demonstrations under Mr. Leishman were still Classes, the students intent on specific fevers or taking notes on the general doctrine of contagion, watching and listening. Now, he felt something of what it would be like to be through with his studies and truly practising.

Tickets to the Royal Lunatic Asylum could be got as well; he had been shown through the Lunatic Asylum on the usual tour. But though he had access he had not returned. Some of the others were over-pleased with the place, and at first went back often; Kerr and McCormach even played with the idea of becoming alienists, and discussed the possible physical causes of lunacy. Dr. Grainger himself encouraged a kind of interest:

"The Scientific Physician must also have an understanding of that science which deals with the higher spiritual nature, of which the body is but the organ and instrument, and yet whose activities are so closely conducted by the healthy or morbid actions of the latter."

Indeed the poor lunatics looked far from fit, many being in the advanced stages of consumption; but it could have been the air itself that did for them, for it stank horribly and Willie had seen rats running along the skirtings.

In the great basement dayrooms some of the lunatics lay on the floor, cripples and others who even when prodded refused to get up. They were extremely white-skinned, never being brought into the daylight. Some were chained, and some left naked because they would tear off even the strongest of garments. Willie saw many physical deformities among them. He remembered particularly a young man with the loop of his bowel exposed so that he was sitting upon it, and a lad with an open bifida. A woman who regurgitated her food was shown to them as a curiosity—a pink pool like "jeelie" in front of her on the floor. They stood about for a time but she had not re-eaten it, though the attendant, who called himself Dr. Macrea, assured them with apparent satisfaction that if they would but wait she would do so, often several times.[17]

The wards were mostly silent but there were distant, repeated cries which for some hours were to persist in Willie's head. A few of the lunatics spoke quietly and constantly to themselves. Macrea told the students that, among intelligent lunatics, religious lunacy was the most entrenched.

"We could do with a few Gadarene swine," Wotherspoon had remarked on the way back. There was a good deal of banter, and silly imitations, the lads letting loose the way they did even during demonstrations and operations; and Kerr actually rolling about among the leaves beside the path. "Oh, the de'il's got hold o' me in a soft spot!" McCormach said that "Doctor" Macrea was a stuck medical student, and as such had no right to call himself a medical practitioner.

"He's stuck with the dafties, then," quipped Kerr.

Willie laughed with them, but wished in passing that he could have discussed the spiritual aspects of lunacy with Robert. He wondered how Robert would have interpreted: "*This kind cometh not out but by prayer and fasting.*"

Every morning after dinner Willie worked on the surgical ward, dressing fresh amputations and removals. Except for Mondays at one when he assisted the Medical Vaccinator with primary vaccinations: numbering the lymph tubes, holding the skinny arms of terrified children. Revaccination fell to the undergraduates; he would be doing that soon himself.

Number 6 Corunna-street stood just at the end of the Kelvinside Road, across Argyle. Sometimes turning into Argyle Willie had used to see Tom on his way to the shop, and if Tom noticed him, which was usual, Willie would cross over, though they were both in a hurry.

"You've no been seen at Elgin Place the last Sabbath or two."

Willie would excuse himself; he said that he attended morning Chapel in the lower hall of the Hunterian each Sabbath at two-fifteen.

"Oh, aye, Chapel is all very well, but our Mr. Batchelor's sermons are out of the ordinary strong. The text for this week was in *Which is your reasonable service.*" Then Tom would begin with his usual ponderous slowness to quote: "*I beseech you, brethren, by the mercies of God, to present your bodies a living sacrifice—*"

Willie would glance at his watch, bringing Tom to consult his own repeater, of which he was justly proud, and pronounce himself late. And Willie would run off more lightly for the encounter.

But now the Spearses were flitted to the Great Western Road, and his cousin Chattie was at Annville, and Tom would be almost next-door to the shop. Willie went the same route still, up through the Park. Corunna-street in the corner of his eye, the second-floor windows side-on from the Argyle-street corner, with a muslin curtain blowing out in the breeze, weightless and transparent against the sun.[18]

In June he filled out his "Natio Glottiana" for the *Matriculation Album, Session 1881-1882*, and signed his name under the Declaration: "*William Alston Brown.*"

He would study Midwifery under Dr. Leishman in the fall and, for the summer course, Operative Surgery, to be followed by lectures on the Principles of Surgery, under Dr. Grainger. He put his name down for a head.

Willie walking across the stone brig over dirty Kelvin River that flowed into dirty Clyde. Now he would no longer step into the gloom and bustle of the Western, but circumvent it and run up the curved path through the newly laid-out gardens, to the new Medical Buildings rising splendidly on the hill. He wore the serious, plain garb befitting the man no longer in Arts, and eyed the *togati* as the mere laddies they were, in their silly scarlet capes, humphing their new books or gathered under the portals like a flock of birds. A Sheltie lad here and there among them, with like as not his fifty-pound sack of oatmeal on his back to do him till Christmas, or his hand-me-down cape askew over ill-fitting Sabbath clothes, and looking about him with eager eyes.

To be the student of Dr. Gairdner—almost, it was a privilege Willie was not ready for. The weeks in the Western had already brought him nearer the great man than lectures could do, and he had witnessed his gentleness with the patients, how he took time to speak personally with them even with Sister chafing in the background. Willie saw especially his minute, even painstaking observation and recording of the facts of each of his cases. He was in his element at the bedside, and could coax a smile from the wannest of faces. He was very fond of his Differentiated Stethoscope, and Willie considered that he'd received a private course in percussion and auscultation, simply by watching him.

"Now this is one of the prettiest results," Dr. Grainger would say, and let Willie "take the voice" after him to prove it—the healthy side and then the side enclosing a vomica. Willie, his ear to the ivory circlet and its far end dipping into unsteady flesh, hoped he could hear a difference. The patient, a dropsical woman, watching them indifferently. But the good doctor stayed to speak with her till she grinned widely, and told him she had ten children, all living. "I've more weans than I've teeth in my moo," she confided, which was indeed the truth.

Pain in his patients Dr. Grainger would not tolerate, and scolded around about him if he met with it, ordering more laudanum; and apologized were he forced to inflict it, as indeed he sometimes was. Willie had then thought himself singled out when the good doctor, with a nod or a quiet "Well done, lad," had acknowledged a satisfactory dressing on an amputation, or turned, if a word of comfort had not made its way to a patient in delirium, his look encompassing Willie with its warmth and pity. "*This frail and fearful tabernacle of the body*," he had said, unforgettably, at one of the lectures.

In his classes Willie soon understood that every student felt, indeed received, this singular warmth. They met in the main lecture room at eleven, Tuesdays and Thursdays, and after a description of the case or cases proceeded to the operating theatre. The class contained of twenty-eight students, though in the theatre it would be much augmented by others crowding in to observe. Sometimes there was nothing scheduled and they received a lecture.

Then Willie contracted what was called milk fever, from bad milk drunk at the student refreshment rooms. It was, if not quite an epidemic, a *smart outbreak*: sixteen came down with it of whom three died.[19] The tainted milk was traced to a farm outside Cambuslang where, with sick children lying, the chanties were emptied directly into "the grip"—a channel running on each side of the passage in the byre, for the cattle droppings. It was presumed the milk had been infected with the contagium. "A *feverish illness, suspiciously like typhoid.*"

Willie lay in his digs three days, having had to leave the theatre, and feeling very weak by the time he reached his bed. The land-lady brought him beef tea made from the best calves' foot at MacGaw's, which he could not stomach; she finally spoke to Mr. Andrew MacNair on the first floor, a member of the *togati* and studying for his preliminaries in the fall. MacNair felt Willie's head and pulse and questioned him about the refreshment room, then told him of the epidemic.

Willie was taken to the Royal in a hansom, MacNair getting him down. He was in a rank sweat, too ill to care that the cabby wanted a blanket on the seat and over the floorboards. The land-lady unwillingly allowing MacNair to fetch the one from Willie's room, and instructing him to bring it back. The cabby meanwhile had jammed his ancient top hat on his head and jumped up.

"The Sanitation will be fumigating my cab again, if I don't take precautions, sirs," he said over his shoulder. "It's the miasma does it. Are you richt?" clicking to the horse.

MacNair however left the blanket wrapped around Willie, who was laid down on the bench in the anteroom.

His clothes were taken from him in the ward and he was washed and put into a hospital shirt and his head shaved. The nurse said, "Dinnae fash about your claes, we've thrown them into cold water the now, and will wash them when convenient."

When he was in bed he said to MacNair, with an effort, "Will you send a post card to Stonehouse, there's a penny on my stand. Tell them a fever is going the rounds and I'll soon have the best of it." His head near to splitting as he spelled the directions out.

CHAPTER 8

In which the Lanimers are celebrated, and Willie endures
illness and convalescence in town.

After the Whitsun term fair came the Lanimers, which was Lanark town's ancient, annual circuit of the Marches or boundary stones. The surrounding villages competed as well in the floats and sports and decking out. Charlotte would not attend, though Aunt Helen said it would be a sad Lanimers if all those who happened to be in mourning stayed within doors.

Charlotte saw them off, Uncle John with a nosegay in his buttonhole, and Helen and Maddie bonnetted lavishly. The Clydesdales coming by, splendid in their peaked holiday collars of shining brass, their manes and tails primped and beribboned, the grush ringing under their great combed fetlocks and lightsome summer shoes. And the floats of all kinds, and an unruly procession of villagers calling out for order and commenting on the decorations, scrubbed bairns with their boots on running about, lads scrambling aboard for a hurl up the Brae. They would all sort themselves before they reached the top.

The front porch at Annville, already so bountifully clothed in yellow roses, had needed no further embellishment, though Maddie that forenoon had tied two great red sateen ribbands—from a shop lot which had got the damp—high on the trellises, with Helen directing from below and Charlotte to hold the ladder. There was a surfeit of blossom to bind over the wicket gate as well, in an arch made from a hazel switch John brought from the river. Helen said she had no quarrel with the colour, for it was closer to rich cream than yellow, and "Glorious John" was the prettiest rose of all, being so plentiful; she guessed there were three hundred blooms in the porch this year, enough and to spare. They smelled overpowering sweet as well, from having planted an onion at the root.

Willie should have been at Annville to make the arch and save his father the trouble. John, fixing the switch with twine, rebuked his wife.

"It was wise of Willie. He's no one to depend on the bursary and be content. *For the night cometh,* John.ix.4."

They had all pricked their fingers. Maddie had to wear her mother's second-best kids to the Lanimers, having put on her own with no court plaister and managed to stain them.

Then Kirkfieldbank was silent all day long, but sometimes with the breeze came the far sound of the pipes and the bells and now and then a mingled shout from up the Brae. Charlotte practised.

It was the second Lanimers for the Browns,[20] and John, who walked the Marches last year, would do so again. After the standard was presented the first circuit set off and he was away among the crowd. Helen, with Maddie in tow, drifted back down the Westport to the E U, and refreshments at the manse.

"You might have been there, Chattie, for you were asked after, and I said, she's concerned about appearing. Mrs. Forsyth said you could have bided at the manse—you'd have seen the whole procession from the Kirk door."

The Reverend Mr. Forsyth was a sandy-haired gentleman much admired by the female members of the congregation, and though off to the Marches in the forenoon he was expected, and a large throng of ladies were on hand to assist Mrs. Forsyth in the kitchen.

"And the wee charity lassies from Mrs. Wilson's Mortification, looking so gay in their great bows and peeping in at the manse door and chasing about the yard—for the rain soon stopped—everyone remarked how the day hadnae started promising but turned out favourable all the same."

"We just took our tea and perambulated back to the High," said Maddie. "For the lifting of the standard bearer—and the Provost, such a great thick man. The Yeomany were very impressive." She touched her laden straw which she had not yet removed, shaking out its beribboned fall across her shoulders.

"We came away however," added Helen. "It was becoming very boisterous. There was a terrible trade at the Clydesdale already." That hotel stood dangerously close to the E U Kirk.

In the evening Charlotte was persuaded by the others to walk the length of the village and look at the decorations. Whoever had returned was out and about. Helen had a comment for each house.

"I've no doubt it was Miss Raines who made that mess over the bothy but you wouldnae wish to prevent them. And the Hotel is a regular heathen bower." They hastened their steps as rough shouts and laughter burst from an entrance almost hid by birk. Already Donnegals sprawled about in the footpath, asleep or worse.

The Gaol was done up proud, and Helen hoped it would not be wanted. Two jaunty fishing-rods crossed like swords over the door and the old salmon on its cracked plaque from the Hall, fixed between them. Wild roses, already wilted, hung their heads along the railings, tied up with fishing line.

"The Anglers have been by to help Roddie Munro. Aye, he wants a woman's hand.

"And will you look at the Miss Pauls'!"

The shades drawn again in the front window of the Grindleys': Helen doubted but that Postmistress Simpson was right, in calling it prideful for but a baby.

Still the wee lassies bounded in their white pinafores, and ran up to greet Charlotte, clinging to her hand to tell her all about the Lanimers. She picked up Jessie Inch, six years old, and kissed her bonnie red cheek, which was sticky. An even smaller lass, one of the Smiths, stood roaring in her door till an arm yanked her inside.

"Oh, aye, it's been a long day for the bairns, and many a sore wame from too many sweeties."

"Whoop!" sounded from the Inn. Here came the last Clydesdales plodding home through the village to Linnmill and Old Orchard, a little less dazzling now but still proud, steady and unfaltering.

Charlotte took her early walk in all weathers. The ways still hung with tawdry bits of ribbon over the dykes and among the hedges. Helen's red sateen they had found not to be fast; when they came to pull it down, the doorstep and some of the roses were spotted from it, which looked very odd. Margaret Tennant scrubbed the porch and Maddie gathered the affected petals up as they fell, for a pot pourri.

Even as early as six o'clock the village was lively, with the strawberry-pulling at its height. Every helper young and old was wanted along the rows. The striped parks rose bright green behind the houses over Ramath, and spread out along the Clydesholme Braes, and all down Clyde, and Charlotte could hear the farmers' piercing birrels blowing near and far.

The sheds against the farm roads brimmed. At Boathill above Ramath she ordered four half-squares, which were great wicker baskets holding four of the ten-pound punnets each, before they were all sent to Carluke. Not that good fruit was lacking at Annville, but Helen liked the sort. The gaffer with his birrell round his grimy neck and a rope of old black in his waistcoat pocket, and "nicky-tams" tying his breeks in under the knee. Promising to set the fruit down at Annville before his van won over the brig. Sunlight lined his cap and shoulders, and his shadow was long cross the road. His squad, away at the far end of the park, standing up to stretch with their hands pressed into the small of their backs, then bending again as they saw him coming. Past them the thick plantings of Corehouse and Castlebank, tucked into the gorge, and the gleaming spires of Lanark along the hill.

She sometimes took The Verge, the old ferry road up to Kirkfield House, that went on to Ayr. The finger-post leaning over now, and the ferry-house inhabited by a collier and his family and but a track down the bank to where the ferry had crossed, just before the parting of the waters among the Inches.

A path from behind the Inn led up the dominions as well, which Margaret Tennant in her usual quarrelsome voice had advised her against: "You'll no be walking up the *hinney muir*," and Charlotte guessed it was a trysting ground. Though children played there and the forenoon would be innocent enough.

Lately, she preferred to walk west the length of the village, and out the Stonebyrnes footpath with Clyde roaring; or she would step quick over the brig and up by Mouse Mill. Mr. Weir lived on the Ramath road. Even the High-street she disliked, the Hotel being just across from Annville, though he was scarcely ever about before the back of twelve o'clock.

He had appeared at the Post Office the Monday as she was returning a book. Mrs. Simpson also operated the shilling library there, the "but" half of her house a wee shop just past the Hotel. Charlotte was pleased her book was not a novel, *Ethics of the Dust* being beyond reproach. But as she went out he was at her shoulder:

"You're a serious reader, then, Miss Spears."

She hardly knew what she replied, or heard his words as she turned away, something about being "over serious, if you didnae take care." She walked as calmly as she could across the road, feeling his eyes on her back.

So did summer come on, and the haying commenced though the fruit-pulling was not yet done, with the Irishmen at their scythes all day and into the bright night, the weather so fine that the hay could go straight from swathe into ricks without turning.

All was new and interesting to Charlotte. The two-wheeled carts, extended by the long harvest frames, were surely piled dangerously high, teetering down the shorn parks to the farmyards. Even the Clydesdales looked quite diminished before them. Margaret Tennant said there was aye more than one wagon spilled at the Tollhouse turn. Some of the parks were even worse with the earth at the gate pitted in dry ruts, and the open-shirted sheavers atop the load would shout a warning or scramble down to steady the load, with only a lad to lead the pair up into the roadway. She saw the aftermath of a tipped load more than once, the hay spread like caught hair in the hedges.

She watched the ricks building in Brig End yard. They cast deep, buttery shadows, almost red, and their sweet scent quite overcame the ordinary reek of the farm. The Brig-End bairns, Jock and Joseph and Mary Ann, too young even to pull strawberries, tottered unsteadily up and down the new lanes and alleys. "*Round the rick, round the rick,*" they chanted.[21]

As Charlotte walked she would endeavour to compose a reply to Mr. Miller's letter, which she had pretty much got by heart. "My dear"! But as she had done nothing about her difficulty, she did not write to him then.

John came in from Stonehouse the Saturday with Willie's card. Drinking a tinnie of sour milk while she read it, in the open back door. "He's sure to be on the mend by now, it came in the first post Wednesday."

"Has Aunt Helen written to the Great Western Road?"

"No, nay, we will wait for another card before we disturb them."

Hanging the dipper back.

Walking through into the kitchen, John said he had never seen the tops so "thrang," or busy, though the weather was said to be too fine to hold. The turnips wanted a good saturation, and the hay was burning up on some of the highest knowes.

The needed rain came at last, one night, in a fierce storm. Charlotte, alone at Annville and waking to thunder, hurried downstairs and threw on her cape and hood, and was in the kitchen groping for the lamp when the sky flashed and crashed all at once—the storm must have been directly overhead. It was already raining hard and she was afraid for the banties—lately, they had taken to nesting up in one of the plum trees nearest the house. It meant rain if the poultry went to high ground, Margaret Tennant said. Brown Eyes was the one who'd started it; she was the tamest. Charlotte had got them in every evening till they'd gone in of their own, but last evening there was Beauty up the tree again and the rest aflutter to follow her, and Charlotte had to poke the besom at her to get her down, and then chase them all to the caivie, swinging her apron. Margaret said, too, that Miss Spears ought to let them be, for it was very bad luck to meddle with poultry after sundown.

Now she was under the plum tree just as a second huge, metallic crackle sounded overhead and the orchard came alight—and there was poor Beauty, low down and sorry for herself, among the clusters of unripe Burnets and the shaking leaves. She let Charlotte take her in her hands, and bear her across to the caivie, and be told on the way she was a bonnie Brown Eyes, with her claws gripped tight and her wee heart dunting.

Back at the house door Charlotte paused, hearing past the pound of raindrops on hard ground a dog's frantic barks, a man's shouts and a woman answering. The rain was warm. Already soaked through, she stood still for a moment. Her night-dress was drawn in against her skin. Strong sweet smell of the earth as it gave over its dustiness. In a picture, softly, she was letting herself down into Clyde by the sandbars, where the children swam below Annville.

She had bathed at Saltcoats, summers gone by. Tom serious and busy with his towers and dams in the sand, tearing about when the tide came in and picked at their crusty edges, till they crumbled despite his efforts. Charlotte and Annie pretended to swim, lying face to face on their wames in the shallows, kicking and laughing. Robert learned to swim. He swam dreamily to and fro, out where they could not follow.

The storm caused no fatalities in Lanark or the villages nearby. But at Newburn Colliery, earlier in the evening, an old man named McGilvarie, according to the *Advertiser*, "*was struck dead sitting by the fire and two children, a girl of seven and a boy of nine, were found lying beside him. The electric fluid had entered his head and shoulder, these parts of his body being quite black. In another house, the electric fluid came down the chimney and went out through the wall, drilling a hole an inch in diameter in its passing through the stone and lime. All the pictures, the looking glass and eight-day clock were broken to pieces. The foot was carried off the cradle and the baby uninjured in it.*"
Stonehouse had escaped the strength of the storm, though John said they'd had a great dump of rain, and in the upper parks there was many a farmer who, trusting the weather, had unhoused his sheaves and spread them out—"They'll have to lie that way a good many days the now." But all the neeps—as he called the turnips—were brairded and looked to be saved. "*The husbandman waiteth for the precious fruit of the earth, he hath long patience for it, until he receive the early and latter rain, James.v.7.*"
Aunt Helen reading the account of the disasters in a high voice, in Annville kitchen with the *Advertiser* spread across her knee. Her stout arms purple from the jelly-making and the whole of the lower flat reeking sweetish and harsh from sugar and hot copper, with the pan to scrub out yet and the tying. It was evening, still light, the windows thrown wide to the wet, cool orchard. The potted geranium plants on the sill, said to discourage flies, were indeed doing their duty proudly as Helen said, there being never more than six or seven flies on the table at the one time for she had counted.
John's cuttie rasped as they considered in silence the extremely rapid transfiguration of the old man and his grandchildren, and Charlotte was sure that both her uncle and her aunt were thinking of their consequent surprise, and were trusting, in the case of the old man, that he had been prepared, though John for once did not offer the familiar quotation about knowing not the hour.
They then dwelt more comfortably on the miraculous saving of the infant.

Helen said, "Aye, when it's big they'll show it the broken cradle, and it will praise God."

John, and Charlotte with him, were inclined to think that a parsimonious collier would have mended the cradle lang syne.

"But there'll be a black crack at the fit, they'd leave that. For it's a grand story, and the baby without a mark on him."

They fell silent again, the burnt bairns brought to mind.

"They are in glory now," said John, putting down his pipe. *"Thanks be to God, who giveth us the victory through Jesus Christ our Lord*, First Corinthians.xv.57."

Willie was soon to be moved from the Royal to lie in a Convalescent Home in the Havelock-road. As his illness abated in severity —for he had been taken very bad, all were agreed—he began to notice his surroundings again and of course in particular his own symptoms, and to make some effort to involve himself in his treatment. The doctors had their own methods and it was difficult for Willie, lying there with his sprouting scalp pricking into the linen, to hear them out with patience. Scraps of what he had learned about *The Continued Fevers* jiggered about in his mind: Tanner's *Index*, the words like wee sharp knives.

Dr. Murchison pronounced it a sharp case of the Enteric Febricula, but not as he had suspected typhoid, there being no facial bronzing or papular rash. There was "a liability to the supervention of pulmonary inflammation." He enquired about the occurrence of phthisis in the family. He was of the opinion that lung disease was inherited, the child who most closely resembled the affected parent being the most likely to carry the taint.

"And are you like your mother?"

"I doubt it, but my sister's very well and she's my mother up the back."

Dr. Murchison looking somewhat cross.

Willie enquired as to the inflammation but was not answered, perhaps because his speech was not yet clear, and the doctor moving on to the next bed.

Dr. Gairdner was hovering over Willie, he saw distinctly the lofty vault, the unkempt side-whiskers, the loving gaze through the round spectacles. Willie thought he had asked Dr. Gairdner some question of great importance, about percussing his brain, but the doctor had turned away, and Willie in desperation had got out of bed and followed him the length of the ward, for he must know the answer—it was something about the Auric Chamber, the brain had four chambers like the heart and one was in danger of filling up with fluid. When he reached the door Dr. Gairdner, who was enormously tall, had turned around and it was not him at all but Mr. Paterson, and Willie had said loudly, "You're no good for complaints of the brain," and woke in his bed, unsure whether he had spoken aloud. With the sheets wringing wet and sweat running down his sides. This was not the worst of his dreams.

Moffatt, who had graduated in '79 and was not more that twenty-five years old, came in of an evening and saw Willie through the worst of his sweats, which were harder to bear even than the aches and pains. He auscultated Willie's chest and pronounced it reasonably clear, the right lung being quite free of matter. "You'll hear old Murchison blethering on about his pulmonary taint to all the patients, it doesnae mean a hoot toot. These fevers express themselves in a great tonnage of symptoms, and disguise themselves into what they aren't, you're no consumptive if that's what you were fashing about."

Willie's shirt and the sheets by this time drenched in sweat.

There was a peculiar sourish smell about, as though the air were infected. He could taste it as well. Later he became used to it.

They gave him cold baths for the fever. The water was to begin at ten degrees below the patient's temperature, being then lowered till it stood at sixty-eight. Willie had endured them at first in a daze of misery; then he had a memory of fighting them, Moffatt holding his shoulders. A jugful of cold water poured in across his knees, a voice, echoing strangely, singing out the temperature. "One hundred and four. One hundred and two point three." Numbers, painfully edged.

Murchison in consultation with Moffatt now said it was the straight forward Crimean Fever, which was also called Remittant Fever,[22] but there was nothing straight forward about it except that the sweats returned morning and night: Willie would begin to shiver and shake and then they were upon him. He did not recognize his hands for the emaciation. In one of his dreams he was tearing them off, somehow using his real hands which would not have been possible.

But the extensors would not break, trailing like white ropes from above his elbows.

Later in the night he slept more comfortably, and in the forenoon felt better, and could avoid depending on the nurses for private matters. He made himself eat, and kept his breakfast down.

But by the end of the forenoon he was vomiting again; the idea of food, particularly of that food he had last partaken, brought on the retching and his head ached. They dosed him with chalk and bismuth for the vomiting. By nightfall the rigors and sweats overcame him.

Yet he improved.

Mrs. Spears, alarmed by a letter from Helen, sent a message that he must come to them and convalesce at the Great Western Road, as soon as he was past the worst. But Willie would not.

The Home would do, and there he continued to improve. He sent to MacNair to bring him in his books, and sat up in the window in the forenoon. He studied Bristowe's *Theory and Practice*, and Findlayson, and the *Index*, the *Acute Specific Fevers* dancing from one diagnosis to the other, till his head ached again. He held down more food. He set himself a date for a full recovery: the end of the second week in July. With hard work he would not lose the term. He would be back in his classes for the reviews and the examination.

The Havelock-street Home had been a private house, and its large rooms each held a row of six stump beds, made of iron. The front windows—Willie was in the preferred second floor flat—looked past the roofs across the street to the spires of the University. The smells of the kitchen at the Royal had put him from taking his meat, but here they scarcely reached him.

There was no qualified attendant. The medical undergraduates doctored themselves, and any others who would let them. They reminded Willie that "returning fever" lived up to its name:

"Sleep, eat when you can, wait with the studying."

But Willie would not wait. He worried a visiting student, whom he did not know, till the man promised to ask for copies of notes from Gairdner's classes, then was frightened when he did not return. "Ask Kerr," he had said, "he'd be more than willing. Kerr or Wotherspoon, John Wotherspoon, he has a wonderful clear hand."

Willie believed that the other convalescents, languid in their beds, were more ill than he; he felt, in the forenoon at least, fit for his books, though he still walked unsteadily over to the bright window, and after two hours or so the print would begin to slide on the page and the burning headache behind his eyes returned. It felt as if they were lined with grit.

A student from the under-flat died so suddenly that Willie first believed he had been discharged. They had been sitting together that morning. He was cramming for the third time for Junior Anatomy, which had comforted Willie.

"'*If a median incision be made through the superficial layer of the fascia above the suprasternal notch, it will be found that access has been obtained to the intraponeurotic space. The anterior jugular veins make their way through the lateral recesses, and breaking through the closing fascia, join the external jugular veins.*' D'you think, if a man were beheaded"—looking up from the illustration of *The Fascia of the Neck*—"he would be conscious of departing this life from his head, or from his body?"

Willie held that the soul would leave the body so instantaneously that there would be no consciousness of separation.

"But if there were. I'm no saying the soul's in one part of the body and not another, I'm just considering whether a man would say to himself, as it were, 'Guid God, there's my body away!' or on the other hand 'Guid God, my head's away gone.'"

"The vagus being severed, you wouldnae have a sensation at all."

The student turned back to page 40, to the illustration of the neck, lateral view, showing distribution and connection of the Vagus Nerve. He read in a high voice: "*The tenth or vagus nerve is much larger than the pharyngeal, and has the longest course of all the cerebral nerves through the neck and thorax to the upper part of the abdomen. It resembles the glossopharyngeal in containing both sensory and motor fibres, mixed with one another at their apparent origin from the brain.*"

The drawing showed the head in profile, faintly Grecian and disproportionately small, with curls of hair over the occiput and only the lateral portion being exposed, as well as all the neck. Tiny numbers were printed on the white page around the figure: *5, 14, 6* just touching the lips, as though whispered.

"A hen would say 'My head's away,'" said Willie, smiling a little, "for sometimes it runs about a bit." The Cuthbertson yard in Stonehouse, wee George's father standing there with the hatchet in his hand, shouting with laughter.

"I was thinking of that. But Cleland would hold that a clacker-hen's no properly conscious at one end or the other. I cannae imagine it. Or rather, I can imagine it, one or the other, d'you ken, as if it could as well be the one, or the other."

Both had taken Cleland's Dissection. Cleland was a passionate Presbyterian with a splendid physique, a solid evolutionist, yet he would never accept Darwin's mechanism.

"*A hen is an egg's way of making another egg.*"

"Ah, you mind that one of Butler's. 'There's my hen away gone,' then. Cleland made you see the divine purpose. D'you mind the way he sawed down Darwin's tree? *The animal kingdom is a temple, not an indefinite growth—*"

"*With many minarets—*"

"*And the greatest, completed dome is the structure of man.*"

The student, who had been looking bewildered, now beamed with satisfaction, and Willie noticed how tiny his pupils were in his flushed face.

Willie, too, had been entranced when he had heard Cleland utter those words, swept away by that great metaphor of reconciliation. He minded big Cleland, who resembled a boxer more than a professor, with his sleeves rolled up and his bloody arms thrust into the mess on the table. He could just mind his own excitement, but cooly now, as if it had happened in a distant time to somebody else.

The talk rambled. They had compared their growing hair, Willie's hand brushing across his own head which was now filled in with a dark pile like coarse velvet. The student had shambled off in the afternoon closing his *Quain's* with a smile and saying he was due for a lie down and some mineral salts, and Willie did not see him again.

That night he dreamed of a decapitation, of reaching after his head, his arms lengthening and lengthening, fingers scrambling at the velvet as he woke.

Each evening a theological undergraduate would come by to take the prayers. Once it was brilliant "Carrots" Gray breezing through, who never had the time of day for Willie in Stonehouse, having gone to the

Free School and being two years older. He stopped at the bedside and gave Willie a strengthening Highland grip, not inaccurately compared to submitting one's hand to a blacksmith's vice. "Willie Brown! I heard how you were gone over to the healing ministry. Now you'll soon be back on the right side of the scalpel again?"

"Oh, aye, you can tell Mr. Paterson I'm already on my feet."

"You'll be able to tell him yourself before I can, I've my sheltification before me, I'm away out now among the kilties. I'll not see Stonehouse before Hogmanay." A little, beaming fellow, but Willie could see by his eye that he did not think any more of Willie now than he had then, when the three Gray laddies were aye up to some grand mischief—like the time they collected all the chanties put out for the night, and piled them in the middle of the Cross. And winning all the prizes besides.

Then there was a theology student who was obviously scared of contagiants, who sidled over to the table at the hearth and read rapidly, barely opening his mouth. Backlit against the unnecessary fire with the lamplight cast upward on his podgy face so his underlip and nostrils were a transparent red. He was very high, and luckily for him there was a high undergraduate in the end bed to supply the responses.

"*Hear us, Almighty and most merciful God and Saviour; extend thy accustomed goodness to these thy servants who are grieved with sickness. Sanctify, we beseech thee, this thy fatherly correction to them, that the sense of their weakness may add strength to their faith, and seriousness to their repentance: that, if it shall be thy good pleasure to restore them to their former health, they may lead the residue of their lives in thy fear, and to thy glory; or else, give them grace so to take thy visitation, that, after this painful life ended, they may dwell with thee in life everlasting: through Jesus Christ our Lord. Amen.*"

"*Amen.*"

Willie by this time aching and sweating, his spine and long bones not so much sore as restless. He would thrust a leg out from under the quilt, giving it momentary relief. He considered the effort of turning his pillow.

When the lights were extinguishing: "Throw up the windows, there's a good lass, it's as hot in here as the bad fire."

"Turn my pillow before you go."

"I'll give you a wet clout for your forehead, sir, if you like."

"No, no, I'm sopping already."

"I'll dry it for you, there. Turn your head."

From the door end: "Come give us a kiss then, Jennie, to help with the sleep."

"Sir, you'll no bide here long if you're up to that sort of talk!"

The servant going quickly about to empty the slops, carrying away the chanties.

CHAPTER 9

In which Willie is obliged to sojourn at Annville, and Mr. Cameron receives a presentation.

Willie came to Annville in August. He was recovered, he said, and need only regain his strength. He would bide a week, and then return to his digs to catch up on his notes, and prepare for the fall Matriculation.

Helen pronounced him shockingly changed, but John said no, that apart from his cropped hair, it was but the usual wrought look of the student, for they were all swarthy and thin like that from the studying.

"D'you no mind how he looked when he went up for the Preliminary Examinations? He was nearly as bad then."

Willie with a trap-plaid over him, in the nice room in his father's chair, drinking strong beef tea. His head down, his eyes darting sideways to take in Charlotte at the piano stool, where she had seated herself after bringing up the tray. She had not recognized him. Then in the glance she saw him for a moment—the young lad—but not again after that once.

Helen going on about his room—how comfortably his cousin had prepared it for him. Charlotte was indeed nearly satisfied. The windows opening west and south made it airy and bright. A gilded looking glass, somewhat tarnished, hung over the fireplace and in front was a tasteful screen, crewel worked on white crash, though the one side was yet bare and the sarcenet bows uneven, and Charlotte had some ideas for improving it. The gate legged table had again made its journey up, and stood in the front window. There was a wardrobe, a straight chair for study, and an armchair with lumpy leather upholstery, on castors so it could be run up to the fire. The Kidderminster carpet from the other bedroom had been moved in to cover the oilcloth.

Long, pale summer curtains of sprigged muslin picked up the warm greens in the wall paper patterning, green or deep gold in all the fringes and cushions and smaller coverings, the candlewick bedspread tufted buff and maroon. She had brought up some shells and pewter from the parlour cabinet and her own shepherdess figurine, to place tastefully about, and laid out Saturday's *Advertiser* and an *Illustrated London News*; but, being a sickroom, had decided against potted plants. A bunch of Glorious Johns—for they had bloomed again, though less copiously—stood on the table.

Later Willie said he would go up and rest, and allowed his father to support him, Helen stepping up just behind them and telling John to take care at the landing and Willie's voice saying something a little sharply.

John came down and said the Willie must have caught a chill on the journey, for he was shivering badly. Charlotte rose at that, and fetched the plaid up, and Helen met her at the stairhead. "He's low, poor lad, and cold as ice. I wanted John to bring down that stomach warmer from King-street but he said we weren't to spoil him."

Willie's voice from within the room: "Dinnae heed me, I'll be warm soon enough." Helen took in the plaid and Charlotte stood irresolute. Later, they wanted her to play a soothing tune on the cottage but she wondered if that would not be welcome above stairs either. She spent the evening talking over Willie's dietary with her aunt. It was not the first time. Helen did not however make any demands; rather she deferred to Charlotte's better understanding and experience. "I'm sure we couldnae go off comfortably to King-street, Chattie dear, unless you were here, I would never leave him to Margaret Tennant."

The Managers hired George Elder, blacksmith, to secure the earth bank. It was building all that summer, its progress followed closely not only by Mr. Steele of the Inn but by the villagers in general, and Mr. Elder had to put up with a fair amount of advice. Old Mr. Elder had been famous for his drystone dykes and comparisons could not be avoided though this, being a containing wall, was another thing entirely. Stone was got from the quarry at Smugglers Brig, the farmers carting it free of charge even though the thrang season. On August First the Managers wrote a general Letter of Appreciation which was read at service after the Intimations.

Charlotte still attended the E U in the Westport, but had begun to take an interest in the Kirk which was to be her employer, and not only in watching the wall's advancement. Once returning from a lesson she had heard the harmonium and looked in; she believed it was Robert Gilchrist practising, "Christian Mariners" being the selection she had set him, though she was a little surprised at the tempo. She had stepped into the porch and then right into the body of the Kirk, the door being open, before she realized it was not Rab Gilchrist at all but an old man with tufty white hair and whiskers, his eye sockets quite black in the gloom. Glaring. The music stopped abruptly as he stood up. Charlotte stepped back and hurried out into the road, imagining him coming down the central aisle after her, mouth working. It was surly Mr. Whiteford.

As she made for Annville she had to recall the furore at Elgin Place when the Musical Committee, dissatisfied, had brought in Mr. Senior the new organist, and Miss Rough.

"Surely I am not like Miss Rough," she told herself, getting through the wicket gate. "I am grieved indeed about Mr. Whiteford's poor health but he is a very old man." She pulled off her bonnet in the porch, loosing a shower of brown petals from overhead. Miss Rough looking so self satisfied. And on the whole not turning out very satisfactory. She had an eye on Robert, who'd been on the Committee, though it was R W who was the moving force. Not a chance of course, even if Robert. Visiting frequently at Corunna-street. Advice asked about the anthem, etc. Her woolly overlip which occasionally, as if magically, was smooth. Odd that she was then even less handsome, that one looked aside hurriedly. As if she'd been erased.

Charlotte heard in a round-about way that Mr. Whiteford was trying to get up a Concert of Sacred Song for September. Mrs. West talking behind her hand to Mrs. Reid at the Hall door:

"For he's saying his year's no out till October and till October he'll stay. No one had an idea he'd live through the summer. Though he has rallied splendidly, he's going at them terrible hard. The Kirk Choir's sore torn, and if he won't go it will be an awful to do, what with the Managers having sent Miss Spears a letter, and I suppose he's had one as well. Oh aye, I'll no say anything about it, for he may die tomorrow, and the fash will be all for nothing."

Charlotte's Harvest Concert would require her to take up her duties September First, to get the Choir in order. Even if the Concert were not to be held till the very end of October, which was about as far into the fall, she thought, as it could be pushed. She prayed, "*Thy will be done*," for if it was the Lord's will to sustain Mr. Whiteford till October, she hoped she would be gracious about it. She was thankful her aunt was as yet ignorant of the possible delay, for she had no wish to have the subject endlessly talked of at Annville.

It must be left to the Managers to decide between, as it were, justice and mercy. Meanwhile she threw herself into her own Classes and pretended she'd heard nothing about it; and no Member, not even one of her three Managers, spoke—though some, in particular Mrs. West, made a great many queer faces.

Later, with the nursing of Willie on her hands, she was glad of the respite.

Kirkfieldbank, 25th July, 1881.

My dear Thomson,

You may be receiving shortly a Letter of Invitation which I hope you will extend to yr good people at Haywood in particular the musical Park's, and of course yr good Self. I write as yet "may," my reasons being as given below.

But firstly, I was pleased that the Lord has granted you a prosperous summer and fine weather for the Sabbath School Treat, we being less fortunate, in fact though we managed some races and kyles, and commenced with ring dancing, it then pelted down with both the canine and feline varieties. We were however not gone far afield as we had but "ta'en the high road", and were merrily sheltered and provided for at Kirkfield House. Now for the tooth of the letter, for the Managers have as it were let themselves in for a new Precentor and the old one being unwilling to step down. You will recall my words about Miss Speirs, whom we in all innocence hired for the 1st September, however Mr. Whiteford whom no one expected to live

long after his astonishing Crash over the harmonium in
June, has reminded us that his full Year does not expire till
the 1st October, he therefore contemplates a "swan song" in
the order of a Harvest Concert—and all the while, it seems,
Miss Spiers busily preparing same herself. I hear this last as
several of my congregation, indeed 3 Managers, are members of both Choirs. The Managers are of course in their prerogative to terminate his engagement at any time but there
being no Fault, this seems rather harsh treatment of the guid
auld man, who would like his Month. We are holding an
Extraordinary Meeting before the Congregational Meeting
Wednesday next, to which yr prayers are begged for a wholesome outcome. There is no chance of Mr. Whiteford taking
himself off, I doubt, as a good fight seems in his case the
right Medicine exactly. Meantime I have unearthed my student sermon taken in Matthew.v.9 which I will read at both
services Sunday next trusting it will not fall on deaf ears.

As far as good news, the earthing is now secured and the
people when appealed to showed their grand co-operative
spirit, there was none of the usual "the cairt cannae be had"
and much assistance volunteered and advice received if not
thankfully by George Elder being in charge of the enterprise and of course for this reason he knows best.

There is also something Afoot among the good Ladies
and I believe it may pertain to my continuing state of
homelessness, I will however remain guileless till all is
revealed John.i.47.

Bye the bye 2 Concerts, would not be a bad thing,
though perhaps coming so close on one another would not
bring in as much as hoped. Yr obt. servant etc.
Walter Cameron.

Charlotte dreamed that the IOGT Hall stood directly across the High-
street from the Kirk, which was much larger and darker, and that both
Concerts had been advertised for the same evening. She was hurrying
across the road to fetch her Members, for they were all gone into the
Kirk, but the new wall was in the way, and there was Mrs. West sweeping past along the top of it in a black gown like a surplice and

announcing, "The Voluntary is about to begin!" That was the Kirk bell ringing, but it had been muffled for the Concert. Thump, thump, thump. She awoke and it was Willie hitting at the upper floor with his staff.

Kirkfieldbank. On Wednesday last, the ladies of the Church presented Mr. Cameron with a handsome pulpit gown, cassock and case of bands, supplied by Messers Middlemas and Company, Edinburgh.

The Hamilton Advertiser, Aug. 3, 1881

CHAPTER 10

*In which Monks and Nuns are examined, and Mr. Weir
turns a slight alarm to his advantage.*

Mrs. West did call, though without a card and without her sisters. She attended wee Sarah who had come for her harmonium lesson. Though voluble at the door, the aunt had apparently been enjoined not to open her mouth otherwise, till the half-hour were over. Even in the lobby, while Charlotte helped her out of her cloak, she kept her lips tight closed. Though looking about to burst, Charlotte noticed with amusement and thought, "She is afraid of her niece!" Which seemed a good thing, silence having been made a condition perhaps, before they came away. Sarah had gone on in to the harmonium and was seating herself, first having turned her clean pinny round to spread between Charlotte's cushion and her plain school frock. Her hair flying and white as straw with the summer, her nose red. And wearing her boots, both for the occasion and to help her reach the pedals.

After the lesson Mrs. West refused tea but Sarah carefully chose a boiled sweetie—for Charlotte had a jar on hand for her younger pupils—and then the aunt, taking a breath, burst out with:

"Monks and Nuns!" And before Charlotte could look her surprise, followed this odd remark with a very long invitation to accompany her to a lecture on the subject.[23] Charlotte agreed.

The ladies set forth early, Mrs. West's sister Miss Taylor making a third and "not being so very quick on her feet, though she loved a good walk." Charlotte noticed that Miss Taylor—blind, but not deaf—must be one of those family members who got herself talked about, and talked past, putting in a word only occasionally, which was then often as not repeated by the others—in this case by Mrs. West—in the same way.

The journey up the Brae was slow. At times, Charlotte offered her arm as well but Miss Taylor, though she would lay a faint hand, in a grayish cotton glove, over Charlotte's wrist for a time, would not be supported. And if Charlotte upped the pace the hand slid away. They kept to the turnpike road, Mrs. West declaring that the Clydesholme Braes would be dirty.

A trap overtook them, Manufacturer Mathiesen and his wife on the same errand, and he offered them a hurl. There would be room for two of the ladies, but Mrs. West though thankful would not hear of their being separated from Charlotte. They were, she said, in very good time as it was. At the Gas Works they fell in with several others bound in the same direction, among them a married couple from Nemphlar with whom Mrs. West was acquainted, perambulating with their mother who was a very old lady in pattens, and the pace was further reduced.

Charlotte had time to stand still while Mrs. West welcomed them, and to look back over Kirkfieldbank in the mist-laden dusk. The dale was blurry, the river hidden and the gray houses almost so, Annville's white gable ghostly among its trees. Away westward the sky lay in long, shredded ribbons of darkish mauve against pink. When she turned to go on, she saw the big moon rising over the town—the promise of a bright night, that would ensure a good attendance.

St. Leonard's stood over against the station. To reach it they must go up Bannatyre-street near the Roman Catholic Church, and this seemed slightly uncomfortable though not what one would have commented on aloud. Mrs. West's "Oh, aye, they'll be sure to have locked that great barred yett up the night" was therefore rather dramatic. Surely the gate was closed each evening as a rule, and any idea of indignant stormings, violently resisted from within, purely imaginary.

They were only a little late, and seats were found for them in a pew near the back and somewhat behind a pillar. Where Mrs. West fussily had her sister sit, "for she'll no need a sight of the minister, you ken," with herself next "and very well able to see, if I lean just a wee bit towards you, Miss Spears." The opening hymn, now indulged, overcame most of this, the depth of the organ's bass pipes thrilling through the floor and up into Charlotte's limbs, and the general echo of the large nave very pleasing, the men's voices in particular swelling like the sea. Charlotte, remembering the organ at the City Hall, felt a pang of regret. It was Luther's grand old hymn, finishing in triumph:

> *And though they take our life,*
> *Goods, honour, children, wife,*
> *Yet is their profit small;*
> *These things shall vanish all;*
> *The city of God remaineth!*

Mr. Hay was not the easiest lecturer to attend to. He was unfortunately very short of stature, and of wind as well so that each sentence while commencing bravely tended to fall away towards its completion, the last words heard as hardly more than a "hurr-umph."

His subject in itself was of course of interest, and most serious— for this reason perhaps, his lack of those choice little anecdotes and humorous turns of phrase, which enliven the best-received lectures, might be excused. He traced the monastic movement from its foundation, and pronounced it to be "contrary to both Nature and Religion, and productive of great evil in all ages and countries in which it was established." He also proceeded to "explode," as he called it, many of the more popular institutions of the Roman Catholic Church, such as the "Redemptorists," of whom Charlotte knew nothing, but learned a very great deal, and the establishment of orphanages. This last was a dig at the Smyllum, of course, the new building outside the town and some fanfare about it in the otherwise piously Protestant *Advertiser.* These organizations Mr. Hay characterized as "designed to overthrow the free and orthodox institutions for which the great patriots of the country had suffered martyrdom." Here the audience was visibly stirred, it being but eight o'clock, for Lanark lay in the heart of Covenanters' country, and the "oot Kirk" of St Kentigern's was the repository of many a martyr's bones, and boasted the new Monument.

Mr. Hay's "explosions" were over-long in the wick, Robert would have said, and many, despite a grand start, failed to come off at all. He continually returned to counselling his hearers "not to be deceived by insinuations arising from the philanthropic pretensions of the promoters of these syst-hrumms."

By nine o'clock Mrs. West had begun to fidget and Charlotte, looking past her, saw that Miss Taylor had fallen asleep and was tipping forward dangerously. Her prayer book dropped to the floor with a plunk. A small and concerned diversion for the nearer portion of the audience was thus created while Mrs. West applied salts; then a way through to the aisle clearing and Miss Taylor helped out while her sister employed the handkerchief and whispered urgently. Charlotte followed and closed the inside doors behind them, Miss Taylor being sat down in the porch for a breather.

"Is your sister no well?" Charlotte, surprised, had found herself talking across Miss Taylor quite naturally.

"Guid Miss Spears, I believe that Maria would most like to go home, for the lecture is muckle long." Mrs. West bending over her sister whose bonnet hid her face, and her muttered words that sounded very cross.

"But dinnae fash yourself, for we wouldnae deprive you of the rest of the entertainment—we'll be home in a moment—I believe, we can get a hire from the Station Hotel."

Charlotte stepped across with them, and found George Kay in his waistcoat but willing; then she waved them away through Mrs. West's thanks and apologies. Being herself determined to see the lecture through for the sake of the closing hymn and the organ.

Mr. Hay continued till well past ten, a grave and steady attention being paid till the last. The hymn was "As Now the Sun's Declining Rays" and afterwards everyone filed out in a subdued manner, Charlotte looking about in the crowd for a familiar face, and encountering Mr. Weir's.

He came forward immediately, though she had turned and hurried into the street, and was passing St Mary's when he gained her side. Some folk were almost scurrying by, some slowing to cast a covert glance into the yard, where two or three sinister lamps gleamed at the windows of a distant building, the church and all else being wrapped in the closest darkness. Mr. Weir's hand at her elbow, steering her around a small group who lingered.

"We're to puzzle about what they are getting up to in there!" he said in his smiling way. "No doubt they have all gone quietly to their beds, which is more than could be said for us, traipsing about the town so late of a Sabbath evening!"

Charlotte, withdrawing her arm, and seeing the Forsyths ahead of them, said she must speak a word to the minister, and, rather rudely she was afraid, got right in beside him through a determined crowd of E U ladies all eager to discuss the lecture. Thus she came down the Westport and turned with them into the lane beside the E U Kirk, and stood a few moments at the manse door. Mrs. Forsyth pressing them all in to a bit of supper and cocoa, and Charlotte really wishing to accept, but the rest declining, it being so late. An intermittent string of folk from Dublin and Kirkfieldbank were passing down into "Jecker's Johnnie," to walk home by Clydesholme Braes. She went in among them, the voices of the couple in front within hearing and two young women close behind.

Jecker's Johnnie was a steep footpath leading down between a hedge of thorn and ash plants on the one side and a paling overhung with beech on the other. The ground was partly cindered, dry under-foot but uneven, and though she held in her skirts the briers would catch at her crape.

Alas, Mr. Weir appeared at her side as she came to the bottom, and she had an inspiration he had run down under the beeches, to have passed the women behind her! But he said he had come by the Butts.

"Such a bright moon, there's no need to keep to the paths at all. One could wander over the parks, or through the plantings, or leip across Clyde at the Inches and see every stone as clear as day."

When Charlotte did not reply he said, "I have a mind I will leave you there at the water, and step over—for you'd be safe home across the brig—do you think I could get across and no wet my breeches?" Like a laddie wanting a dare.

It was best not to respond, for he had a way of turning her words.

He seemed not to mind her silence however, and burst into a snatch of song, and she had to admit he had a good voice:

> *"As he rade ower the hie, hie hill,*
> *And down yon dowie den,*
> *There was a roar in Clyde's water*
> *Wad fear'd a hundred men."*

The footpath was still high above the river, but descending. Charlotte walked as calmly as she could and kept close to the folk in front, but at Clydesbank they turned into the gate. Another figure was visible farther on, and she quickened her step and nearly stumbled.

"Steady, Miss Spears, you'll no want to fall, or you'd be in danger of my helping you to your feet. Take my arm, now, there's no harm in it."

But Charlotte would not, or answer him. After a time he spoke more politely. "We could refer to the lecture, which would be an edifying subject of conversation, though it was over dry, to my mind. Or of the music. They've a braw organ at St. Leonard's. Would you have attended a concert there?" Charlotte ventured to say she had not. "You'd like to get your hands on it, no doubt, for it's very well made, or else it is the acoustic, that brings in the crowds. The puir laddie working the pedal had to be wakened for the last hymn—I was near the front, and saw the beadle going in after him. Nay, Kirkfieldbank has but a harmonium. They'll never provide an organ, Mr. Cameron is far too near.

"You'll find it a wasp's byke, not that I would speak against the Kirk, and you with your strict love of the music, and the method. I must say I am eager to see how you will go on—to be sure excellently, as in all things. Have you discovered when you are to begin?"

Charlotte said that she had not, and did not wish to speak of it, until she had official word.

"Aye, they've treated you badly, Miss Spears, all this with the two concerts, but you will find your Members loyal to you. The only one to watch would be—"

They were just passing under an wild hawthorn, with the park beyond it in a billow down to Clyde, when suddenly as if right in among the foliage a loud, snuffling snort assailed them, and a great shadow separated itself from the dark of the tree and pounded away over the slope.

"Only a gelding, Miss Spears, come, dinnae startle so." His hands, then his mouth a long smear across her cheek as she pulled her head aside.

As far as she could tell, Mr. Weir made good his dare and "leiped" over Clyde. Taking off her bonnet and scrubbing her face and lower lip in the basin, Charlotte was surprised that she was experiencing not anger, but a quite pleasant sense of alleviation, as when a fever, having come to its crisis, is broken. She said her prayers rather quickly not mentioning the episode.

CHAPTER 11

In which Willie improves at last, bee hives are obtained for the garden, and an ecclesiastical crisis is averted.

Annville House, August 7th, 1881.

Dear Mother, Annie and Tom,
Thank you for your welcome letter, which my Uncle and Aunt have heard too on the week-end. We were very glad to hear, of your wee excursion Saturday last, the weather being fine, and Mother comfortable with dear Mr. Batchelor. And I am happy to hear that Jacky is recovered. He is no doubt confused by the more frequent traffic in the Great Western Road, as there was hardly a horse in Corunna-street who did not know his ways. I hope the one swift kick has taught him his lesson. Does he not run away to Corunna-street any more? It is a wonder how Providence has endowed even the dumb creatures with virtues, such as Jacky's constancy here shown, it is indeed a reminder to us. Now he can be a comfort to you Mother. Does he not lie across your feet as he used to do in the evening, at dear Father's?

This was begun and not yet finished, as I am thrang with the Classes, and some wee difficulties about the piano pupils, and Willie is now home recovering from the fever. He is to return to toun soon. He is a good patient and takes his brose in the morning with no complaints, in fact yesterday he was downstairs and out for an hour, however he is a wee bit feverish in the evening and I believe sleeps not quite comfortably as yet. However he is bearing up, and going on very determinedly with his studying. Today he directed a post card to his land-lady that he is to return to his digs Monday next, and Uncle John will be here to put him on the early train.

I was most pleased to hear from you Tom, that the decision about going on with the Anthems has proved successful, even while Summer and many away. I have no need for the frock, or the gloves, because Aunt Helen is most generous with stuffs and articles from the shop, you (Annie) had better let it out both sides, also the over-skirt, it will want a new breadth of Irish poplin in very small tartan, of the same colours, which Aunt tells me is the new Style, or another plain nice cloth, the hat to be similarly trimmed. The colour ought to be something of a match to avoid a perpendicular stripe which, while adding height also increases fullness. I am not the expert! But have it on her good authority sent, of course, with her kindest love.

Will you plan to attend the up coming Sol-Fa Concert, which is to be Bellini's *Norma*. I hope that you will all do so for old time's sake, and send a full report. You have my permission to greet my friends among the Members from me, and of course Mr. and Mrs. W H Miller, if you have the opportunity to easily do so, and tell them I am very well.

Tom, I would like your opinion as to Thompson's Concentrated Nerve Tonic, or could you enquire of Mr. Francis Sprite, as to its efficacy? Willie will not see Dr. Gray, and depends on the remedies prescribed him in toun, which he is very right to do, being a medical student himself with all the newest methods, and has himself walked on the Wards. Uncle John has heard as well, that Dr. Gray though very sound, depends rather too much on the old collier's advice to the new Doctor, which was:—*if you wish to get success, two things you must never fail to prescribe. If an outside sore prescribe rosit, but if an inside sore prescribe whisky.*[24]

With my best love to you all, Chattie

PS. But I do not believe this, I think someone is having a wee joke with Uncle John knowing his Temperance views.

The Extraordinary Meeting was, as anticipated, quarrelsome and inconclusive, despite the pleasant bustle of excitement which had attended the Presentation. Here in the vestry there were no smiling ladies, only the Managers, and Mr. Cameron, having placed his gift in the chest atop the Communion vessels and closed the lid on it, sat down with a fixed smile and tight lips. He looked as if he would let the Managers get on with the business themselves, and the sooner done the better.

Mr. Whiteford unfortunately was not yet gone home, but was out in the Kirk arranging and rearranging his music; his hair sprouted over the choir box like frosty foggage. And looking across at the vestry with a very fierce expression, as reported by Mr. Russell, who had instructions to close the door. Beadle Reid would be wanting to put out the lamps.

Later in the Meeting the strains of "Fight the Good Fight," with all the stops drawn, assailed their ears, followed by a sudden and profound silence, during which the Managers also paused, thinking Mr. Whiteford had perhaps crept up to the vestry door and was listening at it. But they heard the Kirk door slam, and then Beadle Reid put his head in from the dark nave to tell them respectfully that, if no more was required, he'd be away home.

The Managers realized they could hope for no easy, perhaps no possible resolution, though they agreed that a tight rein was required. Most urged that having made the Appointment they ought to stand by it, Miss Spears to assume the office, if not the duties, of Precentor September first, and the rest to be left, for the present, to prayer. A spoken message to Mr. Whiteford by the minister, with no reference to any sort of dispute, "a simple word, with a pleasant reference to his Concert and go away quick, before he begins to reply" would hold him off the now, and the rest was in God's hands.

Mr. Barr could not be denied a word. "It means double wages the whole month however blithely you put it, for Miss Spears will be wanting her fee, depend on it, whether she works for it or nae. We're out of pocket already with various extra obligations—I'm referring to the earth bank, and so on—so that'll be guid money towards the manse thrown away." Spoken with an eye on Mr. Cameron.

Mr. Cameron said as calmly as possible that, Mr. Whiteford's wages being part of last year's accounts and settled lang syne, and Miss

Spears' already voted in, they would do best to live with it, "for you must agree, that terminating Mr. Whiteford's appointment, unless on the grounds of incapacity, of course, would be a sore blow to him, and one he wouldnae take lying down either and he's got a fair support among the Choir."

They ended on this note, Mr. Cameron consenting to speak informally to Mr. Whiteford and lead him as it were into calmer waters. His closing prayer, while it did not actually recommend the removal of Mr. Whiteford from this worldly sphere as the simplest remedy (the Lord being well aware of this already), did touch on "*mysterious ways.*"

And the happy outcome, despite Mr. Whiteford's obstinate and continued well-being, was Charlotte's inability to take up her duties as planned. She must beg the Managers to postpone her Appointment (and of course her fee) one month, till October first, owing to illness in the family. This letter was placed in Mr. Cameron's hand the last day of August, and resolved things to nearly everyone's satisfaction. As well as strengthening Mr. Cameron in his faith in God's provision, which had been sorely tried by the gift of new vestments when he was expecting a manse.

Each forenoon it had seemed that Willie was indeed recovered, for though he preferred to breakfast in his room, he was up and about when Charlotte brought in the tray. By that time Margaret Tennant had been and the fire laid and the room aired, and Willie was dressed or at least into his old Norfolk house-coat and his list slippers, and already at his books. He sat at the gate-legged table in the front window, leaning forward from the big chair, and when she entered would push his papers aside to make room. His freshly shaven cheeks very steep and sunken in the daylight.

By the time Charlotte got back from her walk to prepare his breakfast, Margaret Tennant would like as not have already been down to Clyde. Charlotte would glimpse her beyond the orchard trunks, spreading the linen out on the green; she had been tramping up and downstairs bringing away Willie's night shirts and the armful of bed linen, and sometimes there was vomitus in his basin, and sometimes his supper not eaten, and she would shake her head and grumble.

"Miss Spears would ken nothing about it being off on her perambulations," she said when Charlotte enquired. Margaret Tennant,
when vexed, would address her only obliquely. The flock mattress had
to be turned as well, for which she could have done with a helping
hand, "And all the time Mr. Willie Brown at his picture books in the
winnock and keeking after his breakfast no doubt."

Charlotte, giving the porridge a stir and keeping her eye on the
toast, murmured a reply. It would not do to put the servant's back up
further by telling her how many times Willie had rapped in the night,
and that his bed linen, already soaked and sickly-smelling, had got a
change. "Whatever would they do without Margaret?" was Helen's
constant refrain. Charlotte resolved that she must forego her walk for
the time being, and do more for Willie herself.

Only after she came downstairs again did she take her own breakfast, sitting in the kitchen with the windows open and the geranium
plants nodding in the draught. Willie was indeed looking better and
would surely soon be away.

But every evening he was bad again and though he'd made a fair
dinner about two o'clock, it was often the last food he touched. He
would need his fire piled high for he was terribly cold; as she came near
she could hear his teeth clacketing. He had been lying over on his bed,
for it was disarranged, but now he would crouch over the fire in his
plaid and try to warm himself. Later came his tremors and the sweating.

Helen had given him a staff of John's with a brass ferrule, and if
he wanted anything he rapped on the floor. At first she did not hear it
at once, if she were practising; she heard him at night always. Later it
seemed easy to hear it.

In the evening she brought him a very light supper. Though nine
o'clock he would still be sitting up, a book open in his lap, but the
lamp set at a distance.

She took evening worship with him of course. She carried the
Bible upstairs and read the chapter quietly before she gave him his
supper, and said the Lord's Prayer, and mostly he said nothing and
seemed to pay no heed to the words, being by then too ill.

If he had rapped at night and she had been up to administer his
medicine, neither spoke of it in the morning. Willie had his mixture of
belladonna and tincture of lead, and his laudanum; he dosed himself

if he could. If he could not, he would turn his head aside from the lamp and indicate them in silence.

Charlotte always asked him whether there was more she could do to make him comfortable.

"Thank you, no," he would say. Once he said, "You could learn a page of *Bristowe* for me," and after a moment she understood he was having a joke, and laughed uncertainly.

"Oh, Willie, I would if I could! I will read it to you—" but he said that would not help, he must get it for himself.

Picking apples down the garden, Helen on the ground and Charlotte and John up the ladders, each with a rondel hooked over a branch. White Cluster, Bloodheart, Codling, Whistleberry, Golden Pippin and Lady's Finger were the harvest apples; later would come Bramley, Pearmain, Nonesuch, Pursemouth and Yorkshire Green: Miss Fairlie of Hamilton had planted them said John proudly. Going dunt, dunt into the rondel, though he cautioned Charlotte to place them as soft as eggs.

The two women walked down the garden arm in arm before they went in, Helen pushing at the small of her back from the stooping. Willie was "coming along, was he not?" and Charlotte agreed, saying that though he was at his books more than she could wish, he seemed stronger.

Helen said, "He's no so growly as he was? He is that determined about getting both his examinations. If this fever runs the same course, he'll be free of it same as with the last one. He is most grateful to you, Chattie! how could we ever have done, if you hadnae been here to step in!"

"Of course I am very happy to help! I am only glad how it has worked out, with Mr. Whiteford wishing to stay his month."

"Aye, the Lord provideth."

Then for three nights Willie was wonderfully free of fever and slept deeply; on the second day, the Sabbath and with Helen and John at Annville, he came down into the lobby shaved and dressed, walking quick, and said he would go with them to Kirk. Helen protested.

"It's a long tramp up the Brae, and the day's out of the ordinary cold, John's seen frost on the up parks! He and Chattie will go. And I'll bide home, dear, and get on with the dinner, for I've dressed two nice cockerels, which we kept, for we didnae send them all away." The bantie hens had been sold to Carluke market, even Brown Eyes.

That day Willie walked about the village, and the next forenoon went down to Glasgow.

John Brown tramped up to Carluke with four bunches of white straw on his back, that he had got from the high parks near Auchenheath where they were threshing the wheat. He wanted two skeps sewn, by Pettigrew beekeeper, to stand in the bottom of the garden.

It was Roddy Munro who had suggested it, now that there was aye a body biding at Annville, and such a great good piece of ground; he said there had been bees at Annville at the time of Eliza Fairlie, and the stands were there yet in the back of the shed among the trash. John considered it would be a rare thing to have their own honey; and the skeps if well made could go to the heather near Tintoch when the good of the garden flowers was bye, and stand along the wood. What honey they did not eat they could sell at Lanark market.

"*My son, eat thou honey, because it is good: so shall the knowledge of wisdom be unto thy soul.* Proverbs.xxiv.13-14."

Helen thought he could have got the straw away to Carluke with the apples, when they were sent up, though the Branley were a grand keep-er—despite two left barrels gone bad from last year, she was not sure she would not miss them. She was far from pleased to see John tramp-ing up the hill with the straw bag; she said he looked like a hawker, but John said he wanted a good crack with Pettigrew, which would be more useful to him, and less dear, than ordering a handbook.

The skeps were indeed beautiful when they were brought down, and Charlotte went boldly as far as the green to watch the swarms got in, Mr. Pettigrew fearlessly walking about with bare arms and face among the grosset bushes and making John shift the stands closer into the lee of the east wall. John all muffled up by Helen in gauze from the shop and puffing hard at his pipe—he had made a tear to insert it into his mouth. Margaret Tennant stood up at the kitchen door with her arms folded across her apron, and Helen behind her, Margaret very attentive and serious, almost jumpy.

Later at the table she was uncommonly ready to talk—her father had kept bees and her grandfather, and for all the new Scientific ideas and the Mr. Pettigrew, there were more to bees than what you would learn in a picture book. Mr. Pettigrew sitting meanwhile in the master-chair and pulling on his terrible old Dutch clay. Charlotte had never met a man who reeked so of the black raip; no wonder, as Helen said afterwards, he need not cover himself. Though he told John he'd been stung thousands of times and the bees were long weary of the taste of him.

Now he took his pipe out of his mouth and said mildly to Margaret: "What was it your grandfather said to them, then?"

"Family business. Were we born, and we were, he went first out to the bees about it, before he went to the kirk, and banged on the skeps and said it. And that was us. And the night he died my Dad did the same, told them all about it. Out of respect, for he meant the bees to ken him."

Mr. Pettigrew stared at her complacently. His face behind the bristly whiskers was leather-coloured from the sun, his eyes light as boiled milk.

"Are you doubting I talk to my bees? The last I did, and John Brown will answer for it, was to give the skeps a whack with my keys and say, 'You're flitted to your new home now, and a new master, and you're to agree.'"

Charlotte could not see from his eye whether he was having a joke. John looking suspicious, wondering perhaps whether it would be a kind of papist superstition to knock on hives.

Helen said, "There's no harm in the old country ways, John, and they would no sting you so much being used to your voice."

Then John and Roddie Munro down to watch the bees all Sabbath afternoon, for bees did not rest like Christians. But Charlotte wondered whether they were still angry, having travelled in a box, and then to be fished out like washing on a besom, with bits of themselves dripping off and the edges changing like smoke, and thrust into a new place.

One got into Willie's room with the airing and stung him on the ring finger, just under the first joint. Charlotte wanted to dress it with vinegar but he said she shouldn't bother, a wee sting was the least of his troubles. She brought up some of the extra gauze however and pinned it across his windows.

For Willie was back again. He had gone down to toun in blithe spirits but the new attack seemed even more serious than the last. Helen came in from Stonehouse already the Thursday because Charlotte, worried, had sent a post card. They sat in the kitchen.

"I'll run up and see him when I've drunk my tea. Chattie, you're wearying. Have you slept the night? I said to John, it's no for nothing Chattie would write after me, and Dr. Gray been as well. Is he taken very bad again?"

Charlotte had not written *after* her aunt, though she was very glad to see her. She said that she had not just exactly sat up the night. But she was pleased that Helen approved sending after Dr. Gray, for Willie had been a wee bit against it.

"No, you did the right thing. Poor chield, of course he would want to depend on his own medicines, but I'm no sure whether he's too hard on himself, and went back down before he had his strength, being over-eager."

Willie had such a pain in the limb, that came and went, and was quite a new thing. Dr. Gray, pulling at his moustaches, called it the sciatica which was a kind of gout of the great nerve that went down through the hip joint into the thigh. A neuralgia, he said, could be brought on by over-exertion, for example by Willie's cramming at his books before he was fully recovered.

He was done in by the journey as well. Charlotte remembering his face when he came in, and how he refused the arm of George Kay postilion down from the gate, and almost fell against the trellis, and stood leaning there a moment by the open glazed door. She would have reached out to steady him but he shrunk back: "I'm in pain," not looking at her. George Kay then permitted to go in after him with his rug and bag, slowly behind him across the lobby and up to his room, while Charlotte ran down to the range to rake some eisels into the pan for his fire. He had wanted his laudanum out at once and took a dose, lying full length on the bed in his outer clothes, with his boots on the bedspread as well. After he was rested Charlotte had got him into bed properly.

He was to be kept from his books. But with the examinations approaching, he would have them. Gray was no doubt a grand country doctor but with all the medical words aye jiggling and dancing before his head anyway, the reading would still them.

"It is worse to lie here and think than to open my books," he said. Charlotte was there to relieve him of any other exertion and she could only relent, but looked her disapproval, she hoped. As for his medicines Dr. Gray quite approved while prescribing chalk and bismuth for the vomiting should it continue. The lad came by with the mixture in the morning.

At her prayers, Charlotte asked that Willie be given patience, for he was so eager to be away again and must be so disappointed. Down in the lobby, Dr. Gray had frightened her by saying the sciatica was "excruciating."

She did not tell Aunt Helen this. Or that just as Willie arrived she had been preparing to go out the door, to her Tuesday Class. Then while she was hurriedly switching an egg for Willie's supper, Sub-Inspector Munro had called by, the Members being present at the Hall and Miss Elder reporting the carriage stopped at Annville and sure it must be something serious, or Miss Spears would have been there before them. Charlotte had thanked him eagerly. They must excuse her lateness! They were to choose four monitors exactly as last week and go through the Canon. She would come as soon as she could. She had asked him as well, whether he would get a word to Dr. Gray.

As it turned out she was in time, by running in the footpath, Sub-Inspector Munro coming later and red faced having been delayed by his errand. That next forenoon she had written her letter to Mr. Cameron and the Managers and dispatched Janet Sneddon with it. While she handed it the bairn was staring up into the ceiling, scared by the rap of Willie's staff.

The Concert at the Kirk, which was Mr. Whiteford's swan song, came off satisfactory, though everyone remarked how frail the old man was, waving his stick almost at random it seemed, and the Choir not paying him that much attention, but getting along on their own as well as they could. Charlotte attended of course, and had persuaded her aunt to come, with John left at Annville to see to Willie; they sat well back the Kirk being thronged, with the gas turned up high despite being still daylight. Charlotte looked out for her Members as the Choir got into the box with the usual rustlings and whisperings and last minute coughs as everyone quieted.

There were Mr. Adam and Mr. Carmichael and Mr. Russell, her staunch Managers, and the Paul sisters, and Agnes Elder—who, she saw in the programme, was to sing a Solo. Her big white face, her black wet mouth opening. Charlotte noted with satisfaction that she held her music sheets well up in front of her bosom. Her voice was full and sweet and dark as treacle, but unregulated, slipping about the long notes, finding and losing them.

"*I had Rather be a Doorkeeper in the House of my God, than to Dwell in the Tents of Wickedness.*" Charlotte had to smile.

"I'll bet!"—something dear Robert would have whispered, for he loved a joke, leaning to her ear.

She listened, and folded the Programme afterwards to take away and study it, in her head considering what she should write were she to gazette the performance, which, while not unkind, would refer to the superiority of the Sol-Fa Method and "standards perhaps not quite attained." There was one fearful sharp soprano, a lady she knew only as Miss Henry, having a very thin neck and tendrils of light brown hair teased about the forehead. Looking displeased, Charlotte thought, at not getting the Solo herself, but having to make do, and fiercely, with a short phrase in the last anthem.

Charlotte, alert to the music, almost dozed away during the Intimations and nearly missed herself being named as commencing Precentor, when Mr. Cameron was done his lengthy thanking of the Choir, and in particular Mr. Whiteford, long years of faithful service, etc., etc. To sit at Kirk, to sit down at all, meant giving in to her weariness. The month had been arduous indeed, though she could never complain, being thankful for her strength. She would not neglect her Classes, or her pupils, or her practising. But Willie, being just now truly very ill, must be her first care.

No more did she walk in the forenoon. Up and downstairs was enough of walking. She herself took to rinsing Willie's linen, and found pleasure in doing so, with the air crisp and the orchard leaves curled tight and gold, and chilly dew on the grasses. And the river like ice! She pulled off her boots and stockings as she had seen Margaret Tennant do, the first morning when they'd gone down together. Up against the bushes to be out of view from the brig she tucked up her skirts, then bravely waded in. The sheets reached out hard from her hands, the smell and stain all drifting away. Then getting them out without sand in them, though it would shake off, said Margaret, when they were dry, and wringing them—which had been easier with Margaret on the other end, to twist the knot. Sometimes Margaret would come stamping down the garden to wring them with her properly when she saw Charlotte trying to heave them over the raips.

"Miss Spears doesnae have the wrist for it, being so nice with the piano." If the wet was off the green, Charlotte spread them out on the ground, long blue shadows across them, the sunlight peeping. Unless Margaret had let Gruntie out to root after windfalls and get at the odd potato John had missed. The pig was mottled about haunch and neck with dark spots, and a bluish splash under them, otherwise pink. A pretty piglet she had been, but was big now, placid, soon for the knife. She rocked like a jelly-bag, low to the ground, busy. "Happy pig, bonnie Gruntie," she was called still.

Charlotte stood a moment rubbing at her chilled arms and looking about her, before she rowed down her sleeves and went indoors. Over the river, Nemphlar Wood was changing colour, the highest plantings already brown from the untoward frost. All the ricks were thatched, the wheat was bringing home, and the noise of the threshing machines echoed along the valley. A high sky, almost cloudless. Annville's whited wall rising over the trees.

She made a fomentation of powdered mustard seed and bread crumbs, with molasses to draw away the irritation, and Willie allowed her to place it on his spine—"It's hot as the bad fire, so it's a wee change from the other." His exposed back yellowish and narrow as a child's, with threads of sparse, long black hair growing along it, as if combed. He pulled his breath in through his teeth with a whistle as she laid the flannel down.

The fevers were not so desperate. This was a new illness with a name, and soon to be surmounted. "When I get the better of the sciatica."

But his stomach was as disarranged as before, the sick smell of his fever lingered, and despite the bismuth he could never keep down his supper. Charlotte baked milk in the half-gallon stone jar, covering it with a sheet of writing paper and leaving it all day in the oven. She prepared Helen's raspberry vinegar in barley water, with the juice of a lemon, to stand seven hours. Each day she made a new dish, hoping to tempt him. The sick-room tray to be "invitingly presented and scrupulously clean." She brought his supper upstairs covered with a d'oyley.

But he left it untouched. Dr. Gray had recommended Waterford's unfermented wine to help him sleep, which Charlotte, unsure, decided against introducing. His nights were dreadful. Pulling at his pillows and wringing out the poultices, with the wag-at-the-wa' clock at four and not a trace of daylight showing yet over the Brae, Charlotte pitied him very much, for there was no position he could lie in, that did not hurt him.

She gave him his medicine, asked whether he wanted the lamp left or taken away, or whether she should read to him. Mostly he did not answer, or said with an effort, "You can do nothing for me, I thank you." Sometimes, he was in a little delirium when he woke, and looked as if he did not know her.

"I fancied I was at the old place," he said once. Or: "That's a fair way you've moved the door, I wouldnae get over to the Inns through there," and later, in an unusually open mood, telling her he had thought he was back in his old box bed at King-street and the servant after him to fetch the milk.

"Go away on down, Chattie, or you'll no get any rest at all before old Margaret comes traipsing."

But before she could fall asleep he would be rapping, to be turned on his side and a pillow propped against him.

35, Great Western Road
September 22nd, 1881

Dear Chattie,

Now you must be wondering, when you will hear from us in toun, it being my turn to write. We are all very well. Mother read your letter to us "in a high voice" Tuesday after tea, having got it in the first Post but kept it till I was come home and we were together, and we are most thankful to hear that Willie is pretty nearly recovered, though it may be a time before he regains his full strength and "*rejoiceth as a strong man to run a race*" (Psalm.xix.5).

Norma came off, and I have cut you out a snip from the
Herald but regret we did not attend, Mother not wishing it.
Our summer Anthems at Elgin Place were indeed successful despite decreased attendance, the guid auld Members
holding the fort—*holding forth*, I should rather say. A piece
of news—"WP" is engaged to be married, to Miss (Janet)
Ferguson. Annie claims she is not at all surprised although
I admit to have thought him sweeter on the younger sister
(Lizzie) which shows how blind is blunt old Tom, in the
ways of Love.[25] Of other news, I cannot think of any, but
have as you requested enquired of Mr. Sprite, for I would
not sit down to this letter until I had done so, regarding the
efficacy of Thompsons Conc'd.,—he expressed no strong
opinion of its worth, though selling it in the Shop.
However:—I am sending to you with this Post the two
newest *Papers on Health* by Professor Kirk of Edbr. which
Mr. Sprite endorses very highly, and urges me to have you
read them. The "Barilla" Cure has been known for some
time and tried and true, but not as widely as is yet to be
hoped. I have looked at them myself, and find them found-
ed on sound Christian, as well as Scientific principles.
Whether Willie as a medical man trained by his own
Professors, will agree to the new theories herein pro-
pounded, I cannot tell. They are sent with Mr. Sprite's
hearty recommendation and he will despatch an Order at
any time, and says they would be sure to benefit.

You enquire after Jacky! He was much subdued by his
Adventure, and we hoped (as you) he had learnt his lesson,
however the urgent, may I say *ardent*, requirement to get in
under a dray's hooves has again asserted itself. Mother
therefore keeps him ben, and Annie must walk out with
him on a leathar lead and collar, which he does not like at
all. I think he has forgotten Corunna-street—but I could
not say for certain.

Mr. Sprite has taken on a new assistant to serve in the
Shop and I am now, while still making up the Powders, etc.,
largely responsible for the Accounting, which wrestling
quietly with figures, as you know, suits me exactly. She is

very young, not more I think than fifteen or sixteen.

We have at the commencement of the Fall services admitted into the Fellowship 7 new members, 2 of whom I proposed from the Bible Class, which, and the Soc. for Religious Improvement, having resumed for the season, keep me sufficiently busy.

We are now of course wanting all success for you in your new endeavour! You will think that Tom shakes his head, and wonders if his sister will not get very High? However as I have assured Mother it is not the Episcopal, which she somehow had got into her head, and we trust you will not neglect the "wee kirk up the Brae" entirely.

I am to convey, in closing, Mother's and Annie's best love. Annie says to tell you she has not remade the dress, though thanking Aunt Helen for her advice, but given it to Maggie as she thought it not worth the new stuff (Mark.ii.21) the tartan being too dear.

We send Willie our prayers for his full recovery. It being now my task to read from the Holy Word, I cannot open the auld Ha' Bible without hearing dear Father's voice, and hope I may perform as humbly and reverently. We read in *Ecclesiastes*.

May God bless you and keep you.
Your loving brother
Thos Spears

Charlotte wished Willie well with all her heart, and he was as determined himself. With the sciatica he allowed himself to be ill, which he would never quite acknowledge before. He let her tend him. Only when the pain overcame him could he have been called in any way a difficult patient.

Once, he puzzled her. "Chattie, will you take this post card away over to the Post Office? I would do it myself but here you are with your boots on, and I want to look at my notes. My head is calling me, and I believe I will try to get away to toun tomorrow, if you can get word to the carrier."

He spoke again later in the afternoon of "his head's wanting him in Glasgow"; Charlotte finally understanding, with relief, that he meant the preparation head, the one he had requisitioned, which he was dissecting.

"You see, Chattie, the neck area has many a long Latin name the chemists do not care about, they blether on about congestion of the blood but have no knowledge of the circulatory vessels." Then he would reel off, broodingly, a great list of Latin terms.

"Stay by me, Chattie, and hear my lesson, it's the least you can do, for I've heard your Bible reading and prayers patiently enough, have I not?"

She was grateful when he sometimes let her hear him.

Back in the kitchen she scalded his plate, and surveyed the day ahead of her carefully, as she had done before bed and again on rising. She made notes of his dietary, which she kept in the dresser and added to nearly every day. To Margaret Tennant's disapproval, for if Miss Spears would but write her letters at the escritoire they'd no get the beef tea splashed over them.

Dinner: Sheep's head from flesher 8d. M. Sneddon to fetch and get scorched at the smithy. 3 days.—tomorrow, Broth. Saturday, the dressed head. Sunday Sheep's Head Pie.[26] Today, ham, dressed from Yday, roasted apple. Fire to be kept low to set milk. Soak barley. Greengrocer for arrow-root, Burlow's Extract of Veal. To Brig-End for 12 eggs, order straw. Wash butter. Practise till noon, then Head to be stewed 3 hours. W. dinner. Turn bed.

Lessons,—4 PM. Susan Capie harmonium, half past 4 Katie Ross piano, voice? R. Munro extra lesson, 7 PM. Accounts. supper W.—New broth, with sippets. Pudding. evening Worship 2nd Corinthians.iv.—to be empha-sized—*We are troubled on every side, yet not distressed; we are perplexed, but not in despair, Etc.*

"*Look on the bright side. It is the right side. The times may be hard, but it would make them ten times wearier to wear a gloomy and sad countenance. That would be a dull sea, and the sailor would never get skill, where there was nothing to disturb the surface of the ocean. What though things look a little dark, the lane will turn, and night will end in broad day."*

The *Papers on Health* arrived and Charlotte read them at once. She had to consider whether she should give them to Willie to read, and brought this to the Lord in prayer, and was reassured that all must be open and clear, just as when she said, about his books, "Willie, Dr. Gray believes they are preventing your rest—" giving them to him but letting him know what she felt.

She asked Willie whether he had heard of Professor Kirk of Edinburgh at all and he said he had not.

"Tom has sent on some wee books—tablets—about a soap cure."

Willie said with a bit of a smile that there was soap enough at Annville already.

"You shouldnae interest my cousin Tom in curing me, Chattie, or we will be getting so many parcels with chemist's miracles the press couldnae hold them. I'm fighting off a squad of E U ladies and their awful potions as it is."

But he said he would look at the tablets—"There's no harm in seeing what the chemists are up to, after all."

It was late afternoon when Charlotte came upstairs again, the room darkened by a steady, lowering rain at the windows. Willie was lying quietly on his bed, his hands at his sides, one on each of the *Papers on Health* with their dark red jackets showing under his fingers. The lamp's yellow light fell just there, across his hands. The room felt so very quiet that for a moment Charlotte was almost frightened. Till he turned his head, large eyed and serious, looking at her directly, which was rare for him.

"Are you right, Willie, do you need anything?"

His voice calm: "Aye, I'm right and no, I need nothing. I've taken a keek at these—" his fingers moving slightly on the tablets.

"And your opinion?"

"Oh, it looks like a sure Cure, but awful muckie. All that soap. I couldnae abide it, so I believe I'll be going down to toun instead."

Charlotte not sure she understood him.

"Willie, are you well then? Are you getting your strength?"

"Aye, and I wish to lie still and settle with it an hour or two and no scare it away."

She burst out. "Oh, Willie, how thankful we must be!" hurrying forward to smooth his pillows till his look stayed her hand. She said softly, "I'll just fix the fire and be away down again then—but I will read to you if you like."

"No, no, save your voice. It is pleasant as it is—my head's gone ever so quiet. I believe the words in these wee tablets all about their horrible Cure must have chased all the wild thoughts away." He coughed a little, and Charlotte left him to rest.

He improved rapidly from that day, and at night slept easy, and went down to his Examinations in good spirits. The Matriculation for the winter session was the following week, being the second week of October.

CHAPTER 12

In which Charlotte triumphs, gains an admirer, and is
afterwards prevented from visiting him.

It was a bright, boisterous autumn. The harvest inned, the fattened
calves and bullocks driven roaring uphill to market between the
bright hedges, early frosts, Nemphlar Wood a glory of colour over
Clyde and darkening leaf adrift under the trees.

Every day as soon as Margaret Tennant was done and gone,
Charlotte moved swiftly through the empty rooms. She could not get
enough of airing them, and a sudden gust of hail surprised her so she
must run for the besom and sweep quickly, wee white pebbles melting
under the windows.

Willie's room sweet again at last. He was cramming and doing
well: a card to Stonehouse that he "meant to have a cut for the prizes"
was shown proudly at Annville. Helen and John went down to the
warehouses after the winter patterns, paid a visit to Mrs. Spears and
Annie, missed Willie at his lodgings but had a look at his room and his
landlady. They were thrang with the shop and did not come to
Annville every week-end, now that the apples were in.

Charlotte had five pupils to the piano, seven to the harmonium,
and four to private singing lessons. When she began at the Kirk she
dispersed her Adult Class, making a little speech in the Hall, encouraging any who were not Members of the Kirk Choir to join, at least for
the Harvest Concert, and others (remembering Romish Duncan
McBeau) to come to her for private lessons at a reduced rate.

"For now we must throw ourselves into the Concert as one
Choir."

There were, besides McBeau, a handful of Evangelical Unionists
who would go up the Brae, and Mr. Thomson the law clerk and his

wife announced they'd attend St. Leonard's, which Charlotte generously praised as the superior Choir in the district and offered to write a Recommendation at any time.

Those who followed her were Roderick Munro and Mr. Weir. The latter she no longer feared—one look forestalled him. She had written, after several attempts, a letter to Mr. Miller:

> You will I know be pleased to hear that I have undertaken the Kirkfieldbank Church Precentorship as of October First. Our Harvest Concert, which we are well ahead with already, is set for the 21st November. We are attempting the "Shine, Mighty God" among other selections, and I have assured the children, who have been quite as diligent as the adult Members, a liberal share in the Programme.
>
> I must again, though I have no words, thank your faithful kindness and patience, over a period of nearly eight years of my musical education, for any progress I have achieved. The wee trouble I encountered which you so kindly advised me about is now resolved I am thankful to say.

The Juvenile Class too was brought over into the Kirk, and practised after the Sabbath School.

Mr. Weir had warned of a wasp's nest. But Charlotte was determined to suffer no nonsense and if she should detect a buzz of discontent to smile it away. The first practise, during which she would meet those Members new to her but auld in the Kirk, must show her happy but firm. Already, surveying an augmented choir box while the rustlings and shufflings subsided, she recognized the faces of voices she had heard. Miss Henry in particular, who stood determinedly in her forward spot as chief soprano, two earnest ladies flanking her (she drew in her skirts in a gesture of welcome) while others moved into position. Beadle Reid still walking about the nave, fiddling with the lamps, finally edging into the back row beside a rigid Mr. Barr. Mr. Weir a head taller, making a thing of not caring where he should sit, gazing up into the rafters at being manoeuvred aside by Mr. Barr as if to say: "Whatever silly thing you wish is perfectly agreeable to me."

Agnes Elder at the end of the sopranos coughing loudly into the final silence.

Later, walking back to Annville, she admitted to herself there might be difficulties. She had told the auld Kirk ensemble how very carefully she had listened to their anthems and, instead of plunging into the Harvest Concert work at once, had given half an hour to the anthem for the Sabbath, Gibbons' *Sanctus*, robust and familiar.

Miss Henry's voice was indeed very shrill! Next week Charlotte would urge and encourage the "single organ chord" of the really crack choir—each of the parts singing as one voice.

After the pause she had described the Concert programme. Her own Members were familiar with all but one selection, which everyone would be introduced to now—"Lord of the Living Harvest." She was already practising it with the children, she said as the notes were handing round, but "had no doubt the adults would soon catch them up."

"Would Miss Spears be intimating that the Sabbath School children will sing in the same selection?" This from one of Miss Henry's supporters, the quivery chin on the left.

"Aye, and the grown-ups will be having to mind your p's and q's for the bairns are in great voice already. But we'll no be practising together a while yet."

Charlotte had begun last week with the Sabbath School, and divided them into two groups, the first mostly her own. Wee rocking Bernard she kept with his sisters of course, though a tall lass had pointed at him and complained, "If he willnae sing, why is he no put in the bad choir?" and Charlotte had to spend a few minutes explaining the difference between bad and untrained, and used the example of Bernard (who was hiding under the bench) to illustrate the moral, if not vocal, equality of each.

Would he but sing! For it was his voice indeed she had heard that first evening, and thrice again over at the Hall. It was not then an impediment in his speech, but a degree of shyness quite out of the ordinary, which kept him silent! She heard but a bit of a verse, an echo long after the song was put by and the other bairns well into their scones and milk. He was hunkered down under the modulator whose tassel he liked to touch—hardly more than a phrase it was, yet with such promise of richness! the exact notes, key, words, the sweetness rising!

"Wasna that a dentie coo?
Dance, Katie Braidie!"[27]

Twice again he had sung but never with the others. His sisters shy of Charlotte's interest.

"We do try to make him mind, Miss."

"But you must never prevent him singing! His voice is very beautiful."

"Aye, but he never will sing when he's told, only sometimes at home if he's away at it and we don't want to hear and we say stop it."

Robina glancing up cannily. "But if *you* were to say stop it, Miss Spears, it wouldnae do, for he'd ken what you were about."

Bernie all the while silent between them, his head nodding downward so she saw only a crown of thick, curly, dark brown hair.

Back at Annville with no one to disturb, it was never too late for some practising. She would take her lamp across into the nice room and go through the *Jagdsonata* from beginning to end, before she felt the cold.

Mr. Weir, though he had no success in meeting Charlotte after the Harvest Concert at St Leonard's—she had made sure of the Carmichaels' carriage—on an impulse cornered Precentor Morton in the porch, and urged him to make the short journey down the Brae, and attend her now imminent Service of Sacred Song.

"I'll guarantee you'll be far from disappointed, and I'm no speaking by the lady's leave either, Miss Spears being a very modest person for all her gifts. But it being her first concert, I'm sure she'd be gratified by a report in the *Advertiser* and knowing you're in the way of writing them"—Mr. Morton gazetted his own concerts—"I couldnae think of another who'd do it justice, in the musical sense."

Mr. Morton, flattered, had given his word "though if I do nae like it I will say so. My report will be an honest one."

Mr. Weir, touching his moustache, said it was therefore he had been so bold as to make the request.

So the last practises went forward, with no friction beyond a show of condescension among the ladies when the children were at last brought in, quickly put to rout by their excellence. Bernie, carefully ignored, sang briefly at both the last rehearsals of "Lord of the Living Harvest," Charlotte's baton immediately poised for silence, her fingers providing a gentle harmony with only the *flute* stop drawn:

"So shall Thine angels issue forth;
The tares be burnt; the just of earth,
To wind and storm exposed no more—"

His sweet voice ceased. A quick downstroke and they all rushed in again, the better for having heard him:

"—gathered to their FATHER'S shore!"

Wee Bernie's musical gift! Charlotte would have reached out to him if she could. Dr. Gray had told his mother, who had said it to Mrs. Simpson who had said it to Mrs. West, that such feral children did crop up from time to time, and Bernard needed the attention of a strict institution and be denied music entirely or he would never learn to speak. Charlotte, though her view must be eccentric, could not agree. She was selfishly thankful for the family's lowly estate, which put such a school—if one existed—out of reach.

It was a glorious evening. A high wind had driven away the rain and the face of the big, gibbous moon brightened the High-street as folk streamed towards the Kirk. Its every window was aglow and the bells clanged merrily.

Charlotte had been allowed the schoolroom, the vestry being so small, and Mr. Dunlop had poked up the stove to red-hot. Cloaks and greatcoats were thrown across the tables. Music sheets were clutched, laid aside, restacked, Mrs. West describing to some other ladies how she had put a bit of red ribbon between each selection, then finding them in the wrong order and having to spread them out on the desk. "Oh dear, I'll just move your baton to the chair for the moment, Miss Spears, I've no lost it. It's these ribbands, you see, that willnae hold their place."

Sarah solemnly trying to keep the children out of the adults' way. Mr. Hamilton's loud, slow voice: "There will be no jostling or shoving." He was Superintendent of the Sabbath School.

Beadle Reid peering in to say the Kirk was filling up and then walking back with Mr. Dunlop to see if further seatings were needed.

The Kirk ladies had been decorating all the morning and Charlotte when she looked in before tea had seen a transformation even by dim daylight. It was late in the season yet there were great frothy stacks of chrysanthemum of every fiery hue, and among and between them the last of the beech leaves and the bloodred splash of the haws, for the hawthorn were most plentiful this year.

"*Mony haws, mony snaws*" was the saying and the early storms of hail, one even in August, and the strong frosts, seemed set on proving it.

Charlotte had dressed carefully under her aunt's eye. Helen had tried, with an array of new gowns borrowed from the shop, to tempt her out of mourning entirely, but Charlotte had refused; she chose the occasion to go into half-mourning and even this caused her some pain. But the crape had been unstitched at last, and set with bran-water and oxgall and laid away. Folding it, she spoke in her heart with Robert, as she still liked to do and feel him nigh, and thought he approved the pearl gray cachemere skirt with its wide stripes of slate-coloured satin, and the bodice, tightly fitted in the new fashion, deep violet with an even deeper tone for the brocade. The sudden whiteness of her own mother's lace collar and cuffs, smelling first faintly of lavender and then crisp as toast from Helen's unnecessary ironing, startled her face, when she peered into the glass, with a comparative blush of colour. Her hair, newly washed in rain water, was unwilling to lie flat though she had brushed it as hard as she could and pinned it up securely. Helen, happy to be appealed to, had produced a tight bonnet of mauve silk moiré drawn over felt, which not being Charlotte's size rather hurt her at the temples.

"Now your hair's no to be seen at all, except for the parting, and that's hardly noticed," said Helen. "And dear sister Lottie's lace! I havnae seen it since the day—" brushing away a tear.

Charlotte wore her own mother's jet at her throat as well.

Her uncle and aunt were ready; though Tuesday they were still at Annville, for Helen would never have missed dear Chattie's Concert and John was eager to hear the children, having himself led the Infants' Choir at Stonehouse.

The overheated schoolroom smelled of wet outer garments steaming, and echoed with a tangle of eager talk. Kate, one of Bernard's sisters, pulling Charlotte's head down to say in a loud whisper, "Bernie's come. We didnae say anything, we just came away and he followed us. But our Minnie says he'll no do it."

Charlotte kissed her hot cheek. "We'll see. Just keep him between you, and do allow him to turn his back, or do whatever he likes."

The children staring about, unused to being allowed to talk, to darkness outside the schoolroom windows, to adults overtaking their tables and Mr. Dunlop and some of the men scraping the benches about, getting them away across to the Kirk.

The bells ceased.

Everyone silent, then moving hurriedly into line. Charlotte stood tiptoe at the door and held up her baton. She need not say a word. Before them, sure of them, she led them across the moonlit yard with its black shadows. They would wait in the porch for the first chord of the processional. She smiled at them once, then walked quickly along the side of the Kirk to go in through the vestry. Needing no notes herself, she carried only her baton, tucked under her arm.

As she went in a cold gust pushed at her bonnet and wound the ribbons tight around her throat. She closed the door behind her and stopped to unwind them. The cap was hurting her—surely by now her hair was flat to her head, and she undid the ties and took out the two hatpins. That was indeed an improvement! Laying the bonnet beside the lamp on the table she turned, feeling at her hair. Oh, Mr. Cameron had a wee looking glass behind the door, to have a smirk at himself last thing! She peered into it as he must do, replaced a pin, was satisfied, entered.

Hushed and crowded pews, blazing lamps and a glow of harvest colours. Folk right to the back and some standing. Mr. Cameron in his pulpit and a stranger sitting behind him who must be Mr. Thomson of Heywood, come to do the reading.

"For I mean to be selfish this once and enjoy myself, and leave the work to others," Mr. Cameron had said.

Though he would of course give the Closing Remarks and propose, it was presumed, a vote of thanks to the Choir. Baton still in place, Charlotte drew her skirts to the side and seated herself at the harmonium.

Mr. Thomson's reading was, though clear, quite unmodulated, almost mechanical. He was a slight, beardless young man with light brown hair and long side whiskers that ran into his moustaches, the way Robert's had though of course Robert's were darker, almost black. Mr. Thomson seemed just to pop up and read and get down again as fast as he could. Charlotte could not have explained it, but the following "Shine, Mighty God" with assembled voices, burst forth beautifully in contrast, and lifting her eyes a moment past the heads of her Choir she could see the reverend gentleman seated with his elbows on his knees and his fists under his chin, an unbecoming pose not available to the eyes of the congregation, staring across at her blankly and apparently listening for all he was worth.

Bernie did not sing, and Charlotte must be disappointed though she had hardly expected it. Just as "Lord of the Living Harvest" was begun he left the assembled children, who were stood in front of the box, and went down the side aisle to creep in beside his mother, where he got down on the floor and was not again to be seen. Yet the Choir had heard him in the rehearsals and he had taught the sopranos unawares; and Miss Henry, when given the nod to take his part, sang her solo lines with a hint of the sweetness she had learned from him.

Mr. Miller had come! all the way from Glasgow, and she had not noticed till the vote of thanks that he was there, with Mrs. Miller and Miss Whyte and Miss Esther Tosh from the Select! They had been at the Clydesdale since yesterday and had kept it a secret, in order not to fluster her! In that sea of faces suddenly, at the last, the configuration of his so well-studied face! the white augustan temples, the darkish, streaky beard! his sternly-held head and close-set, penetrating eyes! The final anthem was a blur to Charlotte, but a blur of triumph. A strand of her hair had half escaped the pins, lay in a loop along one shoulder. "My dear," Mrs. Miller saying as they all stood about, "Your hair!" pinning it back for her into the bun sharply.

What congratulations! They were to stay till Wednesday at the Clydesdale, make an excursion of it. Miss Syle-Paton would have come as well, would not have missed it for the world but was unfortunately indisposed.

"Whatever did he mean at the end, the wee man who did the reading?"

"Oh, Miss Spears, I do believe you have made a conquest! Here he comes himself, I declare!"

And Mr. Cameron following the Reverend Mr. Thomson down the nave.

Refreshments were offering in the schoolroom. Mr. Thomson's hand on her arm, so that, she knew not how, she was separated from her friends and came over the yard beside him.

Behind the stove there, Charlotte standing upright and he half leaning against a heap of cloaks, the open grate gleaming red on his side whiskers. He had smallish eyes but set remarkably, so that in the skin around about them there appeared a great deal of light. He spoke low, so she missed some of his words.

But music, of music. "Not since Edinburgh, I assure you. The Parks, splendid people but I am not sure I am pleased or displeased they stayed away for we would have argued about it.

"Hours, all night sometimes.

"No, I am unfamiliar with it in that sense. I'm no a performing musician."

She told him about Bernard. It was delightful to speak, she found, wondering how she could have gone on longer, unable to describe to any one her idea of this child. Glad that Mr. Miller and the others, whom she had a moment before chafed to rejoin, were out of hearing.

"For God's glory only," repeated Mr. Thomson. "And that you had the gift of hearing him—I do understand you.

"When you come to Heywood. The Kirk is small but we have an organ, indifferent but an organ." There would be opportunities surely.

It was Mr. Cameron who thrust himself between them, looking rather cross. "Come, Thomson my good man, if you are to bed down with me the night. You must no monopolize Miss Spears who has a large party from Glasgow to entertain."

Mr. Thomson giving a little rueful laugh, one side of his face twisting. Charlotte noticed that when talking to Mr. Cameron he spoke up quite loud.

"I did say I would have to thank Miss Spears in private. Walter, you are most fortunate, or discerning. You can hardly hope with such talents you will be allowed to keep her long."

Mr. Cameron preening a little, turning away from her, arm in arm with his friend. "Oh, aye, Miss Spears has found fertile ground for her labours here with us. A lady, Drew, after all—however cried up, she must aye have the greater difficulty. The fair sex do not push themselves forward, you see. A position quite out of the ordinary."

Later, Charlotte walking in her rooms, back and forth from bed to front window, rubbing at her bare arms, her stays eased and her dressing-gown flung loose over her shoulders. Too restless to say her prayers, not wishing yet to compose herself.

She was to luncheon early with the Millers and their party, before they were away. The thought gave her no particular pleasure. Mrs. Isabel Miller would store it up to repeat in toun, how her hair had come down—"quite wild," she would say. "Did she not look quite wild, Esther?" Mr. Miller, expecting to be listened to eagerly, would describe to her over the cold meats his successes with *Norma* and the Select, and pat at his mouth with his napkin. The women would gossip of Mr. Tosh and the Syle-Patons. Mr. Miller's Selected! Charlotte knew that she no longer belonged to them or, in any sense, to him, or cared very much.

Charlotte's throat felt tender, her breaths deeper than any she had ever drawn. The noise of the Choir still rang in her head. She could not yet kneel, pray, sleep. A lightness in her body made her trip softly about, rise on her toes, her feet arching with delight. She shivered, wondered whether she were feverish. "*Thou good and faithful servant.*"

Whom did she address? It was not herself she meant by that phrase. Why, it was Miss Henry! A smile, a rush of affection assailed her. Miss Henry and her "cohorts," silly Mrs. West, pompous Mr. Cameron, fierce Mr. Barr, and all the dear children, them all, who had sung at her bidding so wonderfully. Bernie too, though never at her bidding. As though to humble her.

Birds in the woodlands, "*gems of purest ray serene*" who praised God whether they were heard or not. The birds of God. Wee Bernie for all his gifts. Mr. Thomson listening all ears as if the music were performed for him alone. To be given the gift to give such joy.

Mr. Thomson's hand she had thought soft—yet in parting, the firmness of it! That he had returned for a moment in spite of Mr. Cameron, to say goodbye. It was enough. Could time stand still, this moonlit night with the wind blustering around about Annville, clacketing softly in the top slats of the venetians!

All that week the boisterous weather continued, cloud building with the high winds, sharp gusts of sleet and rain, and Clyde a dirty brown with brown foam on its surface, seething out dark as taffy from under the brig. In the day time the wind would abate but at night it rose once more, worrying at the slates and rattling the windows. Nemphlar Wood was stripped bare, and down in the garden all the swept leaves were scattered. On Monday night the storm rose to a keening gale. Charlotte was alone at Annville. Before dark she had wrapped her cloak around her and gone up to the gate, and seen a whole cornstalk blowing past along the road, tumbled over and over like a peerie. But the real storm began later, at the back of midnight, and the noise combined with the roar of the river and the trees and a high, whining wail that rose and fell but never ceased, and seemed to be the sound of the air itself.

Annville shuddered. Unable to sleep, Charlotte took her trembling lamp and went down into the kitchen. She stirred the eisels which started up fitfully in the grate. Then she opened the box bed and took out the spread and hung it over the screen to get the heat, while she fetched down *Waverley*. A sharp pound of hail rattled the windows and the wind shrieked in the chimney.

This would be an interval out of the general passage of time, minding her of nights in her childhood when she had wakened during a storm, and crept into the kitchen to find the others sitting so, close to the fire, wide awake and ears pricked to changes in the wind's sound. She and her brothers all rolled up together in the old plaid in Mother's chair. That might however have been the night Annie was born.

Jacky was dead! A bit of memory out of place, Robert telling it at her bed with big, round eyes, them both waking Tom and then going into the kitchen. Great Hamilton-street. But this Jacky was only nine. How many Jackies had there been? Had they not always had a wee fierce terrier, with a coat like a bristly brush? Now she remembered coming into the kitchen on Arundel-street and only Father there, staring at the grate silently with wide-open eyes and tears running down his cheeks.

"I've a bit of grit in my eye." She thought he had said "greet"—a bit of weeping. It was what he'd meant. Letting her creep, puzzled, into his lap, the wetness of his beard from the tears.

"Oh well, the Lord knows best. My dear wee girlie."

The wind whissled in the chimney, pushing out the acrid smell of the eisels. All her movements, all this last week, slowed and glowing. Roddy Munro at his lesson bursting out, quite animated for him, "You're to be congratulated, Miss Spears! Have you no seen the *Advertiser*,[28] they're fair over the moon." And very red in the face afterwards. The Members coming up of their own accord, their pleasure in how well it had gone.

Kirkfieldbank, 22nd November 1881

My dear Thomson,

This missive but to secure for you, from myself and the Congregation, a *written* word of thanks for your reading Tuesday last, at our much lauded Service of Sacred Song. I hope you have seen the *Advertiser*, if not, I send you the cutting here, Mrs. Capie not having any use for it and the Managers having delivered me two more! Your reading was however noted as *plain*, but that being your inimitable style, and as you last evening confided in me, you did not wish to steal any fire from the Music.

I was of course delighted in your approval of the Concert, while not being myself as it were quite Swept Away, though I believe that a Concert is all very well (the collection in particular being most gratifying, close to 4 Pounds). But the "daily round the common task" must be regarded as the humble obligation of our Profession, and sufficient to "furnish all we need to ask" as the words go on to remind us.

The Managers were immediately decided against any repeat performance, which you had so kindly broached; indeed the weather has set in and continues so terrific that bringing the Choir or any part of them (many Members being of very tender Years) as far as Haywood and in midweek, would be a venture better postponed to a more clement season if at all. Not having received anything further from you on the subject, I trust you are of the same opinion.

We had such a Storm last night, perhaps you will

already have heard that the new Monument to the Martyrs, in the new cemetery was cut in two, the upper part being dashed to the ground. Also, the metal ornaments on the new poorhouse roof were twisted or carried away, and the fencing at the racecourse laid low. Kirkfieldbank High-street is a sorry sight with some slates and chimney cans still lying dangerously about, and we hear that many a fine old forest giant has gone down in the upper parks. The Kirk suffered no more than could easily be remedied, the path now cleared of branches and the road bank undamaged. Haywood being much more exposed, though a snug wee kirk, I trust has weathered the week. God has mercifully preserved life and limb in this district, and now Martinmas Old Term is upon us with the usual flittings, and over-happy faces and well-filled pockets, after which we must hope to proceed quietly, without further Sensations, into Advent, which suits very well
                    your good friend
                    Walter Cameron.

                              Stone Row, Heywood, Lanarks.
                              22nd November, 1881.
Dear esteemed Miss Spears,
    Forgive my temerity in writing to you so immediately after meeting you and our conversation of Tuesday last. My purpose in writing is first, to congratulate you on the very superior concert, which I wish to do in all haste, and 2nd:—to persuade you to bring the Choir, or some members of it (certainly the children!) to Heywood Kirk in order to give our congregation the opportunity of hearing them. I have spoken to our preceptor Mr. Park and he is more than eager to hear any portion of the music from the Concert, though if I had my way it would be "Lord of the Living Harvest" and "Shine, Mighty God." However it is for you to decide.
    The more I have been considering the wee lad and his gift, the more jealous I confess to have become, to hear

him, though whether he will be among those (with his sisters) to come to Heywood I cannot tell. For it would seem, as you said, he will not sing under any kind of persuasion, but rather, for reasons of his own which only our dear Lord is privy to!

Were you to arrange such an excursion, though Advent, I cannot see that any seasonal songs are necessary to be got up, unless a Christmas anthem is preparing. Our Choir are well in train with such, though they are (like our organ) indifferent good.

I would suggest a very early evening concert, which I shall intimate this coming Sabbath:—5 or 6 o'clock on the Tuesday following, so that the home coming would not be too late for the little ones. Heywood lies about 6 miles beyond Lanark so the distance is not unsurmountable in one or two closed carriages. We would of course make good the fee, through a collection.

It will be possible to keep you, yourself, at Heywood overnight, as the house is large. Mrs. Park says that you could sleep with Louise, the wee ones going into the closet with the baby. You will find us a boisterous family, for I count myself almost a member, being somewhere between an older brother and an Uncle, I am not sure which, but do not regard it. You said you are yourself from a family with a sister and brothers (one sadly gone ahead) therefore I do not hesitate to urge you to accept. The reason being quite selfish:—that you could then try out our organ properly after breakfast. I hope as well Miss Spears, that we can get up a fine musical conversation when the concert is bye, for I mind how you smiled when I told you that Parks and I sit up all hours cracking on about music, and as you said, in Kirkfieldbank you are far away from your musical friends and entertainments—who, however, came all the way to hear you, well knowing what they were in for, a real treat.

Again forgive my letter, it is indeed written as quick as can be, without correction to save the time, and I hope with the Lord's will it may succeed. A note from you giving approval of the date will suffice.

Your sincere well wisher
Andrew Thomson (Reverend).

Annville House, Kirkfieldbank,
24th November 1881

Dear Mr. Thomson,

Thank you for your very kind letter. You will mean-while have received a letter from Mr. Cameron, which he referred to while speaking with me today, intimating that the Choir will be unable to sing at Heywood at this time.

I regret the opportunity of trying out the Heywood organ but, it not being my instrument, my playing would match any indifference on its part, I fear.

Please convey my thanks to Mr. and Mrs. Park for their kind invitation.

Yours with sincere best wishes,
Charlotte T. Spears

PS. Bernard sang most touchingly after Sabbath School, I wish indeed you could have heard him.

Charlotte was extremely disappointed. But she dared not write more, being a little in wonder at the ardent tone of the young parson who, Mr. Cameron had hastened to inform her, was but twenty-four years old! Unable to show Mr. Cameron his letter, and confronted with a conclusive interdiction on the part of the Managers (which she suspected was Mr. Cameron's alone, as there had not been a special meeting), she gave way in silence.

Would Mr. Thomson become her musical correspondent, and would she one day be privileged to oust the several "wee ones" and share Louise's bed, and sit up late—as indeed she longed to do—talking music with him and Precentor Park?

With these thoughts to occupy her, she felt the silence of Annville especially, and was half-amused to find, when she sat down to play, that she had conjured up the figure of Mr. Thomson in the horsehair chair behind her—listening hard to every note, with his elbows on his knees and his fists under his chin.

CHAPTER 13

In which the year darkens, and fond hopes come to naught.

Alas, such sweet fancies were to be short-lived; Charlotte's isolation in which to indulge them was broken in upon. Willie failed both examinations. He was seized with fever during the Surgery *viva voce* and Dr. Gairdner himself expressed fears for him, advising him to return to Annville and enforced rest; his febrile debilitation was probably the result of over-exertion as well.

"Whether you will blame yourself for coming in too soon is your own business. I would not—but you must accept this illness for what it is, or you'll never weather it out. The remittent fevers are no easily got the best of and you'll want to steady yourself for perhaps a long fight. And that fight will be against your own nature, which very properly desires to do battle actively. During the periods you are afebrile, work of course. But you must allow this disease its course, and that will require great patience and complete rest."

Annville House itself seemed to grow darker, its inhabitants going about with set faces. Charlotte at the glass, seeing her drawn lips and thinking, "Why, I've got the look of Margaret Tennant on me!" And forcing a smile. All this having befallen them so suddenly, with her uncle and aunt busy at King-street and Charlotte not wishing to worry them unduly. But she could not help her disappointment, or her misgiving, that Willie had not taken proper care of himself—here he was again as if at the very beginning of his illness, and after all he had suffered. She recalled the eagerness with which he had gone down to his examinations!

"If I get the right questions I will do—you are all to pray for me."

And now, his brave reception of the bad news! "It's no the end of the world. Lowrie and Peace and Wotherspoon failed, Wotherspoon

the both, and Peace his Surgical Practise for the second time and without excuse, for he was fit all through the sessions and hardly missed a
lecture. I've a deal of it under my belt and I'll no forget it. Dr. Gairdner
was more than kind, for he knows I ken the work, and he'll give me my
attendance upon the summer lectures. It's most unfortunate of course
to have lost the year—but perhaps to be expected."

They had all concurred, thankful to hear such a rare speech from
him, his Christian spirit shining through unvanquished.

"*We are troubled on every side, yet not disquieted,*" his father read at
the bed side, "*perplexed, but not in despair; cast down, but not destroyed,*
Second Corinthians.iv.8-9." And after that, kneeling as Willie lay white-
faced with closed eyes, from The Epistle of James.xii.12: "*rejoicing in
hope; patient in tribulation; continuing instant in prayer.*"

Later Charlotte tiptoed to Willie's door and heard only the fire
and his quick, uneven breathing, and went down again to the piano
and practised for two hours with the soft pedal pressed, which was no
pleasure to her, or to the now fading ghost of Mr. Thomson in his
familiar pose. It would not do; he was not here, but at Heywood.
Standing up she dismissed him with a little shake of her head.

The post from Lanark brought two letters, Mr. Simpson coming
across with them and remarking on the fine lifting weather, a cloud of
frosty tobacco fume wafting past his whiskers in the sunshine. With a
little thrill Charlotte saw that they were both directed to her, the one
from Glasgow from Mr. Miller, and the other from Mr. Thomson. She
sat down again at the cottage, and opened Mr. Miller's first, her eye
running impatiently down the lines of florid thanks and praise.

"Dear Miss Spears,

"How delightful, etc., etc.!" And near the end:

Your place in the society of the Village now assured,
and any animadversions bravely overcome, I cannot but
foresee a pleasant path before you, in the midst of new
friends and acquaintance whose lives will on their part be
enlarged by your talents. Happy are those, who are permitted to serve! For I count myself among their humble ranks,
and to see your *modest* pleasure in the well-earned Praise
of the *discerning* as well as of the *general* audience, was to

bring back to me my first youthful "triumphs" as they might be called, almost to relive again their innocent charm. The call of Teaching brings now and then such Moments, vicarious as they must be, when someone or other among those one has been privileged to watch over, stretch their Fledgeling Wing, and soars.

We have of course conveyed to the others of the Select an Idea of your concert, and a copy of the Programme has made the rounds—though mine, I have kept for myself. Much well wishing is sent from them, and from all of us, in particular, my dear Pupil, from your constant and admiring Friend
R. W. Miller.

She laid the letter quietly aside. Mr. Thomson's was opened more tremblingly.

Dear Miss Spears,

Thank you for your reply to mine of the 22nd inst. Indeed, Mr. Cameron's last letter did "cross" mine on its travels, toward Kirkfieldbank though not to *him*, and conveyed the disappointing news. A later date, he suggests, to be more suitable, perhaps in connection with a Spring concert, for your choir will not rest on its present laurels I am sure. I have not however given up my hope of hearing you play, and intend very soon to ride to Kirkfieldbank (my old friend Mr. Cameron being ever ready to welcome me) at which time I look forward to hearing something on *your* instrument, the pianoforte, if you will allow me this pleasure. We can then discuss plans for the Spring.
Yours ever,
Andrew Thomson.

The was a second sheet enclosed as well, unsigned and written in an even quicker hand:

I hope you will forgive what I trust is not a breach of confidence, but rather an endeavour on my part to gain knowledge I did not myself possess:—my esteemed Father, with whom I correspond weekly, has heard with interest your description to me of Bernard, which I hope I did not do wrong in writing down for him. He is an Alienist (now however an invalid, as I believe I mentioned to you) and has conveyed to me the following:

"Such cases as these do occur, and if it be not the Musical, it is the Numerical, the mind of these unfortunate individuals being, it would seem, so unwisely convinced of and consumed by the importance of the one Faculty, that all the Energies of the Blood be concentrated into it, to the impoverishment of every other Power in the Brain—in particular, and to a debilitating degree, those of Speech and Understanding."

I do not know whether these words are of any help. I did not mention to my Father, who would never agree with me, that you spoke of a degree of beauty and accuracy in Bernard's voice and musical sensation, such that you could not consider him in any other light (I remember your words) than as an angel of God. Would I could hear him as soon as possible! for I believe I should feel the same.

Charlotte, with no Heywood concert to plan, practised at the Kirk harmonium where Mr. Thomson's attentive ghost awaited her whenever she could come.

There was no extra time, yet she kept well up with her duties, and the weekly Choir practise, in the Kirk now, was concentrated on the Anthem. She had asked Mr. Cameron to invite, in his Intimations, any of the congregation who wished to attend, and several came, including Mr. Thomas Wylie, a wary old bachelor with a red face and a great, raw, true bass, who confided to her that he felt it his duty "to bring the congregation forward."

Charlotte had heard him often enough—his pew was on the left about half way down, where he sat with his two spinster sisters—and his primitive harmonization made it impossible to allow the Choir to try out any other during the hymns. He did not mean to provoke, she must remind herself, but sang as best he could to the glory of God.

During the practise then, he sang from his own pew away down in the darkened nave, and if any new harmony were attempted, he would furiously close his mouth. This would then occur on the Sabbath as well, and such was the power of his voice that the Kirk seemed to ring with silence. Charlotte's basses, combined, could not compete with him.

"Mr. Wylie—" over the baps—"We would be so proud to have you a Member of the Choir!"

"Oh, no, Miss Spears, you'll no beguile me, I'll go up into the box on no account. Whatever would become of the congregation?" With a great, bleary wink.

Her practise with the children came after Sabbath School, the ladies assisting in providing them with cocoa and baps before break-up, which they ate at the back of the Kirk, crowded around her. Bernard, rocking on the floor between his sisters, sometimes sang but she could never predict him. She had come to believe, like his sisters, that he was canny in his own way, and determined to sing only when she had forgotten about him. He would never let her touch or kiss him. His sisters took his hands, one on each side; this he allowed, but only if Robina were on his left and Kate on his right. The older bairns after Charlotte's admonishment had stopped calling him daft and the younger ones, having never got a look or a word out of him, paid him no heed at all.

When he did sing, it was as if a thread of light drew the note upward, over the other children's—his voice was not louder, though she was sure it could be; he had the power. Sometimes he would go on after the others had sung the verse she had required.

> "Or were I in the wildest waste
> So black and bare so black and bare,
> The desert were a Paradise,
> If thou wert there if thou wert there."

Charlotte ached for Mr. Thomson's presence then, seeing him in his place back of the pulpit just as, almost, she saw him when she practised. Could he not have ridden over today, and be standing within the porch? But he was not; he was busy in Heywood.

She decided on a Soirée Concert in the New Year, with the greater part of the program to be given over to the children, and chose the pieces carefully. Mendelssohn's song she would not supply in the programme, or even mention, but half way through the evening she would touch the first chord. And Bernard, surprised by stealth, would sing! Mr. Thomson asked to read again would hear him, listening from the pulpit chair.

She wrote to Mr. Thomson and told him of her plan. She had set the Concert for the 23rd of January. He had not come to Kirkfieldbank as he had almost promised, or written to her again. Were he still eager for her to bring the Choir to Heywood in the spring, she would surely answer this letter proposing it. She also wrote:

> Bernie continues the same. I have high hopes that he will sing at the Concert—for sometimes when I have laid down the baton, he sings on alone, beautifully, and word for word. I am quite convinced he is a clever wee chap, for I am not to notice him or he will close his mouth so tight! The chances to hear him are I would expect better at our last rehearsal, than at the Concert itself.

After some thought she added, "Of course you are free to seek advice about him from your learned Father."

A letter arrived by the return post:

> Dear Miss Spears,
> What delightful news, that the children's concert is underway:—you mention several pieces preparing. I would venture to propose, if it be a secular concert, "Bobbie Shafto" as well, which the Heywood bairns at any rate, love to sing. I did as well as a child, and do so still. If you would like the sheets I can have them sent over. I now await Mr. Cameron's invitation to read, which I have immediately offered (by this post) and will give me a proper excuse to attend!
> Whether I can get to the "dress" rehearsal, which I presume will be the evening before, awaits his reply, I have proposed staying the two nights, and this would also give

me the opportunity of hearing your pianoforte. My intended visit to Kirkfieldbank had to be postponed owing to, I believe, the indisposition of Mr. Cameron's land-lady. I will ride over therefore the morning of the twenty-second February, and hope to pay my respects, if this be convenient, about three o'clock. I wish you a very Happy Christmas.
> Your obliging servant, etc.

Willie recovered, and got away that Wednesday for the five-o'clock train, and Charlotte knew he was happy to be off.

"Goodbye, my dear cousin, take care you do nae cry anyone else in at the first-footing! for I hope I'll no see you again before Old Year's Night, and I'm sure you hope the same! But"—taking her hand—"I know you wish me well, for my own sake."

She allowed him to kiss her, turning her face so his lips just touched her cheek. The carriage lamp jiggling beyond the wicket gate, the horse stamping, the wind come up, shifting the brushed snow back across the path and blowing a gust of it against her ankles.

> Kirkfieldbank, 9th December 1881.
My dear Thomson,

Your kind proposal to read at the Annual Concert, now planning, was of course received with thanks; however, the Managers having decided (with my approval) in calling on the Rev Mr. Turnbull of Lesmahagow to read, and this already undertaken, I am obliged to turn you down. You will not therefore be required to ride out in the inclement weather, which will no doubt free you for the more pressing concerns of your own parish.

Mrs. Capie after whom you so obligingly ask, is doing nicely, I would not however, yet like to impose any extra burden (in the way of a Guest) till I am sure she is quite over the Cough. There is a great deal of this Cough about and while not Diphtheria, it lingers and of course is a sore trial in the reading of my Sermon, the afflicted members of the Congregation saving up their Fusillades (indeed they *make ready the arrow upon the string* Psalms.xi.2) to be launched all at once as it were from all quarters, as soon as I have well begun, in a vain attempt to Mow me Down.

Today is a saddened day: I am called to the Graveside of a child, always one of the most sorrowful Occasions of our profession, as I am sure you will agree, though most for the grieved parents, than for the little innocent Babe who is taken to a brighter Home! Perhaps, in this case, it is a true Blessing, for the child in question has never been "richt", having though he lived till eight years old no speech or understanding, though in good physical health till but two days ago, Dr. Gray giving it out as Meningitis.

On this note I must close, hoping that it will not be long ere we meet in happier circumstances, and take this opportunity to wish you a blessed Christmas-Tide, an example of my Card, which are ordering from More's, will reach you nearer the Day.

Your ever obliging servant
Walter Cameron (Reverend).

Stone Row, December 18th.

Dear Miss Spears—

I will never reproach you, yet had you given me word in time, I should have come. Though I heard him not it seems to me that through your words I have heard his voice in my heart. Now the impatient Angels, jealous of our desire to keep him for ourselves, have taken him to sing in the other Home. I am sure that my friend Mr. Cameron conducted the laying to rest with his usual dignity and charity, yet I must venture to say, from what he has written, *that he knew nothing about this child*, for he called him "not richt." Your presence (as leader of the Psalmody) I cannot be sure of[29]—but perhaps you were at the home in that capacity? I am sure you would have been if you could, and that the chosen Psalms at least were a fitting Consolation.

Your true Friend,
Andrew Thomson

CHAPTER 14

*In which Charlotte is reunited with her old Choir, and receives
a warning. A visit to Glasgow is realized, and Willie
comes to Annville for Christmas.*

The new bills were prominent even in Kirkfieldbank, one pasted
on the Hall door and one in the greengrocer's window. Mr.
Lambeth would grace Lanark with his *Celebrated Choir*!

Charlotte attended with a large party and, on her arrival, was welcomed with heartfelt warmth by her "auld warblers," even the Misses
Syle-Paton, who joined in hurrying her into a borrowed over-gown—
they were wearing their deep purple best—and pressing sheets of
music into her hands. Mr. Lambeth coming forward though as busy as
ever:

"I could not but spy your titian locks amang the throng—of
course you must sing with us."

And Charlotte with heart overflowing, careful to take her cue
from the voices around her, notes held high and scarcely glanced upon
even in the selections which she did not know—getting a line ahead at
a time was no trouble, then with eyes again fixed on the dear old gentleman's face as of old! His familiar flamboyant gestures the crowd
loved and the Members endured, feet dancing and tails flapping, trailing clouds of glory—had he not had printed, in the *Advertiser*, "*as
Performed before Her Majesty the Queen*" to impress the humble folk of
Lanarkshire?

Adeste Fideles! The Members of her own Choir were scattered in
the audience, even Mr. Weir looking, from up here, rather countrified.
How delightful to be "in harness" again, however briefly, to have no
time to dwell on the disappointments and distresses of every day, and

no responsibility except to lose her single voice in the larger whole, safe under Mr. Lambeth's furiously swiping baton, with his lively white eyebrows running as ever up and down his forehead, and his wet lips roundly mouthing through his whiskers!

> *Amen! Lord, we bless thee, born for our salvation:*
> *O Jesus, for ever be Thy name adored.*
> *Word of the Father, now in flesh appearing.*
> *O come, let us adore Him, O come, let us adore Him,*
> *O come, let us adore Him, Christ the Lord.*

Adeste Fideles! They were "raising the roof" and the lamps shivered, all the green boughs trembled. Then the recessional, down between the crowded chairs, a smile unable to hide itself. "Thank you!" in the lobby, "Thank you all, for allowing me to join in!" Hands pressing her own.

Past them by the door, Charlotte caught sight suddenly of Mr. Andrew Thomson. He was speaking with a young lady. Then he was at her side and she turned from Mr. J Westwood Tosh, and followed Mr. Thomson to a bench piled with temperance pamphlets, which he moved aside so they could sit down.

Their eyes meeting and dropping. Perhaps there were no words. He said, breaking across her thoughts: "There is no need to speak of your loss, our loss—but I have regretted so much how angrily I wrote to you, it was not anger with you. Did you lead the hymns?"

"No, Mr. Cameron felt that, being a lady it would not be suitable, and they are using Mr. Whiteford for the funeral services while they can. I am training up a scholar, Robert Gilchrist, who practises in the Kirk already—" her voice, which had been running on, faltering.

He had taken her hand and now pressed and released it, and stood up.

"I am most extremely sorry."

Charlotte could not yet look at him steadily, but strove to recover herself. He said meanwhile, "I must be getting back to Heywood, it's a cold ride over the moor."

"Are you no staying with Mr. Cameron?" Now she could glance into his face, surprised.

"Nay"—diffidently—"though to tell you the truth I was down

over the Kirkfieldbank brig this morning, but you were from home. Walter's no keen on my sleeping with him, you see, till his landlady's on her feet again."

Charlotte was not aware of Mrs. Capie's being off them, having seen her almost daily having her crack with Mrs. Simpson in front of the Post Office.

"Why, I had a lesson up the village between three and four!"

"That is how I missed you then."

She stood and he took her hand again for a moment.

"You've your old friends to speak to and I'll no keep you. It was glorious music." The paleness near his brown eyes, as if light were shining out around them. Now he murmured:

"Such a cross letter—I very much regretted it, that part of it—" and something more, spoken low and rapidly.

Charlotte wished very much to tell him that his letter had been her only comfort and that she treasured it. But here was Mr. Tosh leaning in all smiles at her side.

"I wish you a Merry Christmas—" said Mr. Thomson, going out, running lightly down the step. Could she but have seen him away, riding up the North Vennel for the lonely heath road with the snow blowing!

The Choir were billeted round about in town except for Mr. Lambeth and his secretary, and the Misses Syle-Paton and two other ladies who were lodged at the Clydesdale; Charlotte was easily prevailed upon to join them for a few moments, even if it meant a late walk down the Brae.

When she emerged, her cheeks flushed with the heat of the great lounge fire if not from the fumes of the spirits being indulged in the parlour next door, she saw with a start a young man in a long cloak like a parson's, seated on a dark mare and riding past slowly, examining his gloves or something in his hands. Then she recognized him: it was but young Mr. Cassells who had seen to Gruntie.

And here was Mr. Weir coming happily down the step behind her, his breath, she feared, ready to reveal a state of intoxication; so she very properly cried out:

"I do not wish to walk with you, Mr. Weir, if you have taken spirits!"

"How fortunate then that I have not. I have been seated, I freely admit, in the public parlour, for I would not intrude on your party, but with the door open, and no more indulged than a hot lemon and barley water, noticing that your party had ordered the same."

Charlotte having apologized, they must proceed together down the Westport, but remaining in the road, for the johnnie would be uncommonly dark even with a layer of snow.

After an exchange about the weather Mr. Weir was thankfully silent, and when he did speak again it was to remark on the Concert.

"This gentleman Mr. Lambeth has no doubt a very nice choice of voices, and a grand bass section, but he's a most peculiar way of conducting, to my mind, aye bowing and leiping about so you might be watching a puppetry-show, though I noticed he makes his Members stand very stiff through it all."

Charlotte said they were used to him, and that when she had been a Member she "could not see that his way of conducting as very extraordinary, though perhaps now—" Mr. Weir had not even been privy to Mr. Lambeth's amazing facial antics!

"You do nae copy him."

"It would be most unsuitable in a Precentor."

"It would look very silly anywhere. It's no your style at any rate, which is superior to my mind."

They were getting past the Gas Works. The Brae road wound downward, brushed with white, and a few lamps gleamed faintly in the village below. In the Brig End byre some men could be seen moving about against a lantern. "There'll be a sick beast in there."

"I saw Mr. Cassells the veterinary."

"Aye, called out about it, no doubt."

Charlotte said, "But it has a look of Christmas."

"Oh? Oh, aye, the Christmas story."

They came around the tollhouse bend. Mr. Weir spoke again:

"It's grand how the Choir's rallied round you, Miss Spears, you're a regular Gladstone for the politics, or perhaps Disraeli would be a more suitable comparison, with Mr. Cameron being the Queen, no disrespect of course to either parties. I was nigh certain there'd be they, that wouldnae relent, I mean Miss Henry and old man Barr and now you have them eating out of your hand meek as sparrows. They did whine about the bairns being given all those parts and then it went off very blithely, and as we're to do 'Mothers of Salem' on the Sabbath they will be put in their place." He sang a few lines, trailed off.

"When Mothers of Salem their children brought to Jesus
The stern disciples turned them back, and bade them depart;
But Jesus saw them ere they fled,
And sweetly smiled and kindly said:
Suffer little children—

"You'll be attending the Burns Night I presume? Now that you're no in mourning." After a pause he added, "You'll miss that poor wee laddie."

"I am very unhappy about him, and I cannot yet speak of him, I am sorry."

"Oh, aye, never a word then, never a word."

He went on as they crossed the brig, "Our guid reverend, however, I would like to give you just a wee word of advice: he doesnae like you."

Stopping in confusion Charlotte said, "But I am ready at all times to perform my duties, according to his wishes."

Mr. Weir stopped as well, leaning into a recess, his voice a little raised against the rush of the river.

"Oh, aye, that's just what he doesnae like, so you neednae take it as a criticism. You're too much of a good thing, to his mind, and he's made nervous by it. It's the great success of the Choir, and the Managers that were against you coming in on your side, and all; I'll no say Mr. Barr's changed his mind, he's aye billing and cooing with the Reverend and who kens what they'll be cooking up, it'll no be in your favour I doubt."

Charlotte was concerned. She stood still in the middle of the brig twisting her gloved hands, almost wringing them.

"There is surely nothing I can do, other than to continue as I have done, as well as I can."

"Aye, it wasnae said to distress you. Mr. Cameron cannae well do without you, all the shillings you're bringing in with the music, for he's aye going on about getting his manse built, he's no one to mind the Lord's words about the foxes of the earth and the birds of the air. It's a case I believe of strengthening the Managers. I've a mind to get myself elected, and some others, and am doing a bit of lobbying to that end, on the sly, you'll see!"

A Manager! They walked on.

"But Mr. Weir, you're no a great adherent of the Kirk, I mean apart from the Choir."

"Are you questioning my Christian principles?" He was smiling widely; she could tell from his voice. "Miss Spears, I think we understand each other. I've resolved to take a hand, and what's the harm if it amuses me? I'll have less time to spend loitering at the Hotel, which must be a step on the road—the path of righteousness—you must give me that." With a smug sort of laugh.

They parted—she was forced to give him her hand.

"I will see you to your door, Miss Spears—there's no light kept for you."

"I shall manage, thank you. I shall light the lamp as soon as I am got in."

"Young Willie is on his feet again then?"

On his feet. She remembered stout Mrs. Capie's cough. "All my eye," Aunt Helen would have said to that!

"Aye, he's been in toun these two weeks."

"Then I shall stand sentinel here, Miss Spears, till you drop the sneck. A Christian soldier, mind."

Tired of him, and tired, she again bade him good night.

The ladies—Mrs. Steele to be exact, with embellishments by Mrs. West—had told her of Mr. Weir's intervention to have the Harvest Concert gazetted. Ought she to have thanked him? He did not seem to expect it. He would not set particular store by a word of thanks—as if, she thought, his "*left hand knows not what his right hand doeth.*" He had said that she understood him; if she did, it was a odd kind of sympathy, for he was very unlike her. He did not try to be good, and he was far from innocent, was he not?—a married man! Yet to decide on his merits was, she admitted, beyond her powers.

John had the flesher over to kill Gruntie pig, so they would have a nice fresh side of pork for the holiday. And Charlotte was able to spend four days just before Christmas at the Great Western Road.

Almost, it was less distressing to come to the new apartments, though Father must be badly missed, and everyone perhaps wishing Christmas and Hogmanay could be skipped over that year—festivity must ever make the loss of dear ones the more painful. Mother wanted a few greens of course, and they quietly wrote their cards and received them, and with Charlotte home there was music, but no happy romps or laughter. Mother and Annie she found the same, Tom expansive—quite the man of the house. She saw how much pleasure he took in leading their evening prayers.

"Let us worship God!"

He was a great deal at the shop, which was just along the way at Number 27, and she and Annie looked by more than once on their walks and would purchase two pokes or some new penny item, a lotion or a sweet soap, to explain their presence. Though it was very bustling and they did not see Tom at all.

She could not stay for Sabbath at the auld Kirk, much to their disappointment, but dear Mr. Batchelor visited them one evening and took her hand ever so gently; it almost made her want to scramble up into his knee as they all used to do when they were bairns! One concert she attended with Tom, at the Theatre Royal in Hope-street. Having to wait outside for a carriage afterwards, because of the rain, with all the crowding and pushing, and Tom abstracted and not very attentive.

And there was one Glee Party with both Tom and Annie, a Mrs. Lowrie coming in to sit with Mother. It was quite the high shenanigans with Sir Roger de Coverley up and down the two drawing rooms and Mr. Westwood Tosh taking particular notice and bringing her an ice. Which could not but amuse her. She had never approved of his style, though in former days she must have compared him to Mr. Miller rather than, as now, to an Other. Miss Syle-Paton asking her in the anteroom if she were quite well! and whether the new short skirts, crossing the ankle and ever so liberating to move about in, had not yet reached the village.

Charlotte rattled along in the Caledonian through coarse plowts of sleet that would surely soon turn to snow. She felt on the whole pleased to be returning to Annville. She was quite settled now, she decided. So much so that Glasgow appeared strange to her with its crowds and rushing traffic; even the new apartments in the Great Western Road had looked over-dark and high and pressed together, and they were called so airy.

She had to change at Motherwell, and after Carluke had the compartment to herself. To come into Lanark the train must take a great loop east of town, behind the racetrack and the Regimentary Grounds. Charlotte stood up and, clinging to a curtain, gazed eastward into the high moor country which an early nightfall and driving cloud were fast obscuring. Out there somewhere lay the colliery town of Heywood[30] among its open pits, and a wee street named Stone Row and the Parks' hospitable kitchen! She smiled a little, thinking how much more interesting this direction was become, than Glasgow in the west! The train lurched and she sat quickly down. It was never correct to dream, yet sometimes a dream would suggest itself unawares.

Again Willie's room was prepared for him, and Helen made no comment on a trace of his sick smell, though Charlotte on first going in could mark it faintly still, for all the disinfecting. She had determined not to sniff for it but could not help herself.

Nell said, "That's him then. You've drenched with the Condy's Fluid uncommon thick, Chattie!" Before Hogmanay every drawer in the house was relined and freshened with a pot pourri, the mattresses refilled, and all the linen boiled and ironed. Margaret Tennant helped. Helen had spoken off and on of hiring another servant at the Martinmas Fair, to sleep in the kitchen and be aye on hand, and lighten the work for Charlotte.

But Charlotte protested. "The work is really very light, and I would prefer to care for Willie myself, if he should ever get bad again. We must trust he is well now. It has been nearly four weeks, and he went away in very hopeful spirits."

She had not seen him in toun, though Tom sent a word and an invitation. "He moves in his University circles, of course," had been Mother's comment.

"Aye, well, dear, you were an excellent nurse to him," said Helen now, plumping up the bed so it looked like a great pincushion. "I am sure you could be trusted with an Epidemic."

Charlotte attended the lime light views at the Bloomgate U P, where Reverend Mr. William Logan was lecturing on "*A Run to Florence.*" The views were fifteen feet high and remarkably lifelike. Each met of course with wondering gasps.

Mr. Logan told several anecdotes. When walking up to a picture gallery he had been given to understand, by signs, that it was closed, and he had gained admission only by *"persistent Scottish pluck."*

Willie got in to Annville just before the great storm. Christmas Eve had dawned in a dank fog that turned to clear, lifting weather. The foliage across Clyde looked very queer, being divided into bands, the lowest branches black and untouched, then above them a level stripe about six or eight feet in breadth and completely white, the hoar hung on every twig. Margaret Tennant said that to see the winter "folliery" as white as the flourish was a very bad sign.

Then a sharp wind came up from the southwest, and the trees began casting off shards. Charlotte heard dogs barking across Clyde and looked out, and saw a pack of them in Nemphlar Wood, running excitedly among the trees and baying and snapping at the bits of falling ice.

Willie was got in, and had brought all his books with him, in his box, but Charlotte did not see much of him, or go once to his room. He looked swarthy but not unwell when he was with them, and complained of weakness in his legs.

The storm rose at nightfall and continued the whole of two days. Charlotte battled to Kirk, and John got himself up to the E U in the morning, but Helen kept indoors with Willie and Maddie, and was confirmed in her prediction of a very thin attendance at all the services.

CHAPTER 15

In which Charlotte though secure in affection encounters adversity.

"You'll no be going along to the Kirk this evening, Chattie dear, I'm sure you've no call to step outside the door."

But here was Sub-Inspector Munro stamping in the back lobby, then vigorously applying the besom to the flags where the snow had blown in with him.

"I'll take that, Roddy! Go on in to the fire. Have you been out surveying the village?"

"Ah, in a manner of speaking, Mrs. Brown." Letting Helen take his cloak, but tucking his gloves under his thick arms. He greeted Charlotte with a shy nod. She was standing at the dresser where she had been writing at her dietary.

"And you've found no frozen bodies in the footpath I hope?" said John from his chair by the grate.

"There was a pony over at Linn Farm, and worse up at the railway outside Carluke, if you've no heard about that—a collier walking on the lines, and found lying."

"Ah dear, intoxicated no doubt."

"Oh, we cannae be sure of that. They say there comes over you in such weather, a sort of lethargy, a great desire to lie down in the snow and sleep." Roddy Munro read penny dreadfuls about the Arctic. "The train didnae go over him. It was the cold did for him."

They pondered the collier's fate. He went on—"I'm away over to the Kirk the now—it's the Election of the Managers and Mr. Gilchrist will want a hand with the clearing of the porch."

The chimney roared up suddenly so he had to speak louder. "It all blows back again of course. Easier to melt snow than get up Well Walk for a raik in this weather. You'll no be going over, Miss Spears?"

Charlotte, deciding quickly, said that if she might walk with him she would like to go, Mr. Cameron perhaps expecting her if he desired a congregational hymn.

"To blow the snow out of their lungs," said John. "I doubt there will be many out."

Her cloak and boots were in the kitchen, and she allowed Helen to wrap a shawl well up around her ears and bonnet. They went out by the back door, with Charlotte clinging to the Sub-Inspector's arm getting up along the house wall, where the ground was slippery and oddly bare, leaving them a narrow, scalloped path.

The snow was all curled into wreaths from the wind, the road being in some places quite clean, and ringing under their feet, in some covered by long ridges that they came at unexpectedly in the darkness. Handed through them by Roddy Munro, Charlotte was astonished at how heavy and thick the snow lay despite its curious shapes; it was rather like getting through boiled milk pudding.

They were unable to speak, labouring against the storm which blew falling or drifting snow directly into their faces. The blinds down in all the houses, a few lamps showing very faint. At the Inn a snow-wreathe had pressed itself half way up the door. The leaded windows were however bright from a good fire within, and they could see the shadows of folk moving about, and Charlotte fancied she heard shouts and laughter. In the yard a stable lamp was swinging and she could make out a black tangle of traps tipped on their braces, with the snow already weaving its patterns among the wheels. They would be the Managers' from the out farms, she thought, who must have come in early to have come at all.

They met not a soul on the Kirk path, which was recently swept but filling in again, and the porch was dark and empty. It was largely blown clear, however, with the grush in front dry and hard as iron.

"Will you no come in?" They had to shout to be heard.

"I've no call for it." Roddy stamped in the porch and looked about him, picked up a besom where it stood. "I'll clear off the path, and wait for you if you like. Though I've a mind to go down to Clyde meantime and see if the water's got through." They had been breaking the ice at intervals all day, below Mouse mouth at the shallows.

"No, I thank you but you neednae wait, for Manager Carmichael will be going that way, I will walk with him. The wind will blow itself out surely by then."

She went inside, glad of the comparative warmth and sudden silence. Though the body of the Kirk was brightly lit, there was no one there at all except Beadle Reid, who came towards her down the middle aisle carrying the long brass snuffer upright before him; with his slow, absorbed gait he looked for a moment almost Romish.

"I'm to extinguish the lamps the now, Miss Spears, says Mr. Cameron, for not a soul of the congregation has appeared for the Election, though all the Managers are in the vestry with him, he's out of the ordinary disappointed."

"It's but gone eight o'clock."

"Eight or no, and by his pocket watch it's gone that lang syne."

Mr. Reid began his ritual as Charlotte stood irresolute, and the Kirk progressively darkened.

"Ah, Beadle, you may lock the door and close down the fires now, before you go on with that." Mr. Cameron's voice, sharply, from the vestry door.

Charlotte approached him up the side aisle.

"Ah, Miss Spears. I cannot conceive," rubbing his smooth hands together, "a congregation with less interest in the day to day regulation of the Kirk. Not one soul! And as for its being a bad night, they've the most of them but to step across the road. However"—looking about—"there's nothing lost but the extra expense of heating up the Kirk, and of course the lamp petroleum, which they would never stop to consider, it being a mere pittance, they would suppose. The Annual Election of the Managers not being as interesting, I am forced to admit, as getting up a Concert and being written about all over the *Hamilton Advertiser* and gadding about to Lanark and beyond."

Charlotte waited till he was out of breath and mildly said that she was sure her Members sang for the glory of God and not the *Advertiser* but he hardly let her finish.

"That's as may be Miss Spears but I'm no pleased, the Managers are no pleased at all, with these high-faluting schemes about bringing the Choir around about the countryside, and any idea that they are your Members to wheesk away as you please to Lanark or far beyond to hear you perform in a toun production, even if it were taken to Balmoral and sang before the Queen. We're a humble village kirk, mind, and want no flaunting of ourselves." His eyes darting at a noise, but it was only Beadle Reid putting out the entry lamp.

The Kirk was now in darkness. Mr. Cameron had turned from her towards the vestry, where the door widened for him as if on cue, Mr. Carmichael sticking out his white head.

"You'll no be requiring a hymn then, there being such a thin attendance," said Charlotte, gently but clearly, to his back. "I will wish you a good night." He did not answer.

Beadle Reid met her in the entry with a candle. "Aye, he's in a fair fash," he confided, old tobacco reek hanging on his breath, "but it's no your fault Miss Spears, except that you being the only one there, so you must take the bashing, as the scholar found out when the others ran away, in a manner of speaking as it were. As for the fires, there'd be no great waste of heat with the cheap dross the man orders, so that's one blessing!"

Just as he reached to unsneck the door for her, a sudden great chapping and banging on the outside made them jump back. Again it came, with the addition of loud and angry voices, and the beadle hurriedly opened to a clutch of black figures who pressed their way inside. The meek candle scarcely revealing their faces under capes and scarves, which they proceeded to throw off, shaking snow all over the flags, and were revealed as Mr. Scott and Mr. Weir, very forward and blustery, and a couple of rough-looking younger men, one of them being she thought the former beadle, John Stark.

Charlotte had drawn back against the bench to let them past and they surged into the body of the Kirk, Mr. Weir throwing over his shoulder, in a ringing tone, "You'll see now, Miss Spears, which way the wind is blowing!" She thought she detected a waft of spirits left by his breath.

Out into the snow she plunged, and with the wind at her back made short work of the way home. When she passed the Inn old Mr. Steele was in the door, which he seemed to be trying to close in vain again against snow-wreathes that were persistently bigging. From whence, it seemed, four men had sallied forth moments ago, heartened by who knew what vile potions, to pursue who knew what desperate design![31]

Charlotte now had a strong idea that the visit from Mr. Thomson would be prevented. It being perhaps as well. Though a voice told her that had he really wished to come, nothing was to stop him overnighting at the Hotel. But she saw that this was impossible! Firstly, he was poor and secondly, a parson was aye under the watchful eye of his Managers, if not of his friends. And boarding with his Preceptor—he could not suddenly stand up and announce his intention to ride away for the purpose of talking music in Kirkfieldbank with a lady ten or eleven years his senior!

Still she looked out for him sometimes before she caught herself, and hurried just a little back from a lesson down the village, afraid that she had missed him; and when she practised the pianoforte she seated herself gracefully and allowed, as before, his ghost to sit down and listen.

Suddenly the weather set in very mild, and Clyde shifted away its remaining ice and roared high and taffy brown, pulling at the black weeds along its banks, and there was terrible mud everywhere. Boards had to be laid from the back door to the caivie and the ash heap. On the farms the ploughing was however getting on already and ditches, hedges and byres were mending. The out women could be seen with dutch hoes cutting off the annuals, and pulling out the quick under the berry bushes, their skirts heavy with earth, then carrying the heavy creels away to Clyde. The storms forgotten, old folk now proclaimed there had not been such a mild winter since 1819, which would be sixty-three years.

And now Mr. Miller's Glasgow Selected Choir was to perform in Lanark! It was Miss Syle-Paton who had written, all kindness, to inform Charlotte even before the Advertisements appeared.

> We are so delighted, in particular myself and Westwood Tosh who as Members of Mr. Lambeth's Choir as well, can be certain of the Reception we will receive! We are preparing a most difficult Repertoire, which I will not whisper to you as yet, while our arrival on the very Day of the Concert making a full Dress Rehearsal quite impossible:—we take a late train to Carstairs and the conveyance from Douglas. Thus we cannot alas avail ourselves of your otherwise valued assistance. You will however I am sure bring out your wee village Choir in full force to swell the audience, and we will again expect to have you amang us just as in the auld days,

for a visit at the good "Clydesdale Hotel," should your busy schedule permit.

And should you appear with a Guest, so much the better! But enough said of that!!

We have just had a splendid cookie shine at Mr. Miller's, Mrs. Miller or, Isabel, as she permits we ladies to call her, doing the honours in her inimitable style. So it is not all work and no play at the Select!

We do indeed look forward etc. etc.

But Charlotte, with Mr. Cameron's words still ringing in her ears—though of course forgiven—did not go. She wondered at herself. Who would have thought half-a-year past, that she could treat the relinquishment of such a musical event—the presence of Mr. Miller himself—with near indifference?

Mr. Andrew Thomson had meantime written her a long letter about Schubert and the playing of the "A-Major" Sonata by Miss Helen Hopekirk, whom he had been privileged to hear "for the second time" in Edinburgh. He did not mention coming to Kirkfieldbank. For which last Charlotte, though she did not like to do so, must blame Mr. Cameron. Who, for reasons best known to himself, would not ask his friend to read and seemed determined against receiving him. Widow Capie got about the village meanwhile at her usual speed, which was rather more sideways than straight forward, greeting Charlotte at the Post Office with a broad smile that made two deeply furrowed dimples in her cheeks under the black bonnet. And no sign of a cough.

Miss Syle-Paton as sharp as ever had surely seen Charlotte speaking to Mr. Thomson after the concert. Referring to Mr. Tosh in such proprietorial terms! "Westwood"!

Charlotte got off a card to Mr. Miller wishing them well and saying that it was with great regret she would be unable to attend. And turned to write with renewed tenderness to her own family.

She was answering one of the "plain-Annies," as her sister's letters were affectionately called, and was comforted. Now she recognized her sister's worth, whose life was utterly free of insinuation and female deceit—indeed, Annie could never discover such in others! Even in childhood, when she met the older lassies' teasings with no more than a bewildered look on her butter-dough face. In the close or schoolyard, if Robert were not by to defend her or Tom did not notice their plaguing, Charlotte would do so, even to delivering a slap. Dear old Annie!

Charlotte wrote a long, cheerful letter. She said nothing of missing the Select, or of the Kirk—of what to herself she called her "wee difficulties." A few tears of homesickness wet her sleeve as she wrote.

So the Church Concert[32] was come and gone. Mr. Cameron, unable to get Mr. Turnbull of Lesmahagow—whom in an inspiration he had named to his importunate friend, but had not immediately secured—read the lesson himself.

There was an even greater crowd than at harvest, with benches bringing in from the school and all the vestry chairs, and still folk standing at the back and half way up the side aisles.

Charlotte hardly dared look about for Mr. Andrew Thomson and, seated in her precentor's chair, she felt from the pulpit Mr. Cameron's watchful eye. She must admit to herself now that she had specially trained the Choir to please Mr. Thomson's ear, for there were none in the House of God that night, herself excepting, especially musical, to hear them.

Though general pleasure was of course expected, and got. The programme was light. Though she had not included "Bobby Shafto," which had a verse somewhat questionable all the bairns knew, whether allowed to sing it or no.[33]

She would have wished Bernie's name mentioned. Had Mr. Thomson given the reading she thought he would have done so, but it would never occur to Mr. Cameron. Her bosom nourishing a dislike as strong, perhaps, as his own for her. Not "nourishing"! She must never dwell on it. Always, as adjured in the Scriptures, returning good.

And wee Bernie who might after all have sung, who had in his innocence so easily learned all the words and harmonies—she could not help hearing his voice against her inner ear, a whispered descant. To her assembled choirs before the processional she had named him, as she stood among the children with one arm around each of his doleful sisters.

"Tonight we are singing in remembrance of dear Bernard, and I would ask you all, the adult Choir as well, to sing as sweetly as you can and mind his voice."

"Mr. Dunlop says, Miss, he's listening to us."

"Then we must sing ever so well, Sadie, and perhaps we can keep in our souls a wee listening-place, so we can hear him too."

Charlotte had placed her hand against her bodice involuntarily—there where she sometimes felt spiritual pain.

Mr. Cameron's reading, and indeed his entire conducting of the programme, she felt to be unusually indifferent, his pauses and flourishes studied and oppressive. The children fidgeted, and there was a run of coughing along the pews. How much more acceptable would have been Mr. Thomson's forthright rendering, not choosing to wring every word of its meaning, but trusting the Word to speak for itself, with the music to rise in heartfelt confirmation!

The final anthem, with all voices, swelled and finished. The Choir smiled on each other, and as Mr. Cameron rose for the vote of thanks, three of the youngest children separated themselves from the ranks and ran down to fling themselves at their parents' arms. Others followed—even the big ones—even, at last and shyly, Sarah herself, squeezing in and taking the blind aunt's hand. It was just what Bernie had done, Charlotte recalled, and the best of remembrances.

Mr. Cameron must needs speak above a general rustle of clothing and creak of pews and fond whispers, and more than one upraised bairn's happy voice. He remained however a fund of patience, and all his remarks were delivered calmly. He finished:

"Let us now partake of our well-earned refreshments, not forgetting those who labour with their hands rather than with their voices."

Later, at the back, he came up to Charlotte and wanted a closing hymn. "I would recommend 'The Day Thou Gavest' which we all ken, and will no require the passing out of the hymnaries. If you would be so kind."

Charlotte must accede, though it put rather a dull finish to the music as well as the sociality, with folk still happily milling about in the back with teacups in their hands. Soon all were out in the mud and the dark and homeward bound.

Almost despite Mr. Cameron it had been a success. But her dream-concert, at which Mr. Thomson read and Bernie sang, must ever be set alongside it in her heart, and allow her to be very disappointed.

Her new appreciation of her own family had led Charlotte to urge Willie, when he went off, to visit in the Great Western Road, where Mother and Annie would have welcomed him, and fed him up and comforted him now through his latest fever and disappointment, and strengthened his courage to go on. But they had seen nothing of him.

This onset had been very sudden and severe—he had taken a cab to the Royal and demanded admittance, though scarcely able to get within the door before he collapsed. But they would only keep him overnight on a bench, being very thrang, and Dr. MacMurchie who saw him advised him to be got home in the early part of the day:

"For, being the Returning Fever, there's no more to be done for you here. It won't carry you off, and you ken the medicines as well as I."

The next day Charlotte got Dr. Gray to Annville against Willie's protests. The doctor had with him his assistant Dr. Ewing, whom Willie could not have suffered gladly, thought Charlotte with pity in her heart. A great, red-cheeked chield with the chest of a boxer, already a Medical Graduate and called "Doctor" and away out if not in his own gig, almost as grand, bowling around the countryside with Dr. Gray and no doubt prescribing powders himself with a nod and a word! Charlotte for Willie's sake could not like him either.

Down in the lobby, Dr. Gray allowed Ewing, who had kept a respectful silence, to assist him with his cloak. He had prescribed a febrifuge, and a fresh supply of laudanum to be sent in at the same time. His gray moustaches trimmed short away from his mouth, his long teeth that rather champed his words.

"Even in a well-stoppered bottle, Miss Spears, the alcoholic content will vaporize. Properly used there is no medicine more useful of course."

Charlotte was to administer a half gram each four hours but "only if the pain were of a cutting nature."

Willie complained about the visit for some days, and would use up the laudanum he had, and wondered at her throwing away his father's good money on medicine he already was in possession of. Charlotte must remind herself of his great disappointment, which of course made him impatient with his suffering.

The Select Concert came and went, and Mr. Thomson must have
expected Charlotte, for a letter arrived as soon as it was bye.

It would seem that we are not to meet, at least at present. I read of the success of your Concert of course, but
having my duties here and etc, etc, could really not attend,
though believe me I was sorry indeed. Satisfied however
that you would, in this week following, join your old choir
at Lanark as in December. But you were not there.

I hope you are well, and that nothing untoward either
to yourself or your family prevented you. It was a grand
concert. I over-heard by chance among the choir members
a mention of you:—that they were surprised you had
decided against coming to join them.

I receive *some news* of Kirkfieldbank of course but not
of the musical kind. Mr. Cameron has however mentioned
to me that you have the care of your uncle's son, being as
he informs me "an extremely young man of exactly (my)
own age"—!—suffering from a prolonged complaint
which prevents him from continuing his University studies. My friend voiced his concern whether under these circumstances you will be able to continue your duties, and
evinced your failure to attend the concert of your former
Choir, a warning signal. I hope I have not overstepped
myself in protesting to him on your account, and that you
will agree:—that although nursing the sick is of course
required of your sex from time to time, any one can do it;
whereas a person, of your exceptional talents and education ought not in Christian duty neglect that Profession for
which she is best suited, indeed to which she is *called*. I
hope you are mindful of yourself therefore, in this regard,
and give him no reason to fear you cannot continue the
precentorship.

The plan to bring the children to Heywood for a repeat
performance I have certainly not given up. If you would
suggest a date, I will inform Mr. Park who will join me in
writing an invitation, directed, I believe will be best, to Mr.
Cameron and the Managers.

Will you tell me what you are playing? I would, while in
Edinburgh, where I am to attend the Easter Convocation,
be able to purchase the Sonata I mentioned last, if you
like—or any other music—you must only tell me. On this
happier note I close, being as ever
 Yr most obedient friend
 Andrew Thomson.

"Give him no reason"! Charlotte put aside the letter in vexation.
As for Willie, he would surely soon be well, and gone; and were it otherwise her aunt had more than once spoken of getting a servant.

"Unable"! Not less able on Willie's account! Very able indeed,
with God's help, and no smallest fault could Mr. Cameron find in the
Choirs, or the congregational singing, or in her execution of her
church duties in every respect. Indeed she could not help a tremble of
unchristian indignation, at Mr. Cameron's having pretty much forbidden her to attend the Select, and then complained when she stayed
away!

Oh, aye, Robert would have laughed a good deal, if gently, about
it all—and laughed at her, as well, and teased her (not as Miss Syle-
Paton had done, but fondly) about the superfluity of unsuitable "fol-
lowers" she seemed to have collected about her—a married barrister,
a village constable—for Roddy doted, she knew—and finally a country parson even younger than her cousin Willie!

"Robert, I'm in no danger as you can see. And it would be very
queer for even if I were, Mr. Cameron wouldnae let me!"

She was beating dough for a bun and the flour flew. A shaft of
sunlight lay over Nemphlar Wood and the bare branches looked blurry and reddish, a promise that spring was close at hand. Down the garden the spikes of the snowdrops showed here and there, and in the
Fairmaid pear the blackie was ardently practising—he would get it
right at last. A fall of three fluted whistles, very loud and pure, F, E, E-
flat, and then a liquid downward run of chuckles, and off again in
cheery "tsips" and chirps that rang, and more flutings, and a click-
clickie-click at last, almost as if he were reminding himself that it
would come right if he kept trying, and nothing ought to be taken
over-seriously.

Mr. Weir and William Stark—who was, it turned out, the former beadle's brother—were rebuked and suspended from congregation. From
the back door Charlotte saw Mr. Weir walking to and fro on the brig
on the Sabbath, dressed in a very loud tweed with his stick under his
arm and his top hat set, she thought, at a provocative angle. Later,
Agnes Elder and Euphemia Grindley and one other great lass, all three
more soberly clad and arm-in-arm, walking over and standing to converse with him, twirling their umbrellas though it hardly rained.

She ordered her *"dear Valentines"* from John Morison's in the
Bloomgate and directed them: Tom and Annie, of course, and Maddie
at Stonehouse. One, collectively, to the Select "kindness of Mrs. Isabel
Miller" and, in an after-thought, one to Sarah Hopkins.

> *I thought of One, I thought of Two,*
> *And at last my Dear I thought of You;*
> *The crown is Thine and I design*
> *To choose you for my Valentine.*

   She pondered long, and directed one to Willie, sent through the
post so he should not be forgotten. But in the forenoon it was quite
lost in the large handful for him from Glasgow, eight at least, as well as
two from Stonehouse.
   Charlotte received, besides those expected and those in a childish
hand, four she could not trace. Two were among those handed in, one
was franked from Glasgow and the origin of the fourth she could not
make out. She would have liked to compare the hand to that of Mr.
Thomson, whose letters she kept in the back of her escritoire, but was
ashamed of herself. At her age! At a glance it did look clearer than his
hurried scrawl, more perhaps like a woman's. 'HOPE DEFERRED'
was carefully printed in sloping letters inside the fold. "*Hope deferred
maketh the heart sick,*" recalled Charlotte. Dear Valentine verses meant
nothing of course.

> *The rose is red, the violet's blue,*
> *The honey's sweet, and so are you.*
> *Thou art my love, and I am thine;*

I drew thee to my Valentine:
The lot was cast, and then I drew,
And fortune said it should be you.

Willie, feverish, had wanted his burnt, but she laid them aside for him inside Volume II of *The Causes of Disability*, a medical book he turned to now and then. Later she would paste the prettiest on his screen, the back of which she was gradually covering with decorative and scenic cards, under a coating of oak varnish. Annie being a faithful dispatcher from Glasgow.

Roddy Munro looked she thought a wee bit sheepish and red in the face at his next lesson. No mention of course.

"*I've a Home in Cloudland*," he sang, chest out and head well back. "*Where rivers run o'er golden sand.*" As always his embarrassment vanished while he sang, returned at the finish. His fat hand that had rested on the cottage leaping back behind him. To cheer him she set him to learn "Pull Away Merrily," a rollicking sea air.

CHAPTER 16

In which Willie is forced to a painful decision.

Spring came but for Willie it brought no betterment. His fevers returned and returned. He had fallen into a kind of reverie edged with irritation, which never quite left him, though he was at times well enough to be up and about. Sometimes for as many as three days he was afebrile and the pains in his joints subsided; then he would have his books brought out of his box and would spread them on the gate legged table at the window. But soon he would go from them, and walk up the village, and in the evening the books would be lying open where he had left them. He had registered for the sessions by post but the old fire seemed to have gone out of him; and though twice he was on his feet and decided to get himself to toun, another attack had overcome him before he could get away.

March came in very coarse. But the day the Six O'clock Bell was aye rung in Lanark,[34] the wind took itself and the clouds off and the air lay silky and sweet. Charlotte stood outside like the other villagers—even the weavers had come out of loft and cottage to listen, and hear the far pealing. Bairns were whist and stood still in the street, for whatever the weather this was the sure sign of spring. The bigger laddies ran up the Brae, and when the ringing ceased they joined the Lanark lads and paced through the town, some going "round the ladle" chanting doggerel tunes.

But from the valley only the bell was heard, and Clyde's gentle rushing. With the soft, slowing air on her cheek Charlotte in the porch must pause long, and it seemed the old saying would bear out:

"*March comes in like a lion but goes out like a peacock's feathers.*"

She went indoors at last, and sat down at her escritoire, and reached far into the drawer to draw out Mr. Thomson's letters. She carefully undid the ribband. Usually the first to be reread was the one sent at Bernie's death, the consolation. It lay uppermost. But now she must answer him about the Schubert.

Miss Helen Hopekirk! This was not the first time Charlotte had been, as it were, held up to the mirror of that celebrated lady! Though seven years younger she was forever heard of in Scottish musical society, and heard as well.

She had distinguished herself very early, being the pupil of Liechtenstein in Edinburgh, and had played the *Emperor Concerto* there at the age of seventeen. Then she studied abroad and was away for some years. Mr. Miller was said to have had met her as a girl and predicted great things. There was even a suggestion that he had been approached at the Athenaeum, about teaching her, or perhaps it was Mr. Frank Amor, or that Miss Hopekirk's earlier teachers had solicited an opinion. Though had more come of it, or even that much, Mr. Miller would surely have had more to say.

When Charlotte first received Mr. Thomson's letter she had been impatient with his long effusion and hardly skimmed it; now she set herself to read it properly.

> Miss Helen Hopekirk's rendering of the Allegro was superb, almost frightening. Not knowing the piece at all, when she suddenly halted it was as if she had forgot her place:—but not so! She went on again, and then, the further strange halts, were as questions asked, nay, demanded in a great metaphysical argument:—and were answered, tentatively at first, then more strongly—irrefutably! One was immediately sure that all was *correct*:—I cannot say *well*, for it seemed almost incoherent, at least to my untrained ear. Later I will speak to you of the little Scherzo which to me was even more frightening, but I would want *your* opinion first, in the playing of it, for perhaps I am quite wrong, the party I was with declaring it to be delightful—"fluffy," was the word One used!

She then turned to his last letter, in which he had urged her not to neglect her music in nursing Willie. "Any one can do that." Mr. Thomson's modern views of women were indeed vindicated in Miss Helen Hopekirk. That such a pianist, who performed in the great concert halls of Europe, should spend her time ministering to the sick, Charlotte must almost agree would be to hide one's light under a bushel. Yet it was very difficult.

Charlotte's talents, whatever Mr. Thomson might think, were in comparison insignificant. She was of course content with her lot. David Hartley and Mr. Westwood Tosh had both, at different times, expressed wonder and perhaps a wee bit of disapproval at her "sallying forth" to teach in a remote village, even while removing to a branch of her own family. Mr. Miller encouraged the step, and called her "brave." Yet Mother had to be persuaded, and it was indeed looked upon generally as "independent" and "enterprising," in other words, not quite the thing.

But set against the flashing career of Miss Helen Hopekirk! Charlotte of course would not presume to think, "had I but had the same opportunity," for within her own sphere she had, and had grasped it.

And even Miss Helen Hopekirk would be wrong, were her dear Mother very ill, not to attend her at her death bed! Charlotte, the letters held loosely in her lap, imagined an Edinburgh apartment with a very high ceiling, the silent white sweep of the four-poster and Miss Hopekirk hurrying in from a magnificent Concert, drawing back her veil, leaning over her Mother…too late! Too Late!

Annville House, March 3, 1882

Dear Mr. Thomson,

Thank you for your kind letter. I am grateful for your advice, but I think your friend cannot be completely clear about the management of the household, which is in my charge whether my cousin be here or not. There is a daily servant and my aunt and uncle are here on the week-ends. They are ready to hire a servant to live in, should ever the work become too onerous but thankfully it is not. I can assure you that I would never neglect either my duties as Precentor, or my practising. I was therefore surprised that Mr. Cameron could be in doubt, though after consideration, I would not wish to speak to him, or have it further mentioned, this not being necessary while my duties at the Kirk are fulfilled to satisfaction.

I was sorry to have missed the Lanark Concert but thought it best, Mr. Cameron having very properly reminded me that my duties are to my own Choir, which is a kirk choir of course, not a touring choir like the Glasgow Selected which sings in many places.

Charlotte could not like the tone of her letter, but it must be said. Mr. Thomson would understand that, however she wished it, bringing the Choir to Heywood was impossible.

As for my playing, do you think I would be capable of the Schubert? I would of course like to try, though after what you have written of it perhaps not the Allegro, which might then be rendered with not merely *supposed* incoherence. You must be judge and of course I will recompense you the cost if you will purchase it.

Our Concert was indeed a success. I was able to gather together the Choirs beforehand and made them a little speech, about singing in remembrance of dear Bernard, which I believe the children understood. But I will always regret that he did not live to sing that night and that you were not come to hear him.

There was Willie's staff. She ran up, a clean draught from outdoors entering with her, that had followed her through the lobby and upstairs from her own window. She sniffed nevertheless, the foetor of his sickness just discernible. He was lying dressed on his bed.

"I'm no sure I want you after all, I wasnae quite awake."

"Why, it's no trouble, Willie, I'll be closing the windows at any rate against the night air." She did so, leaving but a narrow opening at the top for the escape of bad air outward.

"Did you hear the Six O'clock Bell?" and when he did not answer: "Will you get into bed?"

"I'm no over-eager to be shifted about."

His clothing was damp and heavy and though he did not cry out, his limbs hurt to be moved, she knew. The sciatica had set in, with pain in his spine as well. When she had settled him she lit the lamp and measured out his medicine.

His case of surgical equipments was very cannily arranged, the row of vials nicely labelled—*Gunia, Vegetable Cathartic, Phosphorus, Arsenious Acid, Sulphate, Morphia.* The wee partitions all exactly to size, and all the various instruments, some long and fearful-looking, some sharp—knives, forceps, catheters, probes, a scurificator, a syringe, his thermometer and a pair of cupping glasses, the differential stethoscope made of polished wood, a miniature saw called a "trephine crown." Some of the steels were discoloured. Like the case itself with its worn velvet linings, they had been bought second hand.

It was kept in his box, in the tray under the lid. Then came the pile of waxed cards with the Illustrations of *The Urinary Path* and *Diseases Peculiar to Females* and so on, none of which she cared to look at, and any of his books not brought out: Quaine's and Bristowe of course, and the *Clinical Manual, Institutes of Medicine,* Tanner's great *Index,* Cleland's *Directory for Dissection,* Huxley, Maclister, Flint and Gee—names and titles so familiar to her now that she knew from look and weight which was wanted. His notebooks, close written, that represented so many, many hours of copying, were there as well.

"Shall I give the instruments a wee shine?" she asked but he said if she kept the lid shut they'd see to themselves.

"You're as busy as Maddie, she would be aye wanting to get into the fancy goods and meddle with them."

"Did you play together then?" Perhaps he would talk to her of Stonehouse days. Helen and John spoke fondly of what a bright lad he had been, and mischievous too. Alas, he was thin and swarthy now! It was difficult to recall the sonsie bairn who once had taken her hand. He said now: "Maddie was in the shop all hours. I cannae mind playing with her." Then before she could ask more he said:

"Shut the blinds tight and take the lamp away down with you, if you please, you rant on and I'm past heeding."

Seed-time came, and potato-planting, and the planting out of strawberry beds. Charlotte was outbye whenever she could, a great straw of Helen's pulled forward to shade her face. Annville garden of course on a small scale compared to the great drilled fields that stretched uphill around the village, but within Kirkfieldbank itself it was the largest, going well on for an acre. The extra fruit was a nice income and this year John would be selling honey as well.

A letter arrived from Tom, and Mother had written a rare page to put into it, that they all three expected to pay a visit to Kirkfieldbank on the Glasgow Fast Day, April 10th.

"My dear, we are wearying to see you. Tom will see to our Travel." Tom elaborated: a cheap train was to be had because of the holiday, and large numbers of people were expected to visit Lanark. He trusted that a carriage could be procured from the station to Kirkfieldbank.

> Though myself and Annie would have walked the distance, as you do yourself. Another Idea is, whether we should not like to take a dog-cart, and see the Corra Linn, which Annie has never seen and I think though so close you have never yourself had occasion to visit. Mother would of course like best to sit in the garden, and as we have persuaded her and she is most agreeable to the Excursion, perhaps we ought not to try for more.
>
> Annie reminds me that, it being the Fast Day, there would be quite a press to get to the Falls and perhaps not comfortable.

On one of his sojourns in town Willie had slipped in late to a Midwifery demonstration at the Western. Leichman the Accoucheur was attending a difficult laying-in: a woman of middle age whose foetus, murmured Kerr to Willie excitedly, was likely to turn out a monster. Between her pains all were permitted to oscillate, and examine its size and position, the sheet laid modestly across her abdomen. Later with the accouchement well forward, Willie was chosen to perform his first internal examination. He could not tell that the head he encountered was extraordinary, having none other to compare it with. The vaginal wall clasped as with a vice.

Forceps were employed. The male infant had a large lateral aqueous tumour in the area of its neck and chin which pressed upon the larynx, and it did not breathe. The mother, who had been chloroformed, was of course not shown the corpse which was hurried to the Dissection Room wrapped in a bag, the crowd of students all thronging in behind. Professor Leichman, as well as Professor Kirk and others who had joined him in the Ward, were present as well.

Willie had attended some living births that fall but he dreamed only of this one. In the dream he was terrified, though at the time he had remained calm, wishing to be seen by his friends as unruffled by the procedure.

But dreaming his hand encountered—and knew it was to encounter—not a presented head but a kind of face, and his fingers would sink into it as though its mass, its half-formed features, were made of a gelatinous substance or congealed blood. It must under no circumstance be allowed to emerge, yet it pressed between his desperate fingers; he could not stop it. He wakened then, always, his heart pounding, his brain full of chattering excuses he was offering to the Professor:

"The pelvis must be elevated. There must be a plug of gutta percha to stop the flow—" and for a few moments his hands were clawing about his bed to grasp at this unsuitable, imaginary object.

Then his mind slowly got clear. His cousin Chattie, if she were in the room, would bend over him, gently ask him what he wanted. What he wanted!

Later he dreamed of the dissection as well. Professor Leichman, or someone more like Professor Coates saying to him severely, "You'll have to do it yourself."

Willie was now admitted to be chronically, perhaps even mortally ill. Dr. Gray, seeing him at his worst, had Ewing shave his head. Like Murchison at the Royal, he said that in susceptible families these fevers progressed to pulmonary disease, such as had claimed Willie's mother those years ago. Any sign of weakness in the chest—and there were now distressing indications—was cause for despair, though Willie's own professors MacMurchie and Gairdner maintained it did not inevitably follow. Willie could not rise from his bed. He was in a delirium at the worst of the fever, Charlotte still determined to nurse him alone though at the weekends Helen attended him, and again spoke of getting another servant, to be hired at the Whitsun term fair.

Both she and John were of course at Annville to receive the visitors from Glasgow. The weather was unfortunately raw and damp, but Mrs. Spears was in grand good spirits. She arrived dressed in full mourning, would perhaps never put it off. The only slight concession to the season was a dark, almost black artificial rose under her bonnet. Annie like Charlotte had put off mourning and half-mourning: she appeared larger than ever in a white sprigged muslin under her drab travelling cape, her placid face enclosed by a light straw with now rather drooping sky-blue ribbons. Beside her mother she would always seem almost handsome, though the two were very alike: Mother's great square face with the strong vertical lines pulling down her mouth, Annie's skin as yet youthfully firm. Tom handing them down, turning about to admire the drive, the house, the front plot. Annie started at the monkey puzzle tree but said the lilies were "dears" and Helen urged her to pluck some, so that she came quite blithely into the lobby with a wet yellow bunch held to her bosom.

Tom had not given up the idea of getting to Corra Linn, despite the weather, with such a large number of public conveyances travelling up and down the Brae, but both Annie and Mother were against returning at once to Lanark and then travelling beyond.

The train journey had been pleasant, though they had been a little crowded—but Lanark station itself was frightful: "The engine shunts six or seven times to allow passing trains in and out, while passengers are jostled backwards and forwards." People darted this way and that, and all was confusion. It was impossible for the officers to get the passengers into the right trains.

The rain ceased however, and it was decided that the young persons should walk down to Stonebyrnes Linn, another awful waterfall not far below Kirkfieldbank and well worth seeing, while Mother stayed for a good crack with Helen and John. The two nieces having already folded away the crash and laid the dining table with new ironed, snowy linen and the best plate.

On the way Charlotte showed her brother and sister the IOGT Hall and the Kirk, and they each smiled to see how some urchins ran up to her in the road to take her hand and walk with her a little way. Jock Duffy, one of the orphans boarding at the McConvilles', a bright lad but with very red hair, stayed with them till the Linn, "so you'll no fall in the Loup," as he explained. He had leapt over it many times himself, he declared, but Charlotte gently reproving him he mended his tale, and assured them there was a Hazelton lad aged fourteen who had attempted it and been swept away.

Charlotte wished to speak to Tom and Annie about Willie but it was not till they had admired the Falls and left Jock there attaching to some touring folk, and got themselves away from the roar of the waters, that she could begin.

Tom must undertake to flit Willie's last things from his lodgings in Enderslie-street, and pay the rent due; he was to get the money from their uncle. After much prayer, John had brought himself to speak to Willie the morning before, about his withdrawal from the University. He did so with a heavy heart, but thought it best. Helen was forever talking of it in Stonehouse, and meanwhile Willie not having said a word, it would be more painful to him should she come out with something incautiously. John had then offered to Willie to write his withdrawal for him, as soon as he was decided of course. And Willie had said:

"It is written lang syne."

And there it was in the front of one of his books only to be dated, which Willie had then done, and so it was sent.

With sad hearts did his cousins return to the house, and the oncoming rain did not help their spirits. Annie looked earnestly out for signs of the flourish and thought she could see something of it already in the early plum, and the gean, as they called the wild cherry, whose tiny white flowers were pushing forth bravely on their black stems in the downpour. Tom had a story from the *Herald* about the Skye crofters who were stoutly holding out against paying their rents, and were now being removed. Then Charlotte could tell them of an interesting local disaster—part of Craighead Mansion House on Clyde bank destroyed by fire Saturday last, in the forenoon, but thankfully with no loss of life. The servants had escaped leaving clothing and belongings to the flames.

"You neednae be so fearful of speaking on my account, and go mincing about in your stocking soles," said Willie the next forenoon. Charlotte, attending to his fire, had not been thinking of him that moment but of her family—the visit had been far too short! But she set about to tell him of the Stonebyrnes Linn as she arranged his toilet, putting out his shaving gear and basin.

Then she took his tray, and saw that he had eaten something.

"Are you feeling better today then?"

"It cannae get worse, therefore you could say I am feeling better. I will try to get up the now, if you will help me."

But he could not. The coughing, which so concerned Dr. Gray, was brought on. "Coughing is a healthful mechanism, serving to clear the pleura." Robert's doctor had said that, but only at first.

So they came again into the full flourish. By early May, the blossom was on the plum all down Clyde, then the pears and early apples, then in a rush all the apples trees. John, for a change, had walked down the Hazelbank Braes. He said that from the upland parks, Clyde's dale looked as if it were filled with white and pink cloud. *"I've a home in Cloudland,"* sang Charlotte softly going down the garden.

No servant was hired at Martinmas, Charlotte still wishing to care for Willie herself. He had improved somewhat but continued despondent. She could not help feeling almost impatient with him, when he would not in any degree be comforted. The easement of his suffering, were it but for a day or days, was a very present blessing and one he must feel—and ought to be thankful for. And such weather and sights abroad, even within the extent of the garden, must serve to turn him from his wretchedness.

Would he but come out into the sunlight! Yet even when he lay easy he said the light hurt his eyes; and nothing cheered him.

"I cannae wake from my dreams."

Mr. Thomson had made the purchase of the Schubert at Wm Laing in the Canongate. He wished to speak to her of it "though he would not presume to explain it in any way, his memory of the rendering being perhaps faulty and, though an Old Notationist, reading anything so complicated as a Sonata was quite beyond him! Yet the massing of the notes in some way recalled what he had heard, and the rises and falls:—her own musicianship would find it out. But he would selfishly wish to deliver it into her hands himself, and trusted that his road would lead to Kirkfieldbank ere long."

If he wrote to Mr. Cameron again and was put off, Charlotte did not know it.

She was out to see the famous comet,[35] though she did not join the watchers "of all classes" on the brig, but stood down the garden on the green. Indeed, the sky was too bright, and though she could hear people calling out about the tail, the comet looked round to her, like a lamp submerged in water. Perhaps she saw its tail, in apparent flashes, but it could have been but the tearing of her eyes, from staring so.

She went on down among the sulphur grossets and passed through the lower gate. The sand-bar was well exposed, Clyde running low in its smoothy swell past Annville, deeper over towards Nemphlar bank, at the place called the Elephant Hole. Innumerable surface wimples folded back and back, wee white smirkies slipping with the current yet remaining aye where they were. Under them the water was sleek as glass. She stood against Annville wall with its cool stones pressed into her shoulders. The brig with a row of heads like a paper silhouette along its high curve. Two arches and the black river coming through. The reeds and trees of the Great Inch pushed up behind the central pile. A splash as something was thrown over, the heads crowding, laughter.

"There's your cap gone then Jimmie!" "Away after it, Jimmie!" Scuffling on the brig. A scrap of dark passing silently out in the current.

1.

KIRKFIELDBANK, LANARK

2.

3.

4.

5.

6.

7.

8.

9.

10.

11.

12.

13.

14.

15.

16.

17.

18.

19.

20.

21.

22.

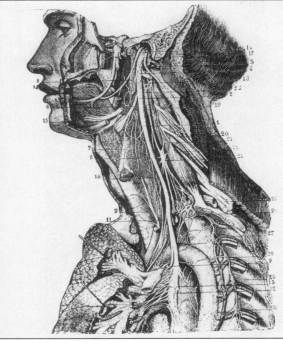

26.

CHAPTER 17

Down in the kitchen Charlotte pored over the *Papers on Health*. She had been up with Willie's brose and he was quiet, drowsy, allowing her to wipe his face and hands, which she did as gently as she could.

"Dinnae move me yet," he had said plaintively. The bed all in disarray from his fidgety night, the room dank and close with the great fire Margaret Tennant had stirred up, despite the partly opened windows. Margaret could not be made to understand the idea of a small, steady fire. Perhaps, a fire in May being quite beyond her comprehension, the great blaze was intended to give her right. Now Charlotte must move Willie, bring away the bad linen, air out the while he was awake and reasonable.

Could he but get himself downstairs an hour or two! He might sit in the parlour, it was aye aired in the forenoon ready for lessons. Perhaps tomorrow, with Margaret Tennant's help.

It was hard on Willie to be moved about when he wished most to lie still. Ought she to wait half an hour? Yet she could not sit down. To stay her impatience she took up one of the red tablets "on Health" from the dresser, sent so long ago. Tom had asked on his visit if the Cure had been tried. If Willie would continue to resist Dr. Gray's regime, he might allow this instead. Where the pages fell open she read:

"*How perfect is the gratitude which rewards the kind helper who gives such a night of peaceful rest instead of the weary tossing of fever!*"

She would speak to him.

She found him asleep but already flushed and restless, and he wakened as she stood, his eyes fixing for a moment on hers with a look of surprise and, she must confess it, dislike. Oh, dear Willie would rather be well and in Glasgow; no one could blame him for that!

"Willie, I must do the room properly and settle you, for it's no been aired yet."

He got himself sitting upright, pushing back the quilt.

"Go out a minute then, while I attend to myself."

When she returned he was seated on the side of his bed, sipping his tea, his ingrowing hair at the crown a curved pattern of ciphers, almost like writing.

"There's hot water for your shave." She took the slop pail and went down, and in the scullery drenched it with lye and carbolic, and left it at the back door for the ash pit.

Willie had got himself over into the big chair. She moved about as quick as she could, standing the screen at his back while she threw up the two windows and let the clear, cool air fill the room. It was a mizzling, windless day. She banked down his fire, then bundled the linen outside the door and closed it against its banging. She heaved over the mattress and remade the bed.

"Now Willie, it is a braw day and you are feeling quite well, would you consider the Barilla Cure Tom sent you, before you are settled? He has asked me about it."

Willie darted her a glance. "You're convinced I'm in for the fevers for all my long sleep. I'd prefer not to welcome bad news that hasnae arrived yet."

His voice was weary, and Charlotte sat down for a moment on the side of his bed. His chair was turned from her towards the window, his bare head looking oddly rigid sticking up over the plaid.

"Oh, Willie, you know I do pray for you to be well. I won't speak of it again. But—"

"Go away with your buts. I'm saying I've no particular pains to complain of and I'll be happy to see the back of you."

"Will you stay there? Will you get into bed?"

"It is the same wherever I am, get away down."

"Shall I give you a book?" For he kept them about him and would listlessly turn the pages even now.

"Would it never occur to you I do nae care to be treated, when my mission in life is to treat? If you will let me have my *Flint and Gee*, and then I wish you out of my sight."

Eagerly she got through the rest, for she could not feel quite comfortable till his basin and the pail were scoured, and the linen on the raips, and herself washed with a clean apron on. Today she would change and air her dress as well.

The rain had stopped, leaving the garden sparkling. New "Wee" Gruntie ran at her heels and she pushed him gently aside with her patten. There was time to practise before the first pupil arrived. Going up the stone steps into the lobby she thought: "This day might Mr. Thomson come." Daylight streamed through the glazed front door, the cathedral glass pattern around the etched urn glowing in gold and ruby and light blue. Her uncle had taken down the winter door and put it behind the porch, in the long black lumber-closet.

Stone Row, Heywood, June 15, 1882

My dear Friend,

You have not replied to my letter of June 1st your reason being I trust, that I had written you of my coming soon to Kirkfieldbank. I am sorry that I have been unable to come, it was certainly my intention:—and I am ashamed to say that your Sonata sheets are still standing on the piano, Mr. Park has even been trying out the Andantino. They are almost dog eared. But that is as much my own fault as his, for turning them about and trying to read them. I assure you Mr. Park soon gave it up! which as I told him I was happy about, and he agreed:—the music being far beyond him and the Park's piano, which stands in the parlour and very damp, in no way suitable.

I expected you among the throng at the Lanimers and a member of your choir whom I ran into, or rather, ran into me, a very pleasant spoken lady Miss West, told me you are much kept at home caring for your cousin.

Thank you for assuring me, that you do not in doing so, neglect your Music. My friend was wrong in saying so, and very wrong in excusing you from the Lanark Concert on those grounds, when as *you* tell me he had himself been set against your going. But you are the wiser of us, in saying there is no need in speaking of it more.

The "hauding of the Lanimers" was noisy and I did not stay it out, in fact I rode down to Kirkfieldbank before turning home, thinking with the many folk going to and fro you might be walking out in your garden. But the house was closed up and no music emerging neither, and in consideration of the invalid I did not presume to knock.

You must shake your head over my reliance on such bits of village gossip as it were at second hand:—"wars and rumours of wars." I hope that Miss West is as sadly misinformed as my friend Mr. Cameron, for she told me that your cousin is despaired of, and suffers a Marching Melancholia, a phrase my dear Father would be surprised at!

Now I must tell you the reason for writing in such haste, that I am called away to visit him:—his health, never good, is now in a decline. How urgent my visit is I do not yet know, and my stay depends upon how I find him, I mean, whether I may not be away some weeks. If it turns out so, which I heartily trust it does not, I will write to you from Renfrewshire.

I have still a stubborn, no doubt childish, wish to put the A-Major Sonata into your hands myself. I leave Lanark for Glasgow on the 10.20 train tomorrow, that is, Wednesday.

> Your ever devoted Friend,
> Andrew Thomson

With Willie very bad and at such short notice, Charlotte was unable to get up to Lanark to see Mr. Thomson off, as she was almost sure had been his meaning. By evening she had his letter pretty much by heart, for it came out of her pocket and into her hand whenever she walked about, and if she were working in the kitchen it would be spread on the board or brought across to the table. Later at the harpsichord it stood on the music rack as she played, her hands running about but her eyes fastened on his words. Night came; he was far away! and it must join his other letters tied up in the back of the drawer. Where Mr. Miller's letter had once been so foolishly cherished!

She blushed, got into bed to half-dream in spite of herself of walking alone in the dusky garden, of Mr. Thomson, Andrew Thomson, spying her as he rode across the brig, then the crush of hooves heard in the drive. He would dismount and come walking around the house. How light, the skin around his eyes! a glow of inward light! She turned over, sighing. She would not think of Lanark Station and the shunting engines and jostling passengers, where he must have looked out for her in vain.

And now, till he wrote or said he was returned, she could not write to him! He had asked her what she was playing and she had not told him! He had only "rumours" of her difficulties with Willie! She blushed again to think of her last, stiff letter.

"My friend was very wrong!" His eyes opened at any rate to the character of Mr. Cameron. Without a struggle he had believed her, his new friend, though he had known Mr. Cameron for many years. The sadness about the station departed, was replaced by more tender sensations. She would write, from now on, with the same candour and openness! Of music, he could not get enough. Later perhaps of her hopes and disappointments about Willie's sickness too—what she felt was his spiritual sickness—for there was no one to whom she could open her heart, not even Mr. Forsyth. Though she did not think Andrew Thomson wanted to hear of Willie particularly, only that her music was not impinged upon. She sat up suddenly at the thought of how cold, almost forbidding, her letter had been. Yet, he had answered her!

All the next day she composed tenderer letters in her head.

The weather continued hot and John coming in from Stonehouse said the drought was affecting the cereals and grasses, and the grazing was getting bare. Clouds would build towards evening, sometimes quite black, but the expected thunder held off. Charlotte thought the sulphurous air must affect Willie for his headache was always worse when the clouds were bigging, and he was nervous and impatient:

"I'm no so bad I want that chemist's cure, you can tell Tom from me." Though she had not again asked him about it.

Then came fiery and cloudy weather, and great pours of rain. Charlotte was caught out in it hurrying across from the Shilling Library in the Post Office, where she had changed *Heart of Midlothian* for *Kenilworth* and intercepted a letter. There was a fragrance on the breezes emanating from the beans that were burst into flower, and she looked up over the village to see the neep fields darkened between the green, springing rills—the dormant turnips had brairded, and the women were bending and singling along the rows, their aprons winking patches of white.

Bridesgate, Kilmacolm
Renfrewshire
June 22nd, 1882

Dear Miss Spears,
    A note as I promised.
    My Father is not in immediate danger. However I have conveyed to the deacons a request for four weeks absence, part of which being my allotted Holiday, so will require no calling in of a replacement excepting the first two Sabbaths. My dear Father is considerably weakened.

Ever your Friend
Andrew Thomson.

To such a letter she could not at once reply, certainly not with the effusions she had been preparing. For some days her disappointment prevented her, then her diffidence: she blamed herself. She had not answered him. She had not endeavoured, as she might have on several occasions, to see him in Lanark. The station—she ought to have gone! Only this last communication, scarcely a note, would she take out now and read as a punishment. It would subdue her and make her as rational as he.

Then she wrote to him, even more briefly, and wished his Father well. How she would have liked to acknowledge his earlier words about Mr. Cameron! "My friend was very wrong"! Yet even to dwell on them was self-indulgence and unchristian. She had already said too much. To have called forth his indignation and caused a breach, perhaps never to be healed, between trusted comr.ades! No more was to be said about it, she and Mr. Thomson had agreed.

At the same time she established for herself a regime of moral and physical improvement. She might not walk, there was not time, yet she could step more quickly down to Clyde with the linen, or going her messages, not loiter vainly about. She denied herself a portion of the sweets she made to tempt Willie, which Janet Sneddon and her sister got instead. Wee Maggie would sometimes peep in though Janet was sharp with her:

"You know fine you're no to come trailing after me meddling with my work."

Charlotte learned that Maggie lived as a kind of servant with the Mathiesons too, though but seven years old.

"Our minnie has three more at home and there's no room for us great ones," explained Janet, her mouth full of seed cake.

Charlotte would work quietly into the evening, not allowing herself those idle moments when dreaming might insinuate. She prayed to be rational, that Mr. Thomson's name might not linger in her thoughts. Scott was returned unfinished and she set herself to read the *Acts of the Apostles*, a portion of the Bible in which Fancy had little chance to spread its wings. Yet, she would have been surprised had she realized how his situation in Kilmacolm had taken shape, though surely unsummoned, in her mind. The tall house, rather dark, the open southern prospect past dense shrubbery, the daily room with its high curtained windows, the old man in his chair! Her imagination might be subdued by her efforts, but was never conquered.

At the Kirk her duties had entered the more lightsome, summer stage. There were two Sabbath services all season, but the Choir being well in hand the practises were less wearying. Mr. Cameron took his holiday. Strawberry-pulling claimed all hands to the beds and her pupils had a respite from music lessons as well.

The Sabbath School annual pic-nic and the Band of Hope's Lanark and Kirkfieldbank outing had given the scholars their romps and pleasures, and now she planned her first Choir Excursion for the adults with care. If the weather were favourable they were to climb to Tintoch Top.

CHAPTER 18

In which the Choir Trip to Tintoch Top[36] is realized,
with an alarming consequence.

The biggest of Kirkfield's hay brakes had been pushed into the mill pond, scrubbed manfully with stable brooms, and filled with new straw. Lindsay Wilson the coachman drove it down from the estate, to meet the Choir at the brig at seven o'clock. The two Clydesdales were decked out with ribbons and raffia, tail and mane. Streamers hung from the harnesses and the brasses sparkled on the martingale. The four hampers from Sunnyside, covered with white linen, were lifted carefully in and then they were away.

Though Roddy Munro had pled off because his injury prohibited a climb, nearly everyone else was there, even cross Mr. Barr in an unlikely tam o'shanter, and carrying a stout hickory stick. It was a tight squeeze and a merry one. Charlotte as leader sat up on the front board behind the coachman and the steep black haunches of the Clydesdales, with Mrs. West on the one side and the younger Misses Paul on the other. They, and Mr. Carmichael, would not go up the Hill but sit comfortably meantime in the Mill garden. Roddy Munro perhaps understandably not wanting to be classed along with them. Weaver James Nugent ought perhaps to be discouraged, yet he would go! and perhaps the high, bracing air was what was wanted for his chest though he looked so white and wan. Charlotte by turning slightly could see him leaning back as if already weary, down in the straw, and from her perch was able as well to keep an eye on Miss Agnes Elder and some of the other more boisterous young Members. She was not so cruel as to forbid Agnes' happy station between James Thomson and Jimmie Henderson on the back board—for this young lady had run out almost too late, pinning her bonnet and waved to by her mother from the airie porch. Though Charlotte had already seen her peep impatiently out the kitchen window all the while folk were climbing up. How much, she thought forgivingly, as Agnes made a laugh of the squeeze, and gathered in her skirts between the two pair of polished, loutish boots, how much depended, on such a summer's day, for youthful hearts, on where one might sit on the slat of a country brake!

They jingled up Ramath road and there was Mr. Weir at his gate in a dapper straw, touching its brim to her, then leaping up into the midst, with the Clydesdales not missing a step. He was now reinstated and had appeared at the last practise not looking at all repentant.

She had seen nothing of him since early spring, Mrs. Simpson giving out that he had been "in London, or such, which he will do on occasion as the mood strikes him, and see his lassies." No Mrs. Weir waved from the porch. That lady who never went about, whom Charlotte would not have recognized, always a shadowy accompaniment to her idea of him.

Very soon they reached the high parks with the countryside opened out around them, and were come farther than ever Charlotte had been on her rambles. Lanark's spires were left behind, and the far hills "skipped like rams." The sun was already warm and several brightly-trimmed parasols bobbed over the brake.

They passed through Hawksland. Mrs. Steele had a sister there and was craning about as they passed a lane. Perhaps she would have liked to spend the day cracking with her sister instead of climbing a mountain? But now she had a sister in Douglas Water as well, and cousins all over the country if she were to be believed. And others were pointing out farms they had family at, or had fee'd to. Mrs. Hastie had once, she said, served a term as byrewoman at Corramore: "She was no sure if it wasnae that steading there, away across the hill." Charlotte was sorry for Mrs. West who being from toun had nothing to do but to exclaim and admire and wonder if Charlotte were not crowded.

"There's 'Paddy with his heuk.'" They had been edging the wilds of Broken Cross Muir, rocking along a rough track with the female occupants occasionally squealing, and were again on a smoother road among fields. Many an apt Irishman with a sharpened scythe might find work and a bothy-bed in this season! All the cutting was done by scythe, women and young lads getting the swathes into sheaves and binding them, the mowers all keeping stroke, entering the hay and bringing round the scythes at the same time, arms moving in unison.

Ahead was "Tintock Tap," at first low and unregarded among the other hills, now growing ever bigger! It rose bluish against the morning sun as if a haze of light hung before it like a transparent curtain. Yet its plain, treeless outline was clear: unbroken to the summit till, as they passed under its western flank, the lower pile of Totherin swelled up from the north, like a footstool.

The road was again hardly more than a grassy track, and bumped through fairy flax and purple moor beside a burn, deep-hidden and winding. A summery hum rose around about, and Charlotte spied a row of blond skeps over against a planting and thought some might be John's. It was hereabouts the bees were taken to the heather.

Wiston Mill was south of the mountain, foremost among a pretty cluster of stone houses and offices glimpsed through well-grown grosset bushes and fruit trees. Behind the house a beautiful giant chestnut, which had shaded many an outing, spread its branches over a meadow. A welcoming tiffin was spread out in the shade on a table covered by a white cloth. The scent of the new-mowed grass overwhelming as they stepped down.

One of the Sunnyside hampers was brought forth as well, though they were warned not to eat too hearty, for the proper feast would be on their return. Nor would they need fear thirst, there being a spring of clear water near the top. Charlotte stood up soon as a signal they must be on their way, and the active parted from the old and thronged across the meadow to the stile. Miller Clarkson in his happy prerogative already waiting there to hand over the ladies.

Some of the party had been down to the burn-side for a pretty stone, others found one near the path. The lads of course choosing large and cumbersome ones to humph uphill. The young ladies whispered about their wishes—they had bits of paper folded tight and deep in their pockets, even those who could not write, to place in the cairn under their stones.

"Have you a wish, Miss Spears?"

Charlotte merely turned away and Mr. Weir did not insist on a reply.

The path began to ascend almost immediately, first in a straight line and then of necessity turning sharply back on itself, for the mountain was steep. The outcropping called Pap Craig towered over them, an almost vertical cliff of red sandstone very bright in the sun. The turn under its easternmost rise was discovered to be dangerous, though in reality quite safe. Skirts and petticoats must however be tended to in the sharpening breeze, and there was a comment in bad taste from Mr. Weir about Tintock's wanting "modesty boards" like the deck of an omnibus.

They went up under the lessening cliff by a path of loose grush and grasses, walking single file, some in "Irish tandem,"—the lady's waist to be grasped, perhaps even encircled, by the gentleman from behind—and Charlotte looking back could not but smile at the lads with the biggest stones, who found themselves unable to join in.

She raised her eyes to gaze forth. How quickly, while they were as yet far from any great height, did the countryside open itself around them! Small summer clouds had formed in the otherwise clear sky, and their passage could be read in their shadows slipping over the fields and hills. But she could glance merely, the others crowding behind her.

The first group indeed out-distanced the others, the great lads almost running up the last and steepest ascent to the "dimple," hurling down their "stanes" on the cairn and flinging themselves full length in the grass.

Charlotte arrived with the largest crowd, the young ladies who with laughter and secrecy began to press their papers deep into gaps and their stones atop to hold them.

The breeze, though not cold, was very fresh and strong and parasols turned out to be unmanageable. The first thing to be done of course, after having "placed one's stane," was to stop and gaze and see whether one could count the twelve counties. Below them through the blue pure air, lowland Scotland from Firth to Firth was spread. The Peaks of Arran were a blurred mist in the West, with Glasgow hid at its thickest. In the East a silver streak was just visible, the Forth with the peak of Berwick Law proudly rising. Southward lay purple moorlands and the blackened bings which marked the collieries. Northward, farmlands and Lanark's spires, with more collieries east towards the Pentland hills. Red roads might be traced, and the modern, straighter criss-cross of train beds and viaducts. A train was discovered and exclaimed at, smoothing its way on the Caledonian Line between Symington and Carstairs. And the upper reaches of Clyde lying as if motionless in lazy serpentines, pale blue amidst sweet fields and plantings.

Such golden fields! Even from such a height they could trace the effect of the distant hay-making, the moving spots of waggons, the even division between the thick gold and the darker bronze of cut fields: here the ripe swathes lying, there the dotted sheaves in tiny lines. Tintock fell away in smooth sweeps of dense gorse and red sandstone, with sparse blackfaced sheep moving here and there. The invigorating wind was a constant susseration, and their own voices were swept away from their mouths.

They gathered around the huge block of granite which William Wallace was said to have lifted with the awful grip of his thumb. The lads must of course have a try, for there was the thumb-dent in the stone, and the hollow cup still damp with morning dews, where he had quenched his thirst.

Agnes Elder chanted, uncertain at first with many a wrong start, then well away and the others joining in:

> "On Tintock Tap there is a mist,
> And in that mist there is a kist,
> And in that kist there is a caup,
> And in that caup there is a drap.
> Tak' up the caup, drink off the drap,
> And set the caup on Tintock Tap."

Then they broke apart, some of the younger ones pushing at each other and laughing. They also chanted:

> "Be a lassie e'er sae black,
> An' she hae the name o' siller,
> Set her up on Tintock Tap:
> The wind will blaw a man till her." [37]

Charlotte seated herself a little apart from Mrs. West and a few other ladies, who had found out some "natural chairs" below the north side of the cairn and sheltered from the strongest gusts. Some of the gentlemen meanwhile were bringing the kettle down to the spring, which bubbled into a little pool among smoothed stones. Soon she saw the bluish smoke blowing off their fire. Tea was a necessary ritual, though most preferred a draught of the clear, cold water. More Members descended to the spring, and snatches of their talk could be heard, the tinkle of tinnies.

A second, almost straight grass track led down that side of the mountain to the village of Tankerton, creeping about the lip of the Cleuch—a steep, western fall—then vanishing over the round brow of Totherin Hill to appear far down the valley. There it followed the thread of a silver burn that passed by a toy farm, under a toy brig. A conveyance crossed over, a dash of whites and darks which, the brig traversed and the brake halted, spilled out into separate, miniature people. Other excursionists, who would surely come walking up the "three Scotch miles" of the longer ascent. Charlotte espied another, single figure already on the track.

Her eyes mounted a fraction to trace the curling burn that in a ribbon of black and gleam moved through the cushiony gorse. She followed a cloud's shadow. There away off was the road they had followed! Almost, she could make out the skeps against the pines.

The lonely figure had disappeared for a time, hidden by Totherin Hill. Her Members were beginning to assemble again on the summit. All pronounced themselves refreshed. Mr. Russell ever courteous arrived balancing two tinnies of tea, and held one kindly towards her.

"I declare, there is a gentleman on his way up."

She recognized him far earlier than she could have recognized him. It was long minutes before someone ventured to guess that it was the young pastor who had read at their Harvest Concert, whatever was his name?

"Mr. Thomson, of Heywood," said Charlotte, her voice steady.

He was carrying a net and slowed a little to fold it up, perhaps wishing to get his breath before he arrived, the last slope being very steeply inclined. Greetings were exchanged. Charlotte stepping forward hardly knew what she said. Then he was being taken about, explained the view by a large group of choristers.

Charlotte stood uncertainly. Mr. Weir, alone unaffected by the arrival, had not risen. He lounged on a stone. Apart from his remark about the modesty board his behaviour had been unexceptionable; if he looked at her at all it was unobtrusively, as a brother or guardian, and it seemed that no other lady among her flock, either, was to be singled out or given cause for offense. He smiled, and smoked his thin cigarettes, the perfume of his tobacco crossing her nostrils occasionally on the breeze. Was he watching her now?

Mr. Thomson being asked whether he had ever been on Tintock Tap. Only once as a lad, he said, with his father. She could not see his face for the crowd of bonnets. Would a shadow have crossed it? Envisioning them suddenly: a small boy in a short jacket, his light hair long and blown about, clinging to the hand of the savage-visaged alienist, who pointed out the counties crossly with his stick.

Her Members, who had become a little languid from inactivity, had many questions for the new arrival. Agnes Elder eyeing the ring-net protruding from his pocket asked him whether he was anything of a botanizer. "Do you ken what this red flower would be Mr. Thomson, for it's quite another colour, hidden away down here deep in the mosses?"

"Ah, that's the soaked blood of the Covenanters." Kneeling among several of the younger Members, the ladies drawing back their skirts in mock horror.

"Oh, it's not! Oh, Mr. Thomson!"

He told them, using his pulpit voice so Charlotte could not but smile, that it was *Erica cinera* or "bell-heather"; and plucking some compared it with the more ordinary purplish *vulgaris*, then sent them off to search for the latter's rare white bloom, which was considered lucky. They spread out then, stooping and chattering.

Charlotte had turned away, and gazed almost unseeing towards the admonishing finger of Berwick Law. Then he was at her side, and walking ahead of her a little farther over the grass, seated himself by a piece of sandstone, his stick extended before him. It tapped at the ground, dislodged a bit of grush, tapped.

His ordinary low, somewhat rough enunciation. "Are you no surprised to see me?"

Charlotte could not answer. She was wondering if she might sit on the stone beside him.

"Since it seems I cannae easily get over to Kirkfieldbank, and

Tintock being about the same distance, and the day being very fine!"

"It is beautiful weather."

"Now, look along my cane, and there is Heywood at the end of it! Can you see the Kirk spire beyond the tips? There it is, there." Charlotte must sit down to look, their heads for a moment very close. She thought she could smell him, a heady, healthful scent, somehow childlike, minding her of best clothes, soap and Sabbath School frolics. She drew back before she could properly attend to his stick with its trembling ferrule, unsure whether she had seen Heywood or no.

Shrieks behind them, where someone had discovered a paper wish blown away and caught among the gorse, reading it in a high voice, and its authorship fiercely denied by several voices.

Mr. Thomson said, "I've brought you the A-Major, and only asking you to forgive me for the delay—I returned Saturday."

Now she must look into his face. "How is your Father?"

"He is the same, but in no danger at all." Charlotte had indeed forgotten how extreme was the lightness around his eyes! Small, pale freckles the size of pins' heads bespattered the open space between his brows, and even just above his eyes. She looked away with an effort, murmured her pleasure at his news.

"I thank you. Oh aye, for about the first week he was to be kept quite quiet, and we thought there was some dullness in his speech—in his forming of the words. Never in his mind! but this cleared away, and after that we had many a grand discussion—" his voice hesitated.

"He was very glad to see you. Is he quite confined? Is he able to sit up again, and be got out?"

Mr. Thomson looking confused. "I have misled you with little information, I am sorry. He's no crippled. He is blind."

They were both glad to look at the roll of music he now produced from the inner pocket of his cloak.

"It is almost worn out! When I got in I found Park had meanwhile gone on with the Second Movement and he's near murdered it. I was glad to get it out of the house. And I was forced to tell him it was for you, which however he said he kenned all along. Here it is—and I hope there's a wee breath of life left in it yet, after his terrible bashing."

Charlotte burst out laughing, and he laughed with her. But their fingers touched in handing it and they were suddenly silent.

"Thank you, Mr. Thomson," Charlotte said at last. "I hope I willnae deal it its death blow then."

Again they laughed. "Not Mr. Thomson please. My name is Drew. And if I may ask—"

But others now joined them, having tired of the tease about the paper, and no lucky heather to be found. Mr. Thomson was in great demand in giving the names of any wee plants and flowers that clung about the summit, and pronouncing the dry little bilberries offering to him as unfit to eat, and classifying as *Artaxerxes* a small brown butter-fly, which he then managed to secure in his net attached to his stick, the young ladies squealing that he would surely tumble over the precipice.

"This is of course one of the Blues."

"But it's no blue at all, Mr. Thomson!"

"A Blue it is nevertheless, and cleverer men than I say so. It is shaped like a Blue, which is what they go by, you see."

He must show them the contents of his pocket-box, and there were further squeals at the sight of three butterflies pinned into the cork, and the wee pincushion suspended by a loop and button inside his coat, from which he removed an entomological pin and secured the newest specimen. He said that the others were two Commas and a Dingy Skipper, caught down in the meadows. The Commas were pro-nounced pretty. "The *Artaxerexes* has blown off course. I have taken many on—" his voice lost its clarity then; Charlotte believed he had said "Arthur's Seat."

All the Members now sitting or sprawling round about, she must exert herself and introduce a merry song—"The Tramp Chorus." One led to another, their voices however very thin in the breeze.

Someone began:

> *"One sweetly solemn thought*
> *Comes to me o'er and o'er:*
> *That I am nearer Home today*
> *Than I ever was before."*

"On Tintock Tap, we are indeed!" said Mr. Weir and some of the ladies laughed. But poor young Nugent coughed and coughed.

The excursionists below were nearly upon them: they had gathered about the spring, among them a black-habited man in a cassock clutching at his round hat! Surely a priest! And looking often upwards as though annoyed by their preoccupation.

Charlotte proposed the descent. No one minded; they were eager to get down again, and there were declarations of great hunger, suddenly felt by all.

They must say farewell to Mr. Thomson whose horse was tethered at Fullburn Farm; though he was urgently pressed to join in their refreshment at Wiston before this was generally understood. He was seen off to the eager wavings of several handkerchiefs, if not of Charlotte's. Her more gentle goodbyes perhaps unheard in the noise of the others, though for a moment his eyes found hers.

She lingered as much as she could in setting off, standing to bind the music roll within her parasol. She could not bring herself to look after him—only her inward gaze might follow him down the green track, along Cleuch's fearful brim, over Totherin mound where his form, brisk and upright, would for a moment be outlined against the distant hills. Then lost from sight, going down and down just as she did this side of Tintock, step below step with the breeze dying, and the shadows lengthening in the valley.

At Wiston the table-linen gleamed like snow, stained by blue patches of shade from the chestnut tree. Mr. Johnstone, Esquire's really excellent repast was spread forth, dressed grouse and great moulded sweets, supplemented by the remaining mountains of Mrs. Clarkson's baps and her strong tea, which last in particular was very welcome to Charlotte.

Then they were into the brake and homeward bound.

Merrily did they bowl along. Song after song was taken up, and some finished, and some dwindling away, and between-times there were great yawns, and exclamations, and climbings about in the straw and changings of place upon the boards, and tappings with parasols, and abductions of bonnets, and protests, and laughter, and sighs, and gentle female murmurings over green-stain on white muslin. The Clydesdales meanwhile plodding along the red road as sedately as if this had all been seen before, as indeed it had, as many times as there were kirk choirs in Scotland and long summer days.

That Mr. Thomson had presented Miss Spears with a roll of music on Tintock Tap did not go unnoticed. But such is youth's indifference to middle age that even among the most perceptive of the younger Members nothing could possibly be thought of it. Mrs. West however would still be talking and asking; on the meadow Charlotte had been forced to show it her before she would be even a little satisfied. Now, safely atop the high seat for the homeward journey, she chatted on to the imperturbable coachman while Charlotte herself sat down in the straw and need not reply.

Mrs. West had cried out at how difficult the music looked: "I am sure only yourself would be able to follow it! And all in the Old Notation!" spoken with an almost indignant shudder, as though over some heathen script.

"The good reverend would be very glad to get rid of it no doubt, and I am sure you will play it very prettily. As I said to Miss Henry, or was it Mr. Barr: Did you see the large roll of pianoforte music Mr. Thomson has presented to Miss Spears?"

The choristers had calmed and there were not a few indolent complaints of tired feet, then a slight reanimation brought on by the sighting of Kirkfield House, and declarations of, though a delightful trip, a wearying to be home. The brake rocked and lulled like a ship. Charlotte, released from further obligations, fell into a reverie.

They were coming down Ramath hill when Mr. Weir, who intended to get off the same way he had got on, sank to one knee beside her and said in a low voice:

"That wasnae very wise, Miss Spears. You'll mind I'm no a Manager to stand up for you. I'm in Mr. Cameron's bad books already. But I wish you well."

Then he was over the side of the brake, and after the confusion of goodbyes at the brig, with the ladies being helped down, and a rousing cheer for Miss Spears at the last, she got somehow into Annville and the day was over.

Kirkfieldbank Church, 15th August, 1882
The Managers met in the vestry on the above date, when
after consideration the following resolution was unanimously
carried—"that the service of Miss Spears as conductor of the

*Psalmody in this church be dispensed with from this date."
Mr. Russell was instructed to send an excerpt of this minute
to Miss Spears. Mr. Cameron was requested to do what he
could to find a person to undertake the duties of Conductor.
There being no other business of special importance the meeting then dispersed.*

Walter Cameron.[38]

CHAPTER 19

In which Charlotte is fallen into scandal.

Kirkfieldbank, August 30, 1882

My dear Thomson,
    You will forgive me that I have not before this inst. enquired again after your excellent Father. Your short letter dated August 10th from Renfrewshire on his *then* steady improvement, ought to have satisfied me. But I would beg one note from you that I might put my mind completely at rest.
                    Your obedient Friend etc.
                    Walter Cameron

Kirkfieldbank, September 9 1882

Dear Thomson,
    Your not having written, though expecting daily some word be it ever so brief, must give me the assurance that you left your good Father well. I was pleased to hear though not from yourself, that you are back in harness and with I must trust no further distresses from that quarter.
    We are at present diligently working up the Deed of Constitution to present to General Assembly. As you know we confidently pray for election into Quoad Sacra within the coming year, as a full-fledged Kirk and Parish. Then there is the manse bond and Endowment, and the Kirk being properly "established." I trust for a speedy outcome for my own "establishment" as well.
    Now one word between friends. You may be surprised to learn that your hill-walk August 14th had an undesirable

consequence. I am very glad to put your presence there to *chance*, which I may now confidently do, not having heard from you to the contrary neither in explanation nor remonstration. Therefore, it shall never be referred to between us further. It would seem that, in a certain Lady, unreasonable hopes might have been raised and therefore a word of warning. To give you some Idea: as late as last week in the High-street some *young* members of my Congregation were loudly chanting the following dogger-el—

"Be a lassie e'er so *reid*,
The Wind will blaw a man till her"—

So you may understand her Behaviour was not unnoticed. The substitution of black by "red," you see.

Believe me, you are yourself completely dis-implicated.

This Lady's Christian energies are now directed into Temperance Work in the Evangelical sphere to which she belongs. Also, she is a solicitous Nurse to her cousin, I say this to her great credit, for he seems to pick and chuse, whether he be an Invalid, or whether he be sauntering up the Village.

Yours ever obediently
Walter H. Cameron

Charlotte had forbidden Andrew—or Drew, as he would be called—to respond.

"There is nothing to be done about it," she wrote against the tide of his contrition, his extreme severity towards his friend. She wrote with great difficulty, but felt she must be firm.

Though I have no reason to demand this of you, will you promise me not to speak of it more, or to protest to Mr. Cameron on my behalf? I know that it will not do any good.

He had promised, though at first he argued vigorously. He had given in after a third letter in which she wrote:

From the words spoken to me some months back by one of my Members, I ought not to have been surprised. Mr. Cameron and I have never been able to get on, and one excuse or other would at last have been made. Though I am very distressed that he should seem to have the right. But, as this pain is to my pride only, I will shortly have got the better of it.

She wrote that she could not allow Mr. Thomson to visit her in Kirkfieldbank, and silently forgave him when he acquiesced. She began the Sonata. In her present darkness the First Movement was almost like a cliff to be assaulted, the pauses like fingerholds over an abyss. But it was a task set whose very difficulty might console her. And it was difficult indeed. She knelt to pen in a possible fingering, tried the worst passages again and again. Octaves in pianissimo to be got through smoothly, the whole to be brought to tempo! Behind her cautious attempts and errors the real music beckoned, almost heard—perhaps unattainable!

She was now leader of the Band of Hope, which met weekly at that old haunt, the IOGT Hall. To be there again, and beginning again! But the children, though some might chant taunting verses in the street, hardly understood what they sang and were still her friends. A juvenile choir could be got up. Temperance songs were plentiful. She must put it behind her as her aunt kindly, and frequently, advised. A village is a wasp's byke, and the Established Kirk was aye busy solemnly admonishing and suspending its congregation, though of course usually there might be cause enough.

Charlotte's list of private pupils had shrunk in. Kirk members, having the excuse of a new season, did not appear or reassign their children. Though the good Reids would still send her their lassies, and Mrs. West could not but allow Sadie to continue when she cried so hard. Besides, it would not do to make a thing of it and upset the household; Mrs. West was very careful not to tell Sophie any particulars—or would have been, had she known how extremely angry Mr. Cameron and the Managers were become. Mr. Cameron's face quite dark red even before she had mentioned the music! And Mr. Barr rubbing his hands! Her sisters shook their heads at it all as a local sensation.

On the first Monday Charlotte waited for Roddy Munro, unsure whether he would appear. She sat down to practise and it was during a pause she heard his chap at the door and got up to cry him in.

"I couldnae make you hear me." Setting his helmet squarely on the ottoman, his shapeless white gloves folded as flat as possible beside it.

She preceded him into the parlour and closed the Schubert, seeing it through his mournful eyes as the mark of her disgrace.

The lesson was short and uncomfortable. When she saw him away she wanted to cry out:

"You'll no desert me too, then, Roddy?"

No, he would not! Though they had not spoken beyond some short exchange about the lesson, and his silences condemned her. Oh, her uncle must not lose a good friend through her mistake!

"I thank you for coming," she was able to say, and he blushed as he set his helmet on his head. Nor did John forfeit his lookings in of a Saturday night, though the Sub-Inspector had then even less to say than usual.

Fortunately for Charlotte there was little time to succumb to regret and self-pity. She looked back on her weeks of Christian discipline as an unwitting preparation for present trials. Now they stood her in good stead. If any in Kirkfieldbank should search her face for signs of misery it must be in vain. Even the freckles and darkened colour, caused by mountain wind and light despite her bonnet, were thankfully fading.

It was fruit time in the orchard, with the apples of all sorts well swollen. The voices of Janet Sneddon and the biggest Smith bairns, Jimmie and Nellie, could be heard calling and quarrelling; they were hired this year to help. John was away all Saturday to Tintock End, and brought back the sharpest-tasting honey, though Charlotte refused it and Helen gave him a look and got ready to say her say and Charlotte wished she had eaten it instead.

"Dear Aunt Helen, we will not speak about it any more," she had said already once or twice. Her uncle took her side at last:

"Now, Nell, you have said yourself what's bye is bye, and will no be spoken of within these walls at least. *For it came to pass*, as it says in the Good Book." Which was his oft repeated, venerable joke.

He pulled on his pipe and turned to "out talk," what he had heard or seen on his long road from Stonehouse. The last reaping of grains and straw was now well forward, and all spoke of the fine weather and how it would hold the week.

Indeed all was inned and "rattling dry" before the end of September. Then Harvest Home became the great topic, and Charlotte began to feel that the interest so painful to her must soon be supplanted by caidlech and public happiness.

How thankful she was, that her own family knew so little!

Mother had indeed overcome her reluctance to taking up the pen and had added a note to Tom's letter: "We have had an alarming note from Nellie and do not know what to make of it." Charlotte replied immediately:

My dear Mother, Annie and Tom,

It distresses me very much that you are made the least unhappy by Aunt Helen's letter. I had intended to write to you first myself, and I regret not having done so more quickly.

There is no need to concern yourselves on my behalf, as I am very well, and indeed, had for some time considered whether the position were not unsuited to me. If Aunt Helen has made you think my leaving it is a great misfortune, she has given it more importance than it merits. Now, if I have not the Psalmody to take up my time, I have plenty of other musical employment, with my pupils, and the Band of Hope, and my practising which I have determined not to neglect. And Willie continuing at home I am earnestly thankful for any leisure hours at my disposal to care for him.

I have been invited to revive the "Hope of Kirkfieldbank" band, which has fallen, despite its name, into a very hopeless state of neglect! It will be quite like old times. Annie and Tom, I will depend on you to supply me with whatever is new in the way of suitable music. The IOGT in Lanark are most willing to assist me and much activity will be carrying on "up the Brae" together with them.

She was thankful most of all that she could speak to Willie before her aunt did.

When the Managers' minute was delivered she was alone with him in the house. After a time she had gone upstairs, and brought the lamp close to the bed.

"I wish to read this to you, Willie, and if you have anything to ask me you must do so. Then I do not want to speak of it again."

"You've been greeting," he had said questioningly, taking it from her.

"I have got over it." Then unfortunately having to go out on the landing and into Maddie's bare room, and stand still and once more get the better.

Willie had nothing much to ask. "They are all a mad crowd in a village kirk anyhow," was his best comfort.

She would have told him the cause had he asked.

"I take it you've displeased the auld men," he had said, and she nodded. "Well, dinnae greet, you're well out of it. Be thankful you're no to be sat six Sabbaths in the front pew for fornication like a poor lassie with short apron-strings. That's what they do at the U P."

"Oh, Willie!"

But he would have heard more since then, up the village.

One day she thought he had gone into her sitting-room in her absence.

"Margaret, has Willie been downstairs the day?"

"I believe he walked down into the kitchen."

It was but an idea, the smallest trace of the smell of him, so slight she could not again retrieve it or be certain she had detected it at all. Though she bent over her chair, and her escritoire, and even went out to the lobby and came in again. The room seemed fresh now, and the letters in the back of the drawer were securely tied.

It was in her brown stuff dress, perhaps, the one she had made a hack of and wore when she nursed him. She had aired and aired it, and was forever changing and boiling the collar and cuffs. Now she held the skirt to her face cautiously. It ought to be picked apart and laundered. In the end, she cut up the picked pieces for rags and boiled them till the colour went out of them.

She took to exchanging her books on a Tuesday when she might intercept a letter from Drew. She asked again for *Kenilworth*. Mrs.

Simpson remarked that "Miss Spears was a great reader the now. But then, you'll have more time than before I expect."

Charlotte had not replied to Mr. Thomson's last letter, and for two weeks now she had not heard from him.

There was a hard, sudden frost. The potato shaws were turned black overnight and the dahlia and the last nasturtiums were over-thrown. Why should he write again when she did not reply? But she dared not!

One evening, when she had settled herself as usual in Willie's chair to open the Bible, he sent her away. From then on he refused to hear evening prayers.

"I'm past all that, go away down and read to yourself, there's a chance for you to repent for all your flyting." His head turning restless from side to side on the pillow.

Later, having read and prayed alone, she closed the Bible and placed it back on the kitchen dresser, and stood herself straight.

"I must go up again and settle him. Oh, may he not say more!"

Mounting the stair very steady with the basin against her stays and the lamp clutched by two fingers at its brim. Taking a deep breath before she entered. Placing lamp and basin on the table, kneeling to mend the fire, not looking at him at once. His voice startling her, not sharp but almost gentle.

"While you're about it you can turn my pillows, there's a great heat coming out of them."

She came and did so; indeed, they were very hot, the linen direct-ly underneath his head drenched, his hair soaked and stringy against his brow. The foetor stronger. Sometimes she thought it would be with her for ever, even when.

A rush of remorse overcame her.

"Oh, Willie—" and she laid her hand over his.

But he pulled away. "You're no to take it all so hard, Chattie. You rant up, and you rant down, and nothing's the better for all that. Attend your own worries, you've enough of them. Just put my gear there and I'll see to myself."

A crash before she was past the landing. The basin gone over, Willie off the bed and leaning against the sliding bedclothes. His head was half hid by his sleeve and outstretched arm, like a penitent.

He had bled from the nose. Lifting him, she saw fresh blood spattered on his collar. It was the first time she was to lift him entirely, though she had so often moved him about washing him or applying the fomentations. She was surprised by a sense of the completeness of him, that this was all there was.

Now she sat for a moment with him resting against her, on the side of the bed. The sourish odour of his fever. His breath harsher and quicker than her own, a-gallop against her shoulder.

"D'you mind auld Robbie while you're nursing me, then? It's no a great comfort to me to think of the way he went, for all your care."

He was indeed worse. Dr. Gray was called in, and said that though his lungs were no further affected he was suffering from congestion of the spine, a progression of the sciatica, perhaps irreversible. The pain was extreme, but the medicine brought him some relief. Charlotte must give him his dose. He was impatient and, she had to admit, more than a wee bit unreasonable.

She did not tell her aunt and uncle how difficult he was become about the powders, and the corked case-bottle they must be added into—how agitated he was about the five minims. Turning her back, counting silently to fifty because her hand shook. Willie, in pain, would not believe the measure was correct, and how could she reassure him? Each night she prayed for patience, for them both but most for Willie, and that the Lord would not chastise him so.

Dr. Gray in the lobby said that Willie also suffered what might be termed an Excitation of the mind. He ought not to read or study, though the Bible or some tranquil verses of a hymn might be read aloud.

But Charlotte believed it was his bad dreams, for he was always worse when he wakened in the night. And sometimes nothing would calm him but to turn up the lamp and bring him across to his chair, and allow him a book:

"Give me *Theory and Practice*, no, *Bristowe's*, the other one, and then get away."

But before she could fall asleep he would be rapping, to be helped back into his bed.

At last Drew wrote to her again. First of the music: she must tell him how she was getting on, "in as much detail as you please, for that is next best to hearing you play." And again begging her to forgive him. He mentioned a coming soirée in Lanark and she understood that he desired to meet her there. Alas, how could she do so?

CHAPTER 20

*In which Willie submits to the Barilla Ash Cure,
and Charlotte is crossed in love.*

Charlotte began the Andantino, unable to prevent a few tears at the thought of Mr. Park's "murdering" it, of how she had laughed. "I cannot bear that pure wind, that pure Day, to have been spoiled!" One of Drew's sentences she must mind and cherish, though she had forbidden herself to reread his letters.

The pace began slow and unbroken, a rocking barcarolle. As she learned it her heart must open, and the tenderness she wished otherwise to repress must flood her heart. The octaves gave her no trouble, and there was no real difficulty till into the second page. From here on no Park could have followed her! But she was determined and attacked it with spirit, as if the mastering of it would somehow eat up the residue of her pain. It demanded indeed all her technical skill, becoming fiercer and faster, great crashing ugly chords—then stopped suddenly as if in fright. "How can one possibly go on after this?" it seemed to ask. Yet it did go on, with no unifying tempo that Charlotte could discern, through disagreeable starts and halts, finally to repeat the first theme, with stammering variations, and resolve it in tempo at last. When Charlotte came through into the last bars her sensation was as if emerging into light.

Willie's fevers had set in, a bout of them that lasted through October. Sometimes he would get downstairs or even out and about in the forenoon, the nervous pain easing or the medicine holding it at bay. But each afternoon would end in misery. And he would not let Charlotte cheer him. Almost, he seemed determined to be as wretched as possible. Poor Willie!

She considered again the Barilla Cure. There lay the parcel from toun unopened in its pigeon-hole in the kitchen dresser. Ought it not to be tried? Being but soap it could never harm him, and Tom's and Mr. Sprite's testimonials, to say nothing of those in the *Papers on Health*, must encourage, couched as they were in Christian terms of charity and relief from suffering!

She put on an extra bed apron and unwrapped the brown paper. It contained of a rough block of soap, dark gray in colour and waxy-looking even while dry. One surface bore the imprint *"BARILLA ASH."* She reread the instructions, then made up a large, cold lather in the basin, beating vigorously with the spurtle. The lather was itself a disagreeable grayish-brown.

Then up she went with the basinful balanced on a pile of folded towels, a sponge and a wee corked bottle of Helen's apple vinegar in one apron pocket and the *Papers on Health*, to give her courage, in the other.

It was that time of day, about two o'clock, when Willie's first chills came over him. He had pulled himself together into the smallest space under the quilts. He was, she supposed, hanging on to himself in order not to tremble, and again she had that idea of the completeness of his body, as when she had lifted it. He was not exactly shivering, but would start now and then quite violently. His face hidden, pressed down almost between his knees, his arms, when she drew back the sheets a little, knotted around them. She tucked him in tighter about his head and heaped on the travelling plaid from his chair. She stabbed at the fire.

He was whispering for his medicines, and got himself up on his elbow and took them, but immediately retched, Charlotte holding the clean chantie close to the bedside as he leaned over though he brought up only a greenish string, scarcely any more than ordinary sputum.

"It's no good, that, is it? It's no good." Lying back, squinting, his eyes shut.

"Are you in pain now behind your eyes, Willie?"

"Aye, and the bad taste coming on."

His face looked pinched, his eyebrows drawn together and lifted in a kind of odd, frightened frown. Such an anxious look!

"Are you feared of anything, Willie? Mind it's but the fever and you'll feel better when it's bye—" gently.

"It's my head racing. It willnae be quiet."

She said then, that she would rub his head "according to the instructions in the *Papers on Health*, for I have learned them," but when she reached out he struck away her hand.

"I'll no be interfered with!" Then, opening his eyes as into sharp light, and making a kind of fearful smile, "You do try, Chattie, but I'll best get quit of it on my own. Let me be, you'll have that less to fash about."

"Willie, it's no trouble, we do so much want you well. Tom says, and Mr. Sprite—"

"Oh aye, it's grand with the apothecaries, how they know all the cures better than the doctors. I should have taken my indentures with Tom and I wouldnae be lying here on my back for stubbornly attending the university—"

She stood up, made herself smile. "You're no so ill you cannae make a joke of it."

He turned his head away. "Close the blinds, Chattie, take the lamp and go away down. Now I've hurt your feelings about auld Tom, go away down and play yourself a soothing tune and forget me a wee."

But she had hardly got into the Andantino before he rapped with the staff and when she ran up he was already wet with the fever.

Charlotte was determined.

"Now Willie," tying the extra apron on, "You must let me try the Cure, if just to please Tom!" He did not answer.

The stuff in the basin had congealed and looked like jellied lamb broth, dismal gray and blackish around the brim. She plunged in her hands and stirred as hard as she could.

> *A fine lather to be spread over the pit of the stomach. The soap to be washed off with a gentle sponge dipped in vinegar, under the clothes. The soaping, and sponging, to be repeated every hour until there is no longer any fever.*

He started as her cool hand, gloved in sapple, reached his belly under the bedclothes, and shivered so much that she could not have made an "even spread" of it. How long ought one to rub? She withdrew her hand and wiped it on a towel. The soap had a tarry, summery scent, strong but not unpleasant. She soaked the sponge in the vinegar and again lifted the sheet, wiped his invisible slippery skin. It was burning to the touch. How she willed it cool!

The soap and vinegar had wet his sheets. She tucked in a towel, dried him, then recommenced. Willie lay now as if resolved to endure it, his face in the shadows, when she glanced up, with closed eyes and tight mouth.

"*A word of Christian truth to give rest to the soul.*" But Charlotte could not think of a word. The pit of the stomach—would that be around about the navel in its wee pit—or, she thought uneasily, from there and downward? The side of her thumb encountered a twist of wiry hair, quickly withdrawing. Something about Robert—pushing that thought aside. A word of Christian truth! Willie had now covered his face with his sleeves.

The cure *to be repeated every hour.*

"I'm to do this hourly, Willie, the soaping and then sponging with a bit of vinegar, and it will bring away the fever." She paused, standing up. "You neednae think about it, just to rest, and we'll just see." He gave a kind of a cough or snort behind his sleeve.

Charlotte was faithful hour by hour, though she taught a lesson between five and six and prepared his supper between six and seven. He would not eat. She ate her portion at his fire, looking deep into the eisels, her eyes drooping for a moment, the smell of the soap heavy and smoky in the room and the fever-smell lurking behind.

Soaping him was easier now for he had thrown off the quilts, and by drawing the sheets up to cover his limbs, she could lather his exposed skin, working gently in her own shadow. His belly was dark yellow in the gloom, the sapple she spread over it almost black. Soap-smell alternating with the sharp scour of the vinegar which she drew gladly into her nostrils. When he seemed unbearably hot she wrung out a cold towel and pressed it against his brow.

Were the hours less long tonight than when she had performed no more than this one task, and turned his pillows?

Down in the kitchen, changing her soaked apron for a dry one, looking hurriedly through the New Testament for a word of Christian truth. "*Behold I am with you always, even unto the ends of the world.*" Which seemed rather desperate, though it was what came to mind.

His fever abated and he took a large draught of barley-water. The night was far advanced; it was almost four o'clock. She had not undressed though she had eased her stays and left off her soaking cuffs. The front of her gown through both aprons, even her underdress, were wet where she had bent over him. She gave him dry sheets, a dry nightshirt, covered him. He was already asleep.

Downstairs, she washed out the basin and scalded it, and put the *Papers on Health* and other items carefully in the dresser. She undid the back lock for Margaret before she went to bed, looked quickly out into the darkness of the garden. Rain fell, the air so black she could not discern even the nearest trees.

"A word of Christian truth to give rest to the soul as the cooling of the night fever has given rest to the suffering body." His belly darkish and knotted under her hands. Now her weary hands lay prone at her sides. She moved them, felt into her own belly, so much softer in its texture, the deeps of its flesh! He ought to be purged. How much would he submit to? Had the fever abated sooner than otherwise, had he suffered any less? "Dear Saviour, may he recover! yet not my will but Thine be done." She fell into a heavy sleep, without time even to turn to her side, and woke with a cough, sitting up, the curious dream a vanishing skirl of voices.

She had been moving her hand over a globe or a map, but the mountains on it were sharp bumps, with the rivers and seas and their names indented, and slippery. "These are the Bavarian Alps. This is the Aegean Sea. This is the Bosporus." She was not to touch Africa:

"You must not touch Africa. It is heathen," a voice had said.

Here was Margaret with the coals.

The next day she would begin with the relieving of his headache, for, as a precursor of the fever, its cure would perhaps affect the fever as well. It required *"but the kind helper to do a very little work in the way of rubbing and cooling the head."*

"Willie, if the headache comes on you'll tell me, for I want to try the other cure, it concerns the moving along of the blood." Surely Willie's headaches were of the sort described: *"marked by an extra degree of heat in the brow, and an anxious uneasy state of the whole mind…."*

"Oh aye, if you'll no blether all the time you may try what you like."

Which was enough for Charlotte, though of course she did not wish the headache on him. But she had the clean towels ready should it come.

The instructions were to stand behind the sufferer, his head to be leaning against the breast. Willie's horsehair chair prevented such intimacy, and Charlotte behind him was able fairly comfortably to move her hands across his brow and scalp in the directions prescribed, upward, back, then inward pressing together, then upward again. Willie however broke it off:

"It may ease the head but it gives a terrible crick in the neck."

Charlotte was sorry, and went on to the four-folded towel wrung out in cold water, *to be rolled half around the head and pressed gently all over, followed by gentle, rubbing friction on the back of the head, which would draw the action of the blood away from the forehead.* She then must rub his head all over the crown with her fingers in among the roots of his hair. The cure stated that *"a great change"* would occur within ten to fifteen minutes, *"the heart released of its load, and all the pain gone."*

After half an hour she lifted off the towel and helped him into bed. His only comment was that she had "managed to spread it about a great deal" which to Charlotte must seem a kind of progress; she kept her hand on his brow as he lay, willing with all her heart coolness and quiet upon him.

Already perspiration was gathering beneath her fingers. She wrung the towel again, and pressed it down, his face in the near-darkness clenched and the strange, fearful look returned again between his eyes.

"Dinnae fash, Chattie, it will go over in the fever. I do believe you're sorrier than I am myself."

That evening and for the rest of the week she read all the stories from Jesus' healing ministry; but she read them alone. Still Willie refused evening prayers. He continued as sick as ever, the headache then the fever coming on every morning, and no food would do. He spoke, but not rationally. In the forenoon he brooded over his books.

He could not be persuaded to come down, though she thought with her help he could have done so.

But one morning he himself asked her, as she was wiping his brow, if he might remain in bed, and if she would rub his head again "properly."

Charlotte was gratified. "You're to sit up, then, for the helper must get in behind you. I'll away after the towels."

She stood the basin on the table and shut the blinds. Willie had seated himself, rather crouched over, on the near side of the bed, with his bare yellow feet on the carpet. She got his list slippers on him and the plaid round him, and surveyed him doubtfully.

"I'm no sure you should sit there, for it says the helper is to stand behind you—I believe I must kneel on the bed, if you cannae go farther across." She walked about the foot of the bed and then, bunching up her skirts, got on it and knelt behind him.

"Have you ever tried anything like this with anyone else then? For it seems very queer to me."

Was he referring to Robert? Charlotte as always fearful that he should name him. But he did not.

"Willie, it is quite the same as in the chair, but without the crick in the neck." She took his head between her hands.

> *Place your hand first on the brow as you stand behind the person who is suffering, and let the head press against your breast, as you press that hand upward so it rubs up over the forehead.*

"Now what?" said Willie.

Charlotte felt a sudden, unreasonable urge to laugh, and had to think hard of her prayers and his poor head swollen with blood. Her knees would sink forward into the floss! Vigorously she placed, pressed, rubbed upward. His head, as she knelt so awkwardly, leaning against her bodice, smelled heavily of his sickness and the pomade he used. "*Follow with the other hand. Very slowly and deliberately.*" *Upward*, she thought as hard as she could. *Drawing away the venous blood*. Willie sniffed loudly. His bony fingers emerging from the plaid he was wrapped in, plucking at the fringe.

"*Then with the hands on each side of the head in front of the ears and temples, press the sides of the forehead together."* Charlotte doing so, over and over.

It was something like stroking Jackie. Willie must have thought the same for he said, "Am I to purr then?"

"Your head is over-warm—the object is to cool it, to draw away the blood."

One knee was quite uncomfortable. The instructions gave no details on how a lady ought to stand, or in this case kneel, behind a gentleman. She felt again his singularity, that he was enclosed by edges. The heat of his head against her bodice.

The headache would be sure to come on by late morning. She would give him his tea and his medicine early, in the hope he would keep them down. The pain made him antipathetic to light, so her ministrations even by day must be conducted in semi-darkness.

In the end she found it best to stand, and the piano stool, carried upstairs and twirled to its highest, was just right. Here Willie would seat himself, all wrapped in the plaids, turned so as to gaze away past the bed into the darkest part of the room.

The lamp was hid by the screen. The firelight flickered, and threads of the day's pallor lined the windows. Charlotte's white hand on his brow, that first pressed his head back against her. They did not speak.

She would finish off with the cold towelling, breaking the silence to step back with a little sigh. She dared not ask him whether the cure had helped. When the sweats came on, he allowed her to "do" the pit of his stomach, and if she were not interrupted by a the Band of Hope meeting or a lesson she tended him hour by hour.

On the weekends they fell into the old routines. Helen was full of fierce energy and liked to do a real boiler wash, and get his linen dry before the Sabbath, the kitchen a haze of steam and a tangle of hanging sheets, the flagstones skiddery. She took over the meals as well, though Charlotte liked to have prepared the meat dish beforehand. Neither Charlotte nor Willie mentioned his refusal of evening worship, and they gathered about the bed while John read the scriptures and said the usual prayers.

November brought Lanark Old Term. The country labourers would be thronging the town for three or four days, wearing their half-year's wages in the cloth shops, humphing their bulky bundles filled with bargains, and looking out for a new place. Helen talked again of hiring a domestic, a "good, stout, steady lass." Charlotte had heard this before and was too busy to take much notice.

She was preparing for her first Annual IOGT soirée,[39] to be held in the Hall. With plenty of advice from the Lanark Lodge, Mr. Munn with the mulberry stain coming down twice with pencil and note book, making her understand that the programme would be in his charge. Her Juvenile Lodge was to give the musical entertainment, however, and she was satisfied at last that they would not disappoint her.

In writing to her family she had not overstated the condition of the "Hope of Kirkfieldbank" when she took them on! The sheep-like Misses Paul had been leading it. Even though the promise of baps and cocoa must aye tempt the poorest, there was much charitable competition regarding their ingestion of such foods! And the sisters were timid and "teedisome," quite unsuited to the charge of children. Attendance had been low, with no Junior Pledges having been signed for more than a year. The singing was dismal, the music sheets torn or misplaced. Indeed Miss Janet Paul had not assisted for many months beyond the tying of her sister's bonnet strings and sending her off on a Friday evening: her chest could not suffer the night air.

They were both then happy to resign the leadership. And if doing so required the closing of one eye to Miss Spears' recent Misconduct— not having climbed the mountain, they had unfortunately missed witnessing it at First Hand—relief overcame their scruples.

Charlotte brought with her into the Lodge a good flock or new and back-sliding Members, and the juvenile choir progressed merrily. Mr. Munn supplied Band of Hope song-books with very little "jeelie" on them and covers reasonably intact, and they contained of many a rousing song. With the campaign pursuing in Egypt, battle-hymns were in great demand by the laddies, who sang lustily and waved invisible flags for the chorus—and would have waved throughout, had she let them.

See the mighty host advancing,
  Satan leading on;
Mighty men are round us falling;
  Courage almost gone!

"Hold the fort, for I am coming,"
  Jesus signals still; ("Flags!")
Wave the answer back to Heaven,
  "By Thy grace we will."

Fierce and long the battle rages,
  But our help is near;
Onward comes our great Commander,
  Cheer, my comr.ades, cheer! ("Hurrah!")

She walked homeward after the soirée beside Roddy Munro. A circle of pale light from his bull's-eye lantern wobbled in the road, and some ragged laddies got in ahead of them, daring each other to step on it. She was very pleased with the reception of the music, and of herself, and she thought Roddy must be pleased as well. He walked somewhat hen-toed, she had noticed in their perambulations. And though never playful, tonight he was turning his lantern from side to side, and she had to smile at the laddies, scuffling and chasing before him to stamp out the will-o-the-wisp.

"Be off now ben," he said finally, and they scattered. These were the bairns the Band of Hope literature was full of—"waifs" from drunken homes in toun. Though whether better off as boarders at miner McConville's, she could not be certain. Peter, James and John. If their stomachs were full of baps, their coats and boots were desperate! Peter and Jock Duffy had each other at least. "*Water for me!*" they had hollered happily with the rest. "*Water, pure water, it's wa-ter for me!*"

Helen did not engage a servant.

"I hope I have done right. You were looking very crushed, lately, my dear, which is not to be wondered at, but I declare there's more spring in your step than there was, and if you really would rather not. It's grand how well the soirée went." Uncle and aunt then conferred, and John approached gently with a further eight shillings to her allowance.

"Take it now, Chattie," he said when she refused. Patting her hand. "It's all to swell your Shilling Savings Bank. You're worth your weight in gold, we've said often enough."

She said she would accept it only while Willie was not well. Doing without an indoor servant was no sacrifice. Indeed, in her present mood she much preferred hard work and the house to herself. As for Willie, only she ought to have the care of him.

She did not give him the Barilla Cure on the weekends when her aunt and uncle were home. Though she mentioned to Helen that she was applying the soap for his fevers and hoped it was useful.

"You must write about it all to Tom, Chattie, as he was so good as to send it and the wee books, and say thank you from Willie for the kindness. Oh, it's grand to see Tom stepping into his place so well as head of the family, for with Matthew and Robert living he couldnae have thought. He was aye a plodder, Tom, but the race isnae aye to the swift—I've a wee idea whether he'll no marry now. Do you mind how he spoke of his friend in his last letter—that he is to be his Best Man? And there's never a Best Man doesnae take it into his head to go the same road."

Again, Mr. Lambeth's celebrated Choir was to perform in Lanark.[40]

"I declare, my dear, it is a full year gone by since they were here before!" Laying down the *Advertiser* in her lap. "It seems but yesterday, and so much has happened."

So much indeed, thought Charlotte.

The family would stay over Monday, her aunt Tuesday as well if Charlotte would like. On Monday the Westport E U were holding a large soirée with several visiting speakers. And the Tuesday night was the Concert, which Charlotte solemnly dwelt upon in her heart.

"Will you go, dear?"

No special letter of invitation, no private encouragement from a female Member had come for her, this year! Charlotte was sure they had heard of her disgrace. The Select as well! She would have been thoroughly discussed, Mrs. Isabel Miller quietly triumphant, the Syle-Patons hardly bothering to conceal their delight. Never more could a letter from Mr. Miller, praising her character and her spirit or calling her "my dear," be expected. He would now decide that he had misjudged her, and another ardent young pupil perhaps was taking her place in piano duets "for four hands" where one's arms crossed so awkwardly. His little murmurs of apology when his fingers slid across a cuff, touched by chance a rounded wrist emerged from its lace border!

A letter arrived with the first post Saturday, handed into the house by Mr. Simpson with Helen getting into the lobby very smartly after Charlotte and surely wondering. At supper:

"You will have heard from your auld Choir then? For as I said I will gladly stay over so you can go up the Brae and hear them."

Charlotte was able to say truthfully that it was indeed a reminder about the Concert. "I have not yet decided."

"I cannot decide!" she thought.

> Again I would beg of you, a word with you if but to enquire about the Sonata:—and to know, to see for myself that you are well. I hear nothing from Kirkfieldbank.

Then:

> You must not absent yourself on my behalf. I would not lose you the Concert. If you do not wish *at this time* to meet me, send but a word and I will not go.

If she did not write to prevent him he would meet her there!

She ought to write at once, but put it off, in the bustle to get away to the Westport. Willie assured by Helen that Roddy Munro was just down in the kitchen, having offered to sit in "except for his rounds, that do nae take but two times ten minutes." Willie receiving this silently from Helen but saying afterwards to Charlotte:

"Am I in gaol then? I hope you enjoy yourselves. You can tell the constable I'll knock his helmet off if he comes up stairs."

She might still choose to stay home tomorrow, Charlotte reminded herself, walking up the Brae with her uncle and aunt, as if rehearsing the steps she would or would not take.

It was a rainless night with the little gathered Kirk thronged.

Precentor McLellan was a meek gentleman with sparse, macassared hair. His performances, if mentioned in the *Advertiser* at all, were given out as "creditable." He came up to Charlotte a little breathless to ask her to assist at the harmonium: "I would be honoured." Perhaps, with his scared look, he was rushing in to do battle, fearful she intended to oust him!

With a Programme marked, and the sheets in proper order on the stand, Charlotte found no difficulty. He conducted in the meantime, turning to give her a stiff nod at the start of each piece, a misplaced lock of hair, like a frayed string, a-wagging at his collar.[41]

The soirée wore on, with the reverend gentlemen almost in competition as to who should speak longest. The last was Mr. McAdam of Carluke, gripping the pulpit fiercely, carrying on in the thickest Aberdeenshire she had ever heard about "Conviction and Consec-rr-ation Viewed in a Rr-eligious Licht." John saying at the end, over the substantial tea, that he had taken the Programme to read "*viewed* in the *lime light.*" Which Charlotte agreed would have been a deal more interesting. None of the lectures was illustrated.

She had not written. She went to the Concert. Had she meant to do so all along? To stay away would cause her friend more pain, perhaps, than she now must face herself. Her night had been nearly sleepless. She had thought herself over the worst, and in the curing of her wounded pride she was. Sadly, pride was the lesser part.

She walked along Clydesdale Brae beside the river, and though there were many on the road she had the path to herself. The sky was overcast, but a light frost made the ground palely visible. She scarcely knew whether the agitation she felt were fear or eagerness. She would not think of him, of anything. She struck upwards behind Clydesholm Green Farm. Then—it was not even a thought! that he would bring her back down Jecker's Johnnie, in the dense narrow darkness between stone dyke and hedges!

It never occurred to her she might be unable to speak to him. At the pause she had gone into the lobby, where many who had risen from their hard chairs were milling around, exclaiming about the delightful

Concert, looking into their programmes—or better, into those of their neighbours. No one accosted Charlotte. The Choir of course sequestered till the recessional, in the room beyond the great IOGT banner at the front. She bent her head over her programme, and then a hand took it from her—his! She knew him immediately, his hand, how he would be standing, just over her own height, even his look, had she dared to lift her eyes!

Then, she thought afterwards, they might have exchanged some sign quickly spoken, some understanding about a meeting after the break-up. His fingers resting in her gloved palm! But two young ladies had pushed their way forward and were attacking him:

"Come, Drew, we have arranged it so that now you may sit by us, we have got the disagreeable Mr. MacDonald moved into the aisle." The girl who had spoken giving Charlotte a frank, careless look before she turned away.

"Oh, Louise—I will come in a moment." But her hands were already twined around his arm and he was borne off as he spoke.

Then Charlotte could see them in their row at the far side, and was sure the lady and gentleman must be the Parks, and the well-grown girl, she thought with relief, their biggest daughter whose bed she had expected to share.

He would be riding; he would be able to escape them!

But it did not turn out so. Perhaps he had looked towards her during more than one loud chorus, but only once or twice at the same moment she looked towards him, and they were too far apart to read each other's faces.

It was she who was prevented, seated nearer the back and brought away precipitously by the crowd. And she had hurried out, slowed only to shake the languid hands of those old friends she could not avoid, and before she need respond to any kind enquiries, or invitations to forgather at the Hotel.

And in the street unable to find him! Unable even to gaze about! He was caught farther back. Already a lad had got the side gate open and the horses were leading out of the stable yard. Shouts, laughter, confusion. She was handed into a carriage before she knew it, at Annville gate before she could find her voice, forced then to thank Mr. Stein and his wife and mother, her benefactors, for what they considered a very charitable turn, carrying off "poor Miss Spears" so she need not walk down the Brae!

She would not go in, she must hurry back, for surely Drew was looking about for her! But the Brae road would already be filled with pedestrian traffic returning, and he knew not the Clydesdale path. Even there, in Jecker's Johnnie, pairs of happier lovers might already be strolling!

And Helen had heard the carriage.

"Come in, dearie, come in! I couldnae mistake the equipage, such superior riding lamps! I said to myself, if the Steins o' Kirkfield will give her a hurl, who's to dare turn up their nose at dear Chattie any more!"

Annville, December second, 1882

Dear friend,

May I tell you at least, the progress of the Sonata, which I assure you is giving me much pleasure, as well as being very demanding, as I had expected. Now I have learned the First Movement. I would dearly like some guidance from one who has either played it or, as you have done, heard it carefully. I do not believe I have it up to Tempo. But I have been going on with the Andantino, and here it begins very deceivingly, and I cannot think Mr. Park enjoyed spelling through more than the first page?

The 3/8 theme continues perhaps with a degree of tenderness, which gives rise to a painful sensation. But the degree of technical difficulty sets me indeed upon my mark! You described the questioning and affirmation of the First Movement. Here in the Second I have found, first, loud affirmation, loud noises at any rate, *then* questioning. Do you recall the passage? You described in your letter a point where the music would stop as if one had "lost the place." It is very modern, with staccato chords like exclamation points. The whole section is quite fierce, but I like very much to attack it, for afterwards it comes through into a most tranquil closure. Then perhaps I sit still for a few moments, and I believe I have some grasp of the whole of it, if not of the First Movement. I hope you will tell me what you think.

The other night, I was handed into the Kirkfield House coach, rather like Rashin' Coatie and could not do anything about it, but was got home before it turned into a Pumpkin! I am indeed very sorry we were unable to speak. I believe you were sitting with some of the Parks family?
> Your friend,
> Charlotte Spears

December came in with hard frost and stormy wind, and the 5th dawned in a heavy fall that settled over the hard ground with no lessening of the cold, though the wind abated. The snow continued.

With Helen and John gone back to King-street Charlotte had resumed the Cure, and that evening came in to Willie's room as usual carrying the barilla-basin. To and fro she had stirred it, to and fro, "with a slow uneasy motion" or so it seemed, till she must give herself a wee shake.

Roddy Munro having just taken himself off, wrapped in a great-coat over his uniform. "The laddies are walking on Clyde below the brig and it's no safe. They cannae see the ice for the snow and it's bound to be thin over by the Elephant Hole, and at Mouse mouth as well."

Willie rapped then and he'd looked upwards. "You're wanted, I'll be away down. I've chased them off once already. I'll let myself out the back door, and see there's none have taken a soaking."

It was already pitch dark with the snow still falling and the wind getting up.

The first thing Willie said when she came in was: "You can take that muck away."

"But, Willie—"

"No more silly sapple. I can't bear the reek." His face very white except for his cheeks, flushed over the bone.

Charlotte set the basin at the stairhead.

"Are you no well enough to come down to the kitchen, Willie? We can eat our supper together at the range, and be warm and comfortable." She poked his fire.

"Roddy Munro's away down the garden," she went on, "to scare the laddies off the ice, they're walking straight over Clyde he says and it's no safe."

In the silence the coals settling with the scratch of the poker.

"You neednae think I'm amused by hearing all that. I'm no here at all except that I must be, I'd be far away the night if I could."

A silence again. "Come down, Willie, do, it will make a wee change and we can say our prayers by the fire." She could hear by his voice he was well enough if he would.

"Oh aye, and I can curl up in the box bed when I cannae get up again. Bring me the writing case and the lamp, and my *Bristowe's* if you please."

Later when she came to settle him, his face turned away from the light, and from her.

"If you'll sit up a wee, Willie, I'll rub your head. I can see you're in pain."

"Leave my note book alone if you please," whispering. As if he'd heard her closing it. Charlotte laying it open again on the night-table, along with the heavy *Anatomy* that had been half-sunk in a fold of the quilt.

She helped to lift him, leaning across the top of the bed, and drew his head back against her. "You're over-hot already."

Her right hand competent now against his brow, then her left that pressed the skin up and back, the wet fringe of dark, straight hair. The bedspread in the lamplight, its tufted pattern rippled with inky shadows, the floor beyond it a black pit. The windows invisible, the fire flaring as it caught a downward draught and the inside of the chimney suddenly reddening like dirty, ravelled wool.

Willie said, "You may think it's only at Annville I have had the pleasure of lying in a woman's breast."

Her hand stopped, then firmly resuming.

"I can assure you it's no a novelty. And they'd no be so wrapped up either, the ladies I am referring to, with stiff aprons and such."

His head pressed more heavily. His pomade, which had reminded Charlotte of Mr. Lambeth's choir and the lobby of the Athenaeum, mixed with the smell of his sickness, almost a taste in her mouth.

"But I do nae care, if only it gives you pleasure. You're no to grieve forever Chattie, if you've loved and lost. I'm all for innocent pleasure."

Charlotte stood up carefully, wrung out the towel, laid it again across his forehead. She would not break off the steps of the cure whatever he said, her fingers deftly moving into his nape, into the roots of his hair. Her throat ached. When she laid him back, he raised a hand to touch her arm. He was perhaps looking at her, but she would not look back.

"Or is it so innocent, for all that?"

In the kitchen she cried, out of anger, pushing the edge of her under apron, where it did not taste of him, against her mouth.

Calm again she prepared the tray, bringing her own supper upstairs as well, and ate silently by the fire while Willie picked over his food. From time to time the wind threw a rattle of snow against the window. He was cooler tonight, not so very bad.

She said in her usual voice, "I saw a lantern down on Clyde and there's folk on the brig as well. I may walk down before I sneck the door, to see if all's right. It'll be the polis keeping the big laddies from going over."

"Will you no come and kiss your cousin and say all's mended?"

She must remind herself he was in a state of Excitation.

"I will bring you your medicine."

"I can manage that myself, come, don't be angry with me, Chattie. I've only said those things to comfort you."

"I am not angry one bit. I am going down to evening worship. You are quite well enough to join me, I know, if you wish."

In the forenoon she met him coming out the back door as she hurried up from the caivie. Two wee gray eggs in her apron, her apron dull white against the luminous snow. It snowed still. Her boots trod between thick feathery wreaths.

Willie had his boots and coat on and had wound a plaid over his ears and shoulders. His face in daylight ill-looking and yellowish.

"I've a mind to go down and see for myself."

When he came in he sat close to the grate and loosened the plaid. He was already shaven. She spooned him a dish of brose and he ate well, asking afterwards for coffee.

"I walked out on Clyde. There was a wee path going over, but no great holes so there's been no disasters." He coughed.

"No, last night it was but Roddy making his rounds, and talking to Jimmie Henderson on the brig."

"You're on great terms with the village lads, who is that chield then? Be canny you do nae take another tumble, with your Roddy's and Jimmies and all!"

She made herself answer mildly.

"He is about fourteen years old. He's employed at the forge, and lives across at Mouse Mill."

She gave Willie his coffee and took some herself, which was rare—it had such a brown, mineral taste. She was sure she never could learn to like it. She had slept badly and now she heard him as if from a distance. He looked shrivelled in the great chair, the plaid pulled around him like an old woman. Perhaps he would sit there all day, making such remarks as his Excitation suggested to him. Well, she had the bread van to meet, and then lessons to prepare and her practising. She could fetch him down his books. She was about to speak.

"Chattie, I'm not well."

Before she could jump up he had fallen forward. She was alone with him! He must be got into the box bed till she could have him moved. She knelt on the flags, gasping, supporting him half upright, staring about. The box bed would be damp, had not been touched or aired since spring. Above him, the fringe of the plaid dragged on the arm of the chair. Suddenly he vomited the coffee, a lumpy hot gush over her arm.

Later he walked up slowly by himself. The fevers returned but she was relieved he was no worse than usual.

"You've a hard road, Chattie, you'd have done better to fly away when you had the chance. Oh aye, you neednae look so cross. I'm sure I am grateful to you that you wouldnae forsake me. You'll carry on, you did for Robbie like it or no and you'll do for me too, though I'm far less patient than he was. Oh aye, there's no help for it."

When he said such things, especially when he said Robbie for Robert, she went out of the room in silence. "I will not answer him, he is not himself." Counting to fifty on the stair before she would go in again, then pleasantly, as if she were in the midst of something. She took to leaving invented tasks at the stairhead—her workbox, a duster for the venetians, music to be learned. A brush and carbolic she could take to the woodwork: a little daily effort here and there against the smell. He would not have prayers, though she still carried the Bible up every evening. *"Behold, I stand at the door and knock."*

"Why do you go on humphing the Bible up here? I've told you I'm past the good of it." or: "Robbie listened to all the prayers in the world and where did it get him?"

Charlotte answering as mildly as she could. "We know where he is, Willie."

"Well, it wasnae for the prayers, I can guarantee you."

Every evening he was agitated again, wanting a rub and a sapple and saying foolish things, which she was determined not to hear. She applied the cool towels and did not answer, or said very steadily she was too busy to do more. "It is the Excitation of his illness, he is not himself."

When he was himself he was contrite: "You'll no object, if I begin to plague you?" She assured him she would not.

But he could as easily send her out sharply: "I'll no have you tripping about with your cheerful smile, when you refuse to be the least bit cheerful to me of an evening."

With the roads blocked there was no letter. And they did not ease until the twenty-second.

CHAPTER 21

In which an understanding is reached; and Charlotte is accused of coddling.

Stone Row, Heywood,
December 4th, 1882

Dear Charlotte,
I have no right to ask anything of you. When I am despondent, I think that your hurrying away can have but one meaning. To meet me after the harm I have caused, must give you pain. I thank you that you came. No more was intended, or to be expected.
Drew

Drew's note did not arrive till Christmas Eve, brought to the door among a handful of Christmas cards. The lad complaining of heavy bundles still to be got out, with extra carriers, from the Post Office in Lanark.[42] Reading it, Charlotte supposed that Drew had not received her letter before today as well. He must write again!

She was unable to spend the Christmas week in Glasgow as she had hoped. Willie was bad and even with the roads eased the weather continued very coarse and the traffic disarranged. Late cards were exchanged, and letters. Annie wrote of the errand-boy bringing in Christmas greens and Charlotte of how Annville need not depend on bought boughs. She had herself gone down through the plowty garden and fetched armsful of natural ivy up from the bottom end, and twined it with red wool to decorate the lamp stands. No holly to be got from the Kirk this year! Instead she used haws for colour, and they hung beautifully among the green, catching the lamp light. Roddy Munro came by on Saturday evening with a another great bunch of haw cuttings from the river braes, some still sheathed in ice. She left them to melt off in the sink and most blackened; in the end she pressed what were left down into the umbrella spill in the lobby, and brought it nearer the door so it looked a gay sight twice over, with the splash of wee red globes reflected in the etched glass.

Madeleine came Christmas Eve, the others to come later and stay over Hogmanay, the shop being then closed.

She told Charlotte when they were alone in the kitchen: "I should not put up with him another minute if he spoke to me like that!" Having heard Willie creating, to have his basin emptied. And gathered up her trimmings quick into the pantry when Charlotte came through. Maddie had been glorifying a hat.

Charlotte scalded and scoured. "Maddie, do come in and sit down, you're no to be angry on my account. Willie is in pain, and we must make allowances."

"I'd never take that from him in pain or no." Her downy arms folded across her clean apron. Her face had got very steep and adult, as if someone had pushed it in, Charlotte thought. She had crimped her dark brown hair and teased a fringe across her brows which were in contrast very straight, like Willie's, and almost met over her nose. She wore a Nottingham lace collar from the shop; for no one cared about real lace any more, she said, it was not modern.

Charlotte sat down. "Of course you must speak out and say aye just what you feel, Maddie, but you will be a dear and not trouble my aunt and uncle? They are grieved enough about him already. And I am quite able to care for him. He is almost never so difficult, unless he is in quite a deal of pain. Dr. Gray says the sciatica is excruciating."

Maddie a bit huffy and saying she was only thinking of her cousin Chattie's good.

"We are very grateful to you I'm sure, and I daresay if you had-nae been here they would have made me nurse him, so you must never think I am angry with you." Kissing her peremptorily and going upstairs to dress for "*New Testament Portraits*" at the Westport E U.

"Is he kind to you, Chattie?" asked Helen. "For he's uncommon grow-ly with me, even, when I sit with him. I've asked John to have a word. You're looking very crushed and I'm feared it's too much for one body, with your teaching duties and the house and all." She paused, gazing at Charlotte affectionately.

"It is my task to be kind to him, not the other way round," Charlotte answered, smiling. "If I can make him comfortable that is my reward."

"But a wee thank you—I've spoken to him about a wee thank you when I came with the tray. I believe however I can explain it, my dear: it's his disappointment! He hasnae got over it, to have given up the University, you see, and he dwells on it."

Charlotte nodded, smiling again into her aunt's eager face. Helen wiped her cheek down which a tear had run, and smiled back. "Aye, it's very puzzling, for the one day he is as right as rain. The Lord is trying his patience. I've a mind to ask John to say a word, however."

"Aunt Helen, not for a thank you! I know Willie is thankful in his heart."

"And what was it he said, so queer, as I was bringing his tray away? 'I am a stuck medical student,' he said, and I said, Why, what's stuck can be unstuck, to cheer him, you ken but he was no having any of that. I wish he would see Dr. Gray!"

Charlotte persuaded her not to trouble her uncle about Willie's behaviour. With his father, Willie was meek and quiet.

"He will think I have complained of him, which I would never do! He is really very forbearing, and it often happens, that I must be in and out just when he would prefer to study or rest. And never once has he complained about the music lessons."

"Nor he should, it's a diversion to him I am sure, to hear some nice singing and playing, when he cannae get out."

Charlotte suspected however that Willie's walks were partly to do with the music, And if he were well wrapped she could not but encourage them. That he admitted to being a "stuck medical student," even for a moment, frightened her. Surely he would not be ill forever! He took up his books! But there was a strangeness in him, a twitchiness or a fidgetiness that she could not excuse by disappointment alone.

"You keep away down in the kitchen and cannae hear me when I want you," he would say.

And sometimes now of an evening when they took their supper together, he'd refer to them as an "auld married couple"—"We've become an auld married couple with nothing to say to each other."

Or: "Take away that silly stool, you can twirl and whirl around in the nice room, at the piano, it's no use to me if you willnae rub my head."

She remained firm. There had been one more try with the cure, Willie asking so meekly for it, to help his burning head; but his mind being quite irritated by the fever, and not being himself at all, he had attempted to embrace her and said words she would prefer not to remember, about how her collar scratched and how soft her breast would feel, if she'd but loosen her garments a wee.

"I am thrang Willie, with the house." She would not excuse herself because of her musical duties. "Roddy Munro would be willing to learn to administer the cure I am sure, if but for respect for Uncle John. He's aye ready to assist the family, and ready to be your friend in particular—he asks after you very kindly." To that Willie had laughed harshly.

"Aye, with you sitting and cracking with him away down in the kitchen all hours, you'll have cured him already too I expect."

At her prayers she forgave Willie.

Dr. Gray looked in from time to time, if he was by, and spoke with Charlotte. But Willie would not see him, and Dr. Gray said he need not trouble to go up, Willie being in the best of hands and doing as satisfactory as could be expected. He was pleased to hear that the chest had cleared: "You must aye be on the look out, however. Are you continuing with the poultices?"

Charlotte, who had not told him about the Barilla cure, said she applied cold towels for the delirium and would prepare poultices as well if he advised.

"They will ease the spine. Do that before the medicine; he's no to depend on opium entirely. You speak of delirium. Is it no rather a general nervous Excitation?"

"In his fevers he speaks deliriously. But he is very often nervous even when he is quite well."

"Aye, it is the Excitation. He must be kept as quiet as possible, and away from his books."

"I think he only turns the pages. He is easier then."

Dr. Gray, who unfortunately was not a Temperance man, advised wine in small amounts and excused himself.

Sighing, she prepared a fomentation, and went up to find Willie seated at the front window, looking out across the road.

"The dafties were having a hey day in the mud. The auld woman's gone after the besom and the auld man's shifting them back into the bothy."

He went on without turning, "Never a dull moment watching the village life. I've been over in the other room and seen a great Clydesdale backed down the ramp to the forge, and then a wagon go over, half way down, that wanted a new wheel. Has the man gone away?"

Charlotte said, "Aye, and he wasnae over-concerned about you at present, and pleased about the chest though I think you ought to have let him listen to it."

"He would have wanted his two shillings if I'd let him near me. I can listen to my own chest, Dr. Alexander Gray."

"He recommended a poultice for your spine. He enquired very kindly for you, Willie."

"More for my soul, I do nae doubt, that's gone a long wandering this last while. I may have left it in toun with my head. Perhaps I should send a post card but I wouldnae ken the direction."

"Will you take this fomentation now it's hot?"

"I would have said no a few minutes back, but aye, the very sight of you holding it forth could bring on the need if nothing else."

He stood up stiffly, the plaid wrapped about him, and got himself into bed, lying on his face and sniffing at the pillow.

She folded the plaid and drew up his bed linen to cover his limbs, and then his night gown, exposing the yellow back, the combing of black hairs.

"I've stirred linseed oil into it to keep the heat—"

"Just get on with it and I'll thank you."

It seemed to soothe him however and he lay easier, his fingers ceased picking at the pillow-casing, his hands at rest each side of his head.

"For all that, you're no a bad wee body, Chattie. Who'd else have put up with me and never a murmur? Maddie threw the basin across the room at Hogmanay, the one time she'd to tend me and she couldnae keep her temper. Mother cleaned it away and said you weren't to know. I'd hardly spoken a word, and I cannae mind now what the word was."

"That is for the best I'm sure."

His eye in profile opened briefly, then closed.

"She's no patience. It's you with your wee white hands." His voice was drowsy though she guessed he was wide awake.

"Give us one more go of it," he murmured and she dipped and replaced the poultice, and he drew back his lips in a wince.

When she was finished she tucked him in. "Can you rest now, Willie? I'll come up with your supper by and bye."

"Have you a lesson?" almost inaudibly.

"Aye, two, Marne Reid and then it's Roddy Munro."

Suddenly and quickly, Willie rolled right over and clasped her, pulling her across him. "You're no wanting to hear that sump singing. Stay here and I'll sing to your bones." His voice hissing, his arm hooked across her throat sharp as a rope.

For a moment she kept very still, then as his arm moved to her shoulder she pulled away and stood up, and quickly arranged her hair. At the door his voice coming after her, with a kind of lost echo in it:

"I'm in here, you ken, but nobody knows."

Charlotte did all she could. She continued the dietary, Annie at her request carefully transcribing sickroom receipts, or anything in the way of remedies Tom found out about in the Shop. Annie also wrote:

> I do not know if I should tell this so do not mention it but Tom is Walking Out, it is a lady from the Shop who is to visit us on Saturday, she is very young called Agnes Jamieson.[43]

Charlotte was delighted.

Willie would try the food but he scoffed at Tom's suggested remedies, calling them "chemist's trash." He would chant "Your Chemist is More than a Merchant," if Charlotte mentioned Tom or the Shop; it was the new slogan for Mr. Francis Sprite's advertisements.

The Westport ladies, too, pressed new receipts and sometimes sweets and bottled draughts into Helen's hands, when she attended the E U on a Sabbath. The Reverend Mr. Forsyth, though he scarcely knew

Willie, came back with them twice after two o'clock service and prayed with Willie, the second time leaving behind him, at Charlotte's request, a set of tracts containing readings to comfort the sick. Willie, who had once loved to argue and tug at war with Robert over theological matters for hours on end, had nothing to say to Mr. Forsyth, and the reverend gentleman, drinking tea afterwards in the nice room, admitted himself flummoxed.

"I cannae see there is very much the matter with him."

"Oh, aye, he's been well enough when you've been by, Mr. Forsyth, but Charlotte will tell you that when his fevers come over him he will be very bad. He cannae eat, and his whole system seems to halt up, as it were. He has his own medicines, I believe it is the laudanum mainly, that relieve him but he suffers a good deal."

Mr. Forsyth sighed. His hand, reaching for the proffered bap, was covered from wrist to fingers with short, sandy hair like fur.

"You wouldnae be over-coddling him I hope, Miss Spears?"

Charlotte sitting down again protested. In the gloom his bushy moustaches and hair, even his eyes, were just the colour of his skin, and his head looked for a moment like one of those neepy-candles the bairns carved out for Hallowe'en. Having chewed and swallowed he said:

"William Brown is a grown man and it seems to me he is not meeting this, his first great trial in life, with Christian fortitude; for surely the Lord tries us to test our strength, not to discover our weakness."

Charlotte burst out: "He has fought bravely for so long! He was aye poring over his books when he could scarcely see for the headache. As for his last examinations, he worked towards them almost alone and with very little hope, and was back and forth more times than you could count—"

"Six times," interrupted Helen.

"—and then to be disappointed in the end!"

"You care for and encourage him Miss Spears, with true Christian solicitude."

"But Mr. Forsyth, I can hardly tell whether it wouldnae be kinder, no to encourage him any more—"

Her eyes filled with tears and her aunt and uncle sat forward, fearful perhaps that she would be making a scene. She calmed herself at once.

"That he must give it up," she finished.

After a thoughtful pause Mr. Forsyth said:

"We must also have the faith to submit, to accept God's will when we do not understand. Whom He loveth, He chastizeth! We know not what plans the Almighty has for this His child, only that he is beloved, and watched over unfailingly, sheltered under the shadow of His wing." Mr. Forsyth wiped his moustaches to and fro, carefully.

Helen added: "Willie was saying exactly the same, when he came back from failing his examinations. He said he'd no forget what he had learned, and that several of his class had failed with far less excuse than he, and it wasnae the end of the world."

Charlotte knew how much she and John cherished those words, to be repeated to their minister with so much pride. But what help were they now? Probably Willie did not even mind he had spoken them.

As she cleared away, she examined her soul and was sure she did not coddle him—why, he would never allow it! She had trouble enough doing what was necessary for his comfort. There was however his going on about rubbing his head. "Mr. Forsyth, you have no idea."

And that night at her prayers she saw, and confessed, that the Barilla Ash Cure had been coddling, and having seen this she understood why she did not like to remember it. Her eager hopes! How she had considered and measured the words she would speak, to persuade Willie to allow her! The earnest instructions in the red tablets—her hands on his skin! The tarry smell of the brown sapple in the darkness returned to her then, and she clasped her hands tighter and was ashamed. What would Drew have said? She prayed heartily to forget.

"*Forgive us our debts, as we forgive our debtors.*" Freely, surely, did she forgive others! And as He had promised the Lord must forgive her, even when she could not forgive herself.

CHAPTER 22

In which Charlotte accepts an assignation, and Willie refuses a visit.

Stone Row, Heywood, January 7, 1883

My dear Charlotte,
First, you must remember to call me Drew when you write, not "Friend," though I am your friend I trust. Or, Andrew if you would prefer it.

I write intending to ride in to Lanark while still morning, and will direct this from the Post Office there, though the wind looks as if it is blowing through snow;—I have several messages to do.

As to the First Movement, you write:—I can find as yet no apparent wholeness. I confess, it is my conviction of Schubert's mastery, more than my understanding, which assures me it is whole. You have the better opportunity, as you will so often be playing and replaying, to find it out. I may in memory have confused what I said about questions and answers, I am sure the Andantino was also in my mind. To write of it makes me very impatient to hear it.

The Concert:—you will forgive my short letter, it was crossed by yours and the snows prevented yours from reaching me till Christmas and even then was lost for a time in a host of Christmas Cards, which made me even less satisfied with this new fangled burden on the poor carrier! Perhaps my letter to you was also lost? I almost hope so, remembering it! The Concert was even so a meeting, if without words. Yes, I was with the Park family and some parishioners. I am glad your Coach brought you safely home:—but I did not find any wee red-leather shoe on the step of the GT Hall.

Now you must correspond with me, Charlotte. You see, that I have twice written *your name*. What will you think of the Scherzo? Sometimes I confess to imagining myself in Kirkfieldbank, and seated near your pianoforte, and that I hear you play. You will struggle with a difficult passage, repeat it perhaps many times! Will you allow me to imagine this? "Loud noises," you write! I would very much like to hear them! and witness your conquering something difficult. And sit still after the ending, with no words.

Charlotte walked up to Melkejohn's to order the piano tuned,[44] and saw the advertisement for the Annual Burns Concert in the window and purchased a ticket. The Congregationalists were in some difficulty about Burns now with the Temperance Movement so strong, and she wondered whether her Uncle and Aunt would be surprised at her wanting to go. But when she told them they had no objection.

"It's grand you've the heart again to go out and about. I wonder whether Willie would be well enough, he used to attend the Musical Concerts in Glasgow from time to time." Charlotte did not pursue this.

John looked at the bill she had brought with her. "Being held in the Grand Templars Hall, the selections will have to steer clear of the strong drink. As for the other, Mr. Paterson who is a great Burns scholar as in all else, explains it as Poetic Inspiration and no offence to good Christians. He mentioned, not in the same light of course, but as a scriptural example, the Song of Solomon. They'll do 'Cotter's Saturday Night.' They aye do."

Willie could not go of course. But he was interested. As she fixed his fire:

"It's the Burns Nicht Concert you're away to then? Take care Chattie, his ballads will fill you with languishment. I wonder you havenae been playing some of them already, instead of that pandemonium you treat us with. But then, somebody said, you've reason to be partial to it." He sang, catching his breath and coughing:

"O-hon! for Somebody!
O-hey! for Somebody!

I could range the world around,
For the sake o' Somebody."

Helen remarked that Willie must be feeling better, to be singing away upstairs as Charlotte went out the door.

It was a crowded Hall that night and all were in a blithe and lightsome mood. Mr. Kennedy delivered "The Immortal Memory" and carried his audience with him through his renderings, delivered without reference to the page and in a clear voice that belied his years. They might be hearing the Bard himself, for he would stride about, kilt swinging, then halt abruptly to clasp his forehead, or gaze upward as though asking the Muse for the next phrase. His last selection was "To a Mountain Daisy, on Turning it Down with his Plough," and left hardly a dry eye in the house.

Ev'n thou who mourn'st the Daisy's fate,
That fate is thine—no distant date;
Stern Ruin's plough-share drives elate
Full on thy bloom,
Till crush'd beneath the furrow's weight,
Shall be thy doom!

Mr. Kennedy perhaps over-pleased to have the words to himself. But he relented, and pipers and soloists replaced him. A fiddler was discovered, and at last the company might sing! The beautiful old favourites rang out lustily:

Meet me in the warlock knowe,
Dainty Davie, Dainty Davie;
There I'll spend the day wi' you,
My ain dear Dainty Davie.

And:

Ca' the yowes to the knowes,
Ca' them where the heather grows,

Ca' them where the burnie rows,
My bonnie dearie.

Charlotte was seated in the side aisle near the back, having lingered outside till the Hall filled, quietly as though awaiting friends.
Some village folk had spoken to her but she sat near no one she knew,
and stepped out before the end, during the loudest singing.

Ghaist nor bogle shalt thou fear,
Thour't to love and Heaven sae dear,
Nocht of ill may come thee near;
My bonnie dearie.

He had followed! He came to her.

They walked with bent heads down Greenside Lane but he took
her elbow gently, turning into the close that ran to the North Vennel.
He was very near! He said:

"I thought you wouldnae come!"

Some young folk pushed past. Then a lantern crossed at the
Vennel and paused there, held like a lifted eye. They turned their backs
to it.

He was speaking quickly and she could not catch every word. In
the dark his voice conveyed very little of him. She wished to see his face
in bright daylight as on Tintock, his clear look, but of course she could
not.

"—that you were angry, which I would, which I must, accept and
understand."

His hand had slipped in between her arm and her side. She said,
breaking into his words:

"Let us not speak of it more. I have begun to practise the
Scherzo."

"I know! I know you have." She thought he said then, "I can hear
you," but he could not have said that. "Are you frightened of it?"

They walked through the close and across the High, bending their
heads as a gentleman hurried past. They turned down the Bloomgate,
following him.

"Are you frightened?" he asked again. "Charlotte?"

"Only of the difficulty. It is so very quick."

"You will not give it up?" He had stopped as he said this but they could not stay, some other folk coming up behind them. They walked on. She had a thought of Jecker's Johnnie, of how narrow it was, of hurrying away down it as fast as she could!

"—but you will never forgive me." As if to himself.

They were passing the mortared wall of Saint Mary's, the church turning its back, its sinister offices and garden. A lamp in a low house opposite, on their right, rosy behind the curtains. Two gentlemen coming up behind them, one speaking in a high irritable manner, obscuring Drew's words.

"—the disgraceful and dangerous condition of the pavement in front of Bailie Watson's on the High-street!"

Drew's gentler voice continued: "...into a room, where we can sit down and speak together like civilized creatures."

"There are several places where you could bury a cat!"

Then the two gentlemen passed and there was no one, and he stood still and put his hand gently against her face. "It will come out right, Charlotte."

She could smell the home-made lye soap, like childhood, in his palm. And under his fingers, that would catch at a bit of her hair, but then she caught some trace of carbolic, some vestige of the sick room that must be from her own clothing or skin. She turned aside and his hand moved to her arm. He asked:

"What are you thinking of?"

"Let us walk a little farther. If we walk a little farther I can go down at the Butts."

"Are you out of your way? I have taken you out of your way." They walked, his hand again within her arm, and he spoke in a low rush. As if his words hurried them, they seemed to step along faster and faster.

"—so wretched about it, that you wouldnae give me leave! I've wanted to break his head. Parks had heard of it. Even in Heywood. He is a good man. He sat me down and listened to me, so there is one, who knows what happened! But he wouldnae advise me. I have prayed! Have you no said the truth of it, even to your family?"

"I have told them the truth, which was, that there was nothing to it. My aunt is very good and does not ask me anything, though she goes on about it in her own way. She means to be kind. She still says, in the midst of it, 'We'll no speak of it more.'"

"You've no told any one then, that it was my fault! I've said it to Park. Charlotte. I had to speak to someone."

"It is now so lang syne. Truly, I regret nothing."

"I wish I could say so! You must forgive me, Charlotte, I cannot be easy till you do."

They were at the Butts and Charlotte to stop him began again about the Scherzo. They spoke of music very determinedly till the footpath emerged into Clydesholm Farm meadows. There, though the night was starless, it seemed very light. They stood still.

"I will go on by myself now."

He took a deep breath. "Kirkfieldbank! I wonder when I will come there again. Oh, I wish I could show you Cameron's letters!"

"Well, you must forgive him as a Christian."

"Charlotte, are you laughing?"

"I am not, of course. I always try to return good for—whatever I get, and I salute him very pleasantly in the street."

"And he doesnae reply? Oh, I could bash the man!" They laughed aloud. "Oh, Charlotte, will you no forgive me for the awful harm I have done?"

"I cannot when there is nothing to forgive." The may-bushes behind his head a black net of branches against the meadow. Then she remembered that this was nearly exactly where Mr. Weir.

It seemed he ought to say something more, but he was silent. She said:

"You must go, you must fetch your horse before they close the stable."

She told him how to get up by Jecker's Johnnie. When she pointed, he took her extended hand, pressed it in its kid glove against his cheek and made to turn it, find out the wee gap under the button, her palm. Oh, he would have kissed her there, had she not remembered the smell of Willie and pulled away!

Alone by Clyde she had an idea of sinking her face into the water and scrubbing it hard. Ice had formed high up the rushy grasses, thick around the stalks, when the water came through big at lousing time from New Lanark. Edges of fragile ice had spread out into the river, clinging to the reeds in the shallows, and at the Inches pale bands of silver encircled the stones.

That night she sank into an anxious, happy sleep.

She dreamed Jacky or a terrier like him was at Annville, but it was not Annville. It was a longer, deeper house and Willie lay in one of the rooms and she must find him. As she went from door to door Jacky leaped about her skirts, nipping at her feet, yapping.

Willie in the morning had a deal of pain in his joints: She remembered her dream when he said:

"It's here, and it's there, and I cannae get away from it."

He was able to limp over to the fire and she gave him his medicine. He sat very restless, gasping now and then while she quickly changed his bed. The clean linen had been boiled vigorously and dried on the kitchen screen, and it smelled of smoke. She pressed her face into it before she shook it across. But his smell was in the floss for all the extra undercovering.

He was quiet as she finished, and let her lead him into bed. His hand was cool.

"I'd go out, if it wasnae for the weak legs. There's aye news to be had up the village. They might tell me about the Burns Concert if you won't."

"Why, I will of course, it was a grand concert. The "Cotter's Saturday Night" was as long as usual and of course Mr. Kennedy couldnae miss one word or he'd be in for it. We all sang "The Soldier's Return" it being suitable with the campaigns and all, but not everyone kenned the words to that. Now, I'm away down to the bread van."

"You're away in a hurry, you havnae told me about all the songs. Did you sing 'A Red, Red Rose'?"

When she picked up the slops and linen he added plaintively: "I suppose I have hurt your feelings yestere'en, Chattie?"

Charlotte had got the linen into her bed apron and turned at the door.

"Aunt Helen said you must have been feeling better, Willie, to be singing."

His look distrustful. That she had answered him.

"I was asking about you yourself, it's none of Mother's business I wouldnae think."

But she closed the door quietly.

Later, in his fever, he sang again.

> *"O-hon! for Somebody!*
> *O-hey! for Somebody!"*

She threw the linen into the boiler, covered it with the two raiks Margaret Tennant had brought in, and quickly got the slops out and the pail scoured. Then she stood still on the kitchen flags, gazed almost unseeing down the garden. The day was very soft; even keeping to the cinder path she could not avoid getting the muck on her hems and stockings.

She raised one arm against her face, where she had rowed up her sleeve. She must wash herself now, down to her petticoats. Her wool gown she would hang in the garden. She loosened a strand of hair, there at her neck where Drew's fingers. Pressed it to her nostrils. She and Annie over their copy books each one with the end of a plait in her mouth. Gritty chew of it. Once Annie had got hold of Chattie's plait and put the tip of it into her own mouth. "It's a red taste. You've a red taste, Chattie!"

Drew's letter would come of a Tuesday, and was usually franked from Lanark. "I am supposed to be at my sermon," he would write, and she smiled. When else in that boisterous household could he assume any sort of privacy? Later, a morning ride into Lanark, which he would find an excuse for. "If you should receive a Dear Valentine and know not the sender, then think of me!" She received however four she could not identify and the three were Lanark franked.

> Dear Drew,
> I would be unwise to send you a dear Valentine, which among the young Parks would excite foolish teazing I fear. Otherwise if but for the old custom's sake I should have done so. This letter as a substitute, and you need not puzzle as to its authoress. Anyhow I am sure you do not lack for them. I am sure the children have overwhelmed you.

Then she could not help thinking of Louise who had shot at her such a saucy stare, or of the "one" of his Edinburgh party who had called the Scherzo "fluffy"—a lady, she was sure. A dear Valentine was too light for what she felt. Yet she would have been disappointed not to have one from him, whichever of these it might be.

"I am like a silly girl," she thought, "I have not command of myself. At thirty-four to be sorting through dear Valentines and trying to discover the hand!"

She added a Post Script: "I hope indeed you do not retain these scrawls from me, for where could you put them?"

But the Park girls, unsuspecting, would never get into his sermons.

The Sonata raged in her head. She had two movements memorized but, as she wrote to him:

> The progression is still puzzling, perhaps because I try away at each phrase again and again and do not go on till I have it. I have not yet got it up to tempo.

He encouraged her:

> Do not despair. The music *is* so, broken with grief. Let what you call the progression be invisible, it will take care of itself. You could tease passion from the rough voices of a village Choir, so I know that you will get it at last.

"My dear Charlotte," he wrote, "My very dear friend."

Now she reread his letters daily. The ribband untied and tied up again so many times it had come unravelled at the ends. Frays of cheap red velvet were scattered on the lining of the drawer among bits of lavender escaped from her sachet. She took everything out, dusted and wiped the scented wood. She found some cotton in her housewife and mended the skirt of her embroidered "lavender lady," an old gift from dear Annie. Carefully she seamed the ribband ends with scarlet silk, bending over her lamp. Then she smoothed the letters and tied them up again, and laid them behind the sachet and her handkerchiefs.

"Somebody!" Whatever Willie had heard in the village was but the old Tintock story. "You're no to grieve." He would surely soon tire of plaguing her about it.

Drew's friendship—she dared not yet say love—sustained her. And that sore place she had conceived as her soul was as if filled. She sang sometimes as she went about her work.

"Love divine, all loves excelling,
  Joy of heaven, to earth come down;
Fix in us Thy humble dwelling;
  All Thy faithful mercies crown.
Jesus, Thou art all compassion;
  Pure, unbounded love Thou art:
Visit us with Thy salvation;
  Enter every longing heart."

Willie watched her broodingly. "Coals of fire, that's what it's about now, coals of fire," he murmured. "You do nae care if I live or die, and that's the truth."

Charlotte, tender, felt this to be so, as if he were now in God's hands. She was faithful in every thing. Daybreak by daybreak she rose with renewed strength. The room gleamed. She gummed a new post card from Annie to his screen: The Kyles of Bute. *"I shall run and not be weary; I shall walk and not faint."*

Mr. Paterson would come all the way from Stonehouse, and visit Willie! Her aunt and uncle were most gratified: a visitation from the great good man would surely be a turning point! Mr. Paterson had never forgot him. He had aye looked out for him, since he was a laddie, had been his tutor two years and awarded him the bursary. There was no one in the world Willie looked up to so!

Charlotte, privately, feared they depended too much upon it.

Now Helen as soon as she came in and not waiting to take off her bonnet was hurrying upstairs.

"Willie, dear, you must hear our good news before anything else. I declare you are looking better and the week has gone well, says Chattie—have you been up and about? For your colour is very good. There, I will let in more light. Now, before we came away"—seating herself on the bed and taking his hand—"we had a visit from Mr. Paterson and he himself told us he will come to Annville. You are much in his prayers, he said, and though we are no longer of his congregation of course having dismissed to the Westport, he wishes very much to make the visitation, and is coming at the end of the week. Now, I will take off my bonnet and give you a kiss, I have no doubt he will get a carriage from the Black Bull at no charge, we would never have asked it of him, but he has determined it himself, and sends his best kind regards to you in advance, and will be with us in person Saturday next."

Willie let her talk on, and his father as well when he came in beaming to repeat in fewer words the same story, then dropped to his knees at the bed side to give thanks, his big raw hands clasping the wan hand Willie would have withdrawn, praying warmly into it.

"Almighty Father, we Thank Thee that in Thy mercy we are again gathered together for the Sabbath. And for Thy servant Henry Angus Paterson, who by Thy grace and aided by Thy strength in his faithful ministry, will make a healing visitation to us Saturday week. May his labours be blessed in all his works, that through him through Jesus Christ we may be led to a surer faith, not doubting, fighting the good fight, having endured trials and tribulations and not been found wanting, for *in His favour is life; weeping may endure for a night, but joy cometh in the morning* Psalms xxx.6, Amen."

Willie refused to see Mr. Paterson and said so as soon as he could. They must convey this to the good man with his best wishes, but he could not, as things stood now, bear to see him.

"I've been hearing Mr. Forsyth with great patience and said not a word, but I'll no see Mr. Paterson, you mustnae even consider it. I will no see him."

Nell, in tears, pressed for an explanation, some excuse she could persuade away. "Are you feared he'll be angry with you about the examinations, Willie? He's no the man to be angry at all! And it wouldnae be the same as Mr. Forsyth, though a good man in his own right—but Mr. Paterson! and if it happened you werenae well, so much the better, and Mr. Paterson that kens you from a wee child! He has your own soul's welfare at heart, by the side of which an examination or two has no consequence."

Charlotte felt almost as much for her uncle and aunt, who could not understand, as for her cousin. Seeing his eyes squint and darken with the effort of making his refusal plain and then, as it were, cloud over and slide away, looking towards the darkest part of the room, and who knows what inward scenes?

Neither Helen's tears nor John's prayers would change his mind. Back at King-street they delayed speaking to Mr. Paterson, on the one hand fearful to let him travel in vain, on the other to prevent him—for surely, as Helen argued, Willie would never refuse him being at the door! Charlotte had promised to get a word to them if Willie relented, but nothing came in the post and it was Friday when John, with a heavy heart, walked over to the wee house on Hill-street[45] and chapped on the garden door.

Mr. Paterson was in his study and could see by John Brown's face that the news was bad—indeed for a brief moment, and with the certainty that had never, till then, been wrong—he augured death. He was therefore most happily relieved to hear that it was only Willie Brown's not wanting to see him.

"We'd no have you travelling all that way for nothing Mr. Paterson. Mrs. Brown is of the opinion to have you come and hope for the best, but I must tell you that Willie is out of the ordinary determined against seeing you—though he willnae tell us exactly why."

"Sit down, my dear good man. No doubt Willie is wrestling with his own soul, and hopes, as does any young fellow of spirit, to come through the night of his tribulation by himself. With God's help of course, but not with mine."

He went on: "Prolonged illness is a great battlefield, whose outcome is not the recovery, or failure of recovery, of the mortal body, but, we must trust, the victory of the Christian soul. Perhaps I did wrong to announce my visitation, as though it were some grand event. I should simply have come."

He rose, and as John stood up awkwardly, grasped his hand. "Will you give your son my most affectionate regards, and tell him that, when he is ready to see me, I am ready to see him as well. Indeed, if you will excuse me a moment, I believe I will write him a short letter for you to take with you, so that my paper and ink, if not myself, may look in on him."

John stood outbye while he wrote, looking across through the trembling buds of a plum tree at the famous old Shed at the back, where Willie with a few other "lads o' pairts" had laboured at their lessons under Mr. Paterson's tutelage. Blossoms had opened and fallen and opened again, year by year. Others sat there now: younger, hopeful lads he could not name. The minister came out with the letter. John thanked him, but had to dry his eyes more than once on his way back to King-street, for he could not think Willie right.

"He's no the lad he was, that he'll no see Mr. Paterson, after all he's done for him, and offered to come all that way."

If Willie were on his feet he was away up the village and Charlotte thought uneasily that he sometimes sat in the Inn. But she was not sure, and she would never mention it to her uncle and aunt. It would have been better had he told her where he was going but he would say, "I have no idea, I am going to get the air."

Sometimes he would say something about her lessons as well. He had taken to remarking about the voices of her various singing pupils and called Miss Sym, who was the new assistant at the schoolhouse, "the bagpipe" and Roddy Munro "the ship's horn," and wee Marne, who was at the age when many a girl's voice got rough and breathy, "the bird's nest."

"Willie, you'll no tire yourself." Remembering how he had collapsed in the kitchen. "How far will you go?"

"Far enough to be out of reach of the ship's horn."

Charlotte had been approached by Mrs. Forsyth to join the Lanark Choral Union but would not. Only her Band of Hope suited her now. Though of course she attended E U services with her aunt and uncle if Willie were comfortable. Her public life was otherwise constricted, and her private life she must keep close to her heart.

At the Hall with the bairns around her she was almost happy. To see a thriveless laddie's eyes widen in wonder when she told a story, how among the eager listeners he would edge nearer her chair, perhaps lean against her knee!

Willie had not before complained about the music. She got the carter to remove her harmonium to the Hall, as much for the children's sakes as to spare him the listening to it.

But he hated the Schubert. One day he said:

"You're aye at it and where will it bring you? You've as much idea of getting that thing right as I have of getting an examination. Oh, aye, you'll go at it as if you did, and I'll look strenuously into my books even so, and we'll both wonder why the world's no kinder to us. We're like an auld married couple nodding at the fire, with the house falling in about our heads."

One day when he was out and she had set herself to scrub his walls, she saw his note book open on his table, half hid by a book. He had copied out the Promissory Oath.

> "*I do solemnly and sincerely declare that, as a Graduate in medicine of the University of Glasgow, I will execute the several parts of my profession to the best of my knowledge and ability for the good, safety and welfare of all persons committing themselves, or commended to my care and direction, that I will not knowingly or intentionally do anything or administer anything to them to their hurt or prejudice for any consideration or from any motive whatsoever.*"

Alas, poor Willie!

Had Charlotte requested it, Drew might have got from his father some learned advice. But after the one advisory Drew had never mentioned Willie again. Mostly he wrote of music, and lightly of Kirk doings, or the latest episode on "Wee Budget" the shopkeeper, who sold *The Weekly Budget* and was tormented unreasonably by one of the colliers, and of the good Parks till she felt she almost knew them, especially Allan whose baby antics Drew recorded with such tenderness!

But Willie's condition was so wretched! She had answered Drew's last letter, but now she reread his older one and added the following:

> You were quite right, Drew, when you guessed good Mrs. West's information to be mere gossip. My cousin is indeed quite ill, so ill that he was forced, much against his wishes, to give up his Medical studies. It is however not a mortal disease, as his own Professors assure him. He suffers from the Crimean Fever, which brings with it a host of other discomforts. Therefore, if he is melancholy (for I never either heard of a *Marching Melancholia!*) it is with good reason,

and I trust with God's help he will soon get the better of it.

Nearly one year is bye since he was forced to withdraw from the University, and he has not yet resigned himself or found Christian peace. Yet I will not call it a Melancholia, first because he has a very good reason to feel disappointed and second, that he is not, as it were, always cast down into despair, but rather, is quite sprightly and teazing sometimes, but cannot fix on anything. He has bad dreams, or perhaps deliriums, and sometimes seems very frightened, yet he refuses the good counsels of Mr. Forsyth, and will not see his own former pastor Mr. Paterson of Stonehouse, who had offered to visit him, and this has made my uncle very sad, Mr. Paterson having tutored him for the University himself and paid the bursary.

Has your Father any acquaintance with this condition? I would not wish to trouble him unless you think, that to consider it would be an interest or recreation for him. Dr. Gray calls it general Excitation of the brain and recommends tonics and complete rest.

I have written the above on a separate page so that, should you think it right, you might send it to your Father.

Her uncle looked older now, and was often sad and silent. He would sit an hour in the kitchen of an evening with his pipe gone out and barely murmur a reply to Helen's pleasant talk. Roddy could cheer him: Roddy was a good, kind man after all. They'd be off down the garden to the bees, now the days were getting longer. John walked as ever to and from Stonehouse but had less to say about what he encountered. Had he seen the flourish at Hazelbank?

"Oh aye, I would have done, for I came down the Braes."

But Willie did not go down the garden with his father! On Saturday, when all was the whitest of white and the pinkest of pink, he was well enough Charlotte was sure, but he kept indoors.

"Do go out, Willie. Your father's down the yard and the sun's shining," she said.

"Aye, and Mother's boiling clothes right and left and everybody is blithe as can be. I'll no stick my bleary mug out among them and spoil their pleasure."

"They would be more that happy to have you with them, Willie, you know that."

"The light's too strong. Close the blinds and take your smile away down with you, you're no as kind as you look."

CHAPTER 23

In which the cause of Temperance is advanced, and Charlotte tells a lie.

The IOGT Hall was thronged to bursting. Charlotte assembled her juvenile Templars in the lobby and on the turning stone staircase at the end, which led to the weavers' loft. They scrambled up happily, the laddies getting as high as possible, legs dangling between the stair rods. And the lassies perched like white birds, gathering their frocks around their knees.

All the while folk were pressing in from the street, and craning to get past the inside door into the Hall. The lecture had been liberally billed, and it was a great coup to have secured the renowned Mr. Clapperton to the village, as Mr. Munn had several times reminded her. The Lanark Templars were therefore down in large numbers, including the Juvenile "Falls of Clyde," who eyed the acrobatics of the "Hope of Kirkfieldbank" enviously as they were got in. They too were wearing their blue ribbons.

When the Hall was filled Charlotte motioned the "Hope" to follow her. The pulpit was back at the far end under a severely brushed IOGT banner, and there sat Mr. Clapperton, an immense personage with cascade moustaches and a great expanse of waistcoat, beside a less significant Reverend Harvey. "Hope of Kirkfieldbank" followed her up the side aisle, clambering over the feet of the people in the roup seats. All chairs were occupied, with "Falls of Clyde" in the front row, where her bairns were expecting to sit.

Mr. Clapperton however, by dint of one fat finger and, it seemed, a little magic, conjured the pulpit out of the way and gestured expansively for the "Hope" to sit at his feet.

"*Suffer the little children come unto me, and forbid them not,*" he boomed cheerfully.

Charlotte was provided with a chair at the near end, and looked along her ranks as they settled. Several of the laddies had stour from the staircase on their trousers. And John Stein, too distant to be got at, had managed to win a chair from "Falls of Clyde" and was busy making room for his brother Archibald, using his elbows vigorously.

Charlotte thought she had passed Willie near the door. Now looking back she saw him seated on the roup seat beyond some colliers. His head was leaning back out of sight but she knew his sharp knees in his shiny trousers, and the way his fingers shifted about on his stick.

Mr. Clapperton was indeed an enthralling lecturer![46] The oration was very long, and yet he had a fine grip on the children, whom he first exclusively addressed. His admonishments were terrific, his anecdotes horrifyingly picturesque. For such a big man he was surprisingly agile, his limbs almost seeming to flow. He would suddenly as it were pour downwards to kneel on one knee and stare at the children directly. The cloth of his trouser-legs then stretched impossibly across thighs whose breadth outspanned their length. The children watched with fascination. Brumestane blazed from his glittering eye. They heard of mice poisoned in bottles of beer, of dipsomaniacs, wife and child beaters, wretched men hanged for murder while under the influence of demon rum. Of dens of iniquity found in almost every Glasgow street, some under the very shadow of a House of God. Of how the weak and unwary were enticed within, of flaring gas lights on frosted globes, brightly gilded spirit casks, mirrors reflecting ragged victims in the midst of pomp and mocking splendour. Denizens of gin palaces recoiled before his tirade, orphans fled, fathers wept, halted at the brink of ruin by a waif's plaintive voice, the tug at their sleeve of a starveling hand.

Another full hour was directed at the adults. Charlotte felt for her bairns, yet they seemed too spellbound or exhausted to protest. At last he was through, and she feared a rush to the front to sign the Pledge and her bairns trampled. But few came forward; the audience in the main were pledged already.

A rousing "Work for the Night is Coming" brought folk to their feet and she quickly got "Hope" into order and turned around. She made her way past them to the harmonium.

She had chosen from Sankey's hymns and they were very well

received. Her Choir was pretty much the same as the Sabbath School's, none more than ten years old. Some had as yet no idea of a tune at all, but these she had taught to be "angel voices," to whisper rather than to sing. That she could train such young children to sing in harmony at all was a source of wonder to the Lanark folk, though the villagers were accustomed to hearing them. And that they sang sweetly as well! The applause was just as great as for Mr. Clapperton and the wee ones smiled with delight.

"Falls of Clyde" then stood up too, and held their banner high before them, and all the children raised their right hands and in the usual sing-song repeated the Pledge and the Juvenile Objective:

> "*Because I want to be my best in every way, I promise, by God's help, never to take Alcoholic Drinks.*
>
> "*I promise that I will not drink cider, beer, wine, spirits or any alcoholic or intoxicating drink. I promise that I will not use tobacco in any form, I promise that I will not use either profane langauge or wicked words. I promise I will not gamble.*"

The final song was set to the tune of "Rock of Ages," though Charlotte raised it a key and increased the tempo in a vain attempt to disguise it. Unfortunately it was common practise among Temperance folk to appropriate a well-known air, and some of these were less suitable than others.

> *Water is the drink for me,*
> *For I would a strong man be;*
> *Water sent in love by God,*
> *To refresh the flowering sod;*
>   *Water, beautiful and bright,*
>   *Emblem of celestial light.*
> *Water from the fountain clear*
> *Will no poor man's conscience sear;*
> *Will not cause to flow a tear;*
> *Like that filthy stuff called beer;*
>   *Water, etc.*
> *Water, water! Oh, how grand*

It doth beautify our land!
Water! Water! Angels cheer,
Who would stoop to filthy beer?
  Water, etc.

Water is the Templar's choice:
Water pure and fresh and sweet;
That he may in water rejoice,
And his Maker's praise repeat;
  Water, BEAUT!-iful and bright,
  Emblem OF! celestial light.

Willie was in the kitchen when she came in. "I'll apologize I didnae wait to get you down the road, but the Hall was over-hot."

"I had a hurl to the gate with the Lanark folk."

He had not lit the lamp though it was dark indoors. She did so now, and poked up the range. "Have you taken any supper?"

"No, I was waiting for you. I believe I have slept. I will want your arm, to get upstairs."

After supper they went up. She did not particularly like his leaning against her, the feel of his hand against her palm—it was at the same time cold, and wet with perspiration. As they turned at the lobby he said again, "I intended to stay and get you home. That would give Roddy Munro something to think about!"

In the room: "Will you want anything?"

"Thank you, I will see to myself. Oh, aye, Chattie, we'll walk the village yet, you and I, if I can step smart enough to keep pace with you."

She need not answer. Going down into the lobby, the glazed door a pale glow in the last of the dusk, telling herself she need not think of his foolish words.

She must indeed be content that Willie should continue to guy her about Roddy. It was no longer an act of self-command to keep silent; she had got into the habit. She need not even to go out to the stairhead. If she turned away it was in pity, to prevent his seeing how little he distressed her. The next forenoon he said:

"You're uncommon blithe the day, Chattie. I'd guess you had a letter, if it wasnae that Roddy Munro lives across the street. Have you a letter in your pocket then?"

She had indeed a letter, and was eager to go downstairs to open it. Settling Willie was a trial of her patience, but anticipation was sweet enough to make her slow and solicitous, and she folded the towels and smoothed his counterpane without haste.

He had got himself sat up, but would not dress, and the anxious lines came and went on his forehead. He would be in a fever before the day was out.

"Willie, whether you like it or no, you ought to eat up your brose." His brows furrowing even more deeply.

"Oh, aye, I ken what I am in for as well as you."

Stone Row, Heywood, March 5th, 1883.
My dear Charlotte,

My sermon being now completed, the text being in Romans.viii.28: *All things work together for good to them that love God*, I may write to you at my ease.

First:—you will be happy to hear that the Temperance Cry has reached Heywood, though in our case the IOGT has been pre-empted by The Church of Scotland. Park and I have got up a Temperance Association, so it was not music we sat up over last night, but the draft of our modest Constitution. We engage to hold an opening meeting in the Victoria Hall, March 9th.

Have I told you of the Hall? It is the heart of the village, though in truth it is only three "but-and-bens" knocked together on the inside, and you would never notice it except for the bills in the window. There is a new floor laid. Our first meeting will be rather light-hearted, despite our serious purpose, with music and recitations rather than lectures and admonishments. Already it threatens to be over-long, the village boasting many voices that like to be heard as well as a concertina and a fiddle. Park thinks it will end in an impromptu assembly, which neither of us would oppose, and will please the young folk.

Now, whether we progress to the Pledge and the rest of the trimmings, I do not know. We are rather uncertain as yet what our tone ought to be for we would rather not be classed among the very militant. The Salvation Army marched through last fall but were greeted with cat calls and worse, though not the general rout which has occurred in some places, but I had some difficulty in persuading my parishioners to leave them in peace. There is promised, also, a set of "tent meetings" by a blind evangelist in June, which while not in any way condemning we should like to get the start of.

What is your opinion, Charlotte? I would not wish you to think us frivolous, being yourself leader of your Band of Hope, but you wrote lately, for I have your letter beside me:—"The Lanark Templars are rather more severe with the children than I like to be." Charlotte, we are of one mind, that *gentle* teaching, and music, and a large supply of wholesome food, are more suitable to their tender age than long winded tales of depravity.

Now to the Scherzo. How different our sensation of the music must yet be! For you it is a present impression, the notes being *heard*, and the progress advanced and improved upon daily. You have no previous hearing of it to mind or compare, all is new;—it is as though you walk in a mountain path, little knowing what awaits you around the next turning. The sheets are your chart, and you read, perhaps, "Here be Monsters!" For myself, having heard but never played it, I have as it were a memory of the path I skimmed as in a dream. It remains in my mind, the Scherzo particularly, like a strange field all textured with colour, which is seen from afar, yet could I come close, these details would be revived instantly. What it is in the field that so frightened me, I know not.

Now here is Allan hauling at the sneck of my door, he can reach it easily and no doubt will be opening it within a week and pulling all my books about;—so I will close.

Your ever devoted
Drew

He did not invite her to the meeting. Indeed, how could she have gone, without making public arrangements and provoking a renewal of the old story? She would of course have refused, but wished he had made some allusion to her coming, if only to regret its impossibility. He did not refer to her page about Willie at all, but on Wednesday a closely written sheet in a stranger's hand arrived, with a note from Drew:

> My father has recently replied to this effect, but it was necessarily delayed as he is forced to dictate it and then to be written out clear. Here it is however, without more delay:
>
> Your good village doctor *is not an expert on the question of insanity, and the particular form of insanity here indicated raises questions of a very delicate nature which are supposed to be above the ken of an ordinary medical practitioner. The condition is a morbid affection of the brain.*
>
> *An over-fullness of blood in the head is caused by over-exertion and over-excitation of the mind, the unreasonable strain on the mind from efforts to cram, great suspense and anxiety, followed by severe disappointment and weighed upon by the debility of a long feverish illness.*
>
> *What is described as deliriums and unnatural fears, and at other times sprightly talk and restlessness, are manifestations of a further condition which may be one of temporary insanity and greatly resembles what is observed in certain cases of epilepsy. It occurs sometimes in epileptics without any bodily convulsions, as if the mental perturbations were taking place of the bodily convulsions.*
>
> *The condition is known as epileptic vertigo or as the French prefer to call it 'petit mal.' This is a mental condition which does not present with convulsions, and the victim of it, is quite unaware of his actions or speech. This modified mental condition involves mental alienation.*[47]

Then on the back of the page, a further note from Drew:

> Charlotte, I do heartily wish you did not have the nursing of your cousin. Indeed your aunt's offer of a servant must be accepted at least:—of a trained nurse, would be best of

all. I have no doubt but that you are an excellent nurse as you are excellent in everything. But even setting aside the time lost and dreary labour involved, the constant companionship of one whose mind is despondent if not at times deranged, cannot but affect your temper as well, and this gives me cause for distress as your friend. You do continue to assure me that you practise diligently and have great pleasure in it. I would however need no such assurance, were your time your own. Forgive me if I over-step my privilege as your friend, I have not at present the right to advise or command you.

Temperance meetings flourished. On the Sabbath evening following Drew's Heywood event Mr. Forsyth came down to Kirkfieldbank and preached a Gospel Temperance sermon in the Hall, Mr. and Mrs. Brown attending.[48] Charlotte, who was to play for the Tuesday Open Meeting scheduled next, met afterwards with Messrs Munn and Reid of Lanark IOGT to look over the musical accompaniments, and was able to assure them that, were the sheets but stacked in the order required, she should have no trouble.

"You'll treat us to a selection, I hope? A set of merry marches would be very suitable." Mr. Munn's mulberry stain dividing his face almost symmetrically while avoiding his nose. The blue eye on the red side appeared paler than the other, almost transparent.

As they piled up chairs she sat herself at the harmonium and went through some well-known Scottish airs, working out transitions so that the one should flow irresistibly into the next.

She would stay with gentler songs but put one march in, "The Battle of Stirling Brig." Most of the Temperance hymns were so very military! The instrument laboured, and she suspected some stour had crept between the keys from upstairs. She would end with "Ye Banks and Braes." In the back of her head the Scherzo tumbled, and she would rather have been at it, at the pianoforte.

March had begun very mild but Tuesday morning dawned to a severe northwesterly gale. The curtain blew about her furiously when she threw open Willie's window and he protested:

"I'll be up and dressed in a wee, if you'd wait with that."

"Are you well, then? I hope you are well! It's a piercing cold day."

From downstairs, the door to the sitting room banged and banged. She mended his fire. He had not rapped in the night.

"Will you come down to your breakfast?"

His look was indeed calmer, his eye less suffused and staring and his brow smooth. But this no longer gave her much consolation. Nor him she was sure, except for such momentary relief, as the expectation of a few days or hours without pain might provide. Too often had his respite been broken in upon, his hope crushed!

She got at the Schubert in the forenoon. She would practise until the post. The Allegro seemed to rush forward yet continually caught her up, tempo and tonality breaking down, and her own vexed outbursts making an even a sorrier mish mash of what she might dare to call Schubert's own. Rests a bar in length! And the Andantino beginning as it did so disarmingly! Then came the difficult passages—wild runs, two-handed trills, staccato chords like furious, indignant crashes! They could not but hurt the ear. She had written to Drew they were like exclamation points. And then, as if wearied but not after all thoroughly discouraged, a single voice in the middle range daring softly to speak, asking for something, though one knew not what. And the theme at last returning, the coming into the light.

Then the Scherzo. Bright, but surely never "fluffy"! Carefully she played through the first theme. There was a "Neapolitan": G-major into D, immediately further modulated into A. Was it not the subdominant of a subdominant? Mr. Miller could have explained it. Immediately repeated as A into F and through into E. These were surely the unexpected, disquieting modulations which had frightened Drew so much, and indeed they produced a thrill of unease in Charlotte as she played them, her old soul-ache for a moment awakening.

"Are you afraid?" Drew had asked, or words to that effect.

Willie put his head in at the parlour door, waited as she completed the sixteen bars and turned to him.

"You'll never get it right, Chattie."

He was gone upstairs again. She had however got it right.

It was long now since she had summoned Drew's presence as she played. She would play for him one day and need not fancy him there.

275 〜

First she must learn it well. She had some idea of getting at a good pianoforte; even the Reids', or the Forsyths' at the E U manse, had a superior tone. There was much to learn yet; she had scarcely glanced into the Rondo!

The budding lilies by the gate were all bowed over in the blast, some stalks quite broken. Returning with her letter she stopped to gather the most hurt of them. The ground looked almost as if frost were setting in. As she quickly got into the house, her skirts caught in the glazed door, and she must open it and close it again. Since John had taken away the winter door the lobby remained day-lit, though dim.

The lilies would open here nicely in a tall jar, and be spared further devastation. After she had arranged them, she might close herself in her room, turn to her letter at last. She would set herself such small tasks almost playfully, deferments of certain delight.

> Our own inaugural meeting went off very well and ended as predicted in an assembly, into which I was pressed to please the Parks, with some trepidation as I am but a poor dancer, but Findlay's fiddle was bewitching. It was indeed an improvement on the usual Victoria Hall doings which are far from abstemious, and I pray will have some gradual effect. Folk took themselves off home quietly. As for Saturday night, to judge from the noise after lousing-time, I doubt that the usual trade was so much diminished!
>
> Now for Lanark. As Park says, I am very faithful in going my messages of a Monday. Charlotte, you will read this tomorrow when, all being well, I will follow it down to Kirkfieldbank, to attend the IOGT Open Meeting as advertised. My perfectly legitimate reason being, as President of a similar Association, to study how such a meeting is best conducted. So I will not write more, in the hope of seeing you, and speaking with you very soon."

Charlotte was to read the account of the Heywood meeting in the newspaper.[49] There had been a Mr. John Rennie, and a Miss Rennie who sang. She could not help forming a picture of Drew being borne off not wholly against his will—smiling with rueful pleasure over his shoulder as he passed the seated Mr. and Mrs. Park—by a determined Louise or a Miss Rennie who sang.

But he was to come! They had not seen one another since January, and she could not trust that his appearance would give her more pleasure than pain. The correspondence had sufficed her, and left no place for dreaming.

Now she was pleased she had washed her hair, which was a rare and laborious operation over the sink. Margaret had filled up the back boiler on the range. At last there was no more sapple in the basin as she wrung out the heavy rope between her hands, and heard the squeak and was satisfied.

She had put it into twenty-five plaits, and all night and day kept it closely pinned under two house caps. Now she undid and sniffed it and could catch no trace of a smell. A fierce brushing subdued the tightest crimpings and she pinned it all back under a clean cap before she went up to settle Willie.

He said he would do very well with some quiet, if she wanted to "rant up the village." His fire, which she now liberally replenished, started up through the eisels fitfully in the draughts from the chimney, and seemed to give off little heat.

"I'll look in when I come home, then, Willie. I hope you will take your beef tea while it is hot. Are you sure you have everything you want?"

"Oh aye, run away with you. You may tell Roddy Munro from me to keep his lantern trimmed, for it's you and me from now on.

> "O lay thy loof in mine, lass,
>   In mine, lass, in mine, lass;
> And swear on thy white hand, lass,
>   That thou wilt be my ain."

He would keep on about Roddy. Though since the Choir was given up, the constable walked with her nowhere. He came for his Monday lesson and looked as if he would like to linger, and every week-end was by for a crack with John. Twice on a Friday he had brought her a trout, in time for her to dress it for the week-end. He was, fortunately, a diffident follower! But what excuse could he find to look by otherwise, unless it were a storm, or some general or particular disaster?

She bathed in her room, carrying up the water herself, shivering, scrubbing every inch. Her summer linen lay ready across the bed, the pillow slips unstitched in which it had been folded away clean in the fall. She put on the new costume from King-street, with the jacket cut in the modern "battlemented" fashion. She had tried it when Helen first brought it down, and at first not thought it becoming but now with the white starched collar it looked very elegant, the clan tartan with its bonnie red stripe somehow suiting her.

"Sad," Drew had written! She was surely not sad! Could she say to him, in a letter if not to him directly: "Drew, you must never be afraid that I am sad, if you are my friend!"

She lifted her sleeve to her face and breathed in through the fresh, new stuff. Oh, if Willie would not rap before she were gone!

He did not. The gale buffeted her along the High-street and her shawl was no protection. She might comfort herself that she was not alone among the ladies who, however inclement the weather, had scrambled into spring clothes at the first pealing of the "wee bell"!

Despite the weather, with the wind as everyone predicted "blowing through snow," the gathering promised to be well attended. She could not guess whether Drew would be kept away by the storm, whether she rather wished him absent than otherwise. Most of the audience were well-kent village weavers and colliers from temperance families. Messrs Munn and Reid as Grand Templars walked about condescendingly, welcoming and nodding, their broad ribbons looking quite gay in the lamplight. One hoped for them an unsteady, desperate figure here and there among the throng. Surely they deserved the satisfaction of new Pledges signed!

She had seated herself early at the harmonium and was playing out of Gledhill's *Echoes from Scotia* as the Hall filled, with only two stops drawn to keep it hushed.

But she did glance up, and immediately discovered Willie! Getting in at the door, with a bare head and his cloak buttoned high at his throat.

Again she glanced, fearfully, almost missing a note, but could see Drew nowhere. Willie meanwhile standing at the back, speaking with Mr. Weir. Where had these two met? Willie sometimes walking in the High-street would have made acquaintances. She felt a wary discomfort at the thought. The idea of his worst times, thankfully known but to herself. In his own room. But his seizure in the kitchen! That he might speak askance, or be taken ill when others were by! Worse, that Drew might see him, or she forced to go to him while Drew was by!

She applied herself to the harmonium and when next she dared to look, Willie had sat down, and Mr. Weir had seated himself elsewhere, though there were as yet empty chairs by Willie. She made herself play an entire page, and when she looked again, these chairs were taken— the one nearest him by Drew!

It was a blessing she must concentrate, if not on the accompaniments which were easy enough, then on which followed which, for there were the usual last-minute changes to be made. If Miss Spears, earnestly whispered at by Mr. Munn, could kindly play "He Comes Not" instead of "Mary's Song," the notes being here somewhere, he believed. Charlotte assured him she knew it. The universal Pledge swelled into an even louder temperance hymn:

> "Strong drinks have cursed our land;
> Souls sink on ev'ry hand—"

Now with the music in some order she earnestly wished she were better prepared. She had been too proud! Old Notation followed Sol-Fa. A song in soprano key attempted by Miss Sym who could not reach it and therefore having as it were in mid-tack to be transposed. Then she must listen to a fulsome introduction by the chairman to her own selection of Scottish airs: "Who needs no introduction." Could she but have sunk away!

She had already rapidly considered the selection and shortened it: she would end with "Scots, wha hae" rather than the yearning tones of "Ye Banks and Braes." But alas, her fingers made the transition before she could stop them. Somehow, she got through.

The call to the Pledge! Reasonably answered by four or five, one no more than a lad—James Thomson who boarded at the Smiths'. It was hardly, as in the illustrated tracts, a fanatical rush to the front, with the ragged and repentant eagerly leaning over the opened book to sign or make their cross, while stalwart Templars clasped their shoulders or stood about in glorified attitudes, casting their eyes to heaven or waving a fist in postures of belligerence. Charlotte replayed the chorus of "Be a Hero!" and dared to glance at last across the Hall as folk settled again in their seats.

The man on the other side of Drew was speaking and Drew had inclined his head. A long face, and a round beard trim as a topiary sticking out of the chin. Had Charlotte seen him at the Lambeth concert—was it not Mr. Park? She must tremble lest Willie, hearing them, should discover Drew beside him. Would Willie but go away home! Surely he would never stay for tea with the room so hot and crowded! He looked very ill indeed. Drew who was well known and would be greeted loudly at any moment by name—impossible if he were not taken notice of! Sitting there in his cassock with a stranger beside him, his presence crying out to be heeded! The ladies now busy with the tea urns would soon be at liberty; chairs were scraping and clearing back, folk starting to move about! William Munn must twice signal to Charlotte to catch her attention, to begin the closing hymn.

She sat on, fearful, wishing Willie away, Drew away if not Willie. A picture rose before her of what occurred often enough in halls and kirks: a resounding crash, then four or five men silently rising here and there to congregate on some unfortunate who had collapsed forward or sideways along a bench or pew. The respectful carrying out of the affected. "It would be the sick Mr. Willie Brown from Annville! He should never have come out! The cold did for him, the heat of the room!"

She knew not whether she should go down or stay where she was. But Drew would come to her if he could, and he must not be allowed to do so! She stacked up the music. Rab Gilchrist, suddenly grown six inches, taking his notes from her, shyly expecting a compliment, though he had but played "Christian Mariners," the same piece he was at over a year ago.

"Well done, Rab!" It was long since he had been her pupil, her most promising one.

At last in the greatest crowd she must move towards the door, and here was Willie at her side.

"I came because the fire went out, Chattie, and I've stayed for your sake, and even drunk the awful temperance tea, and now we may walk home together, just like—"

Mercifully he did not finish. The dread of it was almost worse than anything he might have said. His voice in the general noise was not loud but he always enunciated so clearly.

She kept her head down. They must go and at once. She thought she passed Mr. Weir by the door but could not look at or acknowledge him.

"Mr. Thomson!" and "Mr. Thomson!" she heard, female voices crying out happily as she got Willie into the lobby.

The wind tore at their clothing. Willie's hand within her arm, though not foolishly, for he staggered a little and she must support him. His hand felt like a woman's, clinging. The way Mrs. West's blind sister.

"Put your cloak over your ears, Willie. You should never have come out, or stayed so long!"

She stopped to assist him, pulled her own shawl closer. They went on. It was not even fully dark, the days lengthening though with such cold it could have been in the hawe of winter.

"Dinnae scold. You've no right to scold till we are properly married."

He coughed, and expectorated neatly away from her. She must confess herself wonderfully relieved that he was going on in his familiar strain, however distasteful it was. Would she then escape?

But in the lobby he mentioned it.

"Bye the bye, I was sitting beside a nice pair of gentlemen who seemed over-interested in your playing, and they kenned you as well, for I heard them say Miss Spears this, and Miss Spears that, and the clergyman sat uncommon still when you played.

"You do nae answer me, so I may think what I will, that he is your auld follower from Heywood, who ran away like the black gentleman when—"

Charlotte broke in: "I will answer you of course, Willie. It was Mr. Turnbull from Lesmahagow, and the other man I do not know."

In her room she walked up and down. She would not have a letter from Drew for six days, and could but pray he had not heard Willie speak, or seen him with her at the last. The wind shrieked. Perhaps even now Drew was passing Annville on the road, standing a moment in the saddle to glimpse her lighted window above the palisade, riding disappointed over the brig, that she had not exchanged a quiet word with him at least, or even a look! Oh! Drew must never come to Kirkfieldbank again!

She had lied! Like Peter before the cock crew, she had denied, if not Jesus, a fellow-man. Inasmuch, inasmuch.

She had never lied in her life. "You reek with honesty," David Hartley had said of her once. A liar. She burst into tears.

It was not the sort of meeting Walter Cameron would have attended, and Park being willing it seemed harmless enough. We had a terrible ride home. Park is no horseman and continually regretted our not taking the old trap, which we could have done. He has been laid up these four days with a bronchitis, for which I was very sorry though neither he nor the good Mrs. P berated me as its cause. As for myself, the storm in my face and getting into all the seams of my clothing, held no fears. I should have relished it, had I been alone, as it matched my mood perfectly.

Why did you go away? Were you wanted at home? Now I have had some time to reflect, Charlotte, and acknowledge you were wise. I know you will chide me for having come. But I will look eagerly for your letter as I would rather be reproved than ignored.

You performed excellently as was to be expected. I was only put into further bad humour, that it was the wrong music on the wrong instrument, but I am comforted you must have felt the same vexation. Why did you choose to end with "Bonie Doon" and then refuse to open yourself to it? Was this a wordless admonition?

Charlotte, answer me quickly. I am unhappy, fearing not that I did wrong but that you may teach me to think it so.

Charlotte's part in the meeting was duly mentioned in the *Advertiser*:[50] "*Miss Spears performed skilfully on the harmonium.*" The same edition noted that Mrs. Forsyth had been presented with a handsome gold brooch from the Choral Union. Charlotte had of course heard about that already. Such presentations were all the rage: countless the plaques and books and pocket watches earnestly conferring in ceremonies all over Scotland. Innumerable the huddled meetings, the whisperings, the collecting of pennies that went to them, while the intended recipient looked the other way and pretended to know nothing about it! No, it would never do to covet, and she repressed the thought that it was Mrs. Forsyth's manner rather than her musicianship which earned her such esteem. Dear Robert would have said: "Chattie, that gold brooch is for putting up with the way the ladies mob her husband, never you care." And Drew, too, was straight and clear eyed, despising silliness and show.

Though the precentorship had ended in disgrace she had triumphed musically, and the reward was inestimable for it was Drew's esteem. Her very triumph had led to her material downfall. Mr. Cameron! Mrs. West had told her in confidence that he'd been quite queer and cross about the lovely vestments the Kirk ladies had presented! He had been expecting a manse of course, and Charlotte had to admit she understood him.

"May I be satisfied with this posy brought to me so sweetly by Nellie Smith!" She touched the violets in their jeelie-glass before her on the escritoire. "These are a presentation from the heart!"

Unseasonable snow had followed the wind but the snowdrops and crocus poked their heads through valiantly, and by week-end the sun shone and the air grew warm. Willie had not again referred to Heywood. He could not get out, or hear anything from any quarter, for a cough and a fever had set in. He admitted to having put his fire out himself by overloading it with coals. Charlotte cared for him with much solicitude.

John and Helen arrived. "He should never have gone to the meeting." Dr. Kelso was got, but had no more to recommend than what was going on already with the hot fomentations. Charlotte must admit to being relieved by Willie's being kept in, though it was an unchristian sentiment. She insisted on nursing him while her aunt was there, and stayed up the two nights watching and nodding; it was a penance of a sort and also, she knew not what he might say. His brow was furrowed and fearful as she bent over him and he spoke at random.

"Willie, are you awake? do you understand me?"

She wanted to change his pillow case but he fought her off, his arms jerking, getting in the way. His fingers clutched in her hair so she had to step back to put it up again. Meanwhile he had thrown the clean cover off the bed and it hung half into the slop pail. His eyes were open, but he was dreaming. His voice clear, as clear as it had been in the Hall.

"Take away the light, dinnae look at me, dinnae look at me like that!" and long oaths Charlotte would rather not remember. Somehow she got his medicine into him.

Later he said, "Aye, Chattie, I've been away off in a fever and hardly mind where I was; I believe you were talking to me."

"Don't think about it. It is bye now." She wiped his face.

"I was dreaming of old Watkins in the schoolroom, in Greenside School, who I havenae thought of all these years. He was a drunkard, and one day he fell over the pulpit, and the Board came and carried him out, and that was the last we saw of him."

"Perhaps it was the Meeting brought him to mind? We must trust he has since been led to such a Meeting himself and has become an abstainer."

Willie was looking away past her, his face still anxious, or puzzled.

"We thought it a great joke at the time, the ruination of a man."

Charlotte with flannel and basin was washing his emaciated hands finger by finger.

"He gave me such a look, Chattie, I mean in the dream. He said, I'm done for, and a terrible black blood came welting out of all his apertures."

"Willie, you're no to think about it more. He is in God's hands."

"Oh, aye, that's what we are afraid of, isn't it?"

She could bring a good report downstairs. "He is quiet and thoughtful. I believe the meeting did him good after all."

Charlotte felt such tenderness in her heart towards Willie whenever he spoke gently and rationally, mindful of his own soul! This was the real Willie. She must not forget him.

One night, when he had quietly allowed her to foment his spine, and even murmured, "I thank you" into his pillow, she burst out: "It is I who must thank you! I know you are suffering and I am happy to

care for you always, even when you are cross, for I know that the real
Willie—"

But he stopped her. "Oh aye, the real Willie. He does what he's
bid, meek and mild like a good Christian." As he spoke he was getting
himself by degrees on to his side, his thin neck painfully twisted till he
could look directly at her, his face pale.

"That's no more the real Willie than anything else. It's all a sham,
it's play-acting. You know all about it for you're play-acting yourself
as kind as can be and you'd never half like to give me a swift kick
downstairs."

"Oh Willie, you're no to say such things, I do pity you from my
heart."

"Go on out on the stairhead and compose your face then; do you
think I've no seen your eyes blazing into the fire when you think I'm
too bad to notice."

She prayed for herself, that she had lied, though she could not repent
the outcome. Perhaps Drew was right to have warned her, and she was
changed! Yet the Christian ought never to shrink from the sinner nor
fear contamination; the true Christian was safeguarded, putting on the
armour of Christ. How would Robert have advised her? He had loved
Willie, and Willie for all his faults did not tell lies.

She hoped that the gentle spirit of Robert would say: "It was no
such a bad lie, Chattie, and done for the best." She suspected however
that these were her own words, not Robert's, and that Robert was farther off.

She turned back to her letters for comfort. The one about Bernie yet
brought her to tears. It seemed that then, another course could have
been taken, which now was lost forever!

She was learning the Scherzo.

Could she have written: "Alas, you will never hear me play!" her
tears wetting the keys, sliding between them which could not be good
for the action. "It will be as with Bernie, you will wish to come and
somehow you will always be prevented, and then it will be too late!"
She was not sure how and in which way it would be too late, but felt it
would be so.

CHAPTER 24

In which both Charlotte and Willie visit away from Annville.

A t Term-end Charlotte was to have a proper holiday. Willie would go to Stonehouse all being well, and stay out the week. They fetched him away the Saturday, all the journey by carriage to avoid getting in and out of the train, and John foregoing his walk to assist him. Charlotte got down at Lesmahagow Station and took the Caledonian to Glasgow.

Her aunt wrote to the Great Western Road and reported that Willie had stood the journey well and was "quite comfortable though growly with his aches and pains. We have put him into our bed not wishing to trouble Maddie and his own wee room occupied by Jessie and the boxes. Your uncle and I are in the front room for the time being. Mr. Paterson makes his visitation Thursday, therefore my dear, think of us about four or five o'clock."

Charlotte attended the others to Elgin Place on the Sabbath. It was the Lord's Supper and Tom in his black clothes and white stock and with his great "haundlebars" striped red and gray, carrying the plate and looking, she must admit, not out of place among the other deacons—though she had used to think of them as a set of old men. Then out into the porch with the great columns and wide steps down to Pitt-street[51] and all the bustle of greetings and carriages!

The three of them went to a concert and she ran into David Hartley and a young lady whose name she did not catch and who was determined to carry him off in a hurry, their carriage having driven up. Charlotte saw him wink broadly at Tom just before he got in. Mr. and Mrs. Miller were there as well, her emerald feathers visible through the crowd, with umbrellas being shot up here and there, and Annie asked if Charlotte would not like to go over, where surely her old Choir members would be gathered about them? But Charlotte did not wish it.

Mr. Batchelor visited. Had the others not been there, Charlotte would perhaps have asked his counsel. At the door, her hand clasped between his hands, shaking now though his grasp was firm. The familiar smell of moth pellets that hung about him. They had thought the pellets were hid in his great side whiskers, when they were bairns and forever crowding to get up on his knees! Sparser now though still as well-brushed and silky, his stance still upright but shrunken!

His parlour voice quavered, his sermon voice boomed through unexpectedly: "My dear girl, may the *Lo-ord* keep you!"

Aunt Helen's niece on the other side, Margaret, was staying with them and did the cooking. Annie said she had a sharp tongue. When the housemaid from Number 39 was by on an errand, Charlotte over-heard them at the back door:

"Tom's trysting with a wee thing at Francis Sprite's with great sheep's eyes that's no more than twenty. I saw her at the Chapel, she's most demure and holds her prayer book just so in her white kid gloves. Oh aye, she adores him. She writes poetry! So that's Tom smitten for the first time in his life."

With appropriate exclamations from the other woman.

"There's no fool like an old fool, he's thirty-seven or eight if he's a day, *and* a deacon in the Kirk."

"Oh, aye!"

"And they say too there's a good wipe of the tar brush back in her family."

"No-o!"

"It was an aunt on her father's side went to the Antiguas, or as it were adopted a poor nigger laddie and brought him to Edinburgh to make a gentleman of him, I don't know the connection but there's a squad of wee darkies in Edinburgh all dressed up in pinafores. And W P's Janet says, Tom's lassie has a half-sister with a nose like a squashed plum, though very like her all the same, the same large eye—"

"A piccaninny!"

The Fair in Lanark began the Thursday and Helen was now deter-mined to hire a domestic to Annville. Charlotte came back early in order to receive the new servant and put her into the train of things, before Willie should return.

Helen passed through in the conveyance that would take her to her train, and would just step down, she said, and have a word with her niece on the way. She had been successful, she told Charlotte after kissing her in the lobby, in hiring a "good, stout girl." George Kay out in the drive leaning on the gate to have a crack with Mr. Allan, but she had not quite time for a cup of tea, she must certainly be away to King-street, for she did not wish to leave Willie long. Mr. Paterson's visitation had been such a blessing! Willie was up and dressed and they all sat in the front room, and Mr. Paterson was with them more than an hour, and with Willie longer. But Charlotte, looking into her aunt's earnest face beneath the purple bonnet with its row of China silk rosettes bobbing on the brim, could not believe much good had come of it. Helen saying too, that though she did not like to mention it Willie and Maddie did not get on, and the house was out of the ordinary crowded.

Mr. Paterson had however spoken beautifully of the bonds of family love which proved firm against trouble. Afterwards they had sung "Blest be the Tie that Binds."

Aye, Helen sighed as the carriage bumped up the Lesmahagow hill; she had to admit she looked forward to getting Willie back into Chattie's care, though the visitation was of course a blessing. Mr. Paterson could aye give encouragement to the weary! Willie must face the future with fortitude, he had said, and with pride as well, for it was not every man to whom such a serious challenge was put, to try his strength against.

"Your regular man will choose his path and think nothing of it, or of the temptations he is spared along the way. But God's love is past our understanding. And that man He brings into another, harder path, that man can no longer see his way—that man knows God especially loves him. He looks into the future and thinks there is but a great fog or mist before his face. Look again, Christian! the mist is parting, though to your mundane eye it reveals no certain course! Lay your hand in the Saviour's and allow Him to lead you. You are not lost—it is filled with radiant light."

Willie had said that he was continuing his studies as well as he could, but made no other remark. Helen had kept quiet for Willie had desired her very expressly not to speak: "I'll no be explained and excused and talked about in front of Mr. Paterson. Nor behind my back either."

As she combed his hair. Maddie stepping down from the shop wearing one of the new flounced tweeds and saying, "Well, I'm sure I won't talk about you. How is your brother? Carrots Gray asked me last week, he was at the Cross in his new cassock and enquired after you and I said, I'm sure I don't know the answer to that, you had better ask him yourself."

"He's no been near me."

"He's no here that's why, he's got himself a parish at Aberfeldy and earning his own keep."

"There's those as can."

"And there's those as will. You're no so sick as you make out, I always thought." Touching her lavish bonnet with its Ottoman silk bow.

"Well you thought wrong. Snivelling away in your finery. 'Miracles of Millinery.' It's all borrowed out of the shop anyway and there's no miracle will alter your face, you turned out very plain with the years, Maddie, you're as bonnie as the back of a coal shovel."

"Aye, cough away, we'll be sorry for you then. The trouble with you is there's nobody at Annville will stand up to you and tell you your business."

"Maddie, that's enough."

"Aye, Mother, I have brought on his coughing, I'm very sorry I'm sure."

Willie said, recovering himself, "It's a life of roses at Annville of course. Music and roses and rickety-coo the day long. You'd do with a bit of the rickety-coo yourself, Maddie, it looks like, put a smile on that dead pan of yours."

Helen in the shop had opened the street door. "There's Father has met Mr. Paterson by the Black Bull! They are coming. In you go the both of you, and sit down nicely in the parlour."

CHAPTER 25

In which Catherine Hamilton is introduced; and she enters
her half-term at Annville.

W hen Catherine Hamilton was ten years old, baby Isabella was born and everything changed. Catherine had been till then the only living child. There were no houses and no other bairns nearby, and she must not cross the railway to Lanark Loch where the great bairns played. She had dreamed of a doll but Bella was best. Besides, ten years old was too old for dolls and play. Nursing the baby was grown-up. Mother said, "Put her back in the cradle now Katie" but she preferred to humph her about and Bella got used to it. Katie soon adept as any cottage kimmer at wrapping the baby firmly in a shawl, setting her on her hip and getting on with things. When Bella grew bigger Katie taught her to walk and talk, which took many strenuous, laughing hours. They slept in the same box. The feel of Bella's wee body held close against her own was an ordinary sensation. They "took to" each other, that was how it was.

There was one photograph of them.[52] Their father, a general labourer, had got fast employment with the erection of the Poorhouse, which was building right across the road from the cottage, though well back in its grounds. The day the cornerstone was laid all the squires came driving out in carriages to the Beeches, and Mr. Brown of Clan Tartan Boxwork was requested to take a photograph. Katie was away over to watch, carrying Bella of course, who was then about six months old.

It was a rainless April morning. The masons were got down on their hunkies in front, behind a row of stones. They had their caps and white aprons new laundered for the occasion and held their tools up stiffly, to look as if they were about to smash a stone. The blocks were

arranged in front of them artistically, that is, not in a reasonable pile
as her Dad would have placed them out of the barrow, but all tumbled
about. Andrew Hamilton had not been informed and was in his usual
Irish duck and tattered coat. The gentlemen stood in a row behind the
masons and Dad stood on the right. When old Boxwork was ready
some other folk, who had been weeding in the Bankhead parks, moved
in a little closer, and Katie edged in behind her father. She could still
see the photographic box, which was why she and Bella appeared in
the picture, only partly hidden. Katie's light hair loosely pulled back
from her broad forehead. Her rather short pinny showed too, and her
boots. Bella wrapped away in the tartan so only her wee head stuck out
with a cotton bonnet on it. Later when the photograph was displayed
in the Boxwork window Mrs. Hamilton walked in to see it and said she
was ashamed of them, Dad should have worn his Sabbath suit. Though
it was like him to be standing up, as tall as the squires in their top hats,
taller than most! She admitted that Bella, hardly more than a blur of
white on Katie's arm, looked nice.

Katie was then a scholar at Mrs. Wilson's Mortification in Lanark.
It was a charity school, for not less than twenty-five boys and twenty-
five girls, from families "*of good moral character but not in the receipt of
parochial relief.*" The schoolhouse was a one-storey whitewashed cottage with windows to the street. The E U Kirk ladies sewed dark blue
frocks and white pinafores for the Mortification lassies. In warm
weather Katie went barefoot; her long work in the tattie-fields went to
boots for the winter. Though the year she was twelve her mother's old
boots were pieced over for her and it was Mother who got new ones.
Katie copied her lessons with Bella hanging at her arm. Laboriously,
she had begun to teach Bella her letters.

At fourteen she was fee'd to Corrahouse Farm above the
Hyndeford Bridge to work in the dairy. She was a "stout active girl"
and well-liked. Exactly six months later, on the Whitsun Fast Day of
1883, she flitted like everyone else. There was scarcely a woman nor
man lower than first ploughman who did not flit each half-year at
Term Day, for no more reasons than a general restlessness and money
to spend, or it's being a holiday and fine, changeable weather. Katie
was hired to Kirkfieldbank, by Mrs. Brown of Annville.

She had seen Mrs. Brown before at the E U Westport, and at the
manse as well for Mrs. Forsyth and the kirk ladies sometimes gave a

treat for the school. She thought Mrs. Brown a nice lady. Katie had not wearied of out work or the blethering of the bothy lads, and had intended to fee to a farm at Hyndford, nearer home. But domestic service was of course a step up and Mrs. Brown said she was a neat, great girl, which she took as it was meant. At home, she showed off the dark blue half length of real Victoria lawn for her new worsted, purchased at Andrew Nilson The People's Warehouse because Mother had warned her against buying off the barrows. She brought Bella a gift: a tin peerie with pictures on it that skirled when it was spun. Bella did not want her to go away again and roared when she left. She walked down the Brae. Her box was sent properly with the carrier.

Katie did not see Miss Spears until she came to Annville, being the lady she would be serving under. Miss Spears was busy, as Mrs. Brown had explained, with nursing the man upstairs, as well as a music teacher. Indeed as Katie was chapping at the front door she could hear a terrible blast of piano music coming out the parlour window, and after a time she had gone around to find the back door, being perhaps what was meant, and waited there, which was away down under the house, till Miss Spears came out and found her standing by the step with the banties at her skirts.

Katie had been through the village of Kirkfieldbank before, when the Mortification got a trip to Stonebyrnes Linn, but she had not seen Annville House to notice it, and it struck her from the first as very large and fine. There were more rooms than in Corramore Farm house, though by no means a great house like Castlebank. From the road it was all hidden away, but from down in the garden it stood up three storeys high. There were no offices to speak of except a shut carriage house under the wall at the top, and a wooden caivie and piggery with one pig and a midden by it, and skeps and a glass-house away at the bottom.

Miss Spears if not extremely tall was taller than Katie. She did not look like a lady though Katie saw later that she could if she pleased, all smoothed for the Sabbath with her awful red hair covered up. But for every day she wore a big bed-apron over a day apron and an old drab gown, and a morning cap that did not do its duty; and she was never afraid of the heavy work either, if it had to do with Mr. Willie Brown.

Katie's box had come and been brought in; there it stood on the flags in the kitchen. She was to sleep down there in the set-in bed, and her box to go under it.

Everything being new Miss Spears showed her the appointments and took her up to see the rooms. There was a great lobby at the top of the kitchen stair that the whole of Crosslaw Cottage could have fit inside. Miss Spears walked across to the glazed front door and showed her how it was locked with the key that hung on a nail over the umbrellas, though Katie found soon enough that it, and the back key as well, would be mostly stuck in the doors and left unturned. The door was very beautiful, all etched with a vase and twists of leaves and a square band of coloured cathedral glass around that. There was a bonnie trellis outside and whenever the sun was high enough, the shadows of the leaves and roses danced on the glass and the wee bits of colour danced on the floor. Miss Spears said that in the winter Mr. Brown fixed the real door back on the outside, and Katie thought she would be sorry when he did that, there being not a window in the lobby otherwise, to let in the light.

In the parlour, which Katie saw was very tasteful, Miss Spears showed her how the venetians were worked by cords twined about the pretty nickel fastenings, which she knew already from the parlour at the Westport manse, once when Mr. Forsyth found her wandered in and had demonstrated them to her very kindly lifting her up to try. But now she listened politely of course. They did not go to the upper flat.

Miss Spears was a great one for air, and cool or hot the windows were aye to stand open to some extent, and to be thrown up wide in the forenoon first thing. She was also a great one for laundering which was because of the Contamination.

That first morning they worked together and then Miss Spears sat down with her to tea in the kitchen, and asked her kindly about her family. She also asked if Katie liked to read and she answered yes, thinking what was meant was whether she could read and write, but Miss Spears went on about a Savings Bank and Shilling Library. Katie was sure she did not have a shilling to spend on books. The Mortification scholars had to purchase their school books though the E U Westport gave assistance, and old shabby books they were, and cracked slates as well.

It was no more than two days after Katie took service that Mr. Willie Brown was to come home, and Miss Spears very busy above stairs preparing his room for him though she would have no help except to beat the mattress, on an old table outside the shed.

When they humphed it up again Katie got a peep at his room, which was not like a sickroom at all. It looked like a fairy bower, all light and airy with screens and fresh posies and pictures on the walls, but she had no time to look carefully, and later she could never tell her new friend Agnes Elder much about it, though Agnes pressed.

Katie was in the kitchen when Willie was brought in through the front, and such a bustling up and down did Miss Spears make of it! Afterwards, when she was satisfied, she came into the kitchen and sat Katie down. Looking at her in a very serious way, as if it were a lesson at Sabbath School.

"Catherine"—this was before she began to call her Katie—"You're to understand that Mr. Willie Brown is an ill man."

Katie knew already that she was to do the rough and Miss Spears Willie, because Mrs. Brown had told her. But she nodded, just as serious, and being naturally curious about the man upstairs.

"I'm his nurse, as my aunt has explained to you, and you're no to have any of the care of him at all. I will do his room as well and his fire, unless we're in for a real turn-out when I'll be glad of your help. Oh and I'll aye carry down his slops and ashes to the back step, and bring up his pitcher." She paused.

"I believe you may put his coals on the stairhead, before you sweep the stairs, just as you did this forenoon."

For Willie had a fire though May, which was uncommon extravagant. She went on: "There is no need of your going to the top flat at all, except with me when we do the other bedroom for Mr. and Mrs. Brown."

Katie said, "Yes, Miss Spears," properly.

"You may wonder at this being made a rule, but Mr. Willie Brown is sometimes in a great deal of pain, which must be taken into account."

Agnes saying later, "She was warning you, they aye do, to stay out of the gentleman's way so you'll no be interfered with. So he'll no take liberties with you."

"Oh Agnes, they are Congregationalists!"

Later Katie saw how he took liberties with Miss Spears—all that talk about being married; she would never have liked that. But he never talked to Katie in that way, even if Miss Spears were out at the IOGT Hall or away to Lanark doing her messages, and if he found Katie in the kitchen he'd be as likely to say: "Run away off to the Elders if you like."

"Oh, she's no given me leave."

"I'm giving you leave then, it's my house not hers." Sharply. "Take your wee body out and get some of that fresh air she's aye blethering about."

To please him she might put on her bonnet, and pull weeds under the grossets for a quarter of an hour though there was in work to finish, or till he left the kitchen.

Willie would wander about the house then, into the drawing room to play "There is a Green Hill" with one finger, for he was not musically educated, or even into Miss Spears' rooms; or he came into the kitchen again, picking things up and putting them down, not as if he were looking for anything particular, or was very interested.

"Are you cleaning the steels, Katie?"

"Aye, sir."

"Is the wee lassie no to come by anymore and get a farthing for it?"

"No, but she's by for the out work."

"Go on with you, you're at that as well, it's you that's aye fetching the raiks and tripping after the banties. They've let the woman go as well, that came in before you, sour as a pig in brine she was."

He began to pick up the steels Katie had laid by and examine them and put them down and Katie thinking they must not be bright enough to suit him. Miss Spears made sure he was aye provided with clean linen but close up he had a nasty smell.

"Have you ever seen my kit, it's all lined in velvet, and I've a lancet keener than any of these."

Katie said, rubbing hard with the emery the while, "I've seen a lancet, when the Vaccinator came to do the scholars." Then thought she had said too much, he being sure to know all about the Vaccination as a medical man.

But he had lost interest and wandered out and up the stair, and Katie took the biggest gully into the garden and plunged it in the earth

the way her mother did, which was the best way to get the steels perfectly clean.

"You're no to be startled, Catherine, if you hear him, for he's away off
and must make himself heard, and then I must just run up and see
what he wants."

Willie pounded with his staff when he wanted Miss Spears, but
she had meant, when he created which he did sometimes and which
frightened Katie till she got used to it. At the time she was hired and he
was got in from Stonehouse he was bed rid; it was later he began to
come downstairs.

The set-in bed behind the kitchen door had a lovely dark red fustian
curtain and valance with a rope and tassel, and a fresh pillow and bol-
ster and sweet-smelling sheets. A rag rug lay on the flags for her feet to
land on in the morning.

Miss Spears would entertain her pupils in the nice room and went
in there every day whether she had any body coming or not, to play on
the piano. It was one of Katie's duties each forenoon, to air that room
and dust it, collecting the ornaments carefully first on the table so she
could get at the mantel, and all the brackets and shelves. She dusted the
picture frames with the turkey duster but she was never to touch the
surfaces. The picture by the dining table was very fearful, being a ship
tossed in a storm, with a wee man high up on a mast that was tilted
over in a dangerous way. The rest of the pictures were highland
scenery she supposed; one had a stag in it that looked right back at you
wherever you stood.

She had to shake the smaller rugs and brush the carpet the way of
the pile. The table was French-polished and must never be wetted,
only wiped with the soft flannel. She might rub up the piano however.
Just now the fire-irons wanted but a flick, with the grate empty behind
a japanned screen. Miss Spears did Willie's fire; she left the scuttle at
the stairhead, for Katie to carry down. Katie did the kitchen range of
course, with a lead-block and lamp black, and its brasses with rotten-
stone, polishing vigorously. Sometimes the lead-black would not take
because the fire had not cooled down, and once she burned the heel of
her hand leaning over to get at the brass at the back and had a sharp
red mark for days, and even yet a bit of a red line to remind her to take

better care.

Miss Spears' room was aye airy and clean but Katie gave it a going over even so. And the glazed door—she loved to give it a wipe and a wee polish whenever she was passing, just for the touching of the coloured panes. There were once a week tasks as well like the plate and steels and washing down the stairs, and scrubbing out the kitchen which Miss Spears liked done Friday to be nice for Mr. and Mrs. Brown.

Miss Spears was sometimes from home, for she had her messages to do and her Band of Hope and her musical doings. Apart from her pupils she did not receive visitors however, which made Katie decide she was more a housekeeper than a lady after all. The Browns came in the end of the week, and their room and the whole house must be got ready for them special. Then the polis might come in, old Munro, and sit with Mr. Brown so it was crowded in the kitchen of a Saturday night. But after Katie became friends with Agnes she'd be usually away over the road.

Miss Spears was aye kind and even-tempered. Indeed, when Katie got the way of the house and her tasks, she could go about them pretty much as she chose, and never a word unless it were to open the windows wider, so there was a great draught tearing through whatever the weather with the venetians clickety clicking, or the bang of a door somewhere if any one went in and out. Katie was freer than she had been at Corramore for Miss Spears did not care if she went for a stroll to the brig in the evening even on a week night, and if she had sitting work and it did not rain, she might take it down the garden. After Katie got to be friends with Agnes she would run across to the forge house whenever her work was done and Miss Spears did not care.

Katie was never sure exactly what was the matter with the man upstairs, for he would be ailing the one day and hale the next, but it was all quite clear to Miss Spears. If he were well, he would be down to eat with them in the kitchen. The first time Katie saw him she had decided he was consumptive; he had very white skin and dark hair and his eyes quite sunk into his head. He looked about ages with Miss Spears but she later learned, from Agnes, that he was a great deal younger, being twenty-four. He ate very little though Miss Spears aye

dressed him the prettiest dishes, and he glanced sideaways at Katie the
first time, saying nothing, when Miss Spears told him her name. He
had an odd kind of smile and later Katie saw how he teased Miss
Spears, but not then. Sometimes when he was well he'd go a walk up
the village. But he passed his time mostly above stairs. Miss Spears said
he was studying, and had to rest a good deal.

She assured Katie it was not a smitting kind of fever, so Katie
must never be afraid of catching it, but Miss Spears acted as though it
were even so, with all the scouring and carbolic and airing out that
went on.

On the Sabbath they would walk up to the E U Westport, to the services. There were two in the summer, at 11:15 and 1:45, and they took a
light tea between sermons and ate dinner late. But Willie never went
to kirk whether he were well or no, and he did not attend evening
prayers in the kitchen either, though Miss Spears aye put in a good
word on his behalf. On the week-ends the Browns and Miss Spears
would walk up to the second storey for prayers and Katie in a clean
apron walked after them. The others would kneel about Willie's bed
and Katie behind a large chair just within the door.

"But what's his pictures like, and the screen Miss Spears is
improving? Are there terrible medical books lying about?"

Agnes was over-curious about Willie's room, because Katie had
said it was the most tastefully plenished she had ever seen, but Katie,
with her face against the horsehair and the draught going right
through her skirts, dared not peer around while Mr. Brown was reading the chapter, and squeezed her eyes shut when he prayed.

She got a half day every second Sabbath and it was long enough for
Katie till she and Agnes became friends. The *People's Friend* said that a
Christian servant ought to pass the time reading her Bible, or "*learn by
heart a hymn that she likes; she can write down what she remembers of
the summer. Find opportunities of helping a sick neighbour, teach anything to children. The Sabbath can never be a dull day to one whose heart
is busy learning or teaching.*"

But Katie's free time would soon be spent idly with Agnes, leaning on the brig in fair weather, or at the Elders' parlour window,

though the blinds were drawn down, keeking out at the edges. Agnes might give a long sigh if the brig end provided nothing of interest, and stroll across the room, and turn the ornaments about on the mantel peevishly. Though Katie knew she had but to wait—Agnes would think of something, and it was of course learning, of a sort.

It seemed queer, when the fruit pulling came on, not to be outbye with the women and bairns. Agnes was in a squad, and Mrs. Elder as well, working the rows above Ramath. There were beds at Annville of course and Mrs. Brown pleased with Katie's quick hand among the strawberries. Then came the famous Annville raspberries that, as Mrs. Brown declared, ripened behind you at the top of the row before you got down to the bottom. Katie liked having Mrs. Brown at Annville, and the Saturdays they pulled fruit, and boiled jam, were very agreeable. It was as though Mrs. Brown, walking in dressed up in one fashionable costume after another, brought a breath of fresh air, talking on and on as she did of the new styles and other pleasant things. Miss Spears of course talked cheerfully too but it was never the same.

One thing was, that Miss Spears never complained about Willie no matter what, or scolded him. And one night after the reading, which was in Romans.xii.20, she closed the Bible over-firmly and gave Katie a look, which made her understand that it was a kind of a fight, or a match, between her and Willie Brown, and Miss Spears was going to win it with her Christian charity.

Willie provoked her very much sometimes, and she did a great deal for him which Katie thought he could have done for himself, or that need not be done at all. At first Katie could not understand it, that when Miss Spears was the most provoked she would aye find something extra to do for him, a nice pudding or a pretty card from Lanark for his screen. And never a word did she say.

The worst way he provoked her was to talk about marrying her, and that was in the kitchen while Katie was by; she could tell there was no matter in it, it was only his way of getting at her.

Then Miss Spears would walk out to the scullery to fetch something though Katie was sure it was to keep from opening her mouth, and Willie would glance across at Katie with that smile. But she was not going to share his joke at Miss Spears' expense.

They got each other's back up, and that was them.

"When we're man and wife, Chattie," he would say, and make to take her round the waist, but she would never let him, or answer him. She was that determined, tugging in her lips tight so the skin was white around them.

Miss Spears was what you would call a great reader and was aye lending books at the Post Office. Sometimes she read in a high voice in the evenings, very romantic it was, not at all like a tract, it was called on the dust-jacket *Waverley* and about a fierce highlander and his doings over a hundred years syne, but there was more ponderings than doings all the same, and Miss Spears had to explain to Katie that the mysterious man was Rob Roy, for the poor gentleman supposed to be telling about him could never find it out, though over half the book was gone through already before the Quoad Sacra, and after that Miss Spears must have got tired of it as well for she gave it back.

One part she read and smiled, and read again, as if she liked it, and closed the book in her lap with her finger in the place, and Katie thought for a moment she looked almost bonnie, with the kitchen in the twilight and out in the boughs a blackie singing.

> "*In the meantime, I was lord of my person, and experienced that feeling of independence which the youthful bosom receives with a thrilling mixture of pleasure and apprehension.*"

"We'll stop there I believe," was all she said, but very sweetly almost to herself, as if her thoughts were far away. She sang too sometimes as she went about her work, very softly. Katie thought later that for all she had to do, Miss Spears was happy then.

She was fair for all that; she would never have it that she intended Katie to work as hard as she did herself, and if the day had been over thrang she might send her off early:

"Run away then, if you like," and away Katie would run, the summer evening opening for her, bright and long, and let herself out at the gate and trip along the footpath and across to the blacksmith's airie door.

Agnes Elder was the elder, by almost two years, and pleased to have a lass as ignorant and good-willed as Katie as a friend, for Effie Grindley down the street usually had her wab to finish, and was troubled with a cough now as well.

At first she was called Catherine, later on Katie when she had asked. And hearing Willie always called that she fell into the way of it as well and did not refer to him as "the man upstairs" or Mr. Willie Brown any more.

He was a wee man after his father, and from the sickness very crushed. His skin looked like a chinie doll. She noticed it most when she had not seen him for some days, or had been over at the forge with stout Mr. Elder and Jimmie the joiner, who were so big and hale. When Willie was very ill he did not let Miss Spears shave him and a few days later the basin would be full of longish sharp black hairs, blacker than his head, which Agnes explained was the usual. Agnes had some queer books called *Mother Oracle* and *Mother Shipton's Wheel of Fortune* and they read about *"choosing a husband by the hair."* Black was *"stout and healthy, but apt to be cross and surly."* Which was one half true. And Agnes said about the stubble: "Willie is no such a blackie as all that. Next time you're to get a few of the bristles on the brod, and set them in the sun, and see if they don't dry to brown. My own hair's near black when I wash it."

"Oh no, it is the bonniest light brown!"

"No as light as yours." They put their heads together and compared. One evening when they had the kitchen to themselves, Agnes had the idea of getting their hair singed, which was very healthful. The hair being a thin tube, closing the end preserved the natural juice in it, which was left open and unprotected by being cut across with the scissors. The hair dresser of long experience, explained Agnes, would then pass a jet of gas or some lighted waxed paper across the surface, to catch the ends of the shorter growths. They might try that as well, very carefully of course, with a Runaway match.

She singed Katie's hair first, then Katie singed hers. It made a terrible reek when the candle flared just as Katie was holding a large lock of Agnes' front hair into it, and Agnes screamed and jumped about,

Katie running after her to beat at it with her apron. The ends were awful now, nothing but wee squiggles of ash, and must be cut again and again to get them straight. Then Agnes passed them quick over the candle, and blew it out.

She did not mention the catching of the shorted growths and the girls put up their hair again silently; then Agnes ran upstairs to the looking glass while Katie brushed all the cut bits into the fire, which renewed the reek. Agnes appeared in a cap with short hair sticking out over her brow. She was sniffing and laughing, and threw up the windows.

"You're no to go on about it, Katie, please! I'll show you the Lady's Mile if you'll stop blubbering," she said then, and she rowed up Katie's obedient sleeve and ran her fingers lightly up and down the plump flesh of her inner arm, between wrist and elbow, which Katie conceded was a most queer but agreeable sensation and returned the favour.

"It's no your fault, it's the bad candles from Duncan McBeau," said Agnes kindly. "I will pray my Dad to buy the patented curling pins. I always had an idea to try a fringe!"

Agnes would read, slowly and laboriously, from *Mother Shipton's Wheel of Fortune*. They were in the parlour for privacy, for Mrs. Elder let them go in as long as they did not touch anything, though Agnes often did. They were sitting on the roup seat under the window. It was Saturday night and the summer curtains blew about their heads, for they had the window thrown up and had been leaning on the sill and whispering to each other about any great chield who passed by, and whether he were handsome or no. Now the sun had set down the dale in a sky as white as milk, and the evening star stood over the Kirk steeple, and folk were out in their doorsteps and wee bairns toddling in the road. A burst of laughter came from the Hotel yard.

"*Get nine small keys,*" read Agnes, "*They must all be your own. Plait a band of your hair, fasten it with nine knots, with the garter to your left wrist when going to bed, and the other round your head. Say:*

> "*Saint Peter take it not amiss*
> *To try your favour I've done this.*

You are the ruler of the keys
Favour me then, if you please,
Let me then your influence prove
And see my dear and wedded love.

"*Your dream will be ominous, you will have a fortune as well told as if you had paid a crown to an As—*" here she stared for a moment, then finished triumphantly: "*—trologer.*"

She took Katie by the arm and they ran down to the forge, which Katie did not quite like with the white heat and the noise and the horrible smell of the hoof-parings, but Agnes went straight to her father and interrupted him, begging the bunch of old keys off the wall.

"Are they mine the now? Are they, Dad?" hanging on his neck. Mr. Elder grumbling, "Away with you then and your silly plaguing."

"You have to say they're mine."

"Aye, aye."

In the kitchen, Agnes cut the old tause across and laid the keys out on the dresser.

"There's ever so many!"

"I'll take these eight"—counting them—"with the key to my box, and if I give you the six, and the Annville two makes eight, from the back door and the glazed door. They are yours Katie, do nae be so daft, you are in service, and the ninth you can take out of the caivie, it's you that fetches the eggs."

"But it is very unlucky to disturb the clackers after dark."

"Well, you will no disturb them if you are quiet. Of course you can wait till tomorrow if you please but I'm putting the garters on the night."

This decided Katie and with Agnes at her kitchen window and holding up a lamp to give her courage, she crept past Annville house wall and down the garden and felt for the old key in the caivie door. Her fingers got hold of it but it would not lift out, and suddenly the cockerel started up a terrible clattering. She pulled sharp and it fell out dusty in her palm; she nearly dropped it on the ground and was sure she would never have found it if she had. Up the garden she ran stooping under the branches, for she kenned by now where they hung in the way.

The range was gone out and the kitchen in darkness. Katie lit a candle, which she ought not to do just for getting into bed, and took the key out in a shower of rust, and when she turned her pocket out there was red rust in the seam. She must just take up Miss Spears' bathing water, and wait till the house was quite quiet. Then she got into her night gown, and lifted over the cutty stool near to her bed and stood the candle on it. If only Agnes were there! for the valance hung strangely and seemed to move long after she had climbed in. She knelt on the quilt with the keys laid in a row. Then she must get out of bed again to pull out her box for the scissors, and snip off a strand of her hair. She wished she had plaited it first for it would not heed her fingers, till she licked and knotted the one end and held it between her teeth. Eight more knots, which was easy for it was a long plait—her undone hair hung to her waist. Then she did the part with the garters. The one around her head was out of the ordinary tight!

But, the garter having slid off her head in the night, and the keys being not really her own, Katie did not dream of anything. Agnes said she herself had dreamed of a smartly turned out gentleman with dark brown hair ("*robust, good tempered, fond*") who looked a little like Mr. Weir. Katie quietly putting back the six keys on the Elders' dresser and not quite sure she believed her.

Sometimes they talked about Miss Spears and Katie heard how she had kept tryst with a clergyman at Tintock Tap and been expelled from the Kirk by Mr. Cameron and the Managers.

"But she's old." Katie would not believe it.

"Oh aye, and the parson but a young man, twenty-three. But it is the truth. A handsome man as well, for I talked with him on Tintock myself, he knows all the names of the flowers and birds. But somehow she had got him to come away and meet her there and give her some papers which some say were music but some poetry. At any rate the Managers would never have it though before that day she was Precentor and very respected. I sing in the Choir still but it's sadly fallen off. It was a grand Choir then, very bonnie music we sang, and reported in the *Advertiser* very regularly."

"But a man of twenty-three!"

"Perhaps she cast a spell on him, or it is by way of his being a clergyman, for they are no right in the head, the lot of them. There was one in Liberton hanged himself from the kirk beam, leaving a wife and two bairns. Right over the nave."

Katie told Agnes about Willie and the marrying.

It was Agnes' turn to open her eyes wide. "You are sensational, Katie." And Katie being sensational went back to Annville a little ashamed of herself, but eager to discover more.

She could however find out nothing further about the secret affairs of Miss Spears, and Agnes' proposal—that she look for love-letters in the escritoire when she was doing Miss Spears' room—she treated with the contempt it deserved.

"I would never do that!"

"You could let me in, I would do it."

"No, it wouldnae be right. I'd be sorry for it in my prayers."

"What's prayers for if you've naught to be sorry for?" said Agnes but they came no further and if truth was to be told they could neither of them imagine Miss Spears being in love.

Katie had never thought Jimmie Henderson was anything particular till Agnes began teasing her about him, and she never could discover how that came about, or whether Agnes didnae like Jimmie herself. Agnes declared she had a follower already, a private in the Reserves at Hamilton Barracks and nineteen years old, who had been called out to serve in the Egyptian Campaign and was at the taking of Tel-el-Kebir but thankfully uninjured. He would be on furlough at Hogmanay and then Katie would meet him, a proper gentleman he looked. Agnes seemed to get no letters from him, though Katie would never have asked about that.

Jimmie Henderson at sixteen had outgrown all his clothes, and was covered with the saw dust, for Mr. Elder employed him to mend the tools and farm carts, and anything else of wood that was brought in. He worked in the yard when he could, or back at the other end of the forge where there was but a dirty wee window over the bench to let in the light. When he was chiselling he had his shirt sleeves rowed up and chips of wood caught in the hairs of his arms, which Agnes pointed out before Katie noticed. He had a big nose and a cow lick of straight hair, light brown, out over his eyes. Light brown was "*middling, on the whole bad character*" according to *Mother Shipton*. The apprentice Hamish Souter had red hair however: "*will be artful, cunning, deceitful, a lively temper.*" The best that could be said of Hamish was, he was forever proving his strength with the other lads and could run the Cartland Bridge parapet. And the worst, that he paid no heed to Agnes at all.

Mrs. Elder wanted new shelves in the pantry and Jimmie was doing them, and would take his tea in the kitchen before he went off home. One Saturday he was there late, sanding and finishing up, while Agnes and Katie were fooling with the auguries in *Mother Oracle*, and Agnes writing some of them off in her large, cursive hand Katie so admired, "*Dream of oranges. Most unfortunate. Loss of goods and reputation, every ill that can befall you.*"

Katie was sure she had never dreamed of oranges. Though she had eaten a half orange once at the IOGT Christmas Tree and made a bad mess of it. Mother throwing up her hands at the state of her gown and saying that oranges should be sucked in private.

"Agnes, I wish I could write as beautifully as you."

"Why, you may try. Here's two great letters to copy," Agnes wrote, shielding the paper with her plump arm.

Katie squealed. "I'll no write *them*!"

"Not two letters? Perhaps Great Jay is over-difficult, with the long flourish? Do you no think Great Jay a bonnie letter, Katie?"—loudly— "I am just speaking of the shape of it, mind. Or you could try the—"

Katie covering Agnes' mouth quick with her hand.

Agnes said she was a silly article and wrote "I love you" instead, but Katie would only agree to copy that on a new sheet, and when Agnes went to the dresser Mrs. Elder told them no to be wasting paper with their foolishness. "I could wrap six cheeses in what you've spread about already."

Jimmie grinning and tidying away his tools, and shaking the golden saw dust into the fire from off his apron, the sparks snapping.

Great Jay, Great Aitch. Katie wrote them later with her wetted finger, shyly, on the inside of the smoothest zinc pail, just over the water. Down at Clyde, fetching two raiks for Miss Spears' bath. The pail swung as she lifted it, the water darkening the whole inside and the letters gone as if they had never been.

"The Imperial Yeomanry are holding Brigade Drill on the Lanark Moors. Shall we no walk up, Katie, and see the manoeuvres? The Voluntaries will be taking part." Jimmie was a Voluntary, the drill being considered beneficial for growing lads, smartening up those who slouched in their gait and generally improving health. But Katie would never ask for a half day out of turn and Agnes went off with whomever she could find; she'd tease her mother into the excursion if she could get no one else. Mrs. Brown said Agnes was an "idle girl" but the Elders kept no in servant; the difference was, Agnes could call her time her own if she chose.

One bright forenoon Katie was down the Annville garden hanging up the linen when she heard a familiar voice call to her from the brig. She looked up to see her own dear Dad standing there, with Bella waving on his shoulder.

It was the happiest day of her life. They stayed all morning, and Miss Spears gave her the rest of the day and even helped her pack up a luncheon in a creel, placing a nice d'oyley over it, to eat by Clyde on the sand bar, and the harness rug to sit down upon. With Bella interrupting over and over to have her hand held and go out into the water, and then squealing at the rush and cold of it.

All was well at Crosslaw Cottage. Mother had been a wee bit ailing but was over that, and since the Smyllum grounds were finished Dad had wrought in the Bankhead parks, and he'd got some clearing work out at Bonnington from the morrow.

Her Dad was a gaunt man with long furrows down his face which were white inside, the same colour as his neck below his collar, for they never got the sun. The crowsfoot at the corner of his eyes was the same.

At lousing-time the water came through and they sat up on the grass tight under the wall. Jimmie Henderson and some of the other great lads had pushed a cart down to scrub in the shallows at Mouse mouth, and then they were bathing as well, and after that the Smith bairns came down the johnnie and the big ones went in from this side, naked and squealing. Bella would try, so Katie stripped her down to her shift and held her fast, and she splashed bravely, Katie with the stuff bunched tight in her hands between the wee shoulders, and her own skirts rowed up and feet firm into the sand. Afterwards they wrapped Bella in the plaid and she sat in Katie's lap till Dad finished his pipe and said they must be getting home. Katie walked with them to the middle of the brig and waved at them as they went through the farm and along the path by Clyde, with the warm low sunlight making the brown water sparkle, and a squad of women trailing in from the strawberry beds. Her legs still tingling from the cold water. Here was Jimmie climbing long-legged up the bank behind the toll-house with his wet hair all sticking out, and hailed her but did not walk over. He went up the Nemphlar-road home to Mouse Mill. Agnes would have found an excuse to call him back.

At supper Miss Spears praised Bella and said she was a bonnie lassie and asked Katie if she knew the song? And took her right into the parlour and made her listen to it:

> When smiling Spring comes in rejoicing,
> And surly Winter grimly flies;
> Now crystal clear are the falling waters,
> And bonie blue are the summer skies.
> Fresh o'er the mountains breaks forth the morning,
> The ev'ning gilds the ocean's swell;
> All creatures joy in the sun's returning,
> And I rejoice in my bonie Bell.

Katie loved the song. Standing there with her hands clasped and her bare toes digging into the Turkey carpet, while Miss Spears was playing and singing away, she almost loved Miss Spears too. And resolved not to speak of her again the way Agnes did but to stick up for her, for Agnes must agree when she heard about the half-day, that she was a very kind mistress.

CHAPTER 26

*In which Kirkfieldbank Kirk becomes a Quoad Sacra Church,
and Charlotte is forsaken.*

Willie himself had been too tired to comment when they got him in, as she settled him saying "Well, Chattie, *It came to pass* as Father aye says, and now that's over with."

"Was it no a great refreshment to be home? I am sure it is for me, to visit in the Great Western Road."

He coughed. "Nay, nay, you look about you, and nothing's changed, and it's all nothing for all that, it's all gone."

"Willie, surely not!"

"I'll no be in Stonehouse again till a stone's put over me."

As she was about to go out he said, "Here we are again, Chattie, you and I, and must make the best of it."

Stone Row,
May 28th, 1883

Charlotte, shall I go the Lanimers? I have a mind to ride the circuit this year, as some others from the Association propose. Will you not go up and see the procession? Will you be at the race-ground afterwards for the athletics? Shall I vault with the pole?

I have taken Park into my confidence to some extent, for he knows that we correspond. He cannot see that there is such a difficulty in meeting you and thinks you "nice" but I argue that, being a *village*:—Charlotte, there is no penance I cannot readily agree to, after the unhappy consequence, last year, of my thoughtlessness. You are wise in being "nice." But tell me of the Lanimers. I shall ride, and I shall stay late if there be a chance to meet you.

I am of course delighted that your aunt has hired a servant to live in, and that she is a good, willing girl. You tell me that, your cousin being quite an invalid now, it became necessary. Charlotte, is your cousin worse? You must not be made unhappy. You do not tell me that your burden of nursing him has been lightened, which is what I would wish most to hear:—lightened, or removed entirely.

Dear Drew,

Perhaps we shall meet at the Lanimers. I would not be able to come away for the morning procession, Etc. but when my uncle and aunt and cousin Magdalene return I will walk up, which would be about seven o'clock, if it is a fine evening, by the path I shewed you which joins the Westport beside the E U Church. This unless my cousin is very ill.

As for my cousin, I hope you will not continue to urge me against nursing him, first of all, because I would cause my aunt and uncle much distress, and secondly because I feel this to be my duty at present. He is often in pain from a congestion of the spine, delirious from the fever and unable to take his food. My tasks at these times are not difficult it all being underway. He is unfortunately not suited to the care of a young girl or, I fear, anyone who did not understand him. Your esteemed father has written of the mental perturbation to which my cousin is subject. My uncle and aunt must be spared; indeed, none other than myself ought to attend him at such times. In regard to his physical and spiritual distress my cousin's cross is heavy indeed. Mine in caring for him is much lighter.

Now, I have made too much of a little, in writing so many words! I would not wish to distress my uncle and aunt, that is the heart of it. You are anxious that I might be made unhappy. In being your friend, I cannot. Being happy, I can as it were run lightly through the work of the day which would otherwise be burdensome. In my music, in receiving your letters and writing to you, I am happy indeed.

On the Lanimer Day just after Katie was fee'd to Annville, Mr. Brown again walked the circuit. Mrs. Brown and Madeleine went off too, in high spirits, giving the rain no heed, for did it not aye rain on Lanimer Day? Kirkfieldbank provided some beautiful floats, a "Windsor Castle" which took a first prize, and a grand wild flower display rendered by the Post Office, though Mr. Dunlop had been blarneyed into dismissing all his scholars to botanize for it. Katie watched the floats the length of the brig, swaying high among bells and bannerettes. It was her first whole holiday and she did not know what best to do with herself, knowing nobody to walk with and not wanting to be near Madeleine Brown who looked cross and had not said a word to her from the time she had arrived. Wearing a peacock blue frock with a new Dress Supporter, and showing off its effect though to Katie it looked as if she had got into her grandmother's crinoline and very out of fashion.

In the end Katie decided to go home and visit. Did her parents not go to the Lanimers? Oh, aye, and they would all walk over to the race course together, which was just down the road, and watch the sporting events and the Yeomanry.

Later coming back through Lanark she saw Miss Spears standing at the side of the E U kirk, looking rather distracted.

"Are you away home, Miss Spears?"

"Oh, Katie, how are you?" she had said. "No, I will walk about a little first I believe," or words to that effect, not paying her much attention. And when Katie asked whether she should wait, Miss Spears sent her off very smartly. Katie telling all this to Agnes later after they had become friends.

There was more, because the Tuesday next when the Browns had gone away again, Willie was in the lobby and seized a letter. It came over by Mr. Simpson from the Post Office where, Katie thought, Miss Spears had gone for it and must have crossed him when he was in the Close. Katie from below stairs heard Willie singing and coughing and creating the way he did sometimes, and for a change Miss Spears talking back at him as well.

"Now we'll see who Somebody must be, Chattie, for I can tell from your face it's from Somebody—" and singing a silly song.

From the turn under the stair Katie could not quite hear what Miss Spears answered but she sounded out of the ordinary raised.

"You neednae rant, Chattie, an auld married couple ought to have no secrets from each other. If auld Jock hasnae the right to open letters directed to auld Janet where would we be?"

Then Miss Spears speaking again and a crash as if the umbrella spill had gone over. Katie wondered whether she ought to come right up, and did so, and there was the glazed door wide open and Willie sitting against the stand with his feet out, and one arm stretched up and Miss Spears undoing his fingers, it looked like, to get a paper out of them.

"Oh, Katie, are you there? Willie has got a fall and here's the jessamine-water spilt, will you fetch a flannel and basin?" and as Katie turned away she was saying very calm to Willie, "Come, let me help you upstairs."

His voice clear and whining; "I'm no going upstairs, I'm on my way out the door. And you'll no stop me, for I've grand news to tell up the village the now, secret letters and secrecy, I've no doubt you discuss me behind my back as well, if there's room over from all the rickety-coo."

Willie's taking of the letter had frightened Charlotte very much and she was ashamed that her temper had not stood her well, that she had spoken quite sharply to him. She knew not where she should put Drew's letters any more. Almost in penance for her behaviour, she got up in the night and burned them in the parlour. They left a heap of folded ash that broke to smithereens under the poker. She knew them however by heart.

Though four it was already light. Katie would wonder at ashes in June, and the bit of ribband at the edge which had not caught. She stirred it into the heap.

"I have burnt some old papers in the parlour grate." Which was innocent enough, or ought to have been.

Their meeting by the E U! Charlotte had lingered in Jecker's Johnnie, then reproved herself and gone up to the Westport to stand by the Kirk wall. It was on seven o'clock and Lanark thronged and noisy. Some villagers passed and Charlotte stepped back. A crowd of laddies on their own with flushed, weary faces but still larking about, Jimmie Smith and Peter Duffy pulling birk busks off a gate, dashing them at one other. Loud-talking Dublin men, trailing families getting away home. Four or five vagrants standing at the Hope-street corner, bonnets lowered and close together. Here was Katie on her own, her round, bland face suddenly thrust forward, wanting to walk with Charlotte down to Annville. Charlotte could not attend as kindly as she would have wished.

"Please go on ahead. Go by the turnpike road with the others, so you will not be annoyed."

He had his horse by the reins.

She went on while he stabled it behind the manse, then came after her down between the dusky hedges.

They had wandered through the plantings below Castle Hill, where the paths twisted to and fro, sometimes near Clyde, sometimes by Braxfield Burn that ran down from the High-street. The ground was dirty from the day's rain, the leaf so thick overhead they could not clearly see each other's faces. Both his arms around her waist so they walked turned in towards one other, her one hand curled against his breast within his open cloak, against the slippery fabric of his cassock. Charlotte sure as she could be she was clean and scentless, and when he stopped and undid a lock of her hair she put it up again hardly trembling. In the gloom. He kissed her with his hands in her hair, said something she could not catch.

"—do you not?"

Later on the footbridge over the burn they stood still again, the rail pressed into Charlotte's one side and Drew pressed against the other. Voices. A couple coming down through Gullietudlum to cross Clyde on the stones, the lass kilting her skirts up already, laughing then silent as they went by, their bare feet slapping the ground.

Charlotte and Drew had almost quarrelled going back.

"I've other thoughts, than that you should go on as you are, Charlotte. Mind you didnae engage at Kirkfieldbank to be nurse to an ill man."

"But so it has turned out."

HEATHER SPEARS

"Oh, aye, and that's my fault too, Walter discharging you—"

"It is not what I meant, except that, perhaps it was meant, in a higher way, with my cousin being so sick—"

He said something about "choice," but Charlotte did not think she had a choice. What his other thoughts were he did not say, nor that he loved her. Once he had written, "I have not yet the right to advise you." Not yet—but he advised her very much!

They walked by St Patrick's cottage to Clydesholme Braes, the fields opening, the smell of wet hay in an overcast twilight. Drew would go a little farther with her, and stopped under the same elder bushes where Mr. Weir.

They kissed again. But being unluckily just there she turned away from him. Again he said some words she could not catch.

"—is it so difficult, for all that?"

"I am sorry, I do not understand you."

"You are unhappy! You must not be unhappy."

"I am happy, Drew." His fingers seeking within her glove, moving softly against her palm.

Walking back with a mist of rain in her face, she thought she should have used a different word: "content," rather than "happy." She began to compose a letter. "Perhaps I am not happy, except in dashes, but that is my disposition. To quit my cousin would make me *happy* in that sense, but if I were to do so I would never be *content.*"

When their subject was Bernard or the children, or music or any other thing, they need hardly speak for they were of one mind. But now she felt a sad estrangement from him. She ought not to have asked for his father's opinion. Willie had guessed it: "You discuss me behind my back." She must not speak to him of Willie any more.

"*Content.*" At her bedside she repeated the word, which seemed grayish and sorrowful. A contented life. She prayed for Robert and could scarcely remember his face.

They met again, Charlotte walking up Clydesholme Braes after a lesson to do some messages in Lanark. Drew was waiting at the foot of Jecker's Johnnie and they crossed Clyde at the ford and continued up the farther bank, the low sun sparkling on the water and the plantings soughing softly in the warm wind, and the winged beasties like motes

~ 316

of dust dancing. Drew had brought his net but they saw only one butterfly, which Drew called a "Large Heath and no worth drowning for," dipping far out over the water. The glen was very deep here, and full of trees. Even Lanark's spires were hid, though the steady bang of an anvil reminded them how near the town was, and a shout and a dog's barking.

They sat on a stone and he opened a paper containing of two large slices of wedding cake.

"A parson gets more of this than is good for him! And so do the wee Parks, but I've saved this from Allan's sticky gub." They drank from Clyde, cupping the clear water up in their hands. Drew would drink from hers, then turned her fingers between his own, and called them her "taper fingers." As Mr. Miller, more than once.

Charlotte talked about the Schubert, the Rondo she had begun to learn, though she did not say she nearly despaired of it. More than once she had wept, had almost given it up.

"You said it was like a mountain, Drew. If so, it is very steep, it seems to me more like a cliff."

"You will get it at last."

They walked past New Lanark across the river, and heard the bell and then the mingled voices of the mill-workers as they spilled out at lousing-time. The buildings stood bleakly against the high sweep of the glen, all of a piece like a child's blocks, high and narrow against a rise of cottage gardens: tenements and offices, mill, chapel, school and the Institute of Social Improvement all made of the same grim gray stone. And now they could see adult and child workers going between the buildings very soberly, almost like prisoners in their neat gray garments, sufficient to themselves, as they were intended to be.[53] There was little intercourse between New Lanark and Lanark town. From time to time an accident was reported in the *Advertiser*.

"Have you seen Corra Linn, Charlotte? It is very near!"

The excursionists' avenue, however, went up the Lanark side, and Drew and Charlotte wandered through the plantations for some time, and over the stiles of a farm and through a field of thistles, his hand steadying her, before they at last could hear the roaring of the waters.

Trees hid the chasm, the trace of a footpath descending.

Drew walked ahead of her and stood grasping a tree and looking out over a slope, then turned to smile. She could not hear his words for the noise of the Falls but he seemed to be saying, "It's quite safe, do come!"

They stood close in each other's arms, Drew leaning firmly against the tree. From this side they could not behold the noble breadth of the torrent. Their perch was not so dangerous as she had feared—protected by a second jut of ground and bushes farther down. Through them, as if issuing directly from the wall of a precipice of black stone, the boisterous white water spouted, to be lost in the turbulent sluice below. There was such a constant, fierce noise that the ground under her feet seemed to quiver—it was said that Corra Castle was at times so shaken as to spill water in a glass.

A group of gentlemen were standing about on the farther cliff, leaning on the wooden railings and pointing with their sticks. Above them rose a castellated lookout, which must be the celebrated "tower of mirrors." Indeed, some ladies were to be seen inside with their backs turned, contemplating the dreadful spectacle in comfort through a suspended looking glass.

Below at the ford, Drew and Charlotte found the water big and were forced to wait, and stooped into a grassy dell. Drew spread his cloak down and lay back at the edge of it, sighing. They had not spoken again since the Linn; the great, blirting clamour seemed to have followed them as they walked, his hand gripping hers tightly, sometimes trembling. Now all was suddenly very still.

"Will you no lie down beside me, Chattie?"

He had never called her Chattie before. His face looking up. Willie—a sudden picture of Willie's body, his smell, his voice that said her name. Then gone. For an instant she was frightened, that he had taken a bad turn and she ought to be at Annville. Such "premonitions," she knew, were but the stuff of trashy novels.

"Would you no like me to call you Chattie?"

Though she had turned her face away, Drew's hand sought hers, gave it a shy, urgent pull.

"It seems queer."

"I am more used to saying Charlotte. Perhaps I will call you Char, in the end." Tenderly.

"No one has ever called me that!"

"Char." He sat up then and they laughed, Charlotte seating herself properly beside him, smoothing her skirts over her ankles.

"Will you come away with me?"

Then he said something else very low, and: "I'm no speaking of Heywood, though I have told nobody yet. I am hoping to be called to Perth."

"Perth!" She dared not believe he was serious.

"There is a pianoforte at Kilmacolm, an upright, the tone is very good however. I think my father would make us a present—"

"Oh, Drew, how can I answer you?"

"Why, in the affirmative!"

He cleared some phlegm from his throat, expectorated away from her into the grasses. "It's no till next year. Will you promise me?" Near now, his breath on her cheek.

"I will promise to think very seriously about it."

A year, she thought. She need make no decision now. What could not happen, within a whole year?

He wanted to draw her down beside him then but she would not, getting to her feet. They gathered up the parcels.

The water had fallen. With some difficulty they got across the wet rocks. Her forward hems were well soaked before he stepped her ashore. Under the trees she wrung them, and picked out the worst of the thistle thorns.

"Charlotte, Char, we are bad as a pair of vagabonds. You'll no catch cold with your skirts all soaked?"

"My boots are dry, that is what counts. With dry boots nothing can harm me. But, your cassock!"

"The wind will dry it if I ride fast, and Mrs. Park must brush out the mud. She will think I fell into that hole in the High-street." Then they were laughing. He took her hand quickly and kissed her palm, before she could do up the glove button.

Loud voices now, and a squad of ragged women coming down to cross, two of them quarrelling at the top of their voices. Drew and Charlotte turned away as they passed. From out in the river came a shriek, the two women in gripes, teetering and hanging on to one another.

"Are you meddlin' me? I'll give you more than that before I am done wi' you!"

On the other bank stopping to throw up their arms and adjust their hair, then going at each other again, the other women standing about silent; and finally the whole squad walking in among the trees.

At Annville Katie sat white-faced in the kitchen, but stood up quick when Charlotte at last came in.

"Willie has been rapping these two hours, and I didnae know if I ought to go up."

"Did you go up?" Getting out of her cloak, which Katie took from her and stood holding, opening her mouth.

"I went just upstairs the once, at nine o'clock, he was out of the ordinary raised."

"I had a great many messages. Will you put these away in the pantry? Are the banties in?"

"Oh aye. Oh Miss Spears."

"What is it?" Katie's eyes very round. "Did Willie want you to go into his room and do something for him?"

"You said I was no to go in and he said it was his house and no yours." Katie took a breath. "I said, you would be home soon and did he want his supper and he said aye and I left it on the stairhead on the floor. Where I fetch the scuttle. I just went up again as far as the landing to see if he took it and he did. I fried up two scones for him and there is four left over."

Charlotte sat down.

"Katie, come here. Did he frighten you?"

"Oh, no!" Almost running into the pantry with the packages.

Charlotte walked upstairs. Willie was in bed and seemed to be asleep, his lamp unlit and his supper tray by him on the bed and part of one scone uneaten. She mended his fire and adjusted the windows. When she went close to hear, from his breathing, whether he were feverish, he snatched her arm between his fingers.

"You're no to leave me like that, Chattie."

"Willie, I would never have gone to Lanark if you had been ill. You're no ill, are you?"

"I have given up my supper if you would be interested."

He released her arm. She reached for the chantie and emptied it into the slop pail, grayish sputum and a little lumpy vomitus. Then stood, looking down at him.

"Are you in pain?"

"I am aye in pain, if you are interested."

"Have you taken your medicine?"

"I thought you'd give it to me."

She did so, and turned his pillows.

"That was a great many messages to keep you away till eleven o'clock. You're a liar Chattie, and no a very good one." His voice already drowsy. He had perhaps taken a dose himself and forgotten it. If so, he would sleep heavily the night.

She smoothed his bedspread. "Willie, I am going to go down and fetch a nice sermon."

"I'll no be read to like a baby."

"It will be something to think about, and quiet you, and then you will fall asleep." She hurried out before he could reply, and fetched Dr. Shepherd's *Sermons* from her room, where it was lying out. Katie standing in the middle of the lobby with the lamp, its light under her round chin and stubborn lower lip and rather formless nose.

"I've put in your water Miss Spears, for the morrow."

"Thank you. Will you bring me some supper to my room? Then you can go to bed. I am going to read to Willie to try whether it will settle him. Katie, I am extremely sorry if you were upset! You behaved quite right to be firm, and he was not taken bad at all, only distressed that I was not come home." Charlotte took the lamp from her.

"I will stay home in future, Katie, unless he is very well."

Charlotte kept her word and did not go from the house, unless it were to a lesson or the Band of Hope; Willie did not care if he knew where she was going and if it were but a short while. Drew wrote urgently however, and would see her as soon as she might arrange it.

> I think I must put you up on Gyp behind me and ride away.

> My cousin is worse, and at the moment I cannot leave him.

Yet Willie was sometimes out himself, walking in the village. Whom did he speak with? The Inn! Did he meet Mr. Weir?

He was at his books again, in particular the *Causes of Disability*, spread on his table at the window. If she came in he covered the pages with his hand.

"You've no call to be ranting up here on one of your crusades, Chattie. I can manage very well by myself."

For nearly a week he had kept his food down, and she had a good report of him for her aunt and uncle.

Then he took to sending her letters, in the post, with but an empty sheet of paper inside. Though it was some days before she knew it was he. They were franked in the village and the direction written in plain script in a back-sloping hand, very small. She thought it a prank by the Smith children, for scolding them about the eating of the grossets. But the hand was adult and she had no enemies among the village bairns.

There was one with writing in it. "My dear wee Wifie," it began. She burned it and after that she did not open any of them, and then there were no more.

If he was out of his room she hurried to air and clean it, the reek of the camphor giving her some relief.

> The High-street,
> Kirkfieldbank.
> June 15th, 1883

Dear Thomson,

It is an "unco'" long time since I have had a word from you! However, you will now have received your formal Invitation from Lanark Presbytery to our *Quoad Sacra* ceremonies, and I hasten to add my personal invitation as well. You must *of course* lodge with me the night, and we can have a good long crack like old times after the service. Though unable as yet to invite you to a Manse, with Js. Chalmers digging in his heels about the endowment as usual, the laying of the Corner Stone is viewed by myself with the greatest satisfaction, and opens new vistas in my future plans! Of which I will tell you more when we are together.

The note on the Presbytery meeting in the *Advertiser*

did us no good turn saying quite incorrectly that our endowment was up to 120 pounds! However, I sent a Letter of Correction you may have seen, which amends any mis-apprehension on that score. The cost of the Manse must yet be reached and is by no means secured. We have how-ever hopes for a Bazaar which will write off both these sums.

Life in the village, apart from the Lanimer Holiday of course, continuing very quiet, the more interest is already showing towards the up-coming ceremonies which are indeed viewed hereabouts, as I daresay farther afield as well, as quite an Historical Milestone.

I have decided to use the event as an excuse to present some books to the village Library, my intent being to refur-bish a modern library in the Manse. These books since I arrived have never been unpacked, except for some ser-mons of Wilberforce and Ambrose Shepherd, and a few others I would keep by me that were my Father's. The total is twenty-seven volumes, which ought to swell the wee Shilling Library to bursting. Forsyth's Presentation in Lanark about two weeks ago (of 17 books) put me in mind, and the seed being sown, who among our literate villagers may not reap a goodly harvest? There will be a modest Presentation on Friday.[54]

As for the Quoad Sacra ceremony, please let me have a word as to time of your proposed arrival so that I or one of the Managers may be on hand to meet you. I know your penchant for horse back but in keeping with the solemnity of the day and as befits your station, will expect you by car-riage. Besides, the Procession to Lanark will bring you half home again. You will step down at the Kirk. I would advise an early arrival about ten o'clock. Changes to Vestments Etc, Etc can be accommodated in the vestry.

Your Ob't Servant
Arthur Cameron.

Charlotte must partake as leader of the Band of Hope. She would rather have stayed away! The Grand Lodge of Lanark had charge of the ceremonies and they would be lavish, with pipes and parade and full regalia. They would march down the Brae, the "Falls of Clyde" in attendance as well, and Smyllum Band and the Regimentals piping. Lesmahagow Lodge to meet them marching in from the other direction, down the road at Linn Mill. The "Hope" had instructions to foregather at the Hall.

Drew wrote meanwhile that he would ride to Carluke; he had a matter to discuss with Reverend MacAdam before the meeting of the Parochial Board. Had she no messages to do in Carluke or Nemphlar, to bring her across the brig? Charlotte considered and replied that she would walk up to the Baronald Farm and buy a punnet of white-wood strawberries for her aunt, for they were famous.

"Then I will meet you at Wallace's Cave or that footpath, at about three o'clock."

The day was airy and sunny. Charlotte, in a gray-blue summer gingham and a new Dunstable straw Helen had brought her from King-street, set forth in good time, turning left at the tollhouse into Nemphlar-road as far as Mill Farm, then passing through the yard and into the meadows. As she climbed her spirit lightened. She had hardly glanced at the farm but now she looked back on its roofs nestled low among the summer foliage, a tilted wagon, a lad leading out a dark brown Clydesdale. She heard the dunt of a butter churn. All was far enough below to appear neat and pleasant. The elder-flowers bowed soft around about the edges of the meadow and a lark was singing. She passed under the shadow of a single oak, emerged again into heat and brightness. Sheep moved calmly out of her way. Several bonnie big lambs were crowded on a knowe, like children playing king o' the castle, and scattered as she came near. At the top of the meadow Craig Cottage peeped over the brim and to her left Mouse Water could be heard tumbling through its glen, with the path going darkly into the plantings.

She got over the stile and walked back along the Lanark road to Baronald.

First came the lodge house, then a red avenue overhung with trees, going up past the farm towards the great house. A high wall hid the gardens and greenhouses. There were two long, prosperous barns with offices joining them.[55] As Charlotte walked up a gardener came through the wall gate with a barrow.

"You've come for our white-wood nae doubt, Miss. Would you care to see the rows?"

She excused herself. An old, smiling woman emerged from the offices with two wee lassies at her skirts, and Charlotte got her creel filled and paid for. She had brought a clean d'oyley to lay across the punnet.

"Will you no taste one wee fruit, Miss? They are the sweetest to be had."

She did, and said, "They are so very good, I must ask you for a few more, just a paperful, if they can be put lightly over the others." She lifted the d'oyley, the berries lying in a rosy glow of shade.

The old woman fetched two handfuls into the cloth. "Fold the edge over and they'll come to no harm. No, nay, it's no more for that!"

"Then the farthing must be for the lassies, I'm sure they are big enough to have helped with the pulling."

There was Drew with a book and his net, sitting like an excursionist out on a crag. A turn in the path hid him; then when she rounded it, he nearly ran against her.

"My dear!"

"Where is Gyp?"

"In the meadow at Newsteadings."

They sat close together under the cliff, with Mouse murmuring below hid by green leaves. She unfolded the extra fruit, Drew pronouncing them as sweet, for all their great size, as wild woodland strawberries.

"How hard you stare at me, Charlotte!"

"Oh," looking down: "It's the look in your own eyes, that I so like to see."

"Look, then, and I will look at you."

She dared then, his eyes so kind, his skin so light there still, with the freckles dark and innumerable, like brassy specks.

He wanted to unpin her hair. "Why may I not?"

"It's so red."

"I do nae care if it's red."

But Charlotte tying her bonnet strings firmly. "Would you no rather be keeping company with a bonnie brown-haired lass?"

He kissed her. "There's berries on your mouth, Char." Then: "What are you thinking of, you are pensive?"

"Why, I was recollecting, I suppose—I mind the first time I saw you, how hard you listened in the Kirk."

"Then you told me about the wee laddie with the beautiful voice."

"Bernie."

"Aye, Bernie. Oh, I ought to have married you then before all the rest of it."

"Would I have taken you though?"

Laughing softly, the stone warm on their backs, a thrush they had not noticed gone suddenly silent in the heat, Mouse Water running.

"All the rest of it," he repeated. "It's of no great consequence is it, d'you think? All that?"

It did not seem so now. Her hand curled at his heart, his hand over it, then reaching into her sleeve, touching her wrist.

They parted before they came out into the road and she let him ride ahead over Cartland Bridge, for there was a waggon on it farther along, and folk at the parapet—three great lasses stopped on their way to Carluke with their creels around their elbows. Leaning to look straight down the drop into the gorge, but turning to gaze after Drew as he rode by. Charlotte getting across then and into the planting.

Indeed, he was over-diffident, but so she was herself, and perhaps it must be so. She could neither phrase these musings, nor completely suppress them. There was so much they could not speak of, think of—not yet, perhaps never! "The present is enough," she told herself, going down the meadow in a kind of anxious, happy dream, through the scented grass and a waft of woodsmoke carrying across from Sunnyside. A few small clouds, almost transparent, hung over the Black Hill.

"I said, I have announced our engagement."

Charlotte was at the piano and had not heard Willie enter, or the first thing he had said.

"Aye, now I've got your eye at last, and stopped the infernal noise! I wondered what I must say to get you quiet. It was only in jest, Chattie, and only over at Steele's Inn, so you neednae look so white. I declare—"

Then, putting the salts to her nose, his arm supporting her.

"Are you right again? It's no like you to take a turn for nothing. Here's a braw change, if I'm the one to be treating you!"

She got herself up, holding to the piano stool, the brocade sliding, then to the rack of the piano as he sat back on his heels.

"Are you on your feet then? Better go away in and lie down a wee."

As she crossed the lobby his voice following her:

"And still not a word will you say! I'm sure I never meant to frighten you for all that."

> My dear Charlotte,
>
> We will see one another at the ceremony, but Walter being very set on nurse maiding me through it, we can have no communication beyond, with luck, to look help-lessly towards one another. But do not be afraid of him, he is bound to be so full of his manse and his prosperity that he cannot see farther than the end of his nose. I look for-ward to your wee choir but I can not say to any other part of it for it will be a great Masonic fuss, there are times when I wonder what the Disruption did for the Christian church in Scotland besides settling us queerer in our ways than ever, we are far from the spirit of Galilee.
>
> Surely after it is all forbye I will have a chance to call upon you, the next forenoon, and hear the Schubert at last, but I promise you, I will not do so unless I can be circum-spect.

Hector F Mclean, PGM, in his apron and jewels, was presented with the silver trowel by Bro Js Chalmers, and took the first stab into the ground.[56] Then Mr. Elder getting on with the job properly with his spade, and throwing up a great pile of dirt and divots. After that came the interment of the jar, being a large preserves jar of Mrs. Capie's scrubbed out and polished up which had held in its day many a two quart of strawberry jam. Now what was screwed into it tight were the advertisements and rolls of the newspapers, Saturday's *Advertiser* and *The Glasgow Herald* sent out on the early train and George Kay getting it down specially from Lanark. And an entire set of new coins ordered new minted and never used. The jar would go in under the corner stone itself so could not be got at by thieves. Never to see the light again, as Mr. Maclean put it in his speech, "till all this generation, and their children's children, have joined the Great Majority." Mr. Elder shovelling earth around it and over the brim, smack, smack, before the stone should be laid.

After the speeches folk trod about Widow Capie's parcel of land which she had sold to the Kirk quite dear, it was said, and inspected the beginnings of the manse. It would rise well above both school and Kirk and not be overshadowed, standing on the highest ground with a nice garden planted in the front. Mr. Cameron would marry as soon as he could get into it; he had dropped a number of strong hints in that direction.

The gentlemen removed to the Hotel and were served an early refreshment. A number of patriotic toasts were enthusiastically pledged, but at last all emerged again. The pipers who had brought them down the Brae assembled in the school yard with large crowds to hear them. After them came Miss Spears' Band of Hope, who entertained very sweetly. Which was, as Mrs. West remarked to those nearby, uncommon compliant of her considering last summer. One of the clergymen standing against the Kirk wall the while in the shade and listening very intently.

Agnes pointed him out to Katie: "That was Mr. Thomson, whom Miss Spears had bewitched and didnae he look queer?" but he never went near her, both lasses keeping an eye on him the whole of the morning.

Katie did not march up to Lanark with the pipes and parade. She had taken her half-day and must get back to the lamps and the silver; she watched the procession from the front gate. When she turned to go in she saw Willie at his window looking out between the curtains with his arms on the sill. From up there he could see across the palisade to some extent, the riders and banners and the tops of the hats and carriages. He was bad the now.

Katie changed her gown and put on her work apron to get at the lamps. From the open back door she could hear the pipes skirling all the way up to Lanark, thin at last and then Clyde's noise covering them.

Walter was still carrying on about his manse. In the evening they had walked up and down the meadow, his arm through Drew's and his stick jabbing here and there as he laid out the walks and beds and shrubbery, and would not be satisfied till they had climbed in over the masonry and paced out each room on each flat, for it was to be a two-storey house, and were arrived at the cistern and private arrangements when Drew mildly said they ought to turn in.

He had a mind to chasten his friend about castles in the air, for only the Lord knoweth what the morrow will bring. But it would not be past the Lord to grant a man like Walter Cameron his manse and his wife and a long and prosperous future, whereas Drew's own prospects were yet uncertain—perhaps doomed to disaster, or so he sometimes felt!

Later over a "temperance cordial" left by Mrs. Capie, who had taken herself off to bed lang syne, Drew toasted his friend's expectations and wished him happiness. Happy Walter looked, and smug as well, sprawled there across the best chair with a wide smile on his face. Then suddenly with no introduction he began to relate the worst things, without of course an inkling of causing pain.

"—supposed to be sick but spends a great deal of his time idly walking about the village. He is courting his cousin of course, and I hear is lately engaged. I am told he gets on with his studies privately but I would no put much trust in that, there is plenty of money in the family from the second Mrs. Brown, the purchase of Annville proves it. I am sure I do not know what sort of an illness it may be but that she is out of the ordinary solicitous of him by all accounts and hardly leaves the house. You're well out of that though I cannae believe you were ever in so deep as was suggested at the time."

How Drew wished for Gyp between his legs and a hard ride back to Heywood! Instead he must lie all night in Walter's bed with the man breathing heavily and his round hot back taking up the main part, and a bright early sun glaring in between the curtains, that laughed sleep to scorn. Listening to Clyde, and thrushes, and blackies, and lambs, and at last a milk van and able then to get himself silently up and dressed.

He scribbled in his notebook with his lead pencil, and removed the page and laid it on the bed stand.

Forgive my early departure and thank Mrs. Capie from
me. I am quite well but wish to get home before the heat.

Annville's blinds were down. Was that a sharp, white face showing, at
one of the high windows?

Annville, July 10, 1883

Dear Drew,
I am afraid that your letters have been intercepted, or
that something has occurred. We did not speak when you
were here for the ceremony. I fear you may have heard
something said, and would wish very much to explain or
oppose it if it be so. I do not know what to write, therefore
beg you to write to me again, and ask me anything you
would wish.
I have given up the Rondo for the present, as I am not
ready for it, my hands not having the strength. The rest I
am not ashamed of, and hope soon to play for you as we
have looked forward to, whenever it can be arranged. You
are in my prayers.
Yours ever faithfully
Charlotte.
PS, If you have written, please direct your next letter to
be kept for me at the Post Office, and it would not be lost.

"Are you no away over to the Post Office again, cousin Chattie? You
could do with some air, you are looking peaked lately. You wouldnae
wish to give up your daily excursion. What a great many letters have
come in from the post to be sure, if it is not Tom or Annie it is
Somebody else, though not lately I take it. I would write to you myself
if I didnae have you here day and night, if only to bring the auld light
back into your eye."

Miss Spears was greeting in her room, and it was such a sad noise Katie
had no heart to tell of it to Agnes. At evening worship, kneeling behind
the cuttie chair with Miss Spears saying a prayer about being patient
and good, Katie resolved never to blether about her to Agnes again,
and was heartily sorry for what she had said already, for she believed

Agnes repeated it, and here was Miss Spears with her head meekly bent over her folded hands, and after she said "Amen" lifting her face and such a bleary look! It fairly made Katie want to greet herself.

Though she was sure, still, that Miss Spears did far too much for Willie and put up with more than was needful.

There were about three weeks in July when Willie was as a bad as could be, and Dr. Gray stopped to see him twice and a boy sent with some new medicine which, if Willie did not get it quick enough, he'd be in such pain as to cry out in a fearful way. Miss Spears nursed him day and night and scarcely slept. Katie would willingly have helped her but she would say, if she were down in the night for the fomentations or any other thing, "Katie, go back to sleep. You're no to get up, I will manage."

Once Katie pretending to be asleep saw through the parting of the curtain Miss Spears turn around from the range. It was light already being past five, and Miss Spears' face was all wet and her mouth pulled back the way Bella's would be if she had fallen over and was getting set to roar. But Miss Spears did not roar; only she put the kettle down she was holding, and stuffed her apron across her mouth and held it there and stood bent over a minute getting the better of it, Katie not daring to stir or let on she'd seen. Then Miss Spears standing up straight and smoothing her apron, and pouring the water and replacing the kettle, and going on up. And at breakfast nothing to show for it, Katie already having scrubbed the black off the table.

Katie must boil Miss Spears' aprons and undergarments, and her summer ginghams till there was no colour in them, and rinse them down at Clyde with the village kimmers saying never was there such a washing as that summer at Annville and wondering that Katie could keep up with it. Katie had to fill a fresh boiler though for Miss Spears' things, and never use the same water as for Willie's linens. Sometimes Miss Spears did them, she was not above it, and Katie could never say her own work was more than she could easily do. She thought that, had she not seen Miss Spears in the horrors that night, she would never presume to be sorry for her. For as Agnes said, she went about smiling in the day time and seemed to do what she did because she liked it.

Agnes continued to want to hear about what was going on in

Annville but all Katie would say was, "It's the old thing."

Once Agnes asked her, if she never went up stairs to tend to Willie, if Miss Spears was from home and he wanted anything.

Katie had to say she was told not to.

"She's afraid he will attempt to take liberties with you," said Agnes.

"Oh, he's already done that."

But Agnes though she looked as interested as possible could not make Katie say exactly what or how much he had attempted, and Katie seeming not very concerned one way or the other, decided the girl did not know what was meant.

And their thoughts were otherwise engaged those summer days, cracking about Jimmie Henderson and what a great handsome chield he was, and what Agnes might dare to say to him in the forge to make him blush, and of the other lads in the Voluntaries, and when Katie might come away early to the Moors to see the sham fight or the Highland Light Infantry on review.

CHAPTER 27

In which the Band of Hope takes its Annual Excursion
and Mr. Weir proves a hero.

Willie had come through a bad bout of the fever but a congestion had settled in his chest. Charlotte called it "a relaxed throat" when she mentioned it to Helen, and treated him with alum and water. But he had a deep cough that wearied him and she could not help but mind Dr. Gray's warning that the Crimean fever led to consumption. There was however no blood coughed, his nose bleed from time to time being another thing entirely, which must console her.

She kept him to his bed and he did not oppose her; she did every thing for him.

Mrs. West one morning early at the gate, and all in a flutter and carrying on about Lily Langtry who had been seen, said Mrs. Simpson, at the Lanark Station Hotel and was certain to have a run through the burgh and down the Brae to see Stonebyrnes Linn. By the time Mrs. West had won through to her own home past the Kirk, the road was lined with folk looking out for Lily Langtry. Weavers stood in their doorsteps and bairns dashed across the road and back as excited as if it were a Wee Walk, and they were dashing under the boots of marching Orangemen.

"Willie, if you would wish to see Lily Langtry from your window, she is to have a run through from Lanark, says Mrs. West, very shortly. Would you like me to help you across?"

Willie looked back at her in silence, then as she was turning away said "Lily Langtry," in the mock-serious, high-pitched tone he usually reserved for making fun of the chemists.

"Well, you are quite right of course no to bother about it,"

Charlotte said conciliatingly. "But I wouldnae have it you weren't told, with the whole village in such an uproar."

"No, nay, it is the high point of the week. I will get myself across by and by and see her parasol go past."

Charlotte lingered but he only gave her that look again, so she laid his house coat across the quilt quietly, and placed his list slippers closer to the bed.

"I'll push your chair up to the window then, Willie."

She called Katie from the kitchen, and they took off their aprons and went out, and stood side by side in the doorway, between the two stone urns.

It was a pleasant day to stop the common task and watch a beautiful lady go by. Now came a shout from the brig, that the brake was in sight! They hastened forward to the gate, Charlotte leading. Agnes and her mother could be seen at their open parlour window, and Mrs. Cooper and Margaret Tennant out in front of the Hotel work aprons and all, and the Allens across the way busy keeping their row of dafties from treading out into the road.

Now with a grand rattle the brake came running round the brig end and into the High-street, echoing off the palisade, with George Kay sitting forward merry in his red coat, his whip in the air, and the horses belled and going very smartly. The onlookers had a glimpse of great swooping bonnets and masses of exquisite muslin in the softest of pink and cream, and then Lily Langtry and her party were gone by, leaving a faint, musical laugh behind them to be lost in the breeze.

Mr. Allen, who was a road surfacer by trade, out to rake after the carriage and secure the droppings for his roses.

Charlotte and Katie turned in.

"She did look wee," was Katie's comment.

Willie was at his open window overhead, and was still there when Charlotte went up later to see to him, his hands quiet on his knees, and looking out rather absently.

"Did you see them? Shall I help you back the now?" She wished he had his travel rug, with the cool draught and him right in it.

"I can walk. You'll no need to carry me yet. D'you mind how I would carry Robbie at the end?"

He allowed her to take his arm.

By the bed he stood still: "It's pleasant after all to see a beautiful lady, for all she's come and gone like a summer's butterfly. And never a thought for the folk along the road. Smiling at her and admiring her, and for all that with their own troubles to seek, living lives of misery and pain and she'll never ken it?"

He took a fit of coughing then and Charlotte supported him, his fingers hard in the flesh of her arm.

He lay looking very weak as she administered his medicine, and she did not leave him, but sat by the window till he slept.

The sky had darkened and they were in for a shower. George Kay would have to whip the horses to get on through to Ayr Station before it plowted on them.

"Willie, you know very well not everybody is miserable," Charlotte knew she ought to have said. But somehow, unfortunately, he seemed to be right. One ought to look on the bright side, but it was sometimes too hard. Alas, his was not the only wan face that looked after Lily Langtry that day, seeking a moment's distraction in the brightness of her passing!

The weather was dull but promising, with a high sky, when the "Hope of Kirkfieldbank" set off on their annual excursion.[57] They were to join the "Falls of Clyde" from Lanark. Mr. William Munn on hand to assist in unscrolling the banner as they assembled outside the IOGT Hall. Charlotte helped to adjust blue ribbons on smaller Members. Sadie Hopkins as well, her halo of white hair bobbing among the ranks. The children wore their Sabbath clothes and though summer, some had their boots on. It would be a long trudge for the youngest ones. They set off smartly with Jock Stein carrying one end of the banner as if by right though he'd soon tire of it; and she told him, "to the top of the Brae, then," which would satisfy his pride.

"Falls" were waiting at the Gas Works and stood very smartly, their leaders the two big blackhaired McKnight lads in their kilts, striding up and down the ranks and straightening the stragglers. She was sorry to hear a few Lanark voices calling out about "bare shanks"—the "Falls" being to a man uncomfortably booted—and could forgive a responsive "*Kiltie, kiltie, cauld bum,*" from among the "Hope" though of course turning with a frown.

Mousebank-road led north to the upper wards, climbing through fields and the planting at Croftonhill. They sang. The sun appeared in the high haze, bringing with it a steady increase in heat and glare. But now the road curved down along the thread of a burn to Mouse Water, and the brig by Lockhart Mill.

Ranks were broken, the "Falls" less happy to see the barefoot village lads scrambling down to dip their toes and wade after mennens in the shallows. Charlotte, weary, seated herself beside Mr. Munn on the "ducking stane."

Mouse was low, its bed exposed with the brown lines of weed dried on the rocks. Some of the "Falls" were hurriedly unbuttoning their boots. Mr. Munn held his pocket watch in his palm.

The colours of the shrubs along the banks, even the water itself, had no lustre in the oppressive, even light. The squeals of the children were sharp, almost painful. Charlotte could have wished for the sun to break through clearly. She was as ready as William Munn to be getting on.

The Lockhart Brig must to be crossed properly in file, those already over called back for the purpose, and of course with a rousing song. Charlotte started them off with "King Bibber's Army." She could find little to comfort her, yet still she looked about for it, and here was the hand of wee Mary Reid reaching into hers. The trustful clasp nearly brought the tears into her eyes. She had a wish to take the bairn up and carry her, pressed against her breast and the soul-ache nothing would ease. She would surely do so before the day was done!

"Are you weary, Mary?"

A stubborn look, and a skip to catch up with the marching.

"*Left right left, I had a good job and I left!*"

Some of the older lads sang "a good wife," and snickered.

"We are nearly there, Mary, do you see the planting on the hill? That's Greentowers."

But it looked very far off.

Now they were in the uplands, sheep scattered in great fields lined with stone dykes, and no more trees till Greentowers. Then at last Mr. and Mrs. Muirhead at the gate and William Munn taking up two of the smallest lassies on his arms to walk forward under the trees. The farmhouse and offices stood across a meadow surrounded by orchard on three sides, and a tent was hung at the end from tree to tree and tables set out. Two red-cheeked byrewomen coming forward with broad welcoming smiles.

Though the three men took charge of the races, Charlotte must exert herself now and then to lead in a song. Sarah came and sat by her under the edge of the tent.

"There was some lads going into the byre but I told Mr. McKnight, that one, and they've come back. They oughtn't."

Sadie had grown longer in all her bones, and had got a large chin her face would need to catch up on. Her pinny-front showing two round white mounds. Charlotte asked after her aunts, and about her certificate. Mr. Dunlop had formed a geography class, she said, for the lads in the Fourth after regular school hours, and she had wanted to sit in, she was sure Mr. Dunlop would not care, but Aunt West said it would be unladylike. Her solemn face close to Charlotte's, the white tendrils of her hair shading it almost to luminous green. All of Scotland was covered with ice called glaciers in the Ice Ages, she said, and here and there were great stones lying, called "erratic blocks," that it had carried about.

The hours of games and eating came to an end. They returned by a circular route, down the road through Burgh Wood. Now Charlotte picked up Mary and walked with her a little way, for the bairn was nearly asleep. William Munn wanted to take her but she resisted, clung hard to Charlotte's neck. Then he and the McKnights carried some of the lads on their shoulders, and some big children carried the smallest bairns, but soon tired of it. Archie Stein tumbled out of Jock's grasp and scraped his knee on the sharp grush of the road, but took it manfully: there was not a bairn in Lanarkshire without the scabs of many such an encounter.

They were passing the path to Wallace's Cave.

"I ought to have married you then." She could not look into the trees.

The lads were restless, plaguing their leaders to let them run away in to the Cave "just for a wee minute." No wonder, for they freely roamed the plantings and the crags, cutting whins or bird nesting, and it was hard to be kept in rank all day and scolded for straggling. She had heard too of lads who would run along the parapet of Cartland Bridge for a dare.

"Now we'll march to the Bridge in order, and halt before we part company, for a rousing cheer."

"Hope" would turn aside to go down the steep pasture, the

"Falls" continuing to Lanark. All were wearying to be home. In vain had she endeavoured a smarter step and a cheerful song, and now the opposing rows were crooked and fidgety; the dusty banners drooped and voices were plaintive and faint. William Munn and the McKnights had put down the littlest bairns, and some whined and demanded to be taken up again. Others were clamouring for a turn, and already a few of the bigger "Falls" lads had broken rank and were out on the Bridge itself. As James McKnight shook Charlotte's hand one of them was getting himself up on to the parapet! Mr. Munn's face almost as red as his mulberry stain, thanking Charlotte for a grand excursion, then his bluest eye widening as he caught her alarm. He whirled about.

"Hey, get away off there!" he shouted.

Perhaps frightening the lad, who had stood up and now staggered perilously. A gentleman on foot, crossing from the other direction, came running up, snatched him at the last moment.

They all ran forward. It was Mr. Weir! Brushing off his trousers, a lock of hair out of place on his forehead. Someone picked up his stick and handed it back to him. The lad he had rescued pinned against the stone, head down and expecting a cuff.

"Can you no keep order among your scholars then?" Suddenly seeing Charlotte behind the distraught men he smiled easily, and stepped back.

"I believe this lad thought he was a militiaman—and we know what happens to them![58] So we'll say no more about it. Will we?" He fixed his eyes on the children; and the older ones especially, who had quailed before him at examinations, were eager to agree.

"No, Mr. Weir," loudly, almost in unison.

He would not be thanked, though Charlotte lingered. "I'm away to Carluke. Some matters to bring into order before. Though I would turn and walk down beside you if I thought you needed me. You had a wee fright."

"I wished only to express my gratitude. It was a brave act—resolute!"

"Nay, nay, he'd have been in no danger if the silly man hadnae shrieked. I am sorry to say most of the lads have played on the parapet before they are fourteen and we've no lost one yet. I'll leave you the now, I'm away to London and for who knows how long? Goodbye, for I know you'll no go with me." He gave her a searching look, almost kind.

"For all you're a clever woman, Miss Spears, you're more than a bit of a fool."

So he left her, and she was reproved and strangely thrilled, as if she would have followed him had she known how! In reality she was of course walking downhill through the hot fields to Annville. The children, revived, chattered around her. Bernie's sisters Robina and Kate had taken her two hands. Their narrow feet tripping adeptly between sharp cut stalks. Without attending clearly, for she would have been ashamed, she saw in her mind's eye Mr. Weir saunter towards the upper parks—his life careless and enviable, opening.

CHAPTER 28

In which Sweethearts and Wives are contemplated,
and Charlotte plays at her last Soirée.

Kirkfieldbank, the High-street,
28th September, 1883

Dear Thomson,
The news of your Call to Perth I cannot but receive with the greatest satisfaction. The Lord has indeed blessed you and led you into pleasant pastures. Your regret for present friends is but to your credit, and you will be regretted as well, by all those good parishioners among whom you have laboured so unstintingly. As for myself, we will be sure to meet at Presbytery.

You will have heard of the grand success of the Lesmahagow Bazaar all proceeds towards the furbishing of the Manse. The Managers donated three short webs of tartan cloth manufactured in the village, the finest he had ever seen said Mr. Johnstone of Sunnyside who made off with it at a price I dare not mention. So we do very well without Corehouse who continue in their pique and did not attend.

All is therefore going forward very handily, and I expect to flit from good Mrs. Capie in the course of the winter, not, however in time to receive you in my new abode my good Friend, before you remove. Whether *Another* will then be welcomed here, never to go away again, I leave you to guess!

I am at present hard wrought with my up coming, "*Moral State of Society in the Days of the Apostles*" which I have been invited to read at Lanark as well as at

Kirkfieldbank, being tomorrow evening in Lanark at 7.45 PM, and next Sabbath here at 6 PM.

My subject is a serious one as I intend to treat it, not omitting of course an infusion of one or more light Anecdotes which seem to be relished, and are by now indeed expected, by the Congregation, though perhaps a surprise in Lanark, I cannot tell. However, Society in Biblical times is most relevant to our own times, as I will demonstrate, for Human Nature I am sorry to say continues unabated.

In fact the Managers are much exercised over the lax moral state of the parish, and are decided to put a stop to it by *example*, according to the Directives laid down though not always adhered to, for the public admission of antenuptial congress, followed by Admonition and Absolution. By "*public*" I do not of course mean other than, before me and the Managers, for we of the Established Church are not so over-strict as to make any poor lass sit forward six weeks for wearing her apron high. Or matron neither as the case may be, though the antique members of my *own* Congregation are happily exempted from any scandal in this direction.

I hope that you will find a better character of Congregation in Perth, though I have my doubts.

I cannot expect you before you remove, knowing from experience how much there is to order at such a time, though indeed you are a sorry sort of Friend, I have not seen hair of you since you took off from the Quoad Sacra without your breakfast. Be sure however I bear no grudge, and extend to you my warmest wishes for your future prosperity. I thank you for the new directions and will write to you there, where you may faithfully anticipate an Intimation, ere long, from

Your sincere Friend and well wisher
Walter Cameron (Reverend).

Dear Drew

Forgive me for writing to you once more, as I must believe it is now disagreeable for you to receive a letter from me; if so, you must I beg of you destroy it and read no further. But if you will be patient and read what I have to say, I will not trouble you again.

Several times I have begun a letter to you but set it aside. If you are my friend, in simple friendship send me a few lines, and I will not demand more of you. My wishes for your health and prosperity are all I would send you, and you know you have these already. As we have always understood, though you *then* protested, we were never either by age, nor by the wishes of those interested in us, suited to one another. Perhaps it is but this re-consideration which leads you to a conclusion I have never resisted, and must accept as just and right. But yet I would hear it from you yourself.

That the interest of others, while perhaps well meaning, has led them to say anything to you which is untrue, and has caused this rupture between us, I must however still feel some anxiety over, for otherwise we ought to have continued correspondents.

"It is unlike you, Drew, to be silent! If your anger is towards me, so speak it, I can bear it. It is not in your character to feel an anger you believe to be just, and to keep silent."

Charlotte could not write down these last outbursts of sensibility. Indeed she was unable to finish her letter at all, or to send it, and it was burned with the others she had attempted; surely he knew already what she would wish to say. And as for Mr. Andrew Thomson—closetted from the clamouring Parks, supposed to be preparing for Perth—if he were also wretchedly writing letters and unable to complete them, she did not know it.

After an indifferent summer with the field crops short and the hay about two weeks behind in the cutting, Scotland was treated to what could only be called a "heat wave," the temperature reaching 72

343 〜

degrees in Aberdeen though already the 12th of October, and over 60 degrees in most places. For ten days the weather held and, the moon waxing, each night proved brighter and more beautiful. The ingathering went blithely forward without heed to the clock, for night was as light as day.

Folk spoke of a "ranting" harvest home and even the most sullen temper could not but receive the beneficial influence; smiles were to be encountered everywhere.

Willie's chest was much improved in the warm, dry air, and he left his bed and often walked up the village, his step nearly sprightly. Though never that sure stride of health—looking after him Charlotte could not disregard the falter in his gait, and how he would stop for a moment, and lean on the stick he had been jauntily swinging, and catch his breath. At home he was over-quiet and she could get no conversation from him. His books, which had long been unopened, were again spread about his room. Once coming in she caught him talking aloud in a low, hurried voice. He was standing over behind the bed with his back to her, and turned about with a frightened look. Then stepped around the bed towards her, steadying himself on the post as he came.

"Will you go away, Chattie."

After that she made a good noise coming up the stair and spoke out on the landing as well: "Willie, I am here with your tea," or whatever it was. Though she had never knocked and would not begin now.

In the kitchen, he spread out the *Advertiser* and bent over it.

"Here's a something for us two then," he said in something of his ordinary downstairs voice, the teasing one. "A lecture called *Sweethearts and Wives* at St Leonard's next week,[59] and to be given by Reverend Turnbull of Lesmahagow—why, that's the very gentleman sat by me at the Hall and listened so fiercely to your music! I've no forgot him! Well, we must go and hear him."

The weather being so grand, there was no arguable reason why he might not go, and Helen and John when he spoke of it at the week-end thought it a very good scheme, and would make a pleasant change. John could step across and secure a carriage at the Hotel, and Chattie must buy the sixpenny tickets in Lanark while doing her messages. Mr.

Turnbull being a very steady old gentleman, went on John placidly, there could not be anything unsuitable, in spite of the title.

"I wouldnae have called the man old," remarked Willie.

Here Helen was distracted by a pot boiling over, and no more was said though Charlotte trembled.

Willie otherwise quite reasonable while they were by and afterwards saying to her in a mild way, "You may walk in on my arm, Chattie, if you like, for I've leaned on yours many a time."

Katie at the sink could not help seeing how white Miss Spears had turned—it was the old thing. But Katie had not time to think of Miss Spears, for Thursday was Lanark Fast Day as well, and she and Agnes had trimmed their bonnets and were to walk up the Brae together, and be away the entire morning.

The heat continued, and the stillness intensified, till by Wednesday forenoon the sky overhead had reached an almost singing pink. It was overpowering weather for all the way folk admired it; to Katie it felt exactly as if it were her poorliness coming on, a heaviness and her head aching and wanting that to be over with too, for she was gone longer this time. Mother would aye say it was the weather.

At four o'clock it quickly came on very dark, and looking out the back door Katie saw a shadow standing up behind Nemphlar, blacker than the trees. The down on her arms and the hair at the nape of her neck began to tingle, which was a very queer sensation.

Then the storm broke over the dale. Running with Charlotte to pull the linen off the raips, and chase the banties in, and having to go down again after Gruntie who had got right in under the bee balm, behind the skeps. The raindrops were plowting the earth in great gobs and the thunder clanged directly overhead, with water gushing along the path and no time to seep away. The wind got up as well, and they hurried to close all the windows. The house shuddered and rattled all night, with the lightning and thundering unabated.

Thursday dawned with the wind and rain continuing and the air quite cool and changed. Charlotte lying awake all night could not help exulting; with every bang she thought, for she could not prevent herself: "*That*, is for the end of *Sweethearts and Wives!*" Though it was not at all charitable. "The heavens declare the glory of God—" she repeated the Psalm, which was almost as gratifying to her spirits. Spooning out Willie's breakfast brose, she had difficulty hiding her satisfaction.

He was looking a bit vexed but not desperate.

"Ah well, it wasnae to be. It wasnae to be—you can have that put on my stone, Chattie. And Mr. Turnbull must be disappointed, for you will no want to leave me behind. I believe you've been a mite doubtful about it from the start, and would only have gone to please me. We can give Katie the tickets and she can run away up with one of the village lads—would you no like that, Katie?"

"Oh, if Agnes would go with me, for we are away to the fair at any rate." Looking towards Miss Spears however, though she was turned away to the dresser.

"That's you then. Sweethearting is for the young ones after all, and poor auld Chattie and I must amuse ourselves as best we can nodding by the fire."

Katie and Agnes agreed however that the lecture was uncommon teedisome, though they had stayed it out hoping there would be an improvement. She got in at ten with very wet boots. They'd had a hurl down the Brae with young Mr. Steele, Agnes having gone straight up to him outside St Leonard's and asked. The rain then ceased—almost, Charlotte thought, as if it knew it had served its purpose. She took several deep breaths. "*And there was a great calm.*"

Charlotte was down in the scullery putting geranium cuttings into a box of fresh earth, to stand for the winter. The lamp stood by her on the flags. After she was done she took the besom and gave the floor a good sweep out, for a lot of earth had got in, it was that uneven.

Lifting the lamp, she chose some nice Pippins and Bloodhearts from the rondel by the press, the darkest and reddest, filling her apron.

It was Hallowe'en the night. Bang, bang, Katie mashing swedes over at the kitchen brod. Mother had used to put trinkets in the mash back at Great Hamilton-street. Here in the village, the laddies tore away down the road rattling on the doors with stalks from the kail yards. They had been down cutting whins on the Great Inch that morning, and had busked all the gate posts, even Annville's.

"Please gi' us our Hallowe'en!" they would cry. She had a dish of sweeties ready. Though Helen said the bairns would never like to come to Annville, being too shut away from the road, and John had put up the winter door.

But that evening a few came down the path and rattled shyly, and Charlotte was on the look out and opened both doors, and was just handing the sweeties when Willie stepped forward behind her.

"It's the bogle!" cried out Jimmie Smith, and they all ran up into the street squealing and laughing. She followed to the gate to look after them, and seeing her, Peter Duffy came warily back.

"Share these out with the others then and dinnae be so silly," she said, emptying her dish into his jouks while he stood clutching at his belt and looking ashamed of himself. A neep lantern bobbing by the end of the palisade, near the Smith house, where a clutch of bairns stood in the footpath waiting for him.

Willie was begun to walk about the garden at odd hours, and once from the kitchen both she and Katie heard him laughing. Katie round eyed but Charlotte said, "Willie must be having a joke with the bees," and turned it aside in that way.

Then she had wakened to his footsteps overhead in his parents' room, and thought she heard them later as if descending to the lobby. His voice as well, murmuring low to himself. In the forenoon almost sure of the taint of him, as she stood upstairs, her hand on the sneck of Helen and John's door!

"Katie, has Willie ever come down into the kitchen after something, in the night?"

"No, Miss Spears!" Her eyes round.

"You will wake me at once if he does, so that I can get it for him?"

Perhaps she had frightened Katie by speaking of it.

His sickroom smell seemed perhaps to have spread itself weakly into the lobby, most evident when she first came in from the fresh air and closed the door quick behind her. The distant sharp carbolic, and then past it a faint sourness. Later, sniffing, she was not sure whether she had imagined it.

She began to fancy having a key made to his door, and even looked in on John Anderson Ironmonger in Lanark when she was doing her messages. He said that without examining the lock itself and trying out his spare keys, he could never be sure of a fit. Might she borrow the assortment? She did not want to create a difficulty. He regarded her cannily.

"You'd more likely find it hanging somewhere about the house. Have you looked in the scullery? Or speer George Elder. It is Annville is it not? He'll have seen to that house, or his father."

"Katie, would you look whether there are any old keys about? I've a mind to try them, for there may be a second to the glazed door which would be very convenient."

Katie looking red faced and saying there were none. "Except them for the out doors and the caivie."

"You may declare it is so, but you will never be sure till you look, will you?"

But Katie could not bring her any.

Charlotte made a drawing in lead pencil of the lock but this was of no use to the smith either who recommended the whole changed, which was out of the question.

She gave it up but continued to dream of it. If but a bolt well soaked in oil, to slide across.

"It's my house and I will go where I please."

Which was what Willie would say of course, giving her that quick, sharp look. Then his eyes sliding away.

He would never endure to be locked in! Had her uncle suggested such a thing she would herself have opposed it with all her heart. Oh, that he would lie quiet in his bed! He was surely ill enough.

"Will you no lie down the now, Willie, it is past midnight?"

He was standing over in the corner, beyond the foot of his bed, where the lamp light could not reach him or reveal his look.

"My bed's full of dreams, I dare not."

"Go on, it's new made and aired, I will read you a sermon and you will be quite comfortable."

"It's full of blood." He came slowly forward and grasped the two bed posts. "You may think that's mad talk Chattie, but we're all a wee bit mad in our dreams, are we not? Then when we wake up, it is nothing at all, it is the result of some inflammation, or pressure on the vital tissues." He coughed, and paused as if looking for her agreement.

Indeed, she must agree with him!

"That is very true, Willie."

"Then why would you wish me to sleep? I am sure I will avoid it if I can."

His neck stalk-like sticking out of his night shirt, his two arms stretched to the posts with the loose sleeves almost empty, wrists and hands like dark sticks as well—like a scare crow, Charlotte thought pityingly.

The occasion of Mr. Forsyth's fifth year of his ministry at the E U was now approaching. On the Sabbath before, Mrs. Forsyth came up to Charlotte particularly: would she be so kind as to play at the Soirée? [60] Charlotte had never put herself forward at the E U, with the Misses Allan well entrenched and Mr. McLellan leader of the choir, and had already declined membership in the Choral Union. But she agreed of course.

There was a wee problem in leaving Willie who was not well enough to accompany them. Though Helen thought he might yet, if the weather were good and he were carefully wrapped, for he was up and about for the most and had been disappointed in the *Sweethearts and Wives*. Charlotte did not like to concern her aunt and uncle, who would have expected Katie to remain with him in case he wanted anything. But it would not do. In the end she persuaded them very mildly to let Katie attend the Soirée.

"Willie is perfectly able to take his own supper. I will leave it hot for him if he does not like to wait for us. Uncle, you might just ask Roddy Munro to look in the once, as he is going by—but you'll no wish to mention it to Willie."

A few days ago Willie had begun saying he would fight Roddy if he saw him "meddling about." His parents must be spared the pain of such ramblings. Thankfully, Willie was quiet and rational when they were by.

A dense fog had set in; indeed Matthew Gibson carrier, returning from Glasgow, reported that from Ravenstruther in he could not see the road before the horses, and this at midday, and all traffic on the river was suspended. John for once getting to Annville before Helen, though he said it was ghostly to walk through Auchenheath. A lantern could not pierce the gloom and folk passed by one another like wraiths and could not tell friend from stranger. Helen had sat two hours in the cars outside Lesmahagow there being no getting into the station with all the trains backed up on the Hamilton line. There was a sulphurous smell in the air folk said was carrying all the way from the inversion over Glasgow. Sulphur was however said to have a grand disinfectant effect, and it was hoped that winter fevers would be less prevalent.

With the railways backed up they could never expect Tom and Annie, whose visit had been arranged and was looked forward to.

"You've done all that banging about in vain then, Chattie," was Willie's remark, as Charlotte flattened the fire in the small room where Tom was to have slept, and put away the clean towels.

Willie standing in his doorway, the lamp behind him outlining his figure. So crushed he was now, and pinched, with the short house coat trailing open over his trousers that hung in folds down his shanks, his suspenders barely doing their duty! Almost wild-looking, the way his hair stuck up uncombed, but pitiful as well. His shoulders narrow as a lad's.

"I am sorry it has disturbed you."

He turned back and got himself over to his chair, murmuring, and she followed to arrange his screen.

"When have you done anything but, if it's no that it's the infernal music night and day. You can never wait till I am out of the house, can you, you'll drive me from my own hearth, I'll no find quiet till I'm in my grave."

He began turning the pages of one of his medical books irritably, as if looking for something. It was *The Causes of Disability,*[61] the lamp illuminating the black engravings, the shadow of his hand sweeping them one by one. The gray stippled buttocks of a naked person with a kind of growth like a sea shell stuck between. Charlotte looked quickly away.

"Willie, your father would like to come upstairs to visit with you the now."

"Oh aye," closing the book and sliding it under his notes. "And never a whish, mind, about the coals wasted in the wee room."

Yet before she had turned away he was sobbing bitterly, his fingers clutching her sleeve and his bony face pressed wet into her arm. Had she remained he would soon have pushed her from him. She undid his hand as gently as she could. It would not do to speak. As for Willie, he had got quit of his spell if such it was, and bent to his notes in silence.

Mr. Forsyth in the E U lobby accepting the congratulations of his flock. Mrs. Forsyth at his side to welcome them, her usual rather distant smile. Charlotte noted the gold brooch clasping the stand-up collarette at her throat. It seemed to be in the form of a thistle but she would not look too closely.

Though not yet Advent the gathered kirk was ablaze with candles, as well as the gas lamps turned up full, and busks and tasteful purple ribbons at the ends of all the pews and on the pulpit too. "*And he goeth forth unto a mountain*" was the text of Reverend Alexander Denholm's Tribute, repeated, it seemed to Charlotte, too loudly and too often to retain its first effect. The Mortification scholars were there of course and Mr. Lightbody and his entire Sabbath School.

Foxy Mr. Forsyth asking Charlotte particularly after Willie and wishing to include him in his next visitation, and Charlotte begging him to wait a week or so, for "my cousin is keeping very quiet just the now."

"He is no too much for you, Miss Spears?"

But she could not bear his being kind or his large soft hand that clasped her white-gloved one—red-furred! He had told her once not to coddle Willie.

"I am managing very nicely, thank you, Mr. Forsyth."

And then before he could question her more Helen was upon them, and several other ladies, and Helen saying right off that she hoped he would visit Willie very soon.

Five years! the E U ladies murmuring ardently. Mrs. Forsyth's smile never changed. A most pleasant, active lady! There were no children to the union and her upright figure, very tight laced indeed in a gown of shot green silk lined with fur, was straight as a girl's.

Charlotte was to play first, before the Misses Allan.

"What will you treat us to?" asked Mr. McLellan and she was able to reply, "Whatever you would like to sing," for, as Robert used to say, "Chattie's no been stumped yet"—there was never a tune, had she heard it the once, she could not give again. Though she over ran the first chord of "Fare Thee Well" and blushed and must disguise it and begin again, thankful that Drew had not heard the mistake. She kept her selection short though she could have gone on, the Misses Allan impatient to take over.

The kirk loft rang with merry voices, if a little harshly; and several wrong notes from one or other of the two ladies went unnoticed by the general throng, if Charlotte must hear them.

Going down the Brae in the fog, full of tea and scones, the few lights of Kirkfieldbank unseen, then close at hand swimming to them as through water. They could hear Clyde's rush but must feel their way across the brig. Charlotte's gloved hand brushing along the stones, in and out of the recesses. Oh, she did wish not to be going back into the house! The taste of strong tannin rose in the back of her throat. Helen, ahead of her, carrying on to John about Willie now: how she did believe he was over the worst with his chest, if he could but keep down his food. He must take his tonic that Tom was so kind as to send. Oh, aye, Tom and Annie would be sorry they missed the Soirée, for it was a fine wee kirk for all that, not a candle to Elgin Place of course but very neat and elegant in its way.

Katie walking apart from them. Almost slower than Charlotte, as if she too would have liked to stay outbye a while, dawdling on the brig. The half-term! Aye, that was what lay in Charlotte's mind and irritated, like a sharp bit of grush! She must be grateful that Katie was such a mindful, obedient lass, and had agreed to enter her second half-term at Annville. But Charlotte was ashamed to feel easy about that, knowing Katie did not like to be there. "She has however nothing to do with Willie, that is my business. It is a good place for her after all." Charlotte quickened her step.

"Come, Katie, let us go in and stir up the kitchen fire. It's ever so damp on the brig, come."

CHAPTER 29

*In which Katie attends the Feeing Fair, Charlotte goes up the
village, and Willie walks in the garden; whereafter their paths
meet at Annville with a fearful consequence.*

"Have you no spoken to Miss Spears?"
Agnes was aye after her to have it said and not be worrying at it.

"I've told her I would go to Douglas Water on the Fast Day, and
she didnae say a word, and then about a half an hour later, when I was
beginning to say it again, she said, of course I might have the day."

"I'll miss you if you flit a long way off."

"I've no decided yet."

Agnes staring. "Of course you've decided! You've been decided
since August."

"Aye, but when I am with Miss Spears I'm frightened to say it.
After she made me promise."

"That's neither here nor there and it wasnae a promise, your half-
year's out and you can flit as you please and no one can stop you. Only
don't flit so far you couldnae visit us."

"I'm thinking of feeing home."

"Lanark! aye, that would be best of all."

"But then I would see Miss Spears at the E U, I wouldnae like that
after the way I would have treated her."

"But Katie, you've always said she was fair. And she knows she
cannae say anything about it. Listen to this. You'll get off with the early
conveyance from Ramath, and say nothing about it, and when you
come back you'll be fee'd home and that's you. You'll pack your box
and away."

"I wish I could take my box with me then and no come back at
all." Tears stood in Katie's eyes.

"So pack it up, and say nothing the night. Mrs. Brown will be down from Stonehouse and it's she who pays your hire. You're no afraid of Mrs. Brown."

"No, but she will be very astonished, she doesnae know what it's like at Annville at all. Miss Spears never tells her. Miss Spears always says, the week has gone by very quiet and nice, or some such words, and if Willie's been ranting about in the garden she'll say he's been up and well, and if he's been kept to his bed and creating she will say, he has been just a wee bit indisposed."

Katie had nearly twisted her apron into a knot as she sat, her red hands working and working it. Her head was bent down the while and now she saw the creases and smoothed them out, and looked up at her friend. Agnes had such white, round cheeks and great smiling mouth! And the blacksmith's kitchen, such a rosy glow! Perhaps because it was high up, not hid away under the house. But even its darkest corners were comfortable. When Mr. Elder was in, Agnes though nearly as big and heavy as he, might still fling herself at him, plump herself on his lap and twine her arms around his neck. "Away with you, silly lass!" her father would push her off his knee but not unkindly. It was ever blithe and warm. Katie sighed.

"Will you no come to Douglas with us then, Agnes?"

"I may not. With Dad there hiring there's no pleasure in it, and he'd no let me for he likes to stay, and lie in a cart all night. I'll see you away though, I will lend you my new dolman mantle, if you like."

As it turned out, John Brown was called to do jury duty at the Assizes in Hamilton, and the Browns would not be at Annville in time to pay Katie her half-term. Katie was in a terrible state about that, because Miss Spears would never think it mattered if she did not get all the money right off. Miss Spears might offer her something against the rest but, as Katie said tearfully to Agnes, "It's meant to be, I'm no to flit, the Assizes have got in the way!" Agnes told her John Brown would find himself on the other side of the jury-bench, if he would not pay her in time.

Then on the Wednesday a remittance came through the Post Office from Stonehouse for Miss Spears to pay Katie.

"And that's you," said Agnes with satisfaction, when Katie walked over last thing to show her riches—amounting to ten pounds, four shillings—to her friend.

Katie returned from the fair about eight o'clock, and she had done it— fee'd away from Annville to Cobblehaugh, a farmtoun in the top parks past Lanark, out towards Carstairs Mains. There were two big lasses and she was to help them in the house. She had a half-day every second Sunday and could walk in to Crosslaw, she thought, in under an hour. James Graham of Kirkland Cottage was flitting too, to be fourth ploughman so she would know somebody.

But the day had been stormy and wet, and she had no pleasure in the crowds and merry noise being on needles and pins all the while about how to tell Miss Spears. The only thing she had liked was purchasing a gift for Agnes—a pair of ear-rings, pearl.

Annville kitchen was dark and she lit her candle. Miss Spears had likely gone out to teach her lesson, with Willie the way he was. Katie stood still and listened for him but heard nothing. She unlaced her boots, and stood them close to the range. Then she eased her stays and put on her apron, and spread Agnes' wet mantle over the screen. She took the ear-rings out of the pocket to give to Agnes the morrow, wrapped in their twist of white silk paper. They would never be real pearls, for all the haberdasher said, but they had elegant silvery clamps and Katie had tried them on, just for a moment, and he'd said she was "a picture."

Her box peeped from under the set-in bed. When she'd pushed it back after packing it, the bed valance had come off its ring at the one end, with the cord hanging down. Her own coat folded across the quilt, at the foot, and her box all neat and tied. She was about to straighten the valance when she heard Miss Spears at the front door; and slipping the ear-rings deep into her apron pocket she ran to pull the kettle forward on the range, where it immediately began to purr.

Miss Spears coming in with her own lamp, and giving one of her sniffs, and then pulling her bonnet off the side of her head in the way she had, letting Katie help her out of her cloak.

"Katie, how do you do? Have you been in long? Did you have a pleasant day?" Going quick over to the dresser for her house cap, to cover up her hair, and then forward to the range to sit down.

Katie made the tea and handed her the scalding cup. Miss Spears sitting with it silently, looking into it, warming her fingers. Now it must be said.

"Miss Spears, I've fee'd home, to Cobblehaugh the other side of Lanark."

And Miss Spears white faced looking into her cup and not answering.

Then when Katie burst into tears, she made her draw up the other chair and sit down by her, and drink some tea with sugar in it, and said very kindly that she must of course do as she thought best. Though Katie could see that she was distressed out of the ordinary. Her voice was over-soft and tight, and Katie wished she would take a sip of tea, not sit turning the cup and staring into it so queerly.

"Katie, you know you ought to have spoken to Mrs. Brown, in time for her to make other arrangements."

"But I didnae know myself, whether I would or no!"

After a pause Miss Spears said as if to herself, "You did come to me about it, I confess. And it was wrong of me, to try to persuade you against your will." She coughed.

"Oh, Miss Spears, if you would speak for me to Mrs. Brown? She will find someone to take my place!"

"My aunt will not come till Saturday." Then Miss Spears said almost inaudibly: "She ought not to find anyone else. I must do it myself."

But how she was to manage? Katie, wretched, was sure this was what Miss Spears was thinking; she was in the horrors, for all she held herself so still.

"Has Willie been quiet?"

"Aye." Unnaturally quiet. There was not a sound except the wind in the chimney and the stormy rush of Clyde.

That afternoon Willie had gone into the garden bare-headed, though he had thrown his greatcoat over his shoulders. Again talking and laughing to himself. Charlotte had been out once, with the feed for Gruntie.

Willie brushing past her as she came up through the orchard. His words no worse than what he might say in his febrile delirium. Yet he was not feverish; he was on his feet. When she spoke his name he looked past her. The wind whipped at his coat and it slid from his shoulder, bony under his thin shirt. He wore no collar. She stood, watching him go on down the garden in the twilight. He had been out more than four hours.

"I'll take the worth of it out of you yet!"

Mostly it would be a string of medical terms. An anatomy lesson learned so well the words reeled forth of themselves, like a poem or a hymn. Then the interjections, or laughter.

She would not try to reason with him. He would come in later and sit in the kitchen and be quite himself again, teasing or brooding, as if he had forgotten the episode.

Gently snecking the door, she wished very much for her uncle and aunt! The lamp cast a feeble circle of light on the table and she turned it up full, black shadows billowing above the wall brasses.

Later she heard Willie come in by the front door and go up to his room. She brought him his supper, sniffing once as she entered, in spite of herself. Either he was asleep or feigning; he had got himself under his quilt, even pulled it over his face. She put down the tray.

"Willie, I am away to teach a lesson at the Reids'. You'll no object to being by yourself. I will look in on you when I come home."

It was better now to teach her lessons away from Annville. To forestall Marne then, she would set off for the Reids' well before seven. They were aye welcoming and the younger lassies could look on and learn something as well. Janet played very nicely already, and wee Gracie and even baby Mary would soon be ready to begin.

She could take the modulator along to the Hall now and save herself carrying it next week for the "Hope." It stood behind the front door. As she picked it up she noticed something amiss with the cord. She would see what that was when she got there. She tucked it under her arm as well as she could. No Roddy Munro there to carry it gallantly as in the old days of the Adult Class! He would do so yet, if she stopped by to ask him. But she must manage for herself.

"I should have relished the storm, it matched my mood perfectly," Drew had written; it seemed so long ago. She must agree in her heart, the rain suddenly increasing and the wind lashing her along, with Clyde a steady roar below the houses.

It had been dark since four, and lamps glowed from the windows along the High-street. The Gaol was in darkness, Roddy no doubt "on his rounds," —sitting snug in some ben at the Dublin end with one of his angling cronies.

Mr. Allen had been repairing the footpath and the deepest holes were filled with new grush but even so it was wet, and Charlotte gripping the clumsy modulator stepped up into the road. She passed the flesher's yard. From the darkness within came the sorrowful bawling of a calf. Poor, melancholy thing!

Indeed the cord with its nickel handle, by which to draw the modulator down, had somehow come away. Almost as if it had been cut. Duncan MacBeau would have a bit of curtain twine if it were too late to get a note to King-street so Aunt Helen could bring her a proper length.

"Thank you for allowing me to teach Marne at home this evening, Mrs. Reid."

"No, nay, it is we who thank you, to have come out on such a coarse night. But I am sorry you didnae get word to me, about a fire in the parlour."

Charlotte protested that she had been perfectly warm.

"Mr. Willie Brown is no very well again?"

Charlotte was scrolling up the modulator, and stood with it against her, and looked over it at the good woman, and paused before she smiled in her usual way.

"I thought it best not to disturb him."

They had said goodbye and Charlotte had walked back to Annville against the rain. Willie's lamp almost indiscernible behind his venetians and winter curtains. She could not yet expect Katie. She let herself into the lobby, sniffing the close, sour air of sickness that seemed in the darkness to have crept from the upper flat stronger than ever. A faint glow showed below stairs, and she lit her lamp to carry down. Overhead the house was silent.

And Katie had come back already after all, and was standing by the range to fill the kettle, and Charlotte seeing at once that something had changed. Perhaps she had purchased a new article of clothing? Charlotte, addressing her as cheerfully as possible, had wished it to be that, but she feared it was rather something in the girl herself, the way she stood still and did not turn, a kind of fright or defiance. Then Charlotte knew what it was, what Katie was going to say.

When Miss Spears went up to bed, Katie carefully set out the tea-leaves to dry for the sweeping, and put the cups into the sink. It was strange to think that tomorrow she would no be standing here, doing these simple tasks, she'd be at another place. She must not greet! She had done it! She must think of Agnes telling her how brave she was, and how Agnes would admire the ear-rings, and oh! of the big, airy farm-toun and all the new faces. Not about Miss Spears and Willie, for all this was forbye, all of it! She would never be at Annville again. She took a deep breath, and dried her eyes on her apron.

As she was wiping the sink, she heard an odd noise from the lobby—a bump! And then a scratching as if something heavy were being dragged along the boards. And then she heard Miss Spears make the strangest sound, as if she were trying to call out through layers and layers of cloth. Then came a real, honest crash and a splintering, which must have been her lamp going over.

Katie's first idea was that her mistress had fallen while trying to move the ottoman, for that was what it sounded like, furniture being pulled about. But suddenly she knew what it was: it was Willie, and she stared about her, for scarcely a moment had passed, and he must not be allowed to harm Miss Spears!

The steels were still laid out on the brod, and she snatched up the biggest one, the gully with the black handle, and ran into the lower lobby and up the stairs holding it in both hands before her. She trod on her skirts going up and remembered *Mother Oracle*; it was odd how you could think of something in the middle of doing something else: "*Falling upstairs means a wedding.*"

There was no light ahead of her at the turn. She could hear all the while that awful blurred sound, but she could not make out what Willie was doing to Miss Spears, if he were not choking her; they were in gripes and she could see nothing at all, but then she thought she could just make them out, a kind of denser darkness. But almost not, and her feet in her stocking soles crunched a bit of the chimney glass from the lamp. The Turkey carpet was all rucked, and she could hear Willie breathing and struggling and there was a strange smell, Willie's and something worse. She was there then and she flung herself at Willie and got hold of his short coat, and struck at him with the handle of the gully as hard as she could.

"Let her go, let her go!" He must have for she stopped the noise, but she did not stand up; Katie was sure then he had done her an injury, for she slumped with a thump to the floor. Willie got the gully out of Katie's hands quick as a wink but she thought she had cut him first, or he cut himself, for he shouted in pain.

"You wee devil, you wee devil, coming at me like that. Get on away down or I'll do for you as well!"

But she would never leave Miss Spears, and the whole time he was bending over, Katie was tugging at his coat and Miss Spears under him making that noise again, but suddenly loud, like a cough and a cry mixed together, and nothing more to stop it, her breath coming outwards in two hard, barking coughs; and that was when he did it, with the gully, for she made no more sound after that. And when he gave her the contents of it there was a scrape, and an awful wet blirt, with Katie still hanging on and trying to pull him away. He sat back hard against her, and got himself twisted around and started cutting at her hand with the gully to make her let go.

"Get off my back, you devil!" They were staggering on their knees and were somehow pressed away over against the glazed door, and it was all wet, with the carpet crumpled under them. Which Katie would have to straighten, before Mrs. Brown let her flit to Cobblehaugh. It was wet too, under her hands, a hot wet, and she could not stop him, his one hand getting a grip into her hair now and dragging back her head. And then that heat, aye it was sharp as the range edge but not her wrist this time, it was her throat, her bare throat. It was never pain, it was heat, sensational heat; she was sensational, trying to whisper to him, "Dinnae do that, Willie, please!" and unable to make a sound.

There was a sound. Willie getting himself down the kitchen stair, or falling down it, his voice thin and wild—"Here goes for myself next!"

And Miss Spears beside her in the darkness with the two of them clutching at one another to stand up and slipping on each other's skirts and reaching both at once to get the glass door back, and after that the front door unsnecked. A whiter, open darkness, the night shining through the palings of the gate, and Miss Spears bent right over, ahead of Katie walking ever so slowly up the path. Katie followed as close as she could but when she emerged from the gate, she could not see where Miss Spears had gone. But Miss Spears was dead, she was sure of it.

CHAPTER 30

In which the tragedy is played to its close.

Katie made for the tenements. She felt along the Close wall for the first door, and got at the handle and turned and turned it but no one came. She could not utter, and dared not put up her hand to touch her throat. The front of her dress was soaking, hot and cold at once it seemed, right in through her under garments. Holding to the wall she worked one stocking off, for excepting under the foot it was dry, and carefully wound it round her neck. That was blood pouring down her bodice she was sure. She looked back fearfully and could just see the square of the Close mouth—and just as she looked she heard the rattle of hooves and the hiss of wheels: a carriage coming off the brig. She crept forward as quick as she could, but in no time it was come and gone, the lantern running across the entrance and all pitchy black again, with the noise fading away. Katie creeping into the road then, sharp, cold grush pricking into her bare foot and her foot in the stocking.

But when she won to the Close mouth a friendly beacon appeared—the Elders' dear old lamp, aglow through the curtains in their kitchen window. Eagerly now, though she must think of every tread, she felt along the Hotel front and then crossed to the airie, and step by step crept up into the porch and chapped at the door.

"What's that?"

Almost at once, good Mrs. Elder crying out heartily from within. But when Katie tried to answer, only a unearthly, gurgling noise came out, that hurt her sorely. So she grasped at the door handle instead, and shook it as hard as she could, till her hands slid off from the wet. She chapped again, and spoke out that it was Catherine! Katie! But the gurgling noise sounded nothing like Catherine or Katie at all.

"What's that then? Who's there?"

She chapped again. Silence from within, and Clyde rushing under the brig. Then at last a scratching, over at the parlour window! As if Mrs. Elder were trying to get it up, kneeling on the roup seat the way Katie and Agnes did of a summer's evening, when they pushed back the muslin curtains and let them hang about their heads like bridal veils, to watch for lads passing on the brig. There were linsey-woolsey winter curtains now.

Just then came such a teem of rain, and blast of wind; and Katie felt a terrible, deep cold, as if it had got down into her bones and she would never be warm again. She pressed herself in against the door, as close as she could get. Oh, she wanted most to sink right down, but she must go on chapping till they cried her in. She chapped and chapped.

Perhaps she had fainted away for the next she heard was Mrs. Elder's voice clear out the open parlour window, so close that Katie might almost have reached over and touched her. Mrs. Elder was shouting into the road.

"Hey, who's that there! Will you walk over here a minute please!"

A lad's voice, still high, coming out of the darkness by the brig.

"Liam Chalmers, Mum. I'm no doing anything, I'm just away home."

"Walk over here a wee minute, do, and see if there is someone at the door!"

Steps on the grush, and pausing.

The whiny voice again. "Nay, I cannae see any body."

"Get along with you then, there was somebody before chapping and annoying, it might have been a tramp. Away on home with you!"

"Good-night."

The window slamming down.

Now Katie must rouse herself, and she chapped for all she was worth, clinging to the greasy sneck. She could have greeted for vexation, and oh! she would greet something awful when they had let her in, but not yet. With all the greeting of her blood.

It was silent now inside, and a desperate long time passing by, with Katie so very cold, yet still endeavouring to chap now and then, and also, for she could not help herself, to speak. She begged to be let in, though the noise that came from her mouth was frightful to hear. It was queer she could not speak for her mouth was clean, and quite dry, and she continued to expect that she could, and be sorry each time she would try. Dunt, dunt, dunt.

The parlour window thrown up once more and Mrs. Elder roaring out, "What's that then? What's that?"

Then the inside sneck rattled at last, right by Katie's ear! But at once the window was hurled shut again and Mrs. Elder's voice sounded from inside, angry:

"You'll draw that bolt over my dead corp, Agnes! It's Fast Day thieves!"

Katie could only chap again, pitifully, for Agnes would know it was she. How could Agnes never ken her, when she'd run across so often? Katie had slipped down now, huddled, with her face pressed at the crack of the door where it must open at last.

She scarcely heard the hoofbeats down the length of the brig, or Mrs. Elder throwing the window up again, now quite frightened—"Lads! Stop! Is it you there, Jimmie? Oh, Jimmie, get yourself across to us quick!" Or how they dismounted and came groping up the stair, and one of them saying, "Aye, Mrs. Elder, there is somebody lying in the porch, no doubt intoxicated."

Then one of them, softer: "I'll run over to the Post Office and make them give us a candle."

For Mrs. Elder was out of the ordinary raised, and would no more open the door, or let Agnes open it, till she knew what it was, than if there had been a brigade outside to rescue them instead of three young Voluntaries.

"Mrs. Elder, Jimmie's away for a light and we'll tell you in a minute. It is something like a female."

The first Katie saw of Jimmie Henderson was his polished Sabbath boots and the braid on his trousers, in the stuttering of the lowered candle, and the first she heard him speak was:

"Guid God, it is Katie Hamilton, covered with blood!"

She walked in unassisted. Just as she meant to do, right inside the door, she reached into her pocket and held out her hand. She would like to have said, "Dear Agnes, here is a wee parting gift—" but the words were hid by the awful gurgling in her throat. And her hand was black and striped, and the silk paper hung in shreds, and the ear-rings slipped from her fingers and dropped to the floor. With Agnes backing away and roaring like a baby.

Now Katie need not strive, and she walked into the kitchen and sat herself meekly near the fire, and let herself be laid down on the hearth, and heard as if from a great distance the comings and goings around her. A quilt was brought under her though she would rather not have been shifted about any more, and then there was hot water in a basin, and towels and rags and whisperings, and the door aye banging shut and open, shut and open, and ever so many boots and skirts moving about her head.

Jimmie Henderson now, leaning close over her and asking her who did it? She could only nod, and even that hurt her, and when he asked again, was it for robbery? she held up one finger, and tried to wave it past her head towards Annville.

The second lad, Dickson, had meanwhile gone to rouse Sub-Inspector Munro and was not a minute away when he cried back, and folk all crowded to the door: a carriage was stopped beyond Annville, about opposite the corner shed, and the riding lantern stood on the ground and a man there bending over; then he came running towards them, and bursting in: talking in a very high voice and suddenly low in a whisper:

"There's a dead body face down in the footpath, laying in a great pool of blood—it is Miss Spears!"

Katie could have told them that.

But Dickson after him would not whist, going on about how he saw her first, and now in came old Munro with his face white as a sheet and blinking his wee eyes, with his clapper in the one hand and buckling up his police belt as best he could with the other.

It was George Kay down from Lanark with a late fare who had seen something in the road, and coming back stopped to investigate. He was sent off post haste in his machine to fetch the police officers and medical assistance.

A great many villagers had assembled by now and were trying to gain an entrance, and inside all was confusion again with Agnes in the hysterics and Mrs. Elder not much better, and Mrs. Simpson come across in her shawl and got in by right of the candle. It would be very desperate men, and as it was understood that Katie and Miss Spears and Willie Brown were alone at Annville, very serious anxiety arose concerning Willie as well. The men speaking all at once about organizing a party to search the house.

Roddy was appealed to and chose Jimmie, and the other lad George Day, and Postmaster Simpson, and breathless young Steele who had run all the way from the Inn. Dickson left with orders to keep the Elders' door, and to run out quick and apprehend the officers and the doctor as soon as they should appear. More villagers congregated at the steps, even half-grown shivering lads with their coats over their heads and huge eyes.

When the four men returned they were no longer apprehensive, but out of the ordinary silent. Katie heard them through the ministrations of Mrs. Simpson; her face and cut hand being tremulously wiped, her hair ordered as much as was possible, though it was all loose and caked and soaked with blood and rain, and Mrs. Elder trying to lay a morning cap of Agnes' over it for decency's sake, and saying over and over they ought never to touch her till she was seen by Dr. Gray, and would Agnes only be still.

Jimmie knelt again by Katie's side. Young Mr. Steele going on about the door to Annville standing wide, and a great pool of blood in the lobby right within the door, and blood splashed all over the walls and the glazed door. And a trail of blood down the back stair, and at the foot a great sharp surgeon's amputating knife, it would have been, clotted with blood, and Willie Brown dead in the scullery, all doubled up with his neck stabbed in both sides.

Jimmie was asking Katie all sorts of things and she could not reply. Mrs. Elder saying she ought not to be disturbed, it was too strenuous for her; but when he stopped his questioning Katie began pointing and waving here and there, most towards the dresser. A cup of water was brought, but this she refused, again pointing at the dresser, and trying to raise herself up, and looking very agitated. Her eyes all sunk and darkish around about though the rest of her face was an unearthly white, even her lips, that moved as she tried to speak.

"She wants something. What is it she wants?"

Then Jimmie saw her make a wagging movement with her finger and understood.

"Do you wish to write, Katie? Is it paper and a lead pencil you want?" and her eyes going clear as she saw him.

For he remembered how she and Agnes were aye getting into the pigeon holes after paper and giggling and not letting him see. He stood up.

"Agnes, give us some paper then!" for she was seated by the dresser being attended to by Mrs. Simpson, and throwing herself about. He fetched a sheet for himself, and a bit of lead pencil, and knelt by Katie and put the paper on the floor and the pencil into her hand. She got herself up on the one elbow, and leaned over and wrote in plain letters, having to start the first letter again after Jimmie steadied the paper for her:

Willie killed us both in the house.

She would have liked to write "Get Father" after that, but the pencil slipped out of her fingers. She lay back. The voices in the room came and went in waves, like the organ in St Leonard's when the lad forgets to pump it and then has to give it an extra go. Agnes would be cross that Jimmie held her hand, and she would have liked to say to her it did not matter, it was Dad she wanted. If she could keep her eyes fixed on Jimmie's trouser-braid she could stay awake but it kept blurring, as if unravelling and shining like gold and then would come another dreadful, sidelong pain worse than when Willie did it, and it was easier to let herself drowse away.

Dr. Kelso came first, from New Lanark. He shook his head. Katie was to be made comfortable and that was when the mattress was brought down from Agnes' bed that was afterwards burned, and Agnes roaring and wouldn't stop off till they said she would have to be removed up the stairs by herself with the door closed.

Dr. Kelso putting on his black gutta percha apron and cuffs and laying out his equipment, and saying everyone was to go out or back off. Jimmie had hold of Katie's hand and stayed, but had to squeeze his eyes shut when Dr. Kelso uncovered the wound and sewed it. Dr. Gray getting in then with a grim face and he and Dr. Kelso taking themselves to the other side of the fire and talking very low in medical terms but it was clear there was nothing to be done, Katie being comatose now and sinking fast.

Then Mr. Cassells in the doorway with a fresh, chafed brow shining with rain, and dripping black hair and whiskers, who was the one who thought to fetch her father.

Up at the E U manse the Forsyths were sound asleep when the servant opened the door to Sergeant Hazelton about three o'clock. Rain plowting at the stable doors and Mrs. Forsyth run out into the yard in her night clothes with only a plaid about her.

"It can never be true dear, the villagers have got it up out of all proportion you will see!"

"Well, whatever it is the Lord help his poor parents."

She burst into tears. "Oh—away with you then, Will, quick, quick!" and ran after him into the road though she had but slippers on her feet and no stockings, the servant trembling in the front door with a shawl thrown over her undone hair.

Mr. Forsyth was no horseman and the Brae was slippery but the sergeant kept by him, and they got down seeing all the lanterns below and Kirkfieldbank lit up as if it were Saturday night after lousing time, not past three.

"Mr. Forsyth, she's gone! Her father's by her, will you have a word? Oh what is to be done?" and here he was indoors and taking the poor man's hand—it was Andrew Hamilton, and that would be poor Katie then not Miss Spears, who was lying dead on the floor, looking no older with her hair down than she had been then in the manse parlour, when he had taken her wee body up close in his arms to play with the venetians. Might the Lord forgive him, she was innocent yet!

Doctor Gray was gone over to Annville to see to the carrying in of Miss Spears' corpse, and then Kay was ready in the road with the conveyance, Katie's remains to be removed to Crosslaw. Her father staggering, carrying her himself across the airie and mutely thrusting off those who would assist him. Jimmie who had not left her side got in with them, Mrs. Elder calling out that there ought to be a woman go, with the poor mother to see such a sight; but no one came forward.

Mr. Forsyth accepted a glass of brandy in hot water and drank it down before he realized what it was, a fire of resolution expanding in his breast. Superintendent MacGillivray still tramping about writing his report and the two lads Dickson and Day huddled on the roup seat and told not to move for they would be escorted to the station in

Lanark presently for their statements; and why had Munro allowed young Henderson away when he was a material witness? Turning the pages of his notebook crossly and ready to question the lads at once if he got a chance, for they looked very much as if they knew all about it. Day asleep by then, his head against the curtain and his mouth open.

Sub-inspector Munro sat down by Mr. Forsyth at the fire, his face all puffy and raw red.

"Who will speak the news to John, then, Reverend? If I am ordered by my superior officer, I will go myself."

"Why, it must be done. Dinnae greet man, I'll do it. I will set off at once. Can a gig be got?"

"Steele's." Mrs. Elder making him put on her husband's old greatcoat, for the new one was still at Douglas Water with Mr. Elder in it.

"Oh, oh, it would never have happened at all, if George were come home from the Fair!"

When Mr. Forsyth got to Stonehouse he very wisely called first at Hill-street and roused Mr. Paterson, and they went over to King-street together at about five o'clock.

Reverend Walter Cameron was not an actor in the night's events, being a sound sleeper and Mrs. Capie not daring to wake him till she had cooked his brose though she was fit to bursting; and he was most alarmed to be turned out so long before his usual time though of course forgave her when he understood the cause.

That Sabbath he preached a sermon on the subject, specially improving it, his text being in Matthew.xxiv.44—"*therefore be ye also ready, for in such an hour as ye think not the Son of Man cometh.*"

The End

AFTERWORD

Catherine's half-year was out at Martinmas. A feeing fair at Douglas Water was announced in the *Advertiser*. As a servant Katie would expect a holiday to attend, and most servants flitted every half-term. There is no evidence that she attended the Douglas Fair, or was decided to flit.

The first reports given out of the murders were that Willie cut the two women's throats with his surgeon's knife from his kit; later, that it was a large kitchen knife (a gully) which was lying near his body. Finally that, as a rope was found wound twice around Charlotte's neck, and cut through, that "he *had at first tried to strangle her, and, failing in this attempt, used the knife.*"

All reports agree that Katie and Charlotte were probably sitting in the kitchen before Charlotte went up to bed, as the two chairs were pulled up to the range. Charlotte had then started up to her bedroom carrying her lamp, which was discovered broken in the lobby. Willie "*armed with the weapons of destruction*" had come down from the upper flat and attacked her there. It was surmised from the cuts on Katie's hands that she had run up to defend Charlotte on hearing the commotion. I believe that Katie carried the knife upstairs herself.

The ghost. Mrs. May Morris and her four sisters, who lived in Annville as children, all recall their mother speaking of occasionally seeing a ghost coming up the kitchen stair—a woman dressed in black in a white cap and apron and carrying a lamp. Their mother was "very matter-of-fact about this and if you knew my mother at all you would know that she wasn't the kind of person who would just say something like that. She said that she saw her but that she wasn't frightened by the woman who was just going about her business."

The box bed. A large walk-in cupboard stood in the same corner of the kitchen formerly occupied by Katie's box bed. It was never used because May's mother "thought there was something strange about it. Although my Dad used to laugh at her for this I remember he never went into it either or never stored anything in it."

Elderly people recall being told as children that Annville was "an evil house," and those who did chores in the garden would not enter it. Mrs. Rita Watson of Biggar says she had as a child to put coal sticks in under the stair, and rushed out when she heard ghostly footsteps overhead. The details of the murders are however quite forgotten; Mrs. Alison Rankin next door had heard that the servant had got right across to Sunnyside, and that her last words were "written in blood."

The lesson. Charlotte, reported in the *Advertiser* as teaching in the village that evening, was in fact at the Reids', it having been arranged that Marne would have her lesson there instead of at Annville as usual. The Reids' story always ended with: "And just think, if Marne had gone to Annville she would have been murdered too!" (Told to Mrs. Moira Ireland by the youngest Reid sister, Mary, when an old lady.)

The story of the ear-rings. Mr. and Mrs. Ross, now resident in "The Smiddy," did not know about the murders. The house is renovated though the forge area below remains the same. They showed me the position of the original kitchen and, standing inside where the front door had been (now a window), Mrs. Ross remarked to her husband: "Do you remember when we first moved in, and I was wearing my pearl ear-rings—we were standing about here, and there was that strange gust of wind, and both my ear-rings fell out?"

There is no evidence that Katie bought ear-rings for Agnes, or that the two girls were close friends, though Katie in her distress did proceed to the smiddy, where according to the newspaper reports she had been "a frequent visitor," and knew where paper and pencil were kept. Mother and daughter were alone at home that night, though Mr. Elder's being in Douglas is also conjecture.

Agnes Elder was sixteen at the time and is named in the census of 1881. The rest of the events of that night follow the newspaper reports and what was handed down from Jimmie Henderson's account to his family.

Jimmie Henderson's tale. The then sixteen-year-old Jimmie lived to a great age and told the story to his niece Mrs. Cairnes, of The Butts, Lanark, when she was a child. His sister, aged five at the time of the murders, also told her grandchildren the story; Mrs. Isabel Kerr Wilson writes from Australia: "the whole household was woken when her elder brother returned home and they spent the rest of the night comforting him as he was so distraught by what he had seen." Mrs. Cairnes recalls him as being a lean, tall man, who had married and fathered many children. She remembers him saying: "Willie was a rascal. He wanted to marry Miss Spears for her money and when she would not have him he cut her throat." Mrs. Wilson writes: "Within our family it was mentioned that William Brown was in love with Charlotte but she had refused his offer of marriage and told him she loved someone else."

Mrs. Cairnes told me that her uncle spoke also of a "Bella" with pity, and she thought Bella, not Catherine, was the murdered servant's name. Katie's sister Isabella Hamilton lived till age 26. Another daughter born 1889 ("*Wee Katie*" on the Lanark gravestone), died in infancy. Andrew Hamilton died in 1906, having outlived all his children.

Willie and Robert. From a letter by Robert Spears, convalescing in Egypt, to his family, 23 March 1878 (now in the University Archives, Glasgow): "*I want to devote a sentence to Willie in my last letter, but I fear that in my haste I omitted it. I had no time to read it over, so I cannot remember. However, I am glad to know that he is able to resume his classes, and I trust that his illness has left no weakness of any kind. I want to be very specially remembered to him.*"

The motive. From newspaper accounts:
"*As to the motive for committing such a dark deed, none has been assigned except that the perpetrator and Miss Spears had not been in the most harmonious terms, though there was nothing in this that would have led even to anticipate any violence, far less such a result. Brown had been a long time (eleven sessions) at Glasgow University. He had at first studied four sessions with a view to the ministry and then, changing his purpose, entered for the medical profession. About the time of the milk fever in Glasgow he had been taken ill, and his relations say that he was never the same after that. So much had the state of his health interfered*

with his studies that for the last two years he had been unable to attend the classes. Doubtless his spirits had sunk, and ultimately something of a dejection, if not a phase of melancholy, had come over him. He associated with few or none for some time past, and it is easy to believe he had been the subject of morbid ideas which to all appearances had unhinged his reason....

"His cousin, Miss Spears, who acted as housekeeper during Mrs. Brown's absence, knowing how unwell he was, is stated to have been exceedingly kind to him. Indeed, the appearance of his room bears testimony to the fact that he was the object of much careful solicitude. Before the tragedy of Saturday young Brown's conduct was not such as to cause his friends any anxiety. His father left him in his usual spirits on Tuesday night to walk to Hamilton, where he was to serve as a juryman on the following day. Mrs. Brown remained at Stonehouse to take charge of the business there, and, her husband's duties at Hamilton being over, she was subsequently joined by him, it being their intention to go on to Kirkfieldbank after the business of the week had been got through. The son was left alone with his cousin and the servant in the house at Kirkfieldbank. Nothing strange was noticed about his actions, but several things which he did are now seen to be premonitory to the insane state of mind in which he must have been when he attacked his cousin and the servant. On one or two occasions it is said he was observed walking about the garden surrounding the house talking and chuckling to himself....

"As no motive whatever can be assigned for the deed it is thought that Brown had been suffering under temporary insanity."

Willie's illness. *"The terrific impact (of brucellosis) on the nervous system, both central and automatic...is probably the most significant feature of the disease."* Diagnosis was almost impossible, the disease presenting over 200 symptoms besides the recurring fever, ranging from *"restlessness, impatience of light, loathing of food, diffused eye, sallow skin, bloated tongue, intermittent pulse, rigors, transient pains flitting from joint to joint, digestive disturbances, invasion of the respiratory system, headache, incapacitating arthralgia, disagreeable foetor exhaled from the person and linen"* to *"lassitude, apathy, delirium, anxiety, severe depression, gross tremors, irritability, insomnia, anorexia and latent meningitis."* The fever itself had 2 periods of exacerbation, with complete remission, over 24 hours, but the course of the illness was irregular and unpredictable. A patient might recover quickly or suffer prolonged debility with relapses and repercussions over decades. (Florence Nightingale, bedridden for 40 years, often in excruciating neuralgic pain, is now believed to have suffered from this disease). Symptoms might recur dishearteningly when the patient seemed fully recovered. *"The longer the disease is active, the more deeply entrenched they become…and may have serious repercussions on affect and personality."*

The persistence of Willie's illness, its prevention of his further studies even while at times allowing him to be up and about, and above all the possible neurological aggravation of his already severe disappointment (the newspaper quotes his father as saying *"he was never like the same lad"*), convince me he suffered from chronic brucellosis.

Willie's death. A blood-stained knife was found lying at the foot of the kitchen stair. *"It was a formidable-looking weapon, with a blade six inches in length, lance-pointed, and as sharp as it is possible to make a steel instrument. Judging from its appearance it seems to be a surgeon's amputating knife, and no doubt formed part of young Brown's college outfit. The blade was slightly notched, as if it had come in contact with some hard substance. Judging from this fact and the blood-stains on it, there seems little reason to doubt that it was the weapon with which Miss Spears and the servant girl were murdered. …*

"The store-room on the opposite side of the little lobby was dark. The officers procured a light and on going into the apartment found young Brown lying in the middle of the floor in a pool of blood, which had issued from an ugly deep stab on the left side of his throat. He was doubled up on his right side with his knees drawn towards his chin."

The police report did not survive. There was no inquest, and no autopsies were performed. Willie's grave is unmarked and though he was reported as buried in the Stonehouse churchyard, his remains may have been placed outside the wall on the steep slope to the Avon, where bones are sometimes uncovered. Madeleine Brown flitted to Glasgow in 1884 and any further record of her is lost.

I would have supposed that there was no more communication

between Annville House and the Great Western Road. But the death certificate of Helen Brown, who succumbed to a *"fibroid tumour of the uterus"* in 1891, is signed at Annville by *Thomas Spears.* Tom married Agnes Jamieson in 1887 and she died after giving birth to her sixth child, in 1900. Tom and the children, including my father Robert Bainbridge, emigrated to Canada in 1911 accompanied by his sister Annie, and settled in Vancouver. Tom did not remarry. He died in 1928.

ENDNOTES

1. From the report in *The Hamilton Advertiser,* Dec. 1, 1883. All directly quoted texts are italicized.

2. *op. cit.*

3. *op. cit.*

4. Actually Charlotte's, Tom's and the late Robert's stepmother. Their mother Charlotte Thomson was Helen's sister and had died a few days after Charlotte's birth in 1849; Helen still called Matthew's second wife "Mrs. Spears."

5. From *Your loving Father, Gavin Scott, letters from a Lanarkshire Farmer,* 1911-1917, ed. Ruth Williams. In 1826 the crops were pulled by hand, and the place marked when the labourers went in for dinner, so they could tell when they returned how far they had gotten. Children born in that year were called "*year's bairns.*"

6. For distant relatives, deep mourning was worn for three weeks only.

7. Contemporary Sol-Fa publications gave explicit instructions and endless advice to the fledgling teachers. Before starting up a class, an inaugural Public Lecture was mandatory.

8. This building, with the staircase to the old weavers' loft, still stands.

9. This tree still stands though Annville House was pulled down to make way for the new bridge in 1959. Mrs. May Morris drew me the floor plans for the house, where she had lived as a child, and told me about the woodpecker.

10. The manse fire of August 27, 1924 destroyed almost all the Church records. The *Minutes and General Business Books* survived, being at "The Cottage" across from Annville, home of the late Mr. Tex MacGuinness and Mrs. Margaret MacGuinness.

11. The matter of the subscription, if not that of the venison, is recorded in the *Managers' Books.*

12. *op.cit.*

13. *The Duties of the Precentor.*
I. The Precentor will conduct the Psalmody at all services of worship on the Lord's Day, and at such services on other days as may be held by appointment of the Managers.
II. He will hold a weekly practice with his choir and such members of the congregation as may choose to attend, for at least 8 months in the year, unless specially arranged, at which the praise for the Sabbath soirées shall have prominence.
III. He will, supplied by the choir and friends, provide the musical programme at the congregational soirées.
IV. Generally he will regard it as his duty to interest himself in, and to use all suitable measures to improve the congregational Psalmody.
V. In the mode of conducting the Psalmody, as well as in other matters conducted through his office, the Precentor is subject to the control and bound to obey the orders of the Managers.
VI. Suspension from membership carries with it suspension of office.
VII. Apart from fault involving suspension the engagement will be held terminable by 1 month's notice on either side.
The moral character of the candidate for the office of the leadership of the Psalmody shall be beyond reproach.

14. The Scottish version of Cinderella.

15. A family story, but attributed to one of my uncles, Tom or George Spears, who died in the Great War.

16. As recorded in the Archives of the Faculty of Medicine, Glasgow University.

17. This account of asylum conditions is not Victorian but taken from my own experiences 1954-56, when as a university student I worked summers in mental hospitals in Canada.

18. Number 6 Corunna Street is gutted and boarded up except for the ground flat. Through a gaping window, the stucco ceiling of the second floor room can be seen. Whether Robert actually died in that room is of course not known.

19. The 1880 epidemic listed 508 cases of which 68 were mortal.

20. The Browns had purchased Annville in June of 1879.

21. *"Round the rick, round the rick,*
    There I met my Uncle Dick,
    A stick in his bum and a stane in his belly,
    If you tell me his name I'll gie you a—cherry."

22. An opinion regarding Willie's illness is given in the Afterword.

23. *Monks and Nuns.*
    A lecture on this subject was delivered in St. Leonard's Church
    Sabbath last by Mr. Hay, agent of the West of Scotland Protestant
    Association.... There was a large attendance.
    The Hamilton Advertiser, August 8th, 1881.

24. Gavin Scott, *loc. cit.*

25. In 1889 WP eloped to Montreal with Lizzie, marriage between a widower and his deceased wife's sister being still forbidden in Scotland. He wrote to Tom on that occasion: "*Your kind and long letter has touched me deeply....I was sorry that you must hear the news from other parties but for our own comfort we resolved to keep our own counsel in these matters. But we do feel very keenly the separation from home, from friends, and from the fellowship.*

    "*One element that makes my present step so comforting and natural is its cementing present and past—preserving life's continuity. Lizzie and I not only love each other dearly, but are one in our devotion to the memory of our children's sweet mother. That is something. I pity the man who has a chamber in his heart—the most sacred perhaps of all—into which his present wife cannot enter.*"

26. *Sheep's Head Broth.*
    Secure a nice sheep's head with 4 feet. Scour the head, cut fairly through the middle, clean well. Take H head and 2 feet for 2 days' dinner, put other half away with salt & pepper to keep. Add 1Hd of barley, vegetables, and 2d of potatoes, cut in slices. Cook the other half of the head in the same manner, give each 3 hours' boiling with pepper & salt to taste.
    Sheep's Head Pie.
    Take the remaining meat from the head and hough, cut it up, and put the left-over gravy, which will now be jellied, into a pie dish, with the meat, pepper and salt, parsley, and potatoes from the first day. Bake till

browned.

27. *Katie Braidie had a coo,*
Black and white about the mou',
Wasna that a dentie coo?
Dance, Katie Braidie!

28. *Kirkfieldbank Service of Sacred Song.*
In the Church, here, on Tuesday last, the choir of the Congregation, under the leadership of Miss Speirs, gave a Service of Sacred Song named "Harvest Thanksgiving." The Church was very full in its membership, and the balancing of the various parts was skilfully arranged, except the bass, which was at times rather light. The different sections of the hymn by Watts, "Shine, Mighty God," another, "Lord of the Living Harvest," and the concluding chorus, "Praise the Lord" from Curwen's Anthems, were executed in quite superior style. Training such a number of young members to sing in such a degree of perfection, while most creditable to themselves, was doubly so to their accomplished and painstaking leader. The reading was plainly and effectively done by the Reverend Mr. Thomson, Heywood. The Reverend Mr. Cameron, pastor of the Church, made a few complimentary remarks on the performance of the choir at the close, and, on his proposal, a hearty vote of thanks was awarded to them. As for the reverend gentleman who did the reading, he said he would say his thanks in private. There was a good attendance.
The Hamilton Advertiser, November 21, 1881.

29. Women did not attend funerals.

30. Heywood flourished for only 60 years. Nothing remains but the overgrown pits, a few stones in the windblown grass, and a track leading towards the place of the vanished kirk on the hill.

31. *The Annual meeting for the Election of the Managers met in the vestry, but the Congregation taking no more interest in the proceedings than usual. At a quarter past eight not a member of the church had taken their seat in the meeting, it was moved and carried that those gentlemen already in office as Managers should be re-elected with power to add to their numbers. The meeting was then adjourned till the 16th of January 1882. When the business was over John Weir, followed by John Scott, John Gilchrist and William Stark entered the room. The first having conducted himself in an impudent manner. He disobeyed the ruling of the Chair*

and did his utmost to provoke a disturbance.
Walter Cameron.
Kirkfieldbank Church Minutes, 26th December, 1881.

32. The Annual concert of the Kirkfieldbank Congregation was held January 23rd, *"the Church being filled to overflowing by a respectful and approving audience. The Reading was by the Reverend Walter Cameron. Several choral selections were given by the choir of the Church, under their accomplished leader, and the Sabbath School children sang some of the hymns very sweetly. It was admitted one of the most successful soirées ever held in this church."*
The Hamilton Advertiser, February 3rd, 1882.

33. *Bobbie Shafto's gettin' a bairn,*
For to dandle in his arm,
In his arm and on his knee;
Bobbie Shafto loves me.

34. March 3rd.

35. *A remarkable visitor has been attracting the attention of all classes every night, the only drawback being the lightness of the sky....The great comet of 1882 is now bowling along merrily at a rate of more than a million leagues a day streaming towards the sun. On June 10th if clear it will be visible by day.*
The Hamilton Advertiser, May 27th, 1882.

36. *The Choir of Kirkfieldbank Church under the leadership of Miss Spears had their Annual Trip on Wednesday* (August 14th), *the destination being "Tintock Tap." After assembly at an early hour they entered a brake, which bore them merrily along the road to Wiston Mill, where they realized something of the famed kindness and hospitality of Mr. and Mrs. Clarkson.*

While the horses rested the happy party ascended the hill, and enjoyed to the full the bracing air, the extensive views, and delightful sensations of hill-climbing.

What formed a most important factor to the social happiness was a liberal service twice over of good and very luxurious provisions for the inner man, kindly given by Ronald Johnstone, Esq. of Sunnyside, whose liberality is widely known.

Of course the usual vote of thanks was given with great spirit to Mr. and Mrs. Clarkson.

They in due time got safely home, the pleasures of the day not having been broken by a single jar.

The Hamilton Advertiser, August 18th, 1882.

37. *Tintock chants* from *Notes by the Way*, Archibald C McMichael, Ayr, ca. 1890.

38. from the *Minute and General Business Book* of Kirkfieldbank Mission Church, 1876-1883

39. *Kirkfieldbank IOGT Annual Soirée*
The annual soirée, commemorative of the Institute of the "Hope of Kirkfield" Lodge, took place in the Lodge Hall the evening of Friday last. The Reverend Mr. Forsyth, Lanark, presided, and delivered an excellent address, showing the objects and aims, and struggles and successes, of the order to which they belonged, and the advancement of which they were bound to promote. A most substantial tea was served up by willing hands. During the evening the members of the assembled Junior Lodge, under the leadership of Miss Spears, treated the company to the tasteful singing of some hymns, etc., selected for the occasion, all of which was received with hearty applause, all being exceedingly well presented, and seemed to yield great pleasure to all who were fortunate enough to be present.
The Hamilton Advertiser, December 2nd, 1882.

40. *The Musical Treat of the Season*
Mr. H A Lambeth and his Celebrated Choir, who have twice had the honour of appearing, by Special Command, before Her Majesty and the Consort at Balmoral Castle, will give a Grand Popular Concert in the Grand Templars Hall Tuesday November 29th.
The Hamilton Advertiser, November 18th, 1882.

41. *The Church Choir under the leadership of Mr. McLellan, gave a very creditable rendering of a selection of sacred pieces, accompanied by a harmonium, which was presided over by a Lady.*
The Hamilton Advertiser, op. cit.

42. *The rapidly spreading custom of sending Christmas cards was duly kept up, as the heavy bundles of the letter carriers plainly showed.*
The Hamilton Advertiser, December 30th, 1883.

43. My grandmother.

44. *Pianoforte, Harmonium, American Organ*
Mr. Henderson's Quarterly Visit to Lanark about 5 February. Please leave orders with Mr. Melkejohn, Broomgate, Lanark.

45. Mr. Paterson would not allow his parishioners to build him a manse. He also refused to have a pulpit erected in the otherwise grand new UP church in Stonehouse.

46. *Kirkfieldbank. A Temperance lecture was held in the Grand Templars Hall here, on Tuesday evening, March 3rd. Mr. J Clapperton, lecturer under The Grand Lodge, IOGT, delivered one of his popular orations to a most appreciative audience....What added very much to the attraction of the evening was the singing of Sankey's hymns by a juvenile choir, led by Miss Spears, with her usual ability. It is to be hoped that this, along with their efforts now being made in the village, may have the desired effect of aiding in the suppression of that vice which has long been the bane of honest industry.*
The Hamilton Advertiser, March 10th, 1883.

47. *From the statement of an alienist witnessing at a Glasgow murder trial, 1883, in hand-written court proceedings, The Record Office, Edinburgh.*

48. *Kirkfieldbank. On March 11th at 6PM Mr. Forsyth preached a Gospel Temperance Sermon in the Grand Templars Hall under the auspices of the "Hope of Kirkfieldbank" Lodge IOGT.*
The Hamilton Advertiser, March 24th, 1883.

49. *The Heywood Church of Scotland Temperance Association held its first general meeting in Victoria Hall, on Friday 9th inst.*
Our worthy pastor, the Reverend Andrew Thomson, the president and promoter of the Society, must have been proud to see such a large and respectful meeting. 70 partook of tea. A short but effective speech was made by the Chairman, followed by a lengthy program of readings, recitations, songs and solos by Miss Rennie, and Messrs Denham and Findlay who gave well executed solos on the concerian and violin. Mr. Park, vice president, delivered a telling and effective speech on the evils of intoxication and its effect on young and old. Mr. John Rennie finished with "MacGregor's Gathering" in masterly style. An assembly followed in

which the younger members with their partners took part.

50. March 20th, 1883.

51. Elgin Place Church still stands and is now a discotheque.

52. Lanark Museum. Titled: "*Laying the Foundation Stone at Crosslaw Poorhouse, June 5th 1878.*"

53. New Lanark, Robert Owen's famous social experiment, provided housing, schooling, employment in the mill (from the age of 10 years) and strict moral supervision for its inhabitants. The town is now a museum.

54. The distinction of Mr. Cameron's presentation was unfortunately to be eclipsed by Cranstoun of Corehouse's "handsome donation" on the same date. (Reported in *The Hamilton Advertiser*, June 30th, 1883.)

55. The outbuildings are now in ruins. Baronold House is a thriving restaurant.

56. *Laying a Foundation Stone.*
...The foundation stone of the manse in course of erection at Kirkfieldbank was laid with masonic honours....the ceremony...carried out in accordance with the usual customs and traditions of the order. The musical portion of the programme, being vocal, had a pleasing effect. ....The procession afterwards returned to Lanark, where the Lodge was closed in ancient form. The brethren present included Hector F McLean, P.G.M.; D.A.V. Thomson, acting Substitute; James Swan, acting P.G.S.W., James Scott, P.G.I.W., James Conner, P.G. Secy; Rev. James French, New Lanark, P.G. Chaplain. Bro. Col. James Moffatt, Past Grand Master of Canada, also took part in the proceedings, which were carried out under the supervision of Bros. R.M.Bryce, P.G.Tyler; Capt. Macgillivray, Grand Director of Ceremonies, and the Provincial Grand Secretary.
The Hamilton Advertiser,

57. *The "Falls of Clyde" and "Hope of Kirkfieldbank" Juvenile Lodge of Grand Templars held their annual excursion Saturday last. The latter marched to Lanark in the forenoon under the guidance of Miss Spears and Mr. William Munn, and met the Lanark division under Messrs John and James McKnight. With a fine display of banners, they marched by*

Old Carluke Road and Lockhart Mill bridge to the farm of Greentowers, where they were met by Mr. and Mrs. Muirhead "untiring with their attentions" all day. A service of buns and milk was distributed to all and sundry. Athletic sports were freely and heartily indulged in; other similar distributions made at intervals. After 6 hours of this happy enjoyment, the party was drawn together and hearty cheers were given and votes of thanks to their attendants. Several hymns were sung. They parted at Cartland Bridge and both got home in good time, highly gratified with their day's outing.

The Hamilton Advertiser, August 4th, 1883.

58. On July 14 1883, according to a report in the *Advertiser*, a militia-man called Robert McFarlane was killed falling out of a second storey window at William Robertson's Public House, Wellgate, while reaching for a boy's bonnet that had been thrown on to a projecting part of the building.

59. *On Thursday October 17th, Reverend Mr. Turnbull of Lesmahagow, lectured on the very uncommon, yet everyday subject, Sweethearts and Wives, at St Leonard's Church....(to) a large and respectable audience... (on) the picture of both sweethearting and married life.... The Hamilton Avertiser,* October 20th 1883.

60. This was to be Charlotte's last public appearance: Monday November 19th, 1883.

61. *The Causes of Disability:* these two marvellous volumes were kept in a bookcase behind glass in my father's General Accident Insurance office on Seymour Street when I was a child. I used to get into them if the office was empty, usually while waiting for him to drive me home from Saturday morning classes at the Vancouver School of Art. I had no idea what they were about except that it was something secret and adult about the human body. The engraving Charlotte saw over Willie's shoulder is the only one I clearly remember. Perhaps they were once Willie's, and perhaps Auntie Moo got rid of them when Dad died, for they have disappeared.